REVOLUTION BY CANDLELIGHT

REVOLUTION BY CANDLELIGHT

The Real Story behind the Changes in Eastern Europe

Bud Bultman

A Harold Fickett Book

Portland, Oregon

Edited by Al Janssen
Cover design by Durand Demlow

REVOLUTION BY CANDLELIGHT
The Real Story behind the Changes in Eastern Europe

Published by Multnomah Press
10209 SE Division Street
Portland, Oregon 97266

Published in association with the literary agency of Alive Communications, P.O. Box 49068, Colorado Springs, Colorado 80949.

Printed in the United States of America.

Library of Congress Cataloging-in-Publication Data
Bultman, Bud.
Revolution by candlelight : the real story behind the changes in Eastern Europe / Bud Bultman.
p. cm.
ISBN 0-88070-434-9
1. Europe, Eastern—Politics and government—1945-1989. 2. Communism and Christianity—Europe, Eastern. 3. Europe, Eastern-Church history—20th century.
I. Title.
DJK50.B85 1991
943—dc20 91-5023
CIP

91 92 93 94 95 96 97 98 99 - 10 9 8 7 6 5 4 3 2 1

To the people of the truth—
the men and women of Eastern Europe
whose faith helped change the world

—•—

"If the main pillar of the [totalitarian] system is living a lie,
then it is not surprising that the fundamental threat
to it is living the truth."
— Vaclav Havel, *The Power of the Powerless*

"And you shall know the truth, and the truth shall make you free."
—John 8:32

Contents

FINLAND
NORWAY
SWEDEN
ATLANTIC
OCEAN
BALTIC
SEA
UNION OF
SOVIET
SOCIALIST
REPUBLICS
Gdansk
Berlin
Warsaw
GERMANY
POLAND
Leipzig
Bonn
Krakow
Prague
CZECHOSLOVAKIA
Vienna
Budapest
SWITZ.
AUSTRIA
HUNGARY
ROMANIA
Timisoara
Bucharest
YUGOSLAVIA
ITALY
MEDITERRANEAN SEA

Introduction

When the Berlin Wall fell in 1989 and new democratic governments came to power in at least four Eastern European nations, with a civil war erupting in a fifth, vivid images of city square demonstrations and candlelight vigils shone on the world's television screens. The names of these nations were familiar to us, although many in the United States probably had trouble keeping the capitals—Prague, Warsaw, Budapest, Bucharest, and East Berlin—straight with their countries—Czechoslovakia, Poland, Hungary, Romania, and the German Democratic Republic. The television images that direct our political responses seem to do away with the need for historical and political context and sometimes even to work actively against it. But the story of Eastern Europe in 1989 cannot be told or understood without an understanding of that context.

Briefly stated, the countries of Eastern Europe, with their different cultures and historical experiences, became lumped together into the Soviet bloc largely by virtue of the tag-end events of World War II. For example, in Poland, with the Red Army advancing on the capital, the Warsaw Uprising was launched as a last ditch attempt by

Polish insurgents to overthrow Nazi occupation and keep Poland out of the hands of the approaching Soviets and their Polish Communist allies. The Soviets encouraged the uprising. But as the Nazis brutally crushed the rebellion, carrying out Hitler's orders that Warsaw be "razed without a trace," the Soviet Army purposefully remained encamped across the Vistula River. During the first month of the uprising, Stalin even refused permission for Allied planes carrying supplies to the Polish resistance to land in the Soviet Union.

When the Soviets finally entered the rubble of what was left of the Polish capital six months later, hardly a building was left standing. A once-thriving city with a population of more than a million people was reduced to a desolate wasteland. Two hundred thousand died; the rest were carried away by the Nazis. Any political rivals standing in the way of Soviet interests in Poland had been obliterated.

This tragic episode foreshadowed the way the Soviets would assume control throughout Eastern Europe.

When the war ended, the Soviet Union began to assert its rights to the areas liberated from the Nazis by the Red Army. Stalin viewed the liberated areas in the war's eastern sphere as a buffer zone vital to Moscow's political and military interest. At the post-war conference held at Yalta, the Western powers conceded the region as a Soviet "sphere of influence," in exchange for Stalin's promise to allow "free, unfettered elections" in the Soviet-occupied areas. But those elections turned out to be a farce, a means of imposing regimes subservient to the Kremlin and its Communist doctrine. Moscow set up puppet parties throughout the region, led by either Communist leaders of the local anti-Nazi resistance or by leaders freshly imported from Moscow.

Over the next several years, the Party began taking power. Stalin insured political developments would be to his liking by penetrating the local Communist parties with his own agents who served as his watchdogs. The degree of Soviet involvement in the local parties and the speed with which they came to power varied from country to country. The German Democratic Republic [The GDR or East Germany] was created by the Soviet Union out of the zone of occupation that fell to Soviet control after Germany was carved up by the Allies. In Poland, the Soviet-backed Communist party took power in a rigged election; later Wladyslaw Gomulka, the leader of the Polish national Communists, was denounced, placed under house arrest, and replaced by Bierut Boleslaw, a Soviet stooge who spent most of the war in Moscow. In Romania, the Communist party was one of four parties that took power in a coup in 1944. After a brief period of serving in a genuine coalition government, the Soviet-backed party used bogus elections and harassment of the opposition parties to assume full control. The Hungarian Communists took power gradually, through a divide and conquer "salami" strategy of gradually ousting their political rivals. In Czechoslovakia, the Communists shared power with a coalition government until 1948, when the Communists commandeered the democratic republic founded by Tomas Masaryk in what amounted to a coup.

By 1948, with Eastern Europe firmly in his hands, Stalin began tightening his grip. The Communist party became the means of exerting even greater pressure. It ruled every aspect of life in Eastern Europe. The Leninist principle of the "leading role of the Party" guaranteed the Party's control over the all-important military and security forces, state government, education, workers' unions, and the media. The leading role of the Party was ensured through a system of privilege known as the *nomenklatura*. The Communist party reserved the right to appoint all the top bureaucrats and managers of each country. This elaborate list of appointments included positions ranging from trade union leaders to factory managers, from teachers to judges. The *nomenklatura* was all-encompassing and ever-expanding. In a system based on a classless society, those who held *nomenklatura* positions emerged as the new ruling class. Members of the *nomenklatura* were guaranteed certain advantages: a higher standard of living, access to higher education, and other perquisites. In return they were expected to be absolutely loyal to the Party.

As the Communist party consolidated power throughout Eastern Europe, it began clamping down on institutions and ideas not in keeping with the tenets of Marxist principles. Chief among these were the church and the Christian faith. Marxism teaches that religious faith stands in the way of building a Socialist society. Marx summed it up in the famous line: "religion is the opium of the people." In other words, humanity, according to Marx, simply invented religion to cope with the misery of capitalism's economic bondage. Therefore, he wrote, "the abolition of religion as the illusory happiness of men is a demand for their real happiness."[1]

Religious faith also presented a direct challenge to the Communist party's absolute claim to holding a monopoly on the truth. Marxism's belief in "dialectical materialism," that man is the sum of his immediate surroundings and economics is the determining factor of his destiny, leaves no room for the Christian understanding of human beings as spiritual creatures.

Stalin's sneering question, "How many divisions has the Pope?" foretold the coming confrontation between Christianity and communism. During the early stages of Stalinism, thousands of religious leaders and lay people were put in labor camps, many even executed. After the Stalinist thaw, repression of religion eased somewhat. But the state authorities still maintained control over the church by approving the appointment of religious leaders, regulating the building of churches, limiting religious activity to the confines of these church buildings, and using church leaders to keep any dissidents in line.

The relationship between church and state, like the relationship between the Soviet Union and the various countries, was by no means uniform. Each regime adopted a different attitude. Each denomination, in turn, responded differently, with variations from country to country, and from one decade to the next. In some cases, the church chose a policy of cooperation; in other cases, the church tended more toward confrontation. The church employed a mixture of "discretion and valour" to use Anglican canon Trevor Beeson's descriptive phrase, "with individuals and communities driven to their decisions not in libraries or comfortable armchairs but in the painful torrent of violent social upheaval."[2]

Despite the implementation of atheistic indoctrination, religion still held real sway over the populations of Eastern Europe. Even in Hungary, probably the most secularized country in the region, a 1980 survey showed 50 to 60 percent of the population held religious beliefs, and roughly one-third of all adults attended church regularly.[3] In neighboring Czechoslovakia, 51 percent of Slovaks and 30 percent of Czechs described themselves as religious believers.[4]

In Poland, the Roman Catholic church served as the guardian of Polish culture and tradition throughout its bitter history of partitions and foreign domination. The church symbolized the country's very soul: the romantic Poles viewed their country as the "Christ of the nations," a suffering nation with an almost Messianic mission. To be truly Polish was to be Catholic.

Because of the powerful allegiance the church received from the Polish people, it held a position of power without precedent in Eastern Europe, a position the Communist government ultimately realized it had to accommodate. In 1956, after Gomulka's reinstatement as party leader, the government eased its pressure on the church somewhat, only to reapply it two years later. From 1970 onward, with another change of government, the Catholic church was allowed a high degree of religious freedom as long as it did not directly challenge Communist party rule. The tiny Protestant minority in Poland enjoyed similar protections from the state under the wide umbrella of freedom afforded by the power of the Roman Catholic church.

East Germany, the heartland of the Reformation, was almost Poland's mirror image in this respect. The dominant position of Protestantism and its influence among the population forced the East German government to reach a historic accord with the Federation of Evangelical Churches on March 6, 1978. The government agreed to abandon its policy of trying to wipe out the church in exchange for the church's cooperation in building society as a church "within socialism." That meant adopting a position toward the Communist government that came to be called "critical solidarity." The Protestant church recognized socialism as a *fait accompli* after World War II. The church was willing to give the system a chance, but would resist becoming the puppet of a Marxist regime. "Critical solidarity" meant encouraging positive developments under the new reality, while at the same time reserving the right to denounce what was wrong with the Socialist state. The minority Catholic church, composed of about 1.3 million members, adopted a much different position. It stood completely apart from the government, while at the same time avoiding any open conflict.

In Czechoslovakia, the government took advantage of the historic strife between Protestants and Catholics to exert its own control. The Czech lands of Bohemia and Moravia had witnessed the first rebellion of the Reformation, when reformer Jan Hus denounced the religious and social corruption of the Roman Catholic church of the fifteenth century and was burned at the stake as a heretic. A later attempt at overthrowing Catholic rule and establishing a new Protestant order was brutally crushed in 1620 by the Catholic Hapsburg empire.

When the Communists came to power, they played the Protestants and Catholics off each other. The Catholic church in both the Czech areas and in the predominantly Catholic republic of Slovakia was brutally repressed, setting up a confrontation between the government and the Vatican. Protestants in general received more lenient treatment. Protestant leaders responded by taking a more accommodating line, owing largely to the heritage of Josef Hromadka, a theologian with the Evangelical Church of the Czech Brethren who helped pioneer the Marxist-Christian dialogue.

The Protestant church in Hungary also adopted a more accommodating stance toward the new Communist government, even to the point of collaboration. When party leader Janos Kadar embarked upon a policy of national reconciliation in the 1970s, marked by his almost biblical motto of "Whoever is not against us is with us," there was no question of whose side the Protestant leadership was on. The Protestant hierarchy, particularly the Reformed church under Bishop Tibor Bartha, was quick to show it stood "with" Kadar, offering uncritical support for Hungary's Socialist aims. A theology emerged called "*diakonia*," the Greek word for service, a theology that placed the church at the service of socialism.

The relationship between the Hungarian regime and the Roman Catholic church was marked by conflict and struggle, a battle first triggered when the Communist party seized Catholic property and usurped the church's dominant role before World War II. In 1950, the Catholic church was forced to sign an agreement making it subservient to the state. The isolated figure of Cardinal Jozsef Mindszenty, sentenced to life imprisonment on treason charges, served as a grim symbol of Catholic resistance. During the brief uprising in 1956, the cardinal was freed; he then sought refuge in the U.S. embassy when the revolution was crushed. For fifteen years, he doggedly resisted the suggestion to leave the embassy so that a new primate for Hungary could be appointed. It wasn't until Cardinal Mindszenty finally agreed to end his self-imposed exile that church-state relations began to relax somewhat, and his successor, Cardinal Laszlo Lekai, began pushing for more cooperation with the state.

One glance at Romania's landscape shows the overwhelming influence of the Orthodox church. The rustic countryside is dotted by Byzantine cupolas topped with ornate crosses. Though Romania was founded as a Roman outpost (the country is often referred to as a Latin island in a Slavic sea), its religious heritage is rooted not in Rome, but in Constantinople. Recognizing the Orthodox church's sway over the populace, the country's Communist rulers decided to harness the church's power as a tool to promote nationalism, rather than try to destroy it. A policy of co-existence emerged. The Orthodox church offered its service and support for the regime's foreign and domestic policies in exchange for maintaining its privileged position as a "state church," and the freedom to celebrate its liturgy virtually unhindered.

Other church traditions were not so privileged. The Eastern Rite (Uniate) church, an offshoot of the Orthodox church that still swears allegiance to the Vatican, was banned outright and its members ordered to return to the Orthodox fold. During the 1970s, when the country's Baptist church became one of the fastest growing churches in the world, the Romanian regime used the Department of Cults and the leaders of the Baptist Union to impose restrictions on building churches and conducting evangelism. The leaders of Romania's largest Protestant church, the Hungarian Reformed church, concentrated in the Hungarian-speaking areas of Transylvania, were coopted in the same way.

While the Communist regimes of Eastern Europe were watching their churches, the Kremlin was keeping an eye on the Communist regimes to make sure they didn't stray from the true faith of Marxism-Leninism. To guard against its own version of heresy, the Soviet Union asserted a policy that later came to be known as the Brezhnev doctrine: Moscow reserved the right to intervene militarily where it deemed the interests of socialism were being threatened. Any threat to the cohesion of the bloc's military alliance, the Warsaw

Pact, or any deviation from the central tenets of Marxism-Leninism, such as the leading role of the Party, demanded a military response.

Khrushchev was keeping a watchful eye on sweeping reforms being implemented by Hungarian premier Imre Nagy in 1956. When a popular uprising embraced the reforms and pushed them even further, to the point of sharing power with other parties and pulling out of the Warsaw Pact, Soviet tanks came rolling in.

The Brezhnev doctrine was invoked once again in 1968, when Czechoslovakian leader Alexander Dubcek began introducing gradual reforms designed to create "socialism with a human face." These reforms including allowing more democracy in the Communist party, opening the parliament up to other political parties, restoring civil rights, and declaring an end to censorship. Unlike Hungary's 1956 revolution, the experiment known as the "Prague Spring" was initiated from above and implemented gradually. Dubcek's regime was also careful to assert its intention to remain in the Warsaw Pact. Nevertheless, Dubcek's reforms posed a direct challenge to Soviet political and ideological interests and, in the Kremlin's view, had to be stopped before they infected the rest of Eastern Europe with truly democratic ideals. Warsaw Pact troops led by the Soviet Union invaded, turning the short-lived Prague Spring into a long winter.

But, when Mikhail Gorbachev took over as the Soviet Union's Communist party leader, the mood inside the Kremlin began to change. Gorbachev recognized the need for *glasnost* (openness) and *perestroika* (economic restructuring) in getting the Soviets' decaying house in order. The Kremlin's calls for reform echoed in the halls of power of Eastern Europe, where Communist regimes faced pressure to sweep out the cobwebs of their own economic and political policies. The new attitude within the walls of the Kremlin made it clear that Eastern Europe's Communist leaders could no longer rely on Soviet backing to stay in power.

If there were any doubts about whether the Brezhnev doctrine still applied, they were laid to rest when Soviet spokesman Gennadi Gerasimov pronounced it dead and buried. It had been replaced by what Gerasimov jokingly referred to as the "Sinatra doctrine," after the Frank Sinatra song, "I Did It My Way." The Soviet bloc countries were now free to do it their way.

If not for this hands-off policy toward Eastern Europe, and the reforms of *glasnost* and *perestroika,* it is difficult to imagine that the events in 1989 would ever have occurred.

Deteriorating economic and political situations throughout the region also turned up the heat on Eastern Europe's leaders. The regimes were suffering from a "legitimacy crisis," an erosion of support both from within and without. The people were growing restless, and Big Brother could no longer be counted on to bully the people into submission.

Protest in Eastern Europe began in whispered tones, but as other voices joined in, these mutterings grew stronger and stronger. The cries of priests and parishioners, students and workers, intellectuals and peasants, began to be heard. Carrying only candles of peace, like the children of Israel marching around Jericho with their trumpets, the people of Eastern Europe sounded the trumpet of truth and shouted out their demands. Unarmed and disarming, bathed in the pure light of thousands of candles, the voices of many united together.

And miraculously, the walls started crumbling: the walls of deceit and lies that had fenced these peoples in for decades, the walls of rules and repression that had cut off their basic human rights and freedoms, the walls of an atheistic philosophy that had imprisoned their very natures as spiritual beings. Until, miracle of miracles, the very symbol of the Communist system, the Wall itself, came tumbling down.

Notes

1. Karl Marx, Contribution to the Critique of Hegel's *Philosophy of Right: Introduction*, from *The Marx-Engels Reader*, edited by Robert C. Tucker (New York: W. W. Norton & Co., 1972), 12.

2. Trevor Beeson, *Discretion and Valour* (Philadelphia: Fortress Press, 1982), 22.

3. Ibid., 272.

4. John Anderson, "Courtesy Towards God," *Religion in Communist Lands,* Vol. 18, No. 2, Summer 1990, 106.

Part 1

Light in the Darkness

1

Czechoslovakia

PRAGUE, CZECHOSLOVAKIA
1981

Father Vaclav Maly [VAHTS´-laff MAH´-lee] looked around for any sign of surveillance. The Roman Catholic priest was always careful about being followed while on his way to visit friends. It was one thing to bring the wrath of the secret police down on himself. It was another to get others into trouble. Some of his friends were so afraid of associating with him that when he ran into them on the street, they looked right past him, as if he were a total stranger.

He was counting on the darkness of the night to conceal him. It wasn't always easy to tell if someone was tailing him. He thought he spotted a suspicious looking car, but he couldn't be sure. He turned into an empty street, walked around the corner, then doubled back, sneaking a quick glance over his shoulder. The car had moved on. He continued in the same way, taking a circuitous route to his destination, his broad, boyish face honed by the look of a determined scout.

Maly was built more like a boxer than a priest. That came from years of weight-lifting and jogging even before he had been forced to take manual jobs by the Czechoslovakian authorities. He had been stripped of his clerical collar and banned from performing any priestly duties.

Maly made sure no one was watching when he entered the apartment building and silently climbed the darkened staircase. He knocked softly on the door. It opened on a group of no more than ten people. They had all arrived one at a time, so as not to attract suspicion. There was a small table in the middle of the room covered with a simple white tablecloth. The group sat quietly around the table. They all exchanged greetings in muffled tones.

The table was set with a solitary loaf of bread and a glass goblet full of red wine. What Maly was about to do could cost him two years in prison. He took the bread, blessed it, broke it into pieces and gave it to his friends.

"The body of Christ, given for you."

—•—

Maly was employed as a stoker in the Meteor Hotel, a run-down high-rise in the center of Prague. Every day, he walked past the hotel's peeling facade into an alley strewn with garbage and stooped through the low entrance to the furnace room, a darkened cavern gritty with soot.

It was Maly's job to keep the furnace fed from the mountain of coal piled high in one corner, and then transport the ashes in the steel-gray cans lined up like tombstones against the chipping concrete wall. None of the work was automated. He felt like a machine, struggling up and down the steps, his thick hands calloused by the continual trips, shovel in hand, up and down, up and down, over and over and over. He scraped the ashes from the furnace's gaping mouth into one of the tall, cylindrical receptacles, the gritty dust flying into his eyes, his ears, his mouth. Then he dragged the leaden load of ashes back up to the landing, the steel can scraping and clanging, scraping and clanging, one step at a time. Finally, like a weightlifter doing a clean and jerk, he hoisted the heavy cans through a trap door in the ceiling, grunting and groaning to lift them onto his shoulders and heave them out through the opening.

He had done all kinds of odd jobs since the government suspended his priesthood: cleaning toilets in the city subway, emptying bedpans as a hospital orderly, now working as a stoker. In a way, he didn't mind doing manual work. He rode the crowded trams and buses, elbow to elbow with the people, no longer isolated in a parish house from the man on the street. He never told his fellow workers that he was a priest. But when the secret police would come for one of their regular visits, the people he worked with would find out and ask questions. It gave him a chance to talk about his faith, not from some distant pulpit, but from the proximity of sharing their lives and problems. He learned to respect them, and they learned to respect him. Of course, he was still a priest. He still served God.

It was Maly's childhood dream to become an airplane pilot and drive a sleek Mercedes Benz. Instead, he ended up becoming a priest and driving a cheap, East German-made Trabant. He graduated from high school in 1968, during the heady days of the Prague Spring. The refreshing breeze of Alexander Dubcek's "socialism with a human face" fanned an excitement in him and his classmates about the possibility of political change.

When Soviet tanks rolled in to crush the short-lived reform, they crushed Maly's political dreams along with it. Teachers he once trusted took up the lies of the new hard-line regime. His friends were shattered. They had put all their faith in politics, and that faith had been dashed. That's when he realized he wanted to become a priest.

Maly's parents were deeply religious. His father, a teacher, lost his job because of his faith. He and his three sisters were brought up to believe in God, contrary to the atheistic instruction they were getting in school. Maly was the only believer in his class. After seeing the futility of placing his faith in politics, he wanted a faith that would endure. He called it his "life-hope," and he became a priest to show others the possibility of that faith, even in the most difficult circumstances.

His ministry as a parish priest in northern Bohemia was short-lived, ending less than three years after he was ordained. The government stripped him of his official clerical status after accusing him of violating restrictions and speaking to young people outside his assigned parish. But it was actually his support for the human rights document Charter 77 that drew the wrath of the Czechoslovak government. All nine of the priests who signed the charter had their clerical licenses taken away.

Charter 77, a manifesto protesting the violation of human rights in Czechoslovakia, first appeared on January 1, 1977. The document directed a scathing attack against the government's disregard of rights it promised to uphold in the Helsinki Agreement on Civil and Political Rights ratified the year before.

"Freedom of public expression is repressed by the centralized control of all the communications media and of publishing and cultural institutions," the document read. "No philosophical, political, or scientific view, or artistic expression that departs ever so slightly from the narrow bounds of official ideology or aesthetics is allowed to be published; no open criticism can be made of abnormal social phenomena; no public defense is possible against false and insulting charges made in official propaganda . . . no open debate is allowed in the domain of thought and art. Many scholars, writers, artists, and others are penalized for having legally published or expressed, years ago, opinions which are condemned by those who hold political power today.

"Freedom of religious confession . . . is systematically curtailed by arbitrary official action; by interference with the activity of churchmen, who are constantly threatened by the refusal of the state to permit them the exercise of their functions, or by the withdrawal of such permission; by financial or other measures against those who express their religious faith in word or action; by constraints on religious training and so forth . . .

"Charter 77 is a free informal, open community of people of different convictions, different faiths, and different professions united by the will to strive, individually and collectively, for the respect of civic and human rights in our own country and throughout the world."[1]

Charter 77 was not only a manifesto. It was also the loosely knit community of the thousand or so disparate people who signed the document, the artists and writers, playwrights and rock musicians, Protestants and Catholics, even disillusioned Marxists who could no longer keep silent about the government's repression of basic human rights.

A handful of Chartists, as they were called, would often gather to discuss strategy at the apartment of Vaclav Havel, with its panoramic view of the Vltava River and Prague's Presidential Palace jutting out of the promontory beyond its banks. Havel was one of the Charter's founding fathers. From his early years, the playwright had been at odds with the government. In 1967, he stood up at the Fourth Writers' Congress and denounced government censorship. After the Soviet invasion of 1968, his plays were banned and, like Maly, he, too, was forced to do menial labor.

It was always a risk for the Chartists to meet together, but for Maly, it was a risk worth taking. He saw his fellow Chartists as a community of support. He felt it was important to express the truth, to call things by their real names, and he believed the Chartists had begun to do that. When people looked at them, he thought, they saw real people who were able to live freely. In a society where people said one thing in private and another in public, Maly saw that truth was a rare commodity. The Communists disdained the word. Everyone in Czechoslovakia knew that things were bad. And so to call things by their real names, to express the truth, that was what was most important to him.

Maly grew up in a family where the truth was valued. His parents were always telling him and his three sisters not to be two-faced. "Speak freely," they admonished. "If anyone asks you what we speak about at home, tell them. We don't say one thing at home, and another at school. Always speak the truth. That's where you'll find real freedom."

On December 16, Maly was mechanically going about his duties at the Hotel Meteor. He bent over and scooped up a shovelful of coal. A dull pain spread through his lower back as he straightened up to balance the heavy load. His biceps bulged into a rounded mass under the strain, a spidery network of veins popping into view on his powerful forearms. He staggered down the steps to where the furnace waited below; it hissed and rumbled like a volcano ready to receive a sacrifice. A blast of heat hit him as he shoveled the coal into its red-hot jaws. Then he plodded back up the steps to dredge up another load.

The furnace room was always sweltering. Rivulets of sweat ran down his solid torso. His grubby workshirt clung to his body in the stifling heat.

As he struggled down the steps of the furnace room with another back-breaking load, he heard the rusting boiler starting to sputter. He looked up and saw steam spewing out of the main valve. It was going to blow! He dropped his shovel and rushed over to adjust the pressure, but he reached the valve too late. A deafening blast sent him reeling across the room. He lay there in a heap, too dazed to move.

The police showed up later at the hotel. Maly was arrested and detained for five days on charges of "destroying Socialist property."

Note

1. Translation from *Charter 77 and Human Rights in Czechoslovakia*, H. Gordon Skilling (London: George Allen & Unwin, 1981), 210-211.

2

Poland

August 22, 1980

It was the dead of night when Tadeusz Mazowiecki [Tah-DAY´-oosh Mah-zo-vee-ET´-skee] arrived at the Lenin shipyard in Gdansk with Professor Bronislaw Geremek. Mazowiecki's drawn face looked more haggard than usual, his deep-set eyes cavernous. The pair wandered wearily toward the shipyard gate, Mazowiecki's tall gaunt form hovering over Geremek's smaller, penguin-like figure. Mazowiecki was surprised to see the imposing iron gate ahead of them had been turned into a shrine, an emblem of the Catholic faith of the striking workers inside. The entrance was intertwined with flowers and decorated with religious symbols—crudely constructed crosses, pictures of the Polish Pope, and images of the Black Madonna, the darkly mysterious icon that expresses the heart of Polish Catholicism.

Mazowiecki held in his hands a letter of support for the striking workers signed by sixty-four distinguished intellectuals. The wildcat strikes were set off in July 1980 when the government unexpectedly announced huge hikes in the price of meat. More than 150 strikes broke out, with workers insisting on a list of economic demands, such as restoring the old prices and increasing wages to match the rising cost of living. But when seventeen thousand workers put down their tools and began occupying the huge showcase shipyard in Gdansk on August 14, the wave of strikes took a political turn. The workers were demanding, among other things, an end to censorship and the unprecedented freedom of independent, non-Communist trade unions.

After the flurry of strikes ignited across Poland's tinder-dry political landscape, Mazowiecki felt the intelligentsia could no longer remain silent. The painful history of the gap between Poland's workers and intellectuals was all too familiar to him. In 1968, the workers stood aside and watched in silence during the suppression of student protests and the anti-Semitic campaign against intellectuals that followed. In 1970, it was the intelligentsia who remained silent while the blood of Polish workers was spilled in front of those same shipyard gates. At least forty-five were killed when Polish troops fired on them to put down a similar strike over price hikes. Again in June 1976, the government violently suppressed a workers' protest over rising food prices. Thousands of workers who participated in the strikes were fired. Others were put on trial and received severe sentences. Mazowiecki realized the time was never more right to forge an alliance between the workers and intellectuals—uniting them into the common force needed to get the rusting, broken down machinery of the Communist bureaucracy moving to serve the Polish people.

The two classes were like the energy and pistons of Polish society. The intelligentsia, throughout the partitions of the nineteenth century, had helped preserve the Polish cultural identity. Though a relatively small group composed of the nation's teachers, priests, poets, writers, editors, and other professionals, they were still a driving political and philosophical force.

Poland's huge working class provided the impetus behind Poland's big push toward industrialization. Throughout the 1970s, with a series of sporadic strikes and walkouts over food prices, the workers had paralyzed industries, forcing the government to give in to their demands. The party that billed itself as the "vanguard of the workers" could not ignore their voice. For Mazowiecki, now was the time for intellectuals to add their voices to the workers clamoring for "Solidarity" in the Lenin shipyard.

As editor of the Catholic monthly *Wiez*, Mazowiecki was one of Poland's prominent Catholic intellectuals. *Wiez* means "link" or "bond" in Polish, and the magazine had served to connect not only the community of Catholic intellectuals, but also dissident members of the intelligentsia outside the church. *Wiez* was one of the few havens for dissidents. Those who were blackballed from publishing in the official press could always find a place in the pages of *Wiez*. When dissident historian Adam Michnik was banned from virtually any public activity, his articles appeared in *Wiez* under the pen name of Andzrej Zagozda.

The periodical included essays on Catholic philosophy, politics, and history. Mazowiecki edited it from a small, dust-covered office, simply decorated, with a picture of Don Quixote hanging on the bare walls—a fitting symbol for the periodical. Each issue was an adventure in absurdity, a verbal joust with the ubiquitous government censors. Mazowiecki never knew which items would slip by the censors, and which would need to be excised or rewritten at the last minute. The censors were armed with a long list of "don'ts" they gleefully applied to Poland's Catholic press. There could be no mention of the link between Polish nationalism and Catholicism, nothing about the contribution of the church toward Polish national life, and absolutely no criticism of the religious situation in the Soviet bloc. Just the same, Poland's censors had developed something of a grudging admiration for Mazowiecki and *Wiez*. One of the chief censors once told his underlings it would be a great pity if *Wiez* got into trouble, since no other journal wrote about Poland's history better.

Mazowiecki's job with *Wiez* put him in contact with a broad spectrum of Polish intellectuals. He also had extensive contacts with other Catholic intellectuals through his involvement with the Warsaw Club of Catholic Intellectuals (KIK). KIK was a loose network of the Catholic intelligentsia with chapters in several Polish cities aimed at prodding the Catholic laity into deeper involvement in the life of the country.

When the strikes erupted, Mazowiecki quickly drew up an

appeal to garner the support of the intelligentsia for the strikers and their demands. "The place of all the progressive intelligentsia is at the side of the workers in this struggle," the statement read. "That is the Polish tradition, and that is the imperative of the hour." The appeal urged that the crisis be settled by negotiation, without bloodshed, and called for "the freedom of trade union association without outside interference. . . . Only caution and imagination can today lead us to an understanding in the interests of our common fatherland."

Mazowiecki then gathered together a small group of eight to ten intellectuals to help circulate the appeal.

The next day, the appeal was sent off to the Communist Party Central Committee after gaining sixty-four signatures.

The job of delivering it to the striking workers fell to Mazowiecki and Geremek, a brilliant medieval historian, Mazowiecki had met through the Flying University. The Flying University met clandestinely in different apartments to consider subjects banned from public discussion. These seminars brought together students and intellectuals, both Catholic and secular.

Geremek was chosen to help deliver the appeal by virtue of the fact that he had a good car, a Volvo. Gdansk was virtually isolated, cut off from the rest of Poland, an island of unrest. All trains and buses running in and out of the city were shut down. Virtually the only way to get to the Baltic port was by automobile. The pair left on a Friday morning to present the letter of support to the Inter-Factory Strike Committee (MKS) made up of representatives from all the striking factories in the Gdansk area.

When the two arrived inside the shipyard, they were struck by how well-organized everything seemed inside. They expected to find confusion reigning beyond the gates. Instead, they found an organized community, ruled by unwritten laws. They were received by what seemed to be a welcoming committee of striking workers and ushered past the assembly buildings, where thousands of workers slept on blankets and air mattresses, then led into the assembly hall of the Health and Safety building. Inside the hall, just past the long tables set up for the delegates of the Inter-Strike Committee, they found the mustachioed leader of the strike, Lech Walesa, holding court.

Walesa glanced over the appeal after they presented it to him. "We already heard about this over Radio Free Europe," Walesa said, then handed the document back. "This is very good," he told them. "But we need not only supporters. We need advisers. We are only workers. The government negotiators are educated men. Would you stay on and help us negotiate with the authorities?"

The invitation was unexpected. The negotiations were getting underway the following morning.

"What can we do?" Mazowiecki asked.

"You can organize a commission of experts to advise us and help us in formulating our demands."

The two agreed to stay on, and stayed up late into the night talking with Walesa about the upcoming negotiations. When the late-night session ended, Mazowiecki spread out a blanket to catch what little sleep he could on the cold, concrete floor.

Lying awake on his uncomfortable make-shift bed, Mazowiecki found himself reminded of another time he had been asked to play the role of mediator. The occasion was a hunger strike declared by the Committee for Social Self Defense (KOR), a network set up by intellectuals after the 1976 strike to defend the rights of workers. The hunger strikers occupied St. Martin's Church in May 1977 to demand the release of five workers who were still imprisoned, as well as to protest the recent arrests of nine KOR members. Mazowiecki served as their spokesman, presenting their list of demands to the Council of State, then shuttling back and forth between the hunger strikers and the authorities. That yellow sandstone church in the quaintly renovated Old Town section of Warsaw served as a crossroads connecting the church and the opposition. The collective fast not only secured the release of the political prisoners, it also helped secure the link between Catholic and secular intellectuals, between believers and unbelievers, between workers and the intelligentsia.

When the hunger strikers nervously filed out of the church past the security police stationed outside to end their fast, they vividly remembered how workers from Radom and Ursus were forced to run a gauntlet of truncheon-wielding police as revenge for their protest strike. They braced themselves for some form of violent recrimination, but it never came. Mazowiecki wondered now whether this present protest action, these events swirling all around him in the Gdansk shipyard, would end so peacefully, or whether the bloody cycle of 1970 and 1976 would repeat itself.

—•—

The next morning, after sending word back to Warsaw to recruit a small group of advisers to join them, Mazowiecki and Geremek were led into the great hall, which was now filled with hundreds of delegates who formed the strike committee. The hall was buzzing with preparations for the arriving government delegation. Mazowiecki was escorted to the low platform at the far end of the hall where the leaders of the strike committee sat. He noticed the objects behind the dais—a Polish flag to the right, a life-sized statue of Lenin to the left, and a crucifix in between—three symbols that epitomized the Polish nation in all its contradictions.

Walesa grabbed the microphone set up at the presidium's table, and in his folksy, charismatic style boomed out: "Ladies and gentlemen, we have a matter to take care of. For the union to do its job right in the negotiations before us, we have to appoint a body of experts. After all, we have to be wise and good, right? I think we did the right thing."

While the delegates applauded, Mazowiecki approached the microphone. He looked stilted and ill at ease standing in front of the crowded hall.

"Can you hear me?" he asked tentatively.

"Yes, we hear you," Walesa reassured him.

"First, I'd like to talk about a different matter," he said. "My name is Mazowiecki. I came here with Professor Geremek. We are both signatories of the appeal of the 64 intellectuals, which, if I'm not mistaken, you received earlier. In this appeal, we would like to declare our solidarity with your fight, which isn't just your own affair, but the struggle of the entire nation. After being here, we've become convinced of your great prudence. We hope you'll be able to maintain that, together with your greatest power, your solidarity."

These words of challenge were answered with generous applause. "Now, as far as the committee of experts is concerned, we will do our best to help you, but our role is limited. It's up to us to advise the Presidium of the Strike Committee. But the decisions are up to them."

He sat down to more applause. Later, in the shipyard, he and Geremek noticed a woman from the city carrying a basket full of bread and butter, asking the strikers if she could do anything to help. Her simple act of support convinced them the strike was not just an isolated action by a group of shipyard workers. It was something much larger, an action that brought together all of Polish society.

3

Hungary

BUDAPEST, HUNGARY
1977

On a street corner in the Kispest [KEESH´-pesht] district of Budapest, a crowd of about thirty-five people gathered outside a plain white wooden building. Several leaned against cars parked on the street. A closer look revealed some of them had artificial limbs; others propped themselves up with crutches.

This was a Methodist congregation. The members had arrived outside the church where the congregation had been meeting for 60 years, only to find the door padlocked. It had been sold to an electric company the week before by church officials in collusion with the Hungarian government.

One of the pastors of the congregation, Gabor Ivanyi [GAH´-bore Ee-VAHN´-yee], knew there might be trouble that Sunday. Several days before, two men from the secret police showed up at the door of the church's caretaker and demanded to know if the congregation would try to defy the authorities and force open the doors. The caretaker told them he had no idea what the congregation would do.

When the members arrived for the Sunday service, six police cars were patrolling the area outside the church, making sure their presence was noticed. One policeman walked up and down the street with a walkie-talkie. When Pastor Ivanyi ventured up to the church door and tried it, the police started to move in. Ivanyi hesitated, then told his church members to remain in front of the closed door and hold their worship service there. As they worshiped in the small courtyard, the secret police backed off and kept watch just outside the iron fence encircling the church. The cars barreling by nearly drowned out the faint melody of the hymns. But they continued the service, bowing their heads in prayer and then looking up at Pastor Ivanyi, straining to hear him preach over the noise of the traffic.

Ivanyi was a big bear of a man, a man of towering height and ample girth. His colossal appearance might have been menacing, if not for his gentle eyes and disarming smile, a smile just visible through the forest of his dense brown whiskers. Conflict with the Hungarian authorities was nothing new to him. When he was seventeen years old, Ivanyi wrote a composition entitled, "What Makes a Man Happy," deriving the title from a quote by the famous Hungarian poet Vorosmarty. It was a treatise on his new-found faith. It wasn't money or fame that led to happiness, he argued in the composition, but faith in God. He read the composition aloud in class. During the next break, the director of his high school came to the class and expelled him for "agitation." He now faced a similar persecution for being pastor of a congregation that was illegal in the government's eyes.

The story of Gabor Ivanyi's church was a complicated one. The Kispest congregation was one of several that split off from the three thousand member Methodist church in 1974 after a dispute over the election of the denomination's church superintendent. When Adam Hecker, the current district superintendent, was nearing retirement age, Gabor's father, Tibor Ivanyi, seemed the likely choice to succeed him. The elder Ivanyi was dynamic and charismatic, and he and his wife were popular with the young people in the denomination. But unlike the mild-mannered Hecker, he also had a reputation as a man who wouldn't bow easily to government pressure.

When the Methodist hierarchy decided to postpone the election of the superintendent, Ivanyi denounced the move as a blatant violation of the church constitution. It seemed to Ivanyi and his backers that the denomination's leadership was merely carrying out the orders of the government-run State Office of Church Affairs to keep him out in order to fill the position with a more malleable candidate.

The indefinite postponement of the election set off an acrimonious debate between Ivanyi and the church leadership. Since no new election had taken place, Hecker continued serving as superintendent in an unofficial capacity. Ivanyi was ordered by the Methodist hierarchy to leave his 120 member church in eastern Hungary, where he had been feuding with the local authorities, for another church in the industrial city of Miskolc. Hecker viewed the move as an opportunity for Ivanyi to make a fresh start somewhere else; Ivanyi viewed it as yet another attempt by the church leaders to disrupt his ministry. When he refused the transfer, the church took disciplinary action against him for insubordination and dismissed him from the pastorate. This action paved the way for Hecker's son, Frederick, to succeed him as superintendent.

Ivanyi appealed to the government, but the government ruled the case was an internal church matter, and referred it to the Council of Free Churches (CFC), which predictably sided with the Methodist hierarchy. Ivanyi accused the head of the CFC, Sandor Palotay, of corruption and collaboration with the government and the secret police. The church hierarchy responded by stripping him of his own seat on the CFC's executive council.

The controversy split the Methodist church in two. The ten pastors who sided with the elder Ivanyi in the dispute had their preaching licenses revoked. They continued their ministries with the support of the one thousand members who made up their congregations.

Gabor Ivanyi was one of those who paid the price for backing his father. He, too, was forbidden to preach and harassed for his stubborn disregard of the order. The government not only padlocked the door of his church and sold the building to an electric company, but he and his family were also kicked out of their church apartment, since he was no longer the pastor of a legal congregation. His wife, Kati, took their children to live with his parents in a town 150 miles away, while he stayed on with friends to continue preaching at the Kispest congregation. He began searching for an apartment so his family could be together again, but to no avail. Apartments in Budapest were scarce, with a three to four year waiting list for most.

The Sunday after their church was sold, the same circle was back in front of the closed door. An agent in a blue car parked across the street snapped their photographs as they defiantly worshiped in front of the building that was once their church.

Gabor Ivanyi surveyed the congregation, and saw just how determined they were to continue meeting there, especially the disabled members. Their furrowed faces showed the strength and determination it took as they struggled to keep standing there on their crutches. His church had made a special mission of reaching out to the outcasts of society. Now they were all outcasts. He decided they would hold out and continue meeting outside in protest, even through the freezing winter months. They would not give in to what he considered an unjust decision by the church hierarchy to strip them of their church.

4

East Germany

Leipzig, East Germany
1989

The local Communist authorities objected to the sign posted outside Leipzig's Nikolai Church. It read, "OPEN FOR ALL" in large, block letters. They wanted it to say simply "OPEN" but Rev. Christian Führer, one of the pastors of the church, stood by the original wording. "The church is the roof over the heads of those without a home," he argued. "The sign's an invitation. Our church is an open house with room for all to come in freely and speak as they wish. The sign stays the same."

Every Monday afternoon at 5:00 P.M., the church turned into a veritable open house. A diverse group of people, most of them young, many of them not even believers, wandered in for the weekly peace prayer service or *friedensgebete* and for discussion groups afterward. The church was really the only place to voice their opinions openly. Each service attracted a smorgasbord of political groups, or "basis groups" as they were called. There were groups meeting to try to clean up the environment, others discussing political and human rights, still others arguing over the problems of nuclear disarmament.

Brigitta Treetz [rhymes with "rates"] looked around at the people present in the church that particular afternoon. She was a striking-looking woman, with shoulder length hair the color of a sun-washed beach, neatly swept back from her rounded tan face. Brigitta had been coming to the peace prayer for about six years. She originally started attending because of her concern for the environment. Leipzig was probably the worst casualty of the country's pollution problems, and working with the environmental group meeting at the Nikolai church was one of the few available avenues for doing anything about it. The picturesque countryside of rolling hills south of the city was blotted out by a curtain of smog. Coal-burning power plants and chemical factories belched black clouds of odoriferous smoke. The air in the city was barely breathable; one out of every two children in the city were treated each year for respiratory-related illnesses. Historic buildings that survived the bombing of World War II now were being destroyed by acid rain; the blackened decorative facade of the fourteenth century Old Town Hall was crumbling.

The numbers attending the peace prayer had grown over the years, from a handful to several hundred. There were more and more *ausreisen* now, would-be emigrés who had come to the church to seek support in their bid to leave the country. She was a little dismayed to see so many of them. She saw the service as a place to pray for peace and for her country, to band together to do something about the state and its cruel machinery—to name the political bureaucracy for what it was. The *ausreisen* weren't interested in any of those things, she thought.

She spied two young men wearing black leather jackets in a pew across from her. *Stasi,* she thought—secret police. They were not-too-secret in their leather jackets, de rigueur uniforms for the young members. These two obviously didn't feel comfortable in church. When the members of the congregation folded their hands in prayer, they grinned at one another, covering their embarrassment and discomfort with the unfamiliar situation.

"Stasi" was short for the East German Ministry for State Security. Its presence was pervasive in East German life. The Stasi employed 86,000 regulars and upwards of two million unofficial co-workers, or one-in-eight East Germans: everyday citizens who were coopted into doing some kind of surveillance for the ministry. The Stasi had its own elite military corps and officers in the army, police, and customs. Hordes of Stasi agents monitored the phone, the mail, even everyday life with cameras mounted at intersections. They had reams and reams of files on some six million citizens, a third of the country's population.

There were always Stasi agents in the worship service. *What do they want here?* Brigitta asked herself. Do they hope their very presence will invoke fear? If so, they sent the wrong people. These two young toughs looked so awkward, she almost felt sorry for them.

Fear, she thought. It was what kept people in line. Everyone was so anxious. Otherwise, they wouldn't sit by, hoping the situation would change by itself; the nameless masses seemed to accept holding their peace as their primary civic duty. But she realized she was being unfair. Here in the church, the East German people were learning to put their despair into words, and to express it without hatred. And they were beginning to gain courage from their growing numbers.

5

Romania

TIMISOARA, ROMANIA
July, 1989

The image flickering on TV screens across Hungary at first glance seemed harmless, almost banal: a pastor from Romania being interviewed by Canadian journalists. But in this case, his very presence on the weekly Hungarian program "Panorama" sent out a revolutionary message. Laszlo Tokes [LAHS´-loe TER´-kesh], a pastor of the Reformed church, appeared in order to protest the Romanian regime's treatment of his fellow ethnic Hungarians.

The picture was a little grainy. The interview had to be filmed in secret in Tokes's church in Timisoara [Tim-ih-SWAHR´-ah] and then smuggled out of the country. The Canadian journalists who conducted the interview were later kicked out of Romania.

"You see, gentlemen, I brought you here to the church for we dare not speak in our homes," Tokes said at the beginning of the interview. "According to a friend of mine, even my bathroom is bugged. I don't know if this is true, but in any case, I am afraid to speak except outside, or in corridors."

The thirty-seven-year-old pastor stood against the pews of the church balcony. He had the dark, exotic looks of a gypsy, with coal-black piercing eyes. His broad face was earnest, his rich, bass voice deliberate. "You may wonder why I take the risk of talking to you. It is somewhat absurd, no doubt, for it is not only a sense of responsibility that makes me speak. I also have an irresistible urge to speak out at last, to say finally what I have so often wanted to say. I do not speak for myself, but on the behalf of others. Why should we participate forever in this wall of silence? This wall is much more massive and impenetrable than the Berlin Wall, and I feel somebody has to start to demolish it."

The Hungarian media had been reluctant to discuss the plight of ethnic Hungarians living in Romania. After all, such problems weren't supposed to exist under socialism. Publicizing them threatened to cast a further chill on the already icy relations between the two Communist neighbors.

A strip of barbed wire snaked along the divide between the so-called "fraternal, Socialist" countries of Hungary and Romania, betraying the true feelings of these "allies." Both sides claimed to be the original settlers of the disputed border region known as Transylvania. Ownership of the region had shifted back and forth between the two countries several times between the two world wars before ending up in Romania's hands. The sizable Hungarian minority that remained there, about twenty-five percent of the population of the region, prevented the dispute from ending.

To many Western minds, the name "Transylvania" conjures up an image that flashes into view with a bolt of lightning, a celluloid scene of an ominous looking Gothic castle perched atop a craggy mountain, the home of the famous vampire, Dracula, created by Bram Stoker and later played by Bela Lugosi. In fact, the inspiration for the blood-thirsty fiend lived in Transylvania during the fifteenth century. His castle still stands in Bran, not the eerie Gothic edifice portrayed by Hollywood, but a plain medieval fortress nestled in the lush green forests of the Carpathian mountains. His name was Vlad Tepes, or Vlad the Impaler. And while he didn't actually drink the blood of his victims, his treatment of them justified the metaphor. He was known to have nailed the turbans on the heads of visiting sultans who neglected to remove them in his presence.

His victims included not only his enemies, but his own people and even those in his own court who offended him in one way or another. He often skewered them alive on sharpened stakes, or cut off their heads and put them on public display. His adversaries actually called him "Dracula," meaning son of the devil, and his bloody exploits helped inspire the legend of the vampire.

Now Transylvania was being persecuted by another tyrant. Nicolae Ceausescu, the president of Romania, was waging a campaign to destroy thousands of villages and forcibly relocate the residents to newly-built urban centers. Under this demolition and construction program called "systemization," bulldozers would go into villages with populations of less than two thousand, raze the houses and churches and relocate the residents in newly-built Socialist-style concrete apartment blocks in designated urban tenements. Up to seven thousand of the country's thirteen thousand villages were targeted. The ethnic Hungarians living in Transylvania feared their cultural identity would be wiped out in the process. An estimated fifty thousand of them were to be relocated under the program. Their cultural life revolved around the villages and churches of Transylvania. Ceausescu's relocation program sought to erase any trace of Hungarian culture and assimilate the ethnic Hungarians into Romania.

This measure, this "final solution," had come after several less severe strategies had already been employed. Romanians had already been moved en masse to towns where Hungarians predominated to dilute the Hungarian population. Ethnic Hungarian theater groups were banned from touring; the country's two Hungarian universities shut down. In many towns, Hungarian schools were closed and the students sent to Romanian schools.

Ethnic Hungarians also faced subtle discrimination at school and at work. They complained of getting the worst wages and constantly getting passed over for promotions. Many dared to speak their mother tongue only at home. They were often told, "If you want to eat Romanian bread, then speak Romanian." In the eastern part of the country, school children were fined one *lei* (about a nickel) for each Hungarian word they were caught using.

In the interview, Tokes let it be known that his people's cultural identity was being stripped away. He was tired of his people feeling like second-class citizens. Most of all, he feared for the future of Hungarian-speaking children, particularly his three-year-old son, Mate. After finishing school, Mate faced the prospect of being forced to move to a city predominated by ethnic Romanians, the only place he could find a job under Ceausescu's repatriation plan. Tokes and his wife, Edith, feared that one day, Mate would no longer know what it meant to be Hungarian.

It was a bold interview, a risky one. Not only were millions of people across Hungary riveted to their television sets, but the broadcast was also being picked up by antennas across Transylvania. Most of the Hungarian-speaking residents along the border tuned into Hungarian TV for their news. An electricity shortage limited the Romanian television station to broadcasting only about two hours a night, and even those two hours, filled with driveling tribute to Ceausescu, were too much for most Romanians to stomach.

"The other thing that induced me to take this step is not really new," Tokes said, as he continued talking during the interview. "As a minister, as a spiritual leader, I feel responsible to the people. This responsibility is even heavier, since most of my fellow ministers are silent. I am a minister of the Reformed church in Romania. The clergy, and in particular the bishops of this church, identify completely with the policy which has, among other things, produced this mind-boggling plan to destroy the villages."

Tokes's deliberate voice was louder now, more animated. Point by point, he outlined his opposition to the village destruction campaign, blasting it as yet another method of destroying his people's culture: "During the past decades our institutions have been gradually and systematically wiped out, one after the other. Our culture and our school system have been destroyed. An offensive has been conducted against all possible means of maintaining our ethnic identity. And I feel that it is now the church's turn. [The authorities] are now launching a frontal attack against the Reformed church. And this applies to the Catholic church as well as the Reformed church, for practically the whole Hungarian population in Romania belongs to one of them."

The camera continued rolling as Tokes made his final points. "The destruction of villages actually has a subjective aspect, too, one that affects human rights. . . . In a totalitarian system it seems to be a luxury to think in terms of what I, as an individual, am or am not permitted to do. We have not yet reached the Western level of social development that would enable us to claim [our] human rights . . . the rights stipulated by the basic document of the UN and by the Helsinki declaration are most brutally violated every day."

After the interview aired on Hungarian TV, a rock came crashing through the window of Tokes's apartment. The campaign of intimidation was underway.

Part 2

Flickering Hopes

6

Poland

On October 16, 1978, an event took Poland, and the world, by surprise—an event that galvanized the Polish nation. For the first time in nearly five hundred years, a non-Italian was elected pope, the first pontiff ever from Poland. Mazowiecki could hardly believe the image on his television screen: Karol Wojtyla, the cardinal of Krakow, an old acquaintance, was standing on the balcony of St. Peter's Basilica, wearing the cassock of the pope for the first time. In that image, Poland's past and present flashed before his eyes.

"On October 16, all lights were turned on Rome and on Poland," Mazowiecki wrote of the surprising election. "All Poland looked at herself. In this widespread spontaneous reaction, we felt in ourselves an unusual upsurge of strength and hope. As if history had smiled on us."[1]

History smiled again when Cardinal Karol Wojtyla returned to his homeland as pope in 1979. Faced with the complex tasks of setting up an itinerary, arranging for the mass rallies, and setting up crowd control, the Polish church and the Polish people discovered a competence within themselves, completely independent of the Polish government. The 15 million people who thronged John Paul II's open-air Masses during the nine-day visit surprised everyone with their orderliness and discipline. Church-appointed guards charged with keeping order found their jobs to be almost superfluous.

The pope ended his homily at Victory Square in Warsaw with the words, "May the Holy Ghost descend among you and renew the face of the land . . . of this land." His invocation was being fulfilled even as he spoke. Perhaps for the first time in the country's post-war history, the Polish people realized their solidarity, a solidarity that became incarnate in the Gdansk shipyard a year later.

GDANSK, POLAND
August 1980

Blue-overalled strikers waited for hours outside the conference hall where the talks between Walesa and Deputy Prime Minister Mieczyslaw Jagielski dragged on. The workers watched the proceedings through the hall's large windows, and listened to the discussions being broadcast over loudspeakers throughout the shipyard. They waited, tense with anticipation, as evening came on and darkness fell.

There were growing fears of a violent crackdown on the strike. Rumors began floating through the shipyard that a state of emergency would be imposed if the strike didn't end by September l. Ominous statements appeared in the Party papers and through the Soviet news agency TASS about the "anti-Socialist" forces involved in the strikes.

Mazowiecki's committee of experts had grown. Joining him and Geremek were Andrzej Wielowieyski, head of the Warsaw KIK chapter, Bogdan Cywinski, editor of the Catholic periodical *ZNAK*, two economists and a sociologist, Jadwiga Staniszkis.

Before entering into negotiations, though, Mazowiecki wanted to know exactly where they stood. He suggested to Walesa that the new committee of advisors meet with some of the strike leaders to find out what items were non-negotiable, and which items were crumbs that could be given away. The group stole off to a machine shed that they knew wouldn't be bugged for the frank discussion.

"If the government refuses to give in on the issue of free trade unions, what then?" Mazowiecki asked. "Are you willing to settle for less? Maybe complete democratic reform of the official unions?"

The strike leaders were adamant. They would give up a wage increase before backing down on the matter of independent, self-governing trade unions.

The whole idea of an independent, self-governing trade union was anathema to Communist doctrine. In the first place, according to the Party, it simply wasn't necessary. The Party was the vanguard of the worker. Why, then, did workers need a union independent of it? In the second place, a labor force independent of the Party was a direct challenge to the Party's leading role and its control of Poland's industry and economy. Any attempts at autonomy and self-organization would be a slap in the face to the Party's right to rule every aspect of Polish life. Thirdly, if free trade unions had the right to pick their own leaders and factory managers, what would that do to the *nomenklatura*? In effect, free trade unions would usurp the Party's prerogative to fill vital positions.

While Walesa and the strike leaders negotiated with the government delegation before the whirring cameras and tape recorders of the world press, Mazowiecki met out of the public spotlight in a small working group behind the closed doors of a nearby building. Joining him were two other advisors and three members of the strike leadership. Across from them was a government group of experts led by the provincial governor of Gdansk, Jerzy Kolodziejski. Mazowiecki realized they were walking a tightrope. It was their job to hit on a deal that satisfied not only the strikers and the regime, but one that the Polish government could also sell to Moscow.

The first meeting got underway in a strange, relaxed atmosphere. The two sides addressed each other as equals, in gentle, half-joking terms. They began tackling the idea of a free trade union in hypothetical terms: what needed to happen if a free trade union were allowed. The first snag involved the technical aspects of registering an independent trade union.

"The only legal possibility is to register such an independent trade union within the existing official trade union," one of the government experts insisted.

That was out of the question, the strikers' representatives said.

The government side eventually gave in and agreed to find a way to register an independent trade union outside the Communist-led unions. "But there's no way we can accept your demand that all Poles have the right to organize independent trade unions," the government side said. "If the government approves such a formula, it will look like Czechoslovakia in 1968, when the Dubcek regime was accused of 'encouraging from above.' "

Mazowiecki and his team of advisors realized what the government side was implying. They wanted to avoid any appearance in Moscow's eyes that the Polish regime was promoting independent unions. It had been just that type of liberalism that caused Dubcek's fall in Czechoslovakia. The government would rather be forced into granting only one independent union, even if that meant putting up with strikes breaking out everywhere in each industry over the same issue.

"It will cost a lot of money," the strikers' side warned, but then, that wasn't their problem.

When the first round of talks broke up, both sides walked away amicably.

At the second session of the working group, the government side seemed to be composed of completely different people—their attitude was so different. The atmosphere became deadly serious. They had obviously gotten an earful from Warsaw.

"Your demand for independent unions has become an ideological precedent," the stony-faced government side declared. "What kind of political formula do you have in mind for these unions? Particularly, what's your attitude toward the 'leading role of the Party,' and the 'unity of the working-class movement?' "

One of the strikers' representatives, a warehouse worker named Kobylinski, was taken aback by this new hard-line approach.

"Why?" he objected. "We thought that such problems would be elaborated in practice, step by step. We don't want to play the role of political party."

The government side insisted on a clause spelling out the new union's recognition of the Party's leading role and Poland's existing alliances. It was the only way the regime could grant the unprecedented right to a free trade union.

Mazowiecki wasn't surprised by the demand. He realized what kind of precedent Solidarity represented, and the regime's need to stand its ground in view of the political reality next door.

"I'm willing to accept that," he said, "as long as we make it clear in the language that the Party won't have a leading role in the unions themselves." It was agreed.

Mazowiecki took the compromise to the presidium of the Strike Committee and urged them to accept it.

"Such a political formula doesn't really mean anything," he argued. "So why not use their doubletalk?"

The sociologist, Jadwiga Staniszkis, voiced her objections to the compromise. Accepting the leading role of the Party was a betrayal of the very spirit of free trade unions, she argued. "We should explain the compromise to the workers and let them decide on it," she urged the presidium. "Put it to a full vote of the Inter-Strike Committee."

Mazowiecki objected, "That would amount to making an announcement to the world press. And that could prejudice the negotiations."

In the end, Mazowiecki won out. He and several others formed an editorial group to draft the language of the historic proposal. The eventual agreement was just a matter of time now.

WARSAW, POLAND
August 24, 1980

The news Stanislaw Kania, the Central Committee member responsible for church-state relations, brought to Cardinal Wyszynski was shocking.

"Gierek's had a nervous breakdown," he told the cardinal. "It happened after the Central Committee meeting tonight. He desperately wants to see you."

When the primate arrived at Gierek's residence, he found the Party leader panic-stricken and confused. He listened for more than an hour as Gierek rambled on about the current crisis.

"What these workers are demanding is impossible," Gierek railed. "There will be chaos and bloodshed. It's inevitable that the Soviets will intervene. I need your help in calming the situation."

The archbishop stated his position unequivocally: "I must tell you that the bishops and I are on the side of the workers." But before he left the ailing leader, he promised to do everything in his power to urge restraint in settling the conflict.

Under the long tenure of Cardinal Wyszynski, the Catholic church in Poland had managed to maintain its moral authority with the Polish people and continued to command their loyalty. Wyszynski had been arrested and placed under detention in a monastery in 1953 for his refusal to condemn a bishop and three priests accused of anti-state activity. After his release three years later, he was careful not to confront the regime openly, but his unflinching sermons reflected his unwillingness to compromise over what he regarded as fundamentals.

Two days after meeting with Gierek, the cardinal delivered a crucial sermon from the shrine of the Black Madonna in Czestochowa.

The strikers watched the image of Cardinal Wyszynski on the television screen with rapt attention, as the evening news aired excerpts from the sermon.

What they heard was disappointing. The cardinal began his remarks appealing for calm and prudence on the part of the entire Polish nation.

"I think that sometimes one should refrain from too many demands and claims, just so that peace and order may prevail in Poland; this is hard, especially as demands can be justified and they usually are sound; but there never is a situation where it would be possible to fulfill all the demands at once, right away, today. Their implementation must be gradual."

The strikers listened in bitter silence, stunned that the cardinal seemed to be taking the government side and urging them to abandon the strike. As if to underscore the cardinal's cautious words, the Party daily *Trybuna Ludu* took the unusual step of printing the text of the sermon the next day.

The cardinal's message had barely faded when the conference of bishops went to work to dispel the notion that the church was abandoning the workers' aspirations. They quickly called an emergency meeting to issue a communique backing the workers' demands for independent trade unions. The statement called on the government to respect a litany of human rights, then quoted from the Second Vatican Council: "Among the fundamental rights of the individual must be numbered the right of workers to form themselves into associations which truly represent them and are able to cooperate in organizing economic life properly and the right to play their part in the activities of such associations without risk of reprisal."

The communique was the message the strikers had been hoping to hear in the cardinal's sermon. Large portions of the bishop's statement appeared in the newly created Strike Information Bulletin circulating throughout the shipyard. A battery of priests also rushed into the shipyard to claim that the cardinal's sermon was censored, taken out of context by the carefully chosen excerpts the government aired. If any doubt had been planted in the strikers' minds about the church's support for them, it was now weeded out.

GDANSK, POLAND
August 31, 1981

Jagielski and his government delegation waded through the workers' rank and file for the last time. His team had accepted the political formula hammered out by Mazowiecki's working group. After haggling over some minor points, Walesa and Jagielski finally agreed to the twenty-one points of agreement, and applause rang out from the workers hanging onto their every word.

Shortly after 4:00 P.M., the two marched into the big hall surrounded by the thunderous applause of the strike committee delegates. Walesa made a point of thanking the delegates and the strikers for their patience through the eighteen days of the strike.

"And now with the same determination and solidarity that we showed on strike, we shall go back to work," he said. "As of tomorrow, the life of our new trade unions begins. Let's take care they always remain independent and self-governing, working for us all and for the good of the country, for Poland. I proclaim that the strike is over."

The room rocked with applause, and the delegates jumped to their feet to sing the national anthem.

Then, under the glaring lights of the television cameras, Walesa produced a pen nearly the size of a billy club bearing an unmistakable likeness of the pope and signed the historic accord creating the Soviet bloc's first independent trade union.

Solidarity was born.

Gdansk, Poland
December 12, 1981

Mazowiecki was huddled in the Gdansk shipyard on a snowy, winter's night with other members of Solidarity's National Commission when word filtered in of military movements around Gdansk and Warsaw. The telex machines clattered with alarming reports from Solidarity headquarters across the country. Workers in the union's regional headquarters in Gdansk had been monitoring the police radio and picked up some suspicious orders calling for a massive police presence in Gdansk. There were rumors floating around that some Solidarity activists would soon be rounded up. An attorney friend had warned Mazowiecki earlier that arrests could come as early as that night.

Mazowiecki had been appointed by Walesa as editor of the new uncensored Solidarity weekly, *Tygodnik Solidarnosc*. In its premier issue, Mazowiecki wrote: "As a society and as a union, we have embarked upon a road never traveled before. No plans, models, maps fit our situation. We have to create them for ourselves. We have to be faithful to the hope that has been born among us." That hope was now slowly dwindling.

The National Commission, with its approximately one hundred members, was meeting inside the Lenin shipyard at Gdansk to discuss what to do about the latest deadlock with the government. Tension between the two sides was on the rise. Union members were outraged at the government's use of force to break up a sit-down strike at Bydgoszcz and later their use of riot police to clear out students occupying the Warsaw Firefighter's Academy. In addition, Solidarity charged the government with being too sluggish in implementing the twenty-one demands of the Gdansk accords and in giving workers a voice in running their factories. For its part, the government accused Solidarity of pulling the plug on the country's nearly comatose economy with what it considered pointless strikes.

At the meeting, some of the more radical members of Solidarity proposed breaking the deadlock by staging an active strike, where the workers would actually take over the management of the industries that employed them. Walesa advocated a more conciliatory approach. But the radicals seemed to be gaining the upper hand. The delegates kicked off the weekend with a warning to the government that Solidarity would call a twenty-four-hour general strike if the Central Committee made good on a threat to pass a so-called bill of extraordinary measures banning strikes.

It had already been a long, exhausting day of debate when the delegates took up probably the most radical proposal of all: a call for a national referendum on the government's handling of the current economic crisis. The meeting scheduled to end that afternoon dragged on into the night while delegates haggled over the proposal. It finally passed while Walesa looked on in silence.

When the meeting started to break up, Mazowiecki voiced what was on everyone's mind, "I hear the military is on the move around Warsaw," he told his associates.

Walesa had already heard the rumors.

"It's only a psychological move," he responded with a shrug of the shoulders.

Around 11:00 P.M., the delegates discovered that all the phone and telex lines in and out of Gdansk had been cut. The situation seemed much more serious now. Someone suggested they all stay in the shipyard for safety.

"Two hours ago, I called the police station," Konrad Maruszczyk, the vice-chairman of the Gdansk region, informed them. "When I asked why there were so many police in the region, they told me they're executing an operation called 'Three Rings,' and the arrests are affecting only criminals. Anyway, there's no one left at the shipyard. We need to head out."

It was well after midnight when they straggled out of the shipyard. As the weary delegates crunched across the snow-brittle ground, they joked about what the government might be planning under the cover of darkness—how the moles and the bats might be collaborating. A bit of black humor on a black night.

Walesa went home. Mazowiecki went back to the Grand Hotel

in Sopot, where most of the Solidarity activists were staying. The phones still weren't working. He decided to join some other committee members in the hotel cafeteria to continue the evening's debate. Around two in the morning, someone told them the hotel was surrounded by ZOMO, the elite security unit controlled directly by the Party.

The front window of the hotel looked out onto what had turned into a surrealistic landscape. The front driveway was filled with riot police dressed in stark black and white, standing still in the strange quiet of the falling snow. The futuristic design of their shields and helmets made them look like an alien force that had materialized out of nowhere. Around back, a cordon of ZOMO stretched from the hotel all the way to the ocean. The Grand Hotel was surrounded.

Mazowiecki and twelve other union members were in the middle of a discussion when the police broke into the room and ordered them out one by one. A fat, unfriendly looking officer grabbed Mazowiecki's briefcase, slapped a pair of cold handcuffs on his wrists, and pushed him into a still-empty paddy wagon waiting right next to the hotel steps.

"Things have gone too far," the officer said. "Both sides of the table have to be cleared."

There was an awkward silence. What did that mean? Mazowiecki asked himself.

"Anyway, this won't take long," the officer said in a chummy sort of way. "It's a very small operation."

Each Solidarity activist was escorted to the van by a pair of ZOMOs on either side. The paddy wagon filled up, with two ZOMOs between each detainee. They were making sure no one slipped through the dragnet. Then they were transported to the ZOMO barracks in Gdansk.

Mazowiecki was led out of the van into a huge cellar and forced to line up against the wall with the others. A ZOMO officer armed with a Soviet-made Kalishnikov assault rifle and wearing a handgun on his belt stood between each of them. Every minute, more detainees arrived.

"No talking!" one of the commanding officers shouted.

More and more policemen showed up at the station as reinforcements. Many of them wore a disheveled look as if they had been roused out of a sound sleep to take part in the operation. These were security policemen, different from the ZOMOs who had arrested them. One young policeman seemed particularly angry. Mazowiecki overheard him say he was upset at suddenly being summoned to the station without any explanation.

"I'm called to the barracks on emergency alert," he heard the policeman complain in a voice still gravelly with sleep. "Then I find out that martial law is in effect, and the army has taken over the government."

That was how Mazowiecki found out that martial law had been declared.

Names were called one by one, and the detainees were led out of the cellar for questioning. When they finished with someone, they put him in a separate room and called another. Any Solidarity material was confiscated.

Mazowiecki heard his name shouted out. He was escorted to a room where a couple of security police waited for him like a pair of vultures.

"Martial law is now in effect," one of them said. "You should understand that you have been engaging in activity against the national interest. But you'll be able to go home just as soon as you sign this declaration of loyalty."

He handed Mazowiecki a printed form that read: "I declare that I give up all activity detrimental to the interests of the Polish People's Republic and that I commit myself to abide by the legal order."

Mazowiecki refused.

The officer shook his head as if Mazowiecki's defiance grieved him. "There's still time for you to think about it if you change your mind," he said.

After refusing a second time, Mazowiecki was led to another basement where some of his colleagues already sat, slumped over in exhaustion, waiting for what would come next.

Toward evening, they were finally given some bread and tea and then prepared to be transported to another, undisclosed location. Mazowiecki was led from the large hall to one of several waiting vans. When they were all filled up, the column plowed through the snow piled up along the country roads. Mazowiecki felt a jolt as the entire caravan came to a halt. He heard one of the drivers shout for directions. Apparently, they were lost.

Then the paddy wagon took off again. A little later, Mazowiecki heard the high-pitched whir of spinning tires as the van bogged down in the deep drifts. They got stuck several more times before finally arriving at their destination. The van pulled up in front of a high, gray wall with watchtowers, searchlights and machine guns jutting out of its corners. A sign above the entrance read: "Wejherowo Prison, Social Rehabilitation Center, Strzebielinek."

Mazowiecki's personal "bodyguard" led him into a big room where they confiscated all his possessions. The prisoners were then led out one at a time to be processed into the penal system. He felt like a common criminal when they took his picture, mug shots from all three sides, and then fingerprinted him, staining his hands with dirty ink.

After that, he was escorted through a courtyard surrounded by a chain-linked fence topped with barbed wire, then taken into a pavilion, a building that consisted of one long corridor.

Both sides of the corridor were lined with cells, the ends blocked off by grating that rose from the floor to the top of the ceiling. A guard jammed a key into one of the steel-lined doors. It clanged open with the skin-crawling sound of metal scraping against metal, and Mazowiecki was locked into the shadowy cell beyond it. As his eyes adjusted to the darkness, he made out a row of uncomfortable looking bunks against the wall and two windows, covered with bars. He dropped onto one of the hard cots and immediately fell asleep.

At six o'clock in the morning, Mazowiecki was jolted awake by an unpleasant voice blasting its own reveille, "WAKE UP! WAKE UP!" The grating noise of cell doors creaking open followed. The blinding light slanted straight into his eyes.

After a breakfast of thin, tasteless soup, someone turned the radio on. It stayed on all day, blaring out a never-ending parade of martial music.

WARSAW, POLAND
December 13, 1981

Cardinal Jozef Glemp was awakened in the middle of the night by Kazimierz Barcikowski, a member of the Politburo.

"General Jaruzelski has declared martial law," he told him. "The

Russians gave us an ultimatum: either we do it, or they do it for us."

Jaruzelski, the former Defense Minister, had assumed the mantle of premier in February 1981, after a series of government shake-ups following the creation of Solidarity. Now his army was in charge of the country. Troops swept throughout Poland, sealing off city after city. More than five thousand Solidarity activists had been rounded up; all Solidarity headquarters were shut down. The country's borders were closed off, basic civil rights suspended, a strict 10:00 P.M. to 6:00 A.M. curfew imposed. The armed forces were authorized to use force to maintain calm. In effect, Poland was under siege from its own army.

It was the first real test of Glemp's tenure as archbishop since assuming the position just five months earlier after Cardinal Wyszynski's death. Putting on the miter so long worn by the venerable Wyszynski was not an easy task. Wyszynski had been a formidable foe to the Party during his three decades as Poland's primate, a tenure marked by real authority exercised with caution.

The news of martial law shattered Cardinal Glemp's hope for fostering dialogue between the government and Solidarity. The month before he had persuaded Jaruzelski and Walesa to sit down together to discuss a way out of the crisis. Jaruzelski had been pushing the idea of a power-sharing coalition government that would incorporate representatives from Solidarity, the church, and other segments of society. But his idea of establishing a Front of National Accord as a way of pulling Poland out of its economic political quagmire got bogged down as well in the old demand that the Party maintain its leading role. Solidarity and the church would be consulted and occupy symbolic seats in the Jaruzelski plan, but the Party would still retain all vital positions and make the decisions. In short, the Party agreed to share its problems, but not its power.

On the other side, Solidarity was hesitant about taking part in any coalition that would relegate it to playing a minor role. The union leadership viewed the talks with some suspicion, as a screen to preparations for an attack on Solidarity.

Now, any chance for dialogue between the government and Solidarity had been crushed by Poland's own army. Instead of a Front of National Accord, the government was in the firm grasp of a twenty-one-man Army Council of National Salvation, derisively nick-named crow (*wrona*) after its Polish acronym, WRON. The crow was now at war with the Polish eagle.

As Glemp hastily prepared a sermon to be delivered in Warsaw's Jesuit church that morning, he was painfully aware of his responsibility as head of the church. Information was scarce. Was martial law a necessary evil to forestall a Soviet invasion, as the Politburo member Barcikowski asserted? Was it imposed to restore order before resuming the reform process, as Jaruzelski insisted in his declaration of martial law? Or did Jaruzelski just want to wipe out his opposition? Glemp had no way of knowing his real intentions. And because of the virtual blackout in communications, he couldn't contact Rome. It was up to him to spell out the church's stance on his own.

The Polish people had two choices: open resistance to the new military regime, or accommodating to the new situation. The church hierarchy believed that the process of reform had gone too far to turn back. For the country ever to recover from its economic difficulties, the government would eventually have to open up to a broader governing coalition. For the time being, it seemed wise not to risk through resistance what had already been gained. Martial law was a *fait accompli*. Until Glemp got a clearer picture of the situation, he considered avoiding bloodshed his first priority. When he took the pulpit, he cautioned against confrontation.

"In our country, the new reality is martial law," he said. "Opposition to the decisions of authority under martial law could cause violent coercion, including bloodshed, because the authority has the armed forces at its disposal. We can be indignant, shout about the injustice of such a state of things, protest against the infringement of civil rights and human rights. However, this may not yield the expected results. The authority under martial law is not an authority of dialogue. . . .

"The authorities consider that the exceptional nature of martial law is dictated by a higher necessity, that it is the choice of a lesser rather than a greater evil. Assuming the correctness of such reasoning, the man in the street will subordinate himself to the new situation. . . . Saving life and prevention of bloodshed is the most important matter. . . .

"There is nothing of greater value than human life. That is why I myself will call for reason, even if it means that I become the target of insults. I shall plead, even if I have to plead on my knees; do not start a fight of Pole against Pole. . . . Every head, every pair of hands will be essential to the reconstruction of Poland, which will come, which must come, after the end of the state of martial law."

The military-controlled media played the sermon over and over for the next two days, with its avoidance of any direct mention of Solidarity and its hesitation to condemn Jaruzelski for declaring martial law.

STRZEBIELINEK, POLAND
December 15, 1981

Mazowiecki heard his name read on the radio among a list of the interned. He wondered what criteria the government used in drawing up the list. Actually, there seemed to be two lists: one with the names of Solidarity activists and the other with the names of corrupt officials who had also been arrested. The words of the policemen who arrested him came back to him. Clearing both sides of the table. On one side, there was Solidarity. On the other, those officials without the necessary political clout to prevent them from being served up to the public as scapegoats.

He was later shown a list of names of the interned and the reason for the internment. Under his name, the authorities had written: "He cannot remain free, because he is dangerous to the national security and public order. Free, he would try to continue his actions which would lead the people of Warsaw into anarchy. The citizen will be interned in Strzebielinek Center." Mazowiecki realized he wouldn't be released any time soon.

The second day of detention, the detainees began to resist their captors' rules. The prisoners were required to stand in line twice every day and shout out their names at morning and evening roll call. This never came off. The guards tried to enforce this discipline, but to no avail. They were interned, not imprisoned, the detainees argued. Most of them hadn't even been shown a bill of internment or an arrest warrant, yet they were being treated like prisoners.

They were let out once a day for walks in the courtyard as the

ZOMO guards watched with vacant stares, but the time allotted always varied. No communication was allowed between cells. When the detainees were required to hand over their coats to the prison guards, they rebelled as one.

Mazowiecki tried on his old role of mediator when his cellmates chose him to present a list of fifteen demands to the prison warden. Among other things, they wanted access to a priest, free movement inside the camp, contact between cells, and the possibility of communicating with Lech Walesa, who was also in detention in Warsaw. They also wanted access to books and the right to inform loved ones of their whereabouts.

When Mazowiecki presented these demands, the warden had a ready reply. It wasn't up to him to grant the requests. He would look into them.

Three days later, nothing had changed. Cell Number 35 had had enough. All together, Mazowiecki and his cellmates began banging on the cell door. The incessant pounding brought the guards scurrying. The cell demanded that their list of grievances be addressed. Mazowiecki was given permission to meet with the police commander from Gdansk the next day.

"We can't give you permission to move between cells," the commander told him. "There are strict regulations against that. As to establishing contact with Walesa, we can't authorize that either. He's a private person. We have nothing to do with him. But we can allow you limited access to a priest, and religious activities, within reason, of course."

During the next week, the prison guards relented further and allowed prisoners from different cells to walk together in the courtyard. During one of those walks, Mazowiecki ran into one of the more radical Solidarity leaders.

"Well, Mr. Editor," he said. "I told you. We should have been tougher."

"Well, wiser anyway," Mazowiecki responded.

"All that wisdom of yours, where did it get us?" his friend said sarcastically.

"And that toughness of yours?" Mazowiecki shot back. "It got us to the same place."

—•—

The Roman Catholic hierarchy moved quickly to take a stronger stand against martial law after Cardinal Glemp's cautionary sermon. The majority of Poles viewed it as much too conciliatory. The cardinal was accused of bending too far in the direction of the regime and underestimating Jaruzelski's intentions.

A week after the clampdown, the Episcopate's Main Council issued a statement condemning martial law and the suspension of civil rights; it demanded the release of all political prisoners and the continuation of Solidarity's legal activities.

The church then went to work setting up special committees to help the interned and their families. Local bishops began organizing pastoral care for the Solidarity activists isolated behind the walls of internment camps. Churches served as the central gathering place for packets and parcels to camps and prisons. The church also raised and funneled aid to families struggling to make it through the cold winter because husbands and fathers were either interned or stripped of their jobs. In addition, the church formed a legal section to secure good lawyers and legal aid for those in detention, and set up an information section to document their cases.

Mazowiecki welcomed news of the church's aid, as he languished in detention. "We often think about those beyond our prison walls and gates," he wrote in a letter.

"We have a feeling that their trials are a different kind of hardship, perhaps even greater than ours. Every day, they have to choose their own course of action, often in situations that, no matter what their choice, could be detrimental. Nevertheless, the Polish people know what is evil, what is a lie, and what values are worth defending; their lives are a witness through their solidarity with the imprisoned and those stripped of their jobs, through trying to defend the rights that have been taken away. Not even the events of December 13 could destroy this sense of morality. The best evidence of it is their never-ending solidarity with us. As Pope John Paul II said in 1979 at Victory Square, the history of a nation is judged by how it contributes to humanity; its consciousness, its heart, its conscience. The future of Polish culture will be decided in the same way, by how we pull through this dark era as a nation—whether we'll be a nation aware of the distinct line between truth and falsehood, or whether we'll be a nation shaken out of its moral beliefs and pushed into the prevailing lies. Our lives together and our fight for the rights of humanity and the nation will decide whether we manage to preserve the precious solidarity forged between workers and intellectuals in August 1980, a solidarity that is especially slandered and vilified today. The value of Polish culture, its character and influence on the immediate fate of the nation, hinges on whether in the humiliation we're enduring today, we can have the strength to endure without hatred. . . . I suppose that even when we are forced into silence, our duties are here, in our homeland."[2]

STRZEBIELINEK, POLAND
December 22, 1981

"Mazowiecki, get dressed. We are going home."

The order came from a military functionary dressed in civilian clothes standing in Mazowiecki's cell.

"Right now?" Mazowiecki blinked in disbelief. "But I'm not ready yet." He wanted to buy a little time to say his goodbyes to his fellow inmates.

There was no time. He was escorted from his cell and met by another military officer wearing a civilian jacket and an officious expression.

"I'm a lieutenant from Gdansk," he introduced himself. "From now on, you're in my custody."

Those were strange words if he were being released. He felt twinges of doubt that he was going home.

"Are you really planning to let me go?" he asked.

There was no answer.

He was made to wait on a hard bench while some major shuffled through his papers. While he was waiting there, the prison warden walked toward the bench where he was sitting.

"Bon voyage," he said, and shook Mazowiecki's hand.

The words still sounded foreboding. Why did he have the feeling he wasn't going home?

Then two uniformed policemen joined him. One seemed jovial and easy-going, the other stiff and formal. He remembered seeing them earlier, when he was being escorted through the prison corridor. He saw that one of them was playing with a set of handcuffs. The steel glinted in the light as he dangled them back and forth in front of him. *Why does he need those?* Mazowiecki asked himself. And why were so many officials accompanying him if he was just going home? It didn't make sense.

The major processing his papers was taking too long.

"You won't get your release forms yet," he told him."Someone else will talk to you, probably in Gdansk, but I'm not sure."

Mazowiecki trusted the major. He had an honest looking face. He'd never given him any reason to doubt him when he was in detention. But then, could he trust anyone in prison? It seemed like any time he did, some bureaucratic act or some deceptive trick would shatter his faith. Trust was something he couldn't afford in these times.

Mazowiecki didn't know whom to believe, or what to believe anymore. But as he walked through the corridor surrounded by police escorts, he felt almost joyous. Maybe he was finally being released. He would be in Warsaw soon, in time to spend Christmas Eve with his boys. He looked forward to sharing the *oplatek* with them, the Christmas wafer family members shared on Christmas Eve. He could catch up on news of all his Solidarity companions, and what was happening in Gdansk. He had only gotten snippets of news from the radio broadcasts; word that strikes were being staged across the country to protest martial law. But of course, it was all slanted to reflect the "new reality."

As he left the administration building, and stepped into the courtyard, he felt like the whole world was waiting for him beyond the prison gate. A black Volga was parked next to the gate to take him wherever he was going. For a second, he tried to decide where to sit. Then he realized he still didn't have the freedom to make that decision. He was ordered into the back seat, between the two uniformed officers. The lieutenant got in the front seat, next to the driver. The car was crowded and stuffy. No one spoke. The officers on either side of Mazowiecki were stiff and formal, as if they were standing at attention.

The whole situation was starting to annoy him. Why all this fuss just to take him home? Couldn't they just let him go right there, and let him find his own way back to Warsaw? Patience, he told himself. Just a couple of hours now.

Then the lieutenant in the front seat turned around and said in a firm voice, "Mr. Mazowiecki, I want to let you know that if you try to escape, we won't hesitate to use our weapons. So please don't make us. Understood?"

The words stunned him like a sudden slap in the face. He looked at his captors. They sat in stony silence, with stony faces.

"I have no intention of escaping," Mazowiecki said, taking a deep breath. "Besides, why would I want to do such a thing? You're taking me home."

The lieutenant did not directly dispute his statement. "We have to transfer you to where we're heading now, without any interruptions," he said.

Thoughts were racing inside Mazowiecki's head. What does this mean? Where are we heading? Maybe they're taking me to the police academy in Slupsk to get my papers. Or the one in Lebork. Then they'll put me on a train to Warsaw.

The car bobbed along the narrow, snow-covered road. Through the window, Mazowiecki saw a group of people leaving church. Their faces were full of prayer and meditation. A bit further down the road, he saw light spilling out of houses, so close, so warm and inviting. Life continued on. Despite martial law and its meanings for him, these houses still glowed with love and light. Just a half hour before, he was imagining himself surrounded by familiar faces. Now this seemed so out of reach.

Why did they tell him they were taking him home in the first place? It was a cruel trick. He tried to get a hint of his destination from the faces of his guards, but all he saw were their icy stares. He couldn't make out any familiar landmarks through the window. They seemed to be heading for Gdansk, but then they turned in the opposite direction. They weren't going in the direction of Warsaw, either. He didn't say anything. They didn't say anything. They were obviously keeping his destination a secret on purpose. If they were going to put him in a detention center, why not one in Warsaw, with Walesa? Why were they heading in the opposite direction?

The lieutenant turned on the light for a moment to check the map, then said a few words to the driver. They continued on in silence. Two unpleasant possibilities occurred to Mazowiecki. They could be taking him to an army base. Or maybe a Soviet garrison in East Germany. This last thought presented a horrifying prospect.

"It's suffocating in here," he said, breaking the long silence. "Please let me open a window."

He cracked the window a bit. He felt betrayed. Why had he let them seduce him so easily? Trick him into thinking he was going home? He should have known that after December 13, nothing was as it appeared.

He tried to nod off to sleep. He knew he had to get some rest. Who knew how much longer he would be kept awake, once he reached wherever they were taking him? He shut his eyes, but couldn't shut out the image of the two forms sitting in front of him, taunting him with their silence. He had a rosary in his pocket, one given to him years ago by a sister at the convent at Laski. He always carried it with him. It was too cramped in the car to take it out without calling attention to the rosary, and he didn't want to lose it. He could still pray, though. His mind trod the thin line between sleep and wakefulness, between prayer and desperation.

A refrain from a psalm the detainees sang popped into his mind: "O Lord in heaven, extend your righteous hand."

The car continued slicing through the snow and endless darkness, illumined only by the pale light of the moon and the dashboard. They passed through a small, indistinguishable town, then doubled back. The driver pulled over and the lieutenant hopped out to ask a pedestrian for directions. Mazowiecki wanted to shout out to the pedestrian. His life seemed to be evaporating. He feared he would vanish into thin air, confined in a remote prison camp somewhere, out of sight, where he would slowly fade from memory, like an old photograph.

The lieutenant climbed back in the car and mumbled some directions to the driver. They pulled into a small street, in front of what looked like a house. People were going in and out of the entrance. Then a big car marked "*Milicja*" pulled up. Mazowiecki realized it was a police station. Maybe he would spend the night here.

But then the lieutenant and driver went in and emerged with a third person. He hopped into a car just ahead of them. They began following it past what looked like army barracks into a deep forest. They continued on, brushing past branches bending under heavy snow, until Mazowiecki saw a gate manned by a guard. He strained to see any distinguishing marks, and spied the Polish eagle, the country's symbol. He knew they were on some kind of army base. But which one, where, and why?

They followed on, twisting and turning down a desolate, winding road. Mazowiecki had lost all track of time and distance. There was nothing but the blackness of the forest around them. The small caravan took a sharp left, and looming right in front of them was a gate to a building with a huge sign marked, "Reception."

Was this his final destination? Or would they take him somewhere else from here?

He got out and walked into the building, still in the company of his two escorts. A man wearing a field uniform standing behind the reception desk beckoned him.

"Welcome to Jaworzno prison camp," he said, sounding more like a desk clerk at a hotel than an officer at a prison camp. "You'll be our guest here for a while. I warn you, if you try to escape, you'll end up in bad shape."

"You mean, I'll really be staying here?"

"Certainly," the man at the desk replied. "You'll find lots of your colleagues here. We've got quite a number of detainees. They even have their own mayor."

Mazowiecki was escorted to the next building, where he was welcomed by his fellow inmates. His anxiety began to vanish. He wouldn't be alone, after all.

Things were much more relaxed at Jaworzno than his previous detention center. The inmates called it the "Golden Cage," he discovered. He got a strange reaction when he introduced himself to them. They didn't seem to trust him. He didn't understand it at first, until someone informed him of his "death."

"We heard you were killed by Jaruzelski's storm troopers the day martial law was declared. It was on the radio," one of the detainees told him.

"I assure you, I am Mazowiecki," he told them. "And when I last checked, at least, I was very much alive." The news of his death had been printed in the "Police Bulletin," and even picked up by Western radio broadcasts. As much as he tried to assure them of his identity, some of the inmates still didn't know quite what to make of him, whether he was the genuine article or some impostor sent to spy on them.

Back in his cell, someone brought him a big cup of coffee and three packages that were waiting for him when he arrived. He sipped the coffee. Savoring its rich dark flavor somehow made him feel human again.

Then he began opening the packages. On top of the first one were two letters from home, from his sons. Then his fingers felt a small, thin object, and his eyes began to mist over. It was a little white Christmas wafer, the *oplatek*, and it tasted of everything he loved in life.

Notes

1. George Blazynski, *Flashpoint Poland,* Pergamon Policy Studies, 52 (New York: Pergamon Press, 1979), 357.

2. From letter to Professor Janusz Groszkowski from Mazowiecki, dated 13 March 1982.

7

Czechoslovakia

As an outgrowth of Charter 77, Father Vaclav Maly joined Catholic layman Vaclav Benda in setting up a Committee for the Defense of the Unjustly Persecuted (known by its Czech acronym VONS), established along the lines of the Polish opposition group KOR. In fact, a group of Charter 77 activists secretly met with KOR members twice in 1978 somewhere along the two countries' common border, and the two groups continued trying to support each other after the clandestine meetings.

VONS emerged in May 1978 after more militant Chartists argued for a concrete group to drum up aid for victims of repression and the families of political prisoners. Benda contended that merely monitoring human rights violations was not enough. To him, appeals to state authorities asking them to uphold human rights and the ideals of the Helsinki accords were worse than useless, since they upheld the notion the Czechoslovak government was actually interested in reform. He also felt it was important to create what he called a "parallel community," an alternative system that challenged the state monopoly with its own network of publishing, culture, education, and law.

VONS was established to operate as just such a parallel system of legal aid. The committee kept tabs on the cases of political dissidents facing trial and imprisonment, documented instances of police brutality and government injustice, and organized financial help for the families of prisoners. As a result, the committee members found themselves the target of the repression they were trying to combat.

PRAGUE
May 29, 1979

The police came before dawn, banging on the doors of VONS members. Maly was still groggy with sleep when they entered the tiny apartment where he lived with his parents and dragged him out of bed. He was arrested along with Benda, Vaclav Havel, and seven others on charges of "attempted subversion of the government." The case against them contended VONS was an illegal organization "aimed at undermining the confidence of citizens of the Czechoslovakian Republic in the organs of the state and creating a hostile attitude toward the Soviet system."

Over the past year, Maly and Benda had been spending their days attending trials, carefully jotting down the names of judges, prosecutors, and witnesses, and trying to scrape together money for families of political prisoners. They spent as much time as possible visiting political prisoners and tried to secure good legal representation for them.

Benda had recently attended the trial of a priest accused of saying Mass at a summer camp. The priest, Father Srna, was stripped of his state permit and charged with "obstructing state supervision of the churches and religious associations." He faced up to two years imprisonment. During the trial, the judge implied that Benda was trying to influence the outcome by disseminating information about the case. In the end, Benda's efforts to publicize the case apparently paid off. The priest received only a suspended sentence.

At times, though, it seemed a hopeless battle to Benda. VONS waged its war against the regime armed only with words. And for every typewriter they possessed, the state had at its disposal ten printing presses. Benda felt as if his fellow VONS members were living in a backward time before the invention of the printing press, the automobile, and the telephone. They spent hours running around town to accomplish something that would normally take just two quick phone calls. But they dared not use the phone, for fear it was tapped. They spent thousands of hours repeating and copying factual details to disseminate in their underground communiques, a job that would take mere minutes if they had a copying machine at their disposal.

Despite the monotonous tasks, both VONS and Charter 77 produced a virtual flood of underground typewritten documents. Before the police swooped down on them, the VONS activists had succeeded in smuggling out more than one hundred detailed accounts of unjustly prosecuted cases.

Benda never set out to invoke the wrath of the Czechoslovak authorities. On the contrary, he did all he could to avoid it after being dismissed from his post as a lecturer in philosophy at Prague's Charles University. When he realized he would have to join the Communist party to get a job in philosophy, he retrained as a mathematician. Then he noted that as a believer, he could never be the editor of a mathematical journal, or ever gain any scientific status. So he devoted himself entirely to computer programming. In the end, though, his vocation couldn't escape the web spun by the authorities. The conviction of the Plastic People—a group of rock musicians tried for their outspoken lyrics and performances—convinced him to join Charter 77. He eventually ended up working as a stoker.

His wife, Kamila, abstained from any political activity, and managed to carry on as a mathematician, while Benda divided his time between working in the boiler room, mathematics, philosophy, and his VONS activities. He would often putter around the apartment with the squeals and laughter of their brood of five children providing a beneficial backdrop of noise, considering the bugs that were planted all around. For the older children, the occasional visits from the police were a welcome adventure. They had added two new games to their repertoire: "Belonging to the Charter," and "Being Unemployed."

Benda entertained no illusions that his work with VONS would actually lead to any substantial improvement in all the injustices, illegalities, and social evils he observed around him. For him, it was a simple matter of acting on his religious faith. As he was leaving for work one day before his arrest, he jotted down his reflections on the human rights struggle. "We are right, but we are lunatics. We don't have a chance of winning this fight between a dwarf and a troop of giants. We are voluntarily entering the lions' den and the fiery furnace; a sane person does not risk his neck in such a futile manner. . . . The cry that 'The emperor is naked' can lead to quite uncontrollable and unexpected consequences and can fundamentally change the state of affairs. Of course, in an empire governed by a deceitful tailor surrounded by a host of imperial guards and courtiers—all quite naked as well—only fools or children can insist on shouting that. Well then, I am convinced that to be a fool or a child is the only way to the Kingdom of Heaven—unless you become like those little ones, you will not enter. The wisdom of this world is foolishness and its foolishness is wisdom—but in the present circumstances it is our only temporal political hope."[1]

—•—

After their arrest, the ten VONS activists were thrown in Prague's Ruzyne prison. They were placed in separate cells to keep them isolated from one another.

It was hard for Maly to get used to life in a cell, the lack of light in the day and the lack of darkness at night. Stripped of the freedom to move around, to read, to eat when he wanted, he wondered whether he would be able to endure it. He was confined with his hardened cellmates in one cramped space like rats in a lab cage. Maly's cellmates were two murderers. One of them had cut off the head of a clerk, the other was accused of killing his own mother with an axe.

Maly had always tried to look for the good in other people. These two would present a challenge. They knew he was a priest. That made him a little suspicious. They expected him to be a self-righteous martyr, so he did all he could to shatter that image. Forget the religious jargon, he told himself. Forget quoting the Bible. Talk to them from your life. As the days dragged by, he eventually learned to understand them, and they learned to respect him.

Seven months later, the guards came to Maly's cell. He was free to go. He and three other VONS members were being dropped from the indictment.

Maly's freedom was bittersweet. Havel, Benda, and four others were going on trial. Maly felt a little guilty walking out of prison while his friends remained locked up. It was part of the regime's strategy of dividing the opposition.

Two days before the trial started, the Communist party daily *Rude Pravo* carried an article accusing Charter 77 and VONS of being used by elements abroad to overthrow the social order. The article signaled to the public what the verdict would be—that was the way the government operated.

The courtroom was virtually closed. Only two close relatives of any of the defendants were allowed to attend, and eventually one of them was evicted for taking notes. The room sat only eighteen people, giving the authorities an excuse to exclude the diplomats and foreign correspondents who tried to monitor the trial. Yet a few seats remained empty throughout the proceedings.

During the trial, the defendants were constantly interrupted while trying to justify the legality of their actions under Czechoslovak law. Their appointed counsel made no real effort to defend them. Benda's lawyer even leaned over to the prosecutor and apologized for having to enter a plea of not guilty. No defense witnesses were called. Most of the evidence came from the reports of the preliminary investigation, reports that were stacked against the defendants. Before the trial ended, Havel made one last attempt to defend the actions of VONS in a final statement to the court:

"Mr. Chairman, members of the senate: the international pacts on human rights, which have become an integral part of the Czechoslovak legal system, charge not only the state organs, but all citizens with the responsibility of determining to what extent the rights guaranteed by those pacts are observed in their own countries. I have personally accepted this responsibility as a citizen of this state, for I feel that human dignity, freedom, and justice are genuinely the business of all society, that all of us, without exception, are responsible for them, and that all of us without exception therefore have the right to draw attention to cases in which these basic values are, in our opinion, threatened. Both my work in Charter 77 and my participation in the work of VONS are derived from that right and that responsibility. I do not consider myself infallible and, therefore, I do not know whether I have always carried out well the task I have taken upon myself. But I am certain that I had the inalienable right to do these things without regard for the extent to which what I did was agreeable to the state power or not.

"Behind the harsh words of the indictment brought against us, I sense prejudice and anger. In our texts, there are no such words, because hatred and anger, fortunately, are not the states of mind from which our work emanates. . . . I know the members of VONS who, to my great joy, are still free and I know that they are good people who do what they do out of concern for all who are injured or wronged, care for their fellow human beings, and a longing for a free and dignified life for all people. Behind the work of VONS, there is neither hostility nor hatred but, if I may use the word—love.

"Members of the court, two months ago, while in prison, I was asked whether I would consider accepting an invitation for a working visit to the United States. I don't know for certain what would have happened had I accepted that offer, but I cannot exclude the possibility that I might have been sitting in New York at this very moment. If I am standing in this courtroom now, it is quite possibly the result of my own choice, a choice which certainly does not testify to my hostility toward this country and which comes, among other things, from an intention to state here very clearly that I do not consider myself guilty and that I have not lost faith in justice."[2]

The arguments did no good. The trial was rushed through in two twelve-hour days. Without reviewing the evidence, the judge pronounced them all guilty. Benda was sentenced to four years in prison; Havel got four and a half.

After sentencing, Havel and Benda were transported together with another VONS activist, Jiri Dienstbier, to Hermanice prison in Ostrava, near the Polish border, a hard labor camp run by a sadistic warden who took perverse delight in tormenting them. Havel was put on a detail welding heavy steel mesh. Quotas were ridiculously high, double what they would be outside the prison walls, and punishment meted out if they weren't met.

The three activists got a surprisingly warm reception from their fellow inmates, who shared their food with them and showed them the ropes of surviving prison life. The three helped organize a loose network of cooperation, doling out legal and psychological advice, arbitrating in poker disputes. When the warden found out about it, he flew into a rage.

"I'll be damned if you're going to set up a chapter of VONS in my prison," he yelled at the prisoners.

Havel and Benda were later placed in solitary confinement for writing letters for an illiterate gypsy.

All letters out of the prison were carefully scrutinized to make sure the contents stayed within the confines of a censorship code. Prisoners were limited to one four-page letter home a week. It had to be legible, with nothing corrected or crossed out. There were strict rules about margins and style. No quotation marks. Nothing underlined. No foreign expressions. Humor was forbidden. They could only write about "family matters."

The three activists used to play a game with the censor. They would read each other's letters and try to guess which ones would make it past. They soon discovered there was no logic to the way the rules were applied; it was all subject to the censor's whims.

Benda often used his letters to reflect on his faith. In one letter to his wife, Kamila, he wrote: "What is truth? (Although this question was asked at such an inappropriate moment, it cost the one who asked it his salvation.) If truth were a lifeless stoic formula, I could calmly spit it out, because I know a thousand and one arguments against it, and after all, I too am only human. But if it is the living Christ, then I cannot say no to it and I cannot help following it, though because I am a sinner I will be a little reluctant."

While Havel and Benda were in prison, Maly was under constant surveillance. When he walked out of his apartment on his way to work, a car full of police was always there waiting for him. He was used to their presence by now. The surveillance was even tighter whenever a Western dignitary was in town. The authorities wanted to make sure Maly was kept at a distance.

As Maly left the apartment, the carload of police rushed into action. Their surveillance was anything but subtle. They wanted Maly to know he was being watched. Three of them got out of the car and started following him on foot, just three paces behind, while the car slowly trailed along. When Maly descended to the metro station and boarded the subway train, the three policemen hopped aboard with him. One of them got out his walkie-talkie to let his colleagues above ground know their whereabouts. When Maly emerged from the metro station, another car full of police was already there, dogging him all the way to work.

One evening, Maly decided to have some fun with his ever-present shadows. He left the apartment for his regular run. He knew the secret police assigned to watch him hated his jogging. It was always the same group, and they really weren't in any shape to keep up with him. He usually jogged for about half an hour. Tonight, he decided to extend his run.

After the first half an hour, he heard them huffing and puffing behind him. He kept on running, taking a sort of sadistic delight in their struggle to keep up. Maly led them into a wooded park. They continued jogging behind him, their pace slowing somewhat, the sound of their wheezing growing fainter and fainter. Maly picked up his pace.

After they had faded well into the distance, he ducked behind a tree and waited for them to catch up. When he heard their heavy footsteps approach, he got ready, staying out of sight. Just before they reached his hiding place, he jumped out in front of them and grinned at the sight of their startled expressions.

"Tired?" he called out. He had the gleeful look of an Olympic runner getting ready to run a victory lap.

They could barely gasp out an answer. They were panting for breath, hands on their knees, raining big drops of sweat.

"Have a cigarette?" he offered, pulling out a pack from his sweats.

They nodded, still out of breath. Maly passed out the cigarettes and gave them a light. After they had taken a drag, he turned on his heels and continued his run.

He heard them cursing under their breaths as they took off again after him, still wheezing, cigarettes dangling from their lips.

Prague
1983

When Father Tomas Halik first called on Cardinal Frantisek Tomasek, he found the elderly archbishop almost cowering in his office. He was alone in the room, lost behind a horseshoe-shaped conference table, typing his own letters at an antiquated manual typewriter.

When Father Halik started to speak, the cardinal put a wizened finger to his lips and pointed up at the cone-shaped lamps hanging down from the ceiling. After he switched on his radio, he beckoned Father Halik closer.

"I am absolutely alone here," he lamented. "I don't have a secretary I can trust. All of the people working here in the palace are spies."

Father Halik had come to brief the cardinal on some of the spiritual activities of the unofficial or "parallel" church. The forty-year-old priest was trained as a psychologist and sociologist, and like Havel and Benda, was a student of the philosopher Jan Potocka. Because of government restrictions on seminary enrollment and the licensing of priests, he was secretly organizing religion classes for young people and helping run an underground seminary.

There was no such thing in Czechoslovakia as separation of church and state. The state strictly controlled every aspect of church life. It paid the salaries of priests and pastors, using the amount of the stipends as a carrot-and-stick to gain the allegiance of the clergy. The appointment of bishops had to be approved by the state. So when any bishop's seat became vacant, the state tried to ensure it was filled with collaborating clergy or left empty. Of the country's thirteen bishoprics, ten were still vacant. Religious orders were prohibited from accepting novices and were slowly dying out. Church seminaries were under the control of the Ministry of Culture, and seminarians were habitually recruited as informers by the secret police. The religious education of young people was limited to carefully controlled courses in state schools.

Then there was "Pacem in Terris," the organization of priests formed by the state to encourage government support from the church. Condemned by the Vatican, the association always turned a blind eye to any state restrictions on religion. The name means "Peace on Earth." But the priests were derogatorily dubbed "Pacem Terriors," after their image as the lap dogs of the Communist regime.

When the United Nations selected the group for one of its

International Year of Peace awards, Vaclav Maly wrote an angry letter to the international body protesting the decision: "How can [Pacem in Terris's] talk about peace be credible when they have brought chaos and conflict into their own church? . . . When in their peace statements they merely repeat and expand on the official statements concerning disarmament and peace in the world?"

Halik and Maly had been working with other banned priests to preserve the country's spiritual life through an unofficial network of church activity, another example of Benda's "parallel communities." Clandestine camps and retreats for students and intellectuals were held in private homes and country cottages. Men and women secretly received into banned religious orders were helping organize charitable work.

Maly summarized the aims of this unofficial pastoral activity in a *samizdat* publication published by VONS: "Instead of the mentality of 'we must survive' which set in after the 1948 putsch and lasted thirty years, a new attitude and resolve is starting to emerge: 'We must revitalize, deepen, and radiate our Christian values in society.' These (unofficial) religious activities also have social results, even if they aren't understood as being political in the original sense of the word. They destroy uniformity and strengthen independent thought while defending fundamental rights, making it more difficult for people to be manipulated and creating a framework for alternative attitudes."

Behind the closed doors of the archbishop's office, Halik told Cardinal Tomasek about some of the unofficial church's ecumenical activities. Contacts with other church leaders were developing, he told him. They were not merely tolerating members of other denominations, but looking at them as partners sharing a common aim. The two figures in the vast, empty office presented quite a contrast. An aging archbishop, clad in the black cassock and red skullcap of his high office, conferring with a young maverick priest whose work clothes and Rasputin-like beard made him look like a wild-eyed radical.

Before Father Halik ended his meeting with the archbishop, he said to him, "There is now a large group of priests who are working for the spiritual renewal of the country. You can be assured of our support."

When Father Halik left, he knew how much that support was really needed. The cardinal was virtually a prisoner in his own palace.

Cardinal Tomasek had not always been so receptive to aligning himself with these banned priests and their illegal activities. When he first became Czechoslovakia's primate in 1976, he was careful not to get into politics to avoid any conflict with the regime. But after fellow Slav Karol Wojtyla became Pope and began taking a tough stand for religious freedom in Eastern Europe, Cardinal Tomasek began to follow his lead. He started to abandon the "politics of little steps"—that is, cooperating with the regime for a few concessions, and began to criticize the state more openly.

A controversial letter clinched the archbishop's support for the "underground" church. The letter was sent to the Czechoslovak State Office for Church Affairs in 1983 after a particularly virulent anti-religious broadcast on Czechoslovak TV. The letter denounced discrimination against religious believers at work and at school. It also complained of the obstacles impeding those who wanted to practice religion or receive religious education.

The Western press claimed that Cardinal Tomasek had written the letter. The cardinal denied writing it, and the Czechoslovak regime denied receiving it. The controversy continued until Dr. Josef Zverina came forward and admitted to being the author.

Zverina was a respected priest and theologian who had been interned by the Nazi Gestapo, and later imprisoned for fourteen years under Stalinist rule. As a signatory of Charter 77, he was stripped of his position as a professor of theology and banned from the priesthood.

When the identity of the letter's author became known, the authorities put pressure on Cardinal Tomasek to repudiate its contents. He refused. Instead, he invited Zverina to meet him at the Archbishop's Palace. When Zverina walked into his office, the cardinal shook his hand and congratulated him for the letter. "Every priest who has a conscience should sign this letter," he told him. It was the beginning of a new cooperation.

PRAGUE
December 1988

Vaclav Maly was doing everything he could to gain the release of Augustin Navratil from the closed wing of a psychiatric hospital.

Maly had formed a committee to work for his freedom. He sent out an appeal to the Czechoslovak authorities demanding they stop persecuting him. He issued statements to the West publicizing Navratil's case.

Navratil, a sixty-year-old railway worker from the small Moravian village of Zlobice, had been forcibly committed to the psychiatric hospital after organizing a massive campaign calling for religious freedom. The authorities said he was suffering from what they called "paranoia querulans," a mental condition they say was marked by "excessive complaining."

Navratil had circulated a militantly worded thirty-one-point petition covering almost every aspect of church life. Its primary demand was for the separation of church and state. Among the petition's various points: state interference in the appointment of priests and bishops should end and all priests unjustly stripped of their pastoral responsibilities should be reinstated. The church should have the right to engage in religious education. The authorities should allow the right to import religious literature and copy and publish religious texts. And discrimination against Christians, particularly in education, should end.

This was not the first time the Catholic layman had been placed under psychiatric observation. After gathering signatures for a petition for civil rights in 1977, he was arrested and tossed into a psychiatric ward after being pronounced mentally unfit to stand trial. The report of the medical examiners described him as suffering from "hysterical self-stylization toward the ideal of a strong leading personality and with a strong moral responsibility which the subject understands as 'fidelity to his principles' and an inability to adapt to an adequate view of social reality. The subject thinks that for the truth, one must logically suffer."

After his release, Navratil took up the cause of Father Premysl Coufal, a secretly ordained priest who had been brutally murdered. The authorities ruled his death a suicide. But Navratil circulated an open letter accusing the state security of killing the priest. He was arrested again in 1985, and spent the next two years in and out of prison and mental hospitals.

Even behind the desolate walls of prison, Navratil found hope in his faith. In a letter to his wife and nine children, he wrote:

> So far, I have spent a fair amount of time engaging in what you might call exercises. Yes, spiritual exercises. Partly in peace and quiet, partly in compulsory or voluntary self-denial, partly in prayer and meditation with the help of the rosary. This wasn't possible at home. At home, it was all work, work, work, of one sort or another. There wasn't much time for prayer and contemplation. Here, however, I begin each day not only with my regular prayers, but with all the prayers of the rosary. Only then does my day begin, and it is followed by peace and tranquility: a surrender to the will of God. But there is nothing new about this. I have felt this way at many times in the past when I have been in a difficult position. Just one more thing: I can sense the prayers and petitions being offered up on my behalf to our Father in heaven. You and other believers, close and distant, and those unknown, need to pray. Let us therefore remind ourselves that, in God's hands, no one need be afraid!

After his release, he was assaulted by a group of gypsies in an attack evidently orchestrated by the police. They beat him unconscious and knocked out his two front teeth. But that didn't stop him from launching his petition for religious rights—his most important protest.

Navratil, this simple railway signalman, took his petition all the way to Cardinal Tomasek himself and received his blessing. The primate issued a pastoral letter urging believers across the country to sign the petition to "make their voice heard by the state authorities." The cardinal declared, "Cowardice and fear are unworthy of a true Christian."

Predictably, Pacem in Terris was quick to condemn the document, calling it an unsanctioned action of the laity. People in Slovakia were arrested for gathering signatures for the petition. And the administrators of one diocese, themselves Pacem in Terris members, threatened to withdraw the clerical licenses of any priests who mentioned the petition to their parishioners.

The Party dailies, *Rude Pravo* and *Pravda*, also launched an attack on the petition, suggesting it had been drawn up by "illegal church structures" in collusion with "bourgeois centers" in the West. Lengthy articles accused Cardinal Tomasek of tricking lay people into signing the appeal and denouncing it as an attempt to disrupt talks going on between the Czechoslovak state and the Vatican.

One article in *Rude Pravo* read: "The chief organizers of the action have already proved that they are not striving for religion but to raise the flag of a 'holy war' and to increase tension in our society. . . . The authors of the appeal are seeking to change the laws of the Socialist state, to make it possible for some people in the church to become a considerable political force again."

While Navratil was languishing in a filthy mental ward, the petition was gaining ground. Less than a year after it was circulated, the campaign had gathered 600,000 signatures of both Czechs and Slovaks, making it the most popular civil rights petition in the country's history of Communist rule.

Maly was doing all he could to advance the petition and the cause of Navratil. He felt that the petition's success represented the increasing unity of those opposed to the Communist regime.

—•—

Maly's head slammed against the wall. A flash of light exploded behind his eyelids. He felt the sharp jolt of pain shoot all the way down to his spine.

"Tell us what kind of slanderous information you were propagating at your subversive meeting!"

One of his interrogators was holding him by the hair and beating his head against the wall.

When Maly refused to answer, he punched him in the stomach. Maly doubled over in pain.

"What did you discuss?"

Maly remained silent. The interrogator's fist smashed into Maly's face. The priest's head recoiled from the blow. He felt another tooth crack. His mouth was full of blood. His jaw hung slack, obviously broken.

The interrogations came about once a week now, sometimes relatively painless, sometimes brutal. Whenever they came for him, he was always ready for the worst, prepared for the possibility of being put away for five years. Then, when he was released after just two or three days, being at liberty came as a pleasant surprise. There was a certain freedom in expecting the worst.

Two nights before, the security police had barged in on a gathering of Charter 77 activists and hauled off Maly and six others. He had undergone two straight days of systematic beatings. They were trying to force him to divulge information from the meeting. First came a barrage of questions to disorient him, fired at him in split-second succession, like a machine gun.

"Who was at the meeting?"

"What did you discuss?"

"What kind of subversive activity are you planning?"

"Who are your contacts from the West?"

His interrogators came at him, one after another, mixing in senseless questions to disorient him and get him to talk.

"How many times in your life have you been X-rayed?"

"What kind of car do you drive?"

"Do you drive fast or slow?"

"How fast?"

They harangued him with their relentless questions, but Maly refused to cooperate, answering only, "I'm just a simple Catholic priest who wants to carry out his vocation."

Then came the beatings, coupled with pressure to leave the country. "Either you sign up for voluntary emigration, or we'll finish you off," he was told.

Their tactics only strengthened his resolve to stay and continue his work for human rights. And his resolve only served to infuriate them.

They continued the merciless beatings, kicking him in the groin, pummeling his ribs and nose. Most of his teeth were knocked loose. As he faced his persecutors, bleeding, hunched over in pain, he felt a surge of hatred. He knew they could kill him if they wanted. He felt weak and powerless. From somewhere beyond the despair, he uttered a prayer: "God, help me."

His salvation came with the realization they didn't have any ultimate power over him. *They have the power of might and force*, he thought. But they lack real power, the power of the truth. They're living within the lie, as Solzhenitsyn called it. What they call power—money, might, political gain—held no power over him at all. Though he was powerless in their eyes, he was really the powerful. He actually began to feel pity for them. They didn't know what they were missing.

The authorities let him go after detaining him for forty-eight hours. Before he was freed, an officer thrust a paper at him.

"Sign this!" he ordered.

It was a statement saying that no physical or psychological pressure had been used against him—a document typical of the deceptive legal tactics practiced by the authorities.

When Maly refused to sign the statement, the enraged officer shouted at him, spitting the words in his face: "You're a bastard, just like that Pope Wojtyla of yours!"

Maly regarded the interrogation as a moral victory. Physically he was almost destroyed. But he hadn't given any information or signed anything that could damage himself or anyone else. His conscience was clear. When it was finally over, he had a real sense of who was the powerful, and who were the powerless.

Notes

1. Vaclav Benda, "From My Personal File," *Svedectvi*, Keston translation, 58, July 1979, 273-276.

2. H. Gordon Skillings, *Charter 77 and Human Rights in Czechoslovakia* (London: George, Allen, & Unwin, 1981), 305-306.

8

Hungary

Gabor Ivanyi spent six years trying to get his outcast congregation legalized. His persistent lobbying finally paid off. In 1981, the State Office of Church Affairs offered the Methodist splinter group recognition as a separate denomination called the Hungarian Evangelical Fellowship. After years of weathering the elements, the group could start worshiping together legally in a church building of its own.

The legal recognition was a sign of an encouraging shift in church-state relations, as Hungarians began to enjoy a relative amount of expanding freedom and prosperity. Well before Mikhail Gorbachev's glasnost *policies, Hungarian Communist party leader Janos Kadar introduced a gradual program of liberalization. The modernization campaign was aimed at placating a population that resented the way he was placed in power after the Soviets crushed the 1956 uprising. Kadar embarked on an economic plan of "goulash communism" that began to mix the Marxist idea of a command economy with the capitalist qualities of private enterprise and foreign investment. The economic experiment succeeded in stocking*

Hungarian shelves with an abundance of consumer goods, though it later turned out to be a recipe for economic disaster when a worldwide recession squeezed foreign investment and left Hungarians with the age-old problem of capitalist consumers—incomes that couldn't keep up with skyrocketing prices.

At the same time, Kadar began to ease cultural and religious restrictions, gradually earning a degree of popular support. The increasing amount of religious freedom enjoyed by the church served for the most part to keep it pacified. Under this relative prosperity, Hungarian churches began turning their attention to their less fortunate relatives in Transylvania. Hungary was being stampeded by thousands of Romanians seeking political asylum, and the Hungarian church began taking an active role in publicizing their plight and lending them aid. In 1986, a group of Hungarian religious leaders sent an open letter calling on churches to express their solidarity with the Hungarian minority in Romania by establishing a relief fund. Another letter in 1988 from the Hungarian Ecumenical Council protested Ceausescu's village demolition program. Extensive networks of aid began springing up on both sides of the border, with Christians often at the forefront. One of the churches taking part in the relief activities was the newly recognized Kispest congregation.

HUNGARIAN-ROMANIAN BORDER
1982

It was after sunset when Gabor Ivanyi reached the Hungarian-Romanian border. He always waited until dark to take these trips. The darkness provided better cover, and lessened the likelihood he would be observed once he reached his destination. As he pulled up behind the line of cars waiting to go through the small sleepy border crossing, he uttered a quick prayer of protection. His car was crammed with food and about eighty Hungarian Bibles, hidden out of sight, bound for Hungarian-speaking churches in Transylvania.

The Hungarian pastor traveled the long road to Transylvania frequently. He usually tried to cover the three hundred miles there and back from Budapest in one day. His church had a storehouse in Eastern Hungary filled with donations of religious literature and food brought in from the West. Every month, couriers set out for

Transylvania to deliver the needed items to believers there who took the risk of being visited.

Unlike many who made this trip, Ivanyi refused to bribe his way past the border, though he didn't judge those who did. It was an easy thing to take advantage of the corrupt border guards, a simple matter of placing a discreet packet of "gifts" on the hood of the engine before stepping away to fill out the necessary paperwork to get across the border. When you went back to the car, the packet had vanished, and you were free to go after a token search. A young professional smuggler he had once traveled with boasted that he could bring in a piano right under the border guards' noses.

After nightfall, the border crossing glowed like an oasis of light that rose suddenly out of a dark desert. There was nothing for miles around. The hollow sounds of trunks slamming and border guards shouting orders seemed amplified in the vacuum of inactivity, jarring Ivanyi's already jumpy nerves.

As he watched the gray-uniformed border guard poke around the cars in front of him, he felt his mouth go dry. The steering wheel was slippery from his sweaty palms. No matter how many times he made the trip, his heart still pounded before each customs search. The Bibles he was carrying were concealed, but a careful search could easily uncover them. If discovered, his car could be confiscated and there was a chance he could be imprisoned.

The border guard waved the car ahead of him through and walked toward him. Ivanyi rolled down the window.

"Do you have anything to declare?" the guard asked.

"No," Ivanyi replied, trying to suppress any nervous gestures that would make him look suspicious.

"Do you have any drugs, weapons, or books?" the guard asked perfunctorily.

Ivanyi swallowed hard. Should he lie?

"What kind of books?" he asked.

"Mass books, prayer books."

"No, I have no mass books or prayer books," he replied. Technically, at least, he was telling the truth. The guard didn't say anything about Bibles.

The border guard ordered him out of the car and motioned for him to open the trunk. Ivanyi obeyed. His pulse raced as he watched the customs official sift through the carefully arranged luggage in the trunk and pull out a cardboard box lying underneath. He struggled under the weight of it.

"What's this?" the customs official asked suspiciously as he dropped the box on the nearby inspection table with an incriminating thud.

"What?" Ivanyi replied, stalling for time.

"This," the guard scowled, producing a Hungarian-language Bible from the box.

"It's a Hungarian Bible."

"You can't bring them in here."

"They're gifts. What's wrong with bringing them into the country? I thought there was religious freedom in Romania."

"We have no need for them in our country," the guard said as if he were reciting from a rehearsed script.

"Who are you kidding?" Ivanyi shot back without thinking, then held his tongue.

After the customs official conferred with several other border guards, presumably higher ups, Ivanyi was ordered to turn around. He breathed a sigh of relief. He was fortunate this time. No interrogation. They didn't seize his car. They didn't even confiscate the Bibles he was carrying.

Ivanyi drove away. When he was well out of sight of the guard towers overlooking the border, he got out of his car and rearranged the Bibles in his trunk, then resolutely drove toward the next border crossing. A sense of deja vu flashed over Ivanyi as he waited to go through customs there. Would he be stopped again? The same feelings of fear flooded over him as he watched the customs official walk toward his car. This time, after a cursory search, he was waved through.

—•—

Ivanyi's church was part of a growing ministry in Hungary to help ethnic Hungarians from Romania on both sides of the border. Every Friday night, hundreds of Romanian refugees swarmed to the Community of Reconciliation, a church center on the fringe of Budapest, looking for advice, jobs, food, clothing. They found solace there, talking to others who were dispossessed, who knew the same pain of separation from friends and family that continually gnawed at them.

The ecumenical ministry was started by Geza Nemeth, an avuncular pastor of the Reformed church and part-time art dealer. Nearly every inch of the walls of his business office was covered with paintings done by local artists, everything from gaudy seascapes to primitively drawn religious icons. Tablecloths, vases, and other objects in the exotic, floral patterns typical of Hungarian handiwork cluttered the bookshelves, tables, and desks occupying the two rooms. Nemeth was quite a wheeler-dealer. He sold the art work to help finance the ministry he started in 1987 when three refugees showed up at his doorstep. At first, the Hungarian government frowned on taking in refugees, so they were quietly hidden away with Hungarian families. But when Hungary began to be inundated with ethnic Hungarians coming out of Romania, the authorities eased up on the restrictions on church social work and gave official approval for the refugee work. Nemeth's tiny chapel was soon overflowing with refugees, and he was given permission by his bishop to transfer the ministry to a larger church.

A steady stream of refugees showed up at the ministry's relief center. As they sifted through clothes or combed the bulletin board for job postings, they poured out their anguished stories of life in Romania. A young woman told of how she had been jailed for singing the Hungarian national anthem. A young man recalled how he had been forbidden from studying in his mother tongue. One couple named Eva and Lajos Oszvath recounted the story of their dramatic escape into Hungary.

Carei, Romania
March 1989

As Eva told it, it was always dark there. After dusk, a murky twilight descended on their village of Carei and then smothered the villagers in a deep darkness. Streetlights lined the dusty roads of the border town, but they were useless, yet another casualty of the Romanian regime's austerity program. Electricity was a luxury, rationed like everything else in the country. The authorities often cut off power from six to nine in the evening, and indiscriminately throughout the night. The people never knew when the lights would go out, plunging the entire village into a suffocating blackness.

Eva and Lajos fought to ward off the chill that had taken permanent residence inside their four-room home. Their heat was turned on for just seven hours a day, hardly long enough to keep them warm through the freezing winters. One sardonic joke making the rounds: Why should you keep your windows closed during the winter? Because people passing by outside could catch their death of cold. Humor, the blacker the better, seemed to help make the bitter situation more bearable.

Eva worried not so much about herself, but their four children. Trying to feed them under the ridiculous constraints of monthly quotas was nearly impossible. They were limited to just over one pound of meat, a little over one pound of cheese, two pounds of sugar and just ten eggs every month. And that was when they were available. She often looked longingly at the goods you could buy on the black market, those smuggled in from Hungary. But they were prohibitively expensive, five times as much as Romanian products. Her children had never even known the sweet, creamy taste of chocolate, and probably never would. One candy bar on the black market cost a quarter of a month's wages.

Running water trickled through their rusty pipes only a few times a week, hot water only once a week, if they were lucky. So they always had containers standing by to make it through the days the tap was dry. Even then, there was never enough to wash clothes.

Sometimes Eva felt she would collapse under the strain of the austere conditions. There was such a heaviness, an oppressive shadow, that seemed to weigh down their lives. The very air seemed to press against her. Even the simplest task became a burdensome responsibility. Shopping turned into an endless wait in endless lines, only to discover once inside the shop that the window displays bore no resemblance to what was actually stocked on store shelves. She and Lajos often talked about leaving the country, emigrating to their homeland of Hungary, just a few kilometers away. They had tried for years to emigrate legally, waging a long bureaucratic battle to get a passport, a fight they ended up losing. The authorities simply said no.

They couldn't even get a thirty-day tourist visa to visit Hungary, a means thousands of Romanians were using to turn into a permanent stay. The only route available was taking the risk of making an illegal dash into Hungary. What a difference a few kilometers make, Eva thought.

—•—

Eva knew the minute Lajos was missing that he had headed for the border. She felt desolate, abandoned. But the worst part was not knowing whether he had made it. She went to the police station. Nothing. In a way, that was good news. The waiting continued without any word until a stranger showed up at her door. He had just come from Budapest. Lajos had sent him to let them know he was safe. He was already working as a welder. He was also working on getting the children and her out of Romania legally.

The news was like cold water to parched lips. From that point, Eva was determined to join him. She couldn't wait for the legal process. That could take years. She knew of people who worked as human smugglers on the black market. They were professionals, trained to sneak groups of Romanians across the border. But their price was high—sixteen thousand Hungarian *forints*, or more than three months' salary. She scraped up all the money she had saved and together with some money Lajos sent from Hungary hired a black marketeer who knew the best route into Hungary.

She could only take along her thirteen-year-old son. Her sixteen-year-old had broken his arm, making the difficult journey out of the question for him. Besides, Eva needed him to stay behind to help take care of the two younger children, eleven and nine. She arranged for them to stay with an older woman in town until she and Lajos could get them out legally. She knew it was impossible for all of them to escape together. The two younger children could endanger the entire group. But that didn't make it any easier to leave without them.

Eva embraced each one of them, wiping away their tears along with her own. "You know your father and I will get you out as soon as we can," she said between sobs. "We'll be together before you know it." The words were directed as much at convincing herself as they were at reassuring the children.

It was a moonless night in April. There were fifteen of them altogether, all of them clad in black. A drenching rain was falling. Though it was bone-chilling, they welcomed it as an additional cloak.

They waited until 10:00 to start the trek, staying close together and close to the ground. With each step, she was haunted by the memories of others who had tried this risky route and failed. One villager caught trying to flee the country was paraded to the front of the police station. Eva had seen it herself, watching from the back of the crowd that gathered there as the escapee was beaten on the station steps. It was a warning for everyone to see. His bleeding body was then tossed into a cell, where he went without water for days.

Eva pushed the image out of her mind as the group made its way toward the border concealed under the cover of heavy brush. Eva was on her hands and knees, crawling a few hundred yards at a time. The prickly leaves jabbed into her face; her hands were bleeding from the briars and sharp sticks that made up the heavy underbrush. She glanced around to make sure her son was making good progress. Suddenly she froze. A few hundred feet away she spied the khaki-colored uniform of the border patrol. She motioned for her son to stay still, then held her breath as she watched the high-topped combat boots march straight for them. The sentinel stopped, then headed left, his submachine gun slung over his shoulder. He was just making his routine patrol. Eva remained motionless, her muscles aching from the paralysis. She didn't dare move. After what seemed like hours, he was out of sight.

Now the group crawled toward a clearing just ahead where the terrain dropped off into a deep canal. Eva wriggled to the edge of it and looked down the slippery precipice into the icy water below. The group leader slid down the steep slope and eased himself into the dank water. He beckoned for the others to follow. Some of the group balked at lowering themselves into the deep ditch and turned back. Eva was tempted to join them. The chasm below looked like it would swallow her up.

Her son sidled up to her and urged her on.

"I'm not sure I can do this," she whispered in a shaky voice. She was only five feet tall and slightly built. Already her muscles were in revolt, nearly shutting down under the strain.

"I'm on the swim team, remember, Mama?" her son reassured her. "I can help you once we're in the water."

She knew they couldn't go back now. She nodded and the two of them began to clamber down the muddy bank. They had to watch every step, careful of their footing so they wouldn't go splashing into the water below. Any suspicious noise could summon the sentinels patrolling the area.

Once down the slope, Eva eased herself into the black water. The frigid temperature almost choked the breath out of her. She wanted to gasp for air, but couldn't allow herself. Her son quietly paddled over to her and helped tow her to the other side. With all the strength she could muster, Eva began climbing the steep ascent out of the canal. Every step took enormous effort. The slick wall seemed to rise straight up out of the water. She inched forward, hoisting herself up with her arms, searching for good footing so she wouldn't slip back into the ditch. Finally, she reached the top and pulled herself over and onto level ground. Her arms ached from the effort.

When she lifted her head, she could make out the form of a guard tower rising ominously ahead through the constant rain. There were only six left in the group now. They were on their bellies, dragging themselves like snakes, slithering forward a few feet at a time. She could taste the mud. They had to crawl right under the watchful eye of the border station. Once past it, they were home free.

Her mind flashed back to another horrifying story of an unsuccessful escape. She had heard about a family that was nabbed while trying to cross the border illegally. They, too, were beaten in public, even the pregnant wife. A Hungarian Reformed pastor in the crowd witnessing the brutal beating tried to intervene. He too was beaten severely. Two hours later, he was dead.

Eva tried to shake the unnerving story out of her mind. She was almost there. As she approached the border station, a chilling sound pierced the quiet darkness. The vicious rapid-fire bark of a guard dog. The low-pitched staccato sound filled Eva with terror. They were discovered, she thought. The dog's yelps grew more high-pitched, more incessant. It must have picked up their trail. It sounded like it was coming straight for them. As she strained to listen, the barking began to drift off into the distance. Then, suddenly, silence.

Eva breathed in the welcome quiet. She continued slogging through the muck, her short-cropped dark hair plastered to her head, her face blackened with mud. She was soaked and cold and hungry. Her muscles screamed at her to stop. But she kept plodding ahead on her bloodied hands and knees until, at long last, five hours after they started out, she was across the border. She pulled her thirteen-year-old son to her aching body and wrapped her weary arms around him. "We made it," she whispered. "We're in Hungary."

Eva was reunited with Lajos the next day, and the couple began a desperate attempt to get their other three children out of Romania legally. Eva showed up at the emigration office several times a week, but it was always the same story: wading through more people, more paperwork, more bureaucracy. She would collar a sympathetic-looking bureaucrat and tearfully plead for help in getting her children out, only to hear the same refrain: don't get your hopes up; we're processing papers for hundreds of other families. In the meantime, they found a friend who agreed to deliver food and clothing to the children during his trips to Romania.

But Eva couldn't sleep nights thinking about the children she left behind. She lay awake in their closet-sized room, pressing her face against a pillow damp with tears, wondering how the children were doing, what they were doing.

Five months passed. They had nearly given up hope of ever seeing them again when she and Lajos received word their papers had gone through. It had been five months of torture, from their frantic escape to the painful separation. But Eva believed it was worth it to escape the hell that was their life in Romania. She couldn't imagine ever going back.

9

Romania

When Laszlo Tokes gave his surreptitious interview to the team of Canadian journalists, it wasn't the first time he had spoken out against the Romanian regime. In the early 1980s, Tokes contributed to the Hungarian language samizdat *publication* Ellenpontok *(Counterpoints), one of the first unofficial opposition periodicals in Romania. There he wrote articles accusing the church leadership of collaborating with Romania's Communist authorities. That won him no points with either church or state. But his criticism was not unfounded.*

When the Communists came to power, they wrested control of every aspect of church life. A law passed in 1948 placed the church under the Department of Religious Affairs, which saw to it that those appointed to church leadership positions were willing to toe the government line. The appointment of pastors, the building of churches, even minor church renovation had to be approved by the department. The state recognized the church as a social institution that could help promote its policies and build socialism. In return, the church saw its role as one of service to society. In reality, though, the church became subservient to the state, not its servant.

On the forty-fifth anniversary of Romania's liberation from the Nazis, leaders from the Reformed church along with the country's other religious leaders sent Ceausescu a congratulatory telegram, praising him for having "taken the Romanian people to the highest level of civilization," and for his "unique achievements for peace and justice," and calling him the "greatest hero" of Romanian history.

Tokes also called into question the dearth of Christian literature in Romania. The regime regarded any religious material as a danger to the state's official atheistic ideology. During the 1970s, the Romanian authorities turned a massive shipment of Bibles legally imported from the West and earmarked for Hungarian churches in Transylvania into toilet paper. In fact, legible verses were still visible on some fragments of the toilet paper. But when Tokes issued an appeal to church leaders for more Hungarian Bibles and hymnbooks for his parish in Dej, and asked them to arrange for more printing, the hierarchy accused him of "sowing discord."

He raised the wrath of the Romanian regime when be began organizing Bible studies for the congregation's high school students. While the activity was technically legal, in practice it was forbidden. One by one, the young people were called before their teachers, before Communist party officials, and finally before the dreaded Securitate, where they were pressured to inform on Tokes and sign statements accusing him of using mysticism to brainwash them with Hungarian Nationalistic ideas.

The Securitate also began putting subtle pressure on the church leadership to do something about this renegade pastor. After a series of disciplinary hearings, Bishop Gyula Nagy ordered Tokes's transfer to a tiny village of 150 people, despite the objection of his congregation. When Tokes refused, he was fined and suspended. Though he was never defrocked, he was kept from ministering as a pastor. He spent the next two years without a job, often in hiding, staying with friends who would put him up for the night. He ended up living at the home of his father, Istvan, a Reformed theologian who had been forced into early retirement from his job teaching at the Protestant Academy in Cluj because of his own outspokenness.

In 1986, Tokes was given another chance. Bishop Laszlo Papp offered him a position where he would not be able to stir up much trouble, it was thought, as assistant pastor of a dying congregation in Timisoara, a city of about 350,000 on the western edge of the country.

TIMISOARA, ROMANIA
July 1986

Tokes arrived in Timisoara to find a church in ruins, physically and spiritually. He stood on the corner of Cipariu Street surveying the dingy, yellow-bricked building that housed the church. It cried out for repair. Anyone getting off at the busy tram-stop across the street could easily pass by without even knowing a church stood there. There was no steeple, no cross, no ornate stained glass windows. The only tell-tale sign was an unobtrusive plaque at the entrance around the corner identifying it in Hungarian as the Reformed Church of Timisoara. The most noticeable thing about the building's facade was a crudely drawn poster in dirty shades of brown and yellow depicting a pair of eyeglasses that advertised the optician in the same building.

The church itself was situated on the second floor of the three-story building, just above the apartment that served as the parsonage. The interior of the church was stark, even by the simple standards of the Reformed church, which eschews any pictorial representation of Christ. Simple-patterned windows in subdued tones rose to meet the high-vaulted ceiling. Uncomfortable looking wooden chairs and splintery pews lined the rough-hewn floor. The furnaces to heat the frigid church stood against the wall.

Membership had dwindled down to just a handful under the head pastor, Leo Pauker, a man derogatorily called a "red" priest because of his suspected ties to the Communist government. Services were limited to only one on Sunday morning. The only life outside the Sunday service revolved around death, that is, the burial of the dead. Six months after Tokes arrived, Rev. Pauker died of a stroke, leaving Tokes in charge of the congregation.

The first Sunday Tokes climbed into the pulpit as the congregation's sole pastor, the sanctuary looked even bleaker then usual. It was a disheartening sight. He peered out at a sparse congregation of forty to fifty people, most of them elderly women. They barely managed to warble out the hymns. It was almost painful to hear them dragging out the melodies, dirge-like, to the wheezing accompaniment of the pipe organ in the choir loft behind them. As the thirty-seven-year-old minister surveyed this anemic group, he stared into the face of the work that lay ahead of him.

But Tokes began to breathe new life into the moribund congregation. He started an amateur drama group that became something of a center for Hungarian cultural activity. His fiery sermons drew on biblical injunctions to point out the injustices of the Romanian regime. From Sunday to Sunday, the church was filled with more and more people drawn by Tokes's dynamic personality. Before long, five to six hundred people regularly jammed together inside the small sanctuary for Sunday services. He attracted students, intellectuals, even ethnic Romanians and members of other denominations.

At the same time, he also attracted the attention of the Securitate. They were watching the nondescript little church in Timisoara very closely.

Arad, Romania
September 6, 1988

Well before his interview aired on Hungarian TV, Tokes had been trying to rouse his fellow pastors to take a stand against Ceausescu's systemization policy. He and an old friend from seminary, Janos Molnar, got together and drafted a carefully worded resolution calling the demolition plan into question. Over the summer the two traveled throughout the church districts of Cluj and Oradea to drum up support for the protest. The pastors they spoke with were reluctant to take a stand; they knew the kind of reprisals they faced if they did. But by the time of the Reformed church's annual church district meetings in September, the two pastors thought they had lined up someone on their side in nearly every district.

Tokes and Molnar were apprehensive as the meeting of their own church district opened in Arad. They had no way of knowing just what kind of support they could expect from their colleagues. The meeting seemed to drone on and on.

Finally, after all the formalities, Molnar stood up and asked for permission to address the meeting. Dean Jozsef Kovacs nodded his assent. Molnar then began reading from the protest resolution Tokes and he had drawn up. His voice trembled as he called on the Reformed church leadership to set up a "summit" between the country's religious leaders and state authorities to discuss the demolition plan.

"The destruction of villages means the destruction of the past," he told the pastors assembled in the meeting room. "Any people would become rootless if its past were wiped off the face of the earth."

The appeal met with stunned silence at first. Then two pastors jumped up to voice their support for the idea.

Tokes added his own bold suggestion. "I think every Reformed congregation should use its Sunday services to pray for each of the villages targeted for destruction by name," he said. "My congregation in Timisoara has been praying for a long time to stop the demolitions."

The group took a vote on adopting the resolution.

"All in favor?"

Fifteen hands shot up.

"Opposed?"

No one. Four pastors opted to abstain. Tokes and Molnar were overjoyed that the resolution passed unanimously.

But their church district was the only one out of thirteen Reformed deaneries that dared to speak out. At the deanery meeting in nearby Cluj, one of the pastors started to read the statement of protest aloud. He was stopped in mid-sentence and prevented from reading any further. The other church districts remained silent.

Three days after the deanery meeting, Tokes, Molnar, and the others who supported the memorandum were summoned to the office of their bishop, Laszlo Papp. Papp, a member of the Socialist Democracy and pro-government Unity Front in Bucharest, was suspected of having ties with the Securitate. He had a reputation at any rate for carrying out the wishes of the state. The bishop acquiesced to the government's strict limitations on the number of candidates who could attend seminary, and refused to do anything about the severe shortage of pastors in rural areas of the country. His role seemed one of keeping the church in check, rather than aiding in its growth. Any pastor who went beyond the church's proscribed role was subject to his reprimands.

When Tokes arrived for the meeting, he was greeted by Papp and a government inspector involved in the government's village destruction policy. Tokes and his fellow pastors listened incredulously as Papp defended the plan, almost parroting the government line that a new environment was needed to build a new society.

"Gentlemen, it could be to our advantage if some congregations disappear when the population is resettled," he argued. "It's not that important if the churches are pulled down. After all, it's not the stones that matter, but the services held inside them."

Then he turned to the dean of Arad, Jozsef Kovacs, and declared, "Reverend, even if they pulled down the Reformed Church in Arad, people could still pray in meeting houses in the suburbs. Even that would really be no great loss."

Timisoara, Romania
April 1989

It was a day Tokes dreaded, but one he knew would inevitably come after his outspoken interview with the Canadian TV crew the month before. Kovacs ordered him to his office in Arad and handed him an official notice suspending him from the pastorate. The order came on April 1, Tokes's birthday.

The next day, a Sunday, the dean showed up unexpectedly outside Tokes's church in Timisoara accompanied by the militia to bar Tokes from taking the pulpit. Kovacs rapped on the door of the church apartment downstairs from the sanctuary right before the service was set to begin.

"Since you are no longer the legal pastor, you are no longer allowed to preach," Kovacs informed him. "I am taking over the service."

The militia were posted at the church door to keep Tokes from entering. But the pastor took a hidden way through the building's basement to the church, reaching the sanctuary before Kovacs arrived.

When Tokes informed the congregation of the dean's intentions, the service turned into a showdown. Kovacs took the pulpit, but he was shouted down by the angry parishioners who demanded that he let Tokes preach. Their indignant shouting chased him away from the church. The congregation had won round one. Tokes knew, though, he would hear soon from his higher ups.

In mid-May, Bishop Papp handed down the order for Tokes to be transferred to the tiny, remote village of Mineu. The transfer was part of an all-too familiar pattern. Pastors regarded as troublemakers were moved to insignificant locales, out of sight, where they could have little impact. When Toke's congregation got word of the transfer order, they were incensed.

Members began swamping the bishop with letters and telegrams protesting the decision. It was illegal under church law, they argued, since the congregation alone had the right to dismiss their pastor. When their appeals went unanswered, they dispatched a team of eight members to pay Papp a personal visit.

The delegation from Tokes's church arrived at the office of Bishop Papp in Oradea in May with its petition in hand. Two of the members who were spearheading the campaign, Zoltan Balaton and Erno Ujvarossy, approached the ornate residence and asked to see the bishop.

Papp's deputy, Jozsef Zsigmond, looked at them and smelled trouble brewing. "And what do you want to see the bishop about?" he asked with that haughty air underlings often assume when visitors drop in unannounced.

"We're from the Reformed congregation in Timisoara," Balaton answered. "It's about our pastor, Laszlo Tokes."

Zsigmond ducked inside and returned after several minutes.

"I'm sorry. The bishop is a very busy man. He doesn't have time to see you today. Perhaps you could come back later."

Balaton felt his face flush with anger. "No, we can't come back later. We've traveled all the way here from Timisoara, and we're not leaving until we see the bishop. We'll wait until he's free."

Once again, the deputy disappeared. He was gone much longer this time. He finally reappeared with a look of bureaucratic determination.

"It's simply impossible to see the bishop now," he snapped. "And I've been told to tell you if you insist on staying, we'll have to call the authorities and have them remove you by force if necessary. Now please go." Balaton and Ujvarossy felt the force of the threat as the door slammed behind them.

TIMISOARA, ROMANIA
August 1989

Zoltan Balaton's ten-year old son, Bruno, kept an eye on the policeman standing guard outside Tokes's church apartment. He had a soccer ball with him. The grimy clothes he was wearing gave the impression he had been playing the game all day.

Bruno began kicking the ball toward the church building. He seemed engrossed in his private game, his stout little form chasing the ball, using his feet to pin it to a stop, toying with it like a kitten with a ball of string. He rhythmically kicked the ball from foot to foot, intent not only on balancing the ball, but also on juggling his attention between the ball and the guard. That was the real game he was playing, one that pitted him against the watchful eye of the policeman. The guard glanced at him, but didn't pay him too much attention. So Bruno began deftly maneuvering the ball, kicking it back and forth, positioning it closer and closer to the church building's entrance. When he was just in front of the door, Bruno quickly glanced over his shoulder to make sure the guard wasn't looking, and slipped inside.

Once inside, he pulled a message from his father concealed under his dirty jersey and gave it to Pastor Tokes. He waited inside Tokes's apartment until darkness fell, then slipped out again carrying letters and cassettes from Tokes to deliver to his friends and family.

This was one of the methods devised by Tokes and his congregation to communicate under the state of siege imposed on them. After Hungarian TV aired his outspoken interview on July 24, state and church authorities began waging a war of intimidation and relentless persecution against him.

The Securitate had set up a constant vigil outside the church building to isolate the popular pastor from his congregation and family. At first, any visitors to his church apartment were subjected to searches and questioning. Later, no visitors were allowed in at all, and Tokes was placed under an unofficial state of house arrest.

Armed guards accompanied him everywhere he went. Contact with members of his congregation was limited to Sunday services. And each Sunday, uniformed police formed a gauntlet outside the church, pointedly fiddling with their handcuffs as churchgoers passed by to enter. Some twenty to thirty people were singled out every week and prevented from attending the service for no apparent reason.

When Tokes's relatives tried to visit him, police headed them off at the Timisoara train station, questioned them, and then forced them to take the next train out of the city. His father was detained overnight after arriving from Cluj. Police accused him of coming to Timisoara to do illegal business on the black market and escorted him back to his hometown.

The authorities also confiscated Tokes's ration book, leaving him without any means to buy bread or meat or fuel. Members of his congregation had to smuggle in food and firewood. His phone was cut off. But in an Orwellian ploy, the authorities occasionally turned it back on to deliver death threats, then billed him for these calls at long-distance rates.

He and his pregnant wife, Edith, began to fear for the safety of their three-year-old son Mate after he just missed being hit by rocks tossed through their windows by "vandals."

The harassment was starting to take its toll on Tokes. In a videotape smuggled out of the country, the strain he was under showed on his haggard-looking face. "We live with daily violence and intense emotional strain, but enduring this enforced isolation is the worst," he said. "They've broken our windows every day. Now they've started breaking them in the church as well. Our friends sleep here now. The nights are terrible."

Tokes knew the pressure the entire congregation was under, and he felt responsible for what was happening to them. He never wanted to make his church members the casualties of his own battles. But he realized he couldn't face the authorities alone. He had consciously worked at building a sense of community in the congregation, forging a fellowship of the powerless to help fight the powerful. Now that solidarity was being put to the test. His parishioners were paying the price.

—•—

Zoltan Balaton was often stopped five times in a single day for questioning. In town. On the street. At work. Without cause, the police would grab him and ask him inane questions: "Who are you? What are you doing here?"

One morning, a car screeched to a stop in front of the technical institute where Balaton worked as a teacher. Two tough-looking men emerged and dragged Balaton back to the car. They drove him to the local state security headquarters and marched him into a barren-looking room occupied by only a single table and two chairs. They deposited him on one of the chairs and left him there without saying a word. Balaton sat alone for about two hours, his mind terrorized by the fear of what awaited him.

Then the door opened and a rather friendly looking officer entered. He acted as if he and Balaton were the best of friends. "How's your family?" he asked. "Tell me about your work." He engaged Balaton in innocent conversation for about a half an hour, then left. It was the classic good cop-bad cop routine, Balaton realized. He braced himself for the bad cop.

An hour later, another officer threw open the door. He was almost a caricature of the "bad cop." Aggression seemed to smoke off his shoulders as he stomped into the room. He took a menacing position at the table opposite Balaton and began hurling questions at him: "What's your connection with this revolutionary Laszlo Tokes? You know he's an agent of the Hungarian government, don't you? All this talk about the destruction of the villages comes straight from Budapest."

He pulled out a stack of paper and slammed it on the table. The sound was nearly deafening in the bare enclosed room. "You'll be free to go if you just put in writing what you know about Tokes and his friends, how they're working for forces outside Romania to overthrow the government. We already know this. We're just asking you to state it in a written declaration."

Balaton glanced down at the document before him and politely pushed it away.

The officer erupted in fury. "You refuse to cooperate?" he screamed. "You must be a foreign agent, too, just like your rebel leader Tokes."

With that he picked up his chair and brought it crashing down on the table, splintering it into pieces. He grabbed one of the legs that had flown off and held it above his head, towering over Balaton, as if he were going to crush his skull with it.

"Don't you know I could kill you if I wanted to?"

Balaton crouched down and threw his hands over his head instinctively, readying himself for the beating. But there was none. He watched in relief as the officer pitched the make-shift club against the wall and stormed out of the room.

A little later, the "good" cop returned and began asking Balaton about his wife, Mary, and son, Bruno. Balaton answered the questions matter-of-factly. As the conversation continued, he was gripped by a chilling realization. They knew every detail of his life: where he was on certain days, what his wife and son were doing then. When he was finally released, the officer called after him, "Take care of your family."

—•—

Erno Ujvarossy was in charge of supervising the reconstruction of the church building. It was badly in need of repair; plaster was chipping away, paint was peeling, the roof was sagging. He was the perfect man to head up the project, a building engineer and architect by profession. Even better, he had the knack of knowing how to pull the right bureaucratic strings to get what he needed. And in a country where you had to have permission from Bucharest for everything—even a simple project like putting on a new door—pulling strings was a valuable skill, and doubly so because of the red-tape tightly constricting any church construction.

Because Ujvarossy was also a staunch defender of Tokes, the Securitate zeroed in on him right away. At first, it was just phone calls, warning him to abandon the project. Then he was picked up and taken to the Communist party headquarters. "Are you trying to make a revolution?" the Communist party boss asked him. "No," came the simple reply. "We just want to keep our pastor."

The sporadic warnings turned into a barrage of threats against him and his family. Ujvarossy gradually became afraid even to leave his home. The car full of watchful eyes was always parked outside, waiting for him. He felt their sinister stares following him, threatening him. He was becoming despondent, fearful. The Securitate could sense his psychological weakness, like sharks smelling blood. They began to escalate their war of terrorism, ready to move in for the kill.

Tokes got a visit from Ujvarossy's son on September 13. He was visibly shaken, barely able to talk about why he had come. The day before, he sputtered, his father had left home at 7:00 in the morning. But he had not returned that evening, and he hadn't been seen since.

Tokes tried to calm him, but any words of reassurance were just that, empty words, full of false promise. He had heard Ujvarossy allude to threats made against him, but never said anything specific, though others in the congregation had come to Tokes with concerns about his well-being.

He was admittedly worried. Tokes immediately fired a letter to Bishop Papp expressing his concern over Ujvarossy's disappearance and accusing him of responsibility for the campaign of terror being waged against his church members: "Attempts are being made, directly or indirectly, to drive a wedge between the congregation and me. Members of my congregation are continually threatened. These threats are part of a worsening atmosphere of fear. Because of this campaign of terror, Ujvarossy had become dispirited and afraid. Now I fear for his safety."

Three days later, Ujvarossy's body was found in a forest near town. He had been dead for two days. Traces of poison were discovered in his body. Police ruled his death a suicide.

At the funeral, Zoltan Balaton noticed a red car parked conspicuously next to the cemetery. When the two men inside saw him looking their way, they got out of the car, pulled out their cameras, and very obviously began to snap his picture. It was another threat. Today, Ujvarossy. Tomorrow, you and your family.

—•—

A month later, Securitate agents swept through the city, pounding on the doors of the elders of Tokes's church to drag them to a suspicious meeting hastily arranged by Bishop Papp. Only eight could be located. They were forced to attend under threat of arrest. The rest were in hiding.

The orchestrated meeting took place in the corridor outside Tokes's locked office. A vote was taken to dismiss Tokes as pastor of the congregation. The results were not surprising. With the prospect of detention hanging over them, all eight voted to remove him. Though there was no quorum, Papp now had what he needed to get rid of Tokes.

The next night, police broke into the apartment of Bela Sepsi, the husband of one of the church elders.

"We know you're dealing on the black market," the security agent bellowed while two of his comrades ransacked the apartment.

"I don't know what you're talking about," Sepsi protested.

"Don't give us that." The official's bellicose face was just inches away from Sepsi's, so close Sepsi could feel his hot breath. "We know everything, how you've been working as a foreign agent and dealing in illegal currency speculation for years. And we know you've got the money stashed away here."

"I don't have any foreign money."

"We'll see about that," the security officer said, spitting out the words. Sepsi's papers and books were strewn on the floor. Then they threw open drawers, shuffled through papers, and grabbed books off the shelves, riffling through them and then tossing them aside.

One of the officers walked over to a map on the wall. He surveyed it intently, as if he were trying to pinpoint some location, then reached behind it and produced 300 German marks.

Sepsi's eyes widened, his mouth agape in astonishment. Where did that come from? "That's not mine! I never saw it before."

"Then what's it doing in your apartment?" the officer asked. "You're under arrest for illegal currency speculation." He turned to the other officers. "Take him in for interrogation." That night, Bela Sepsi had a stroke. He spent the next several months in a Timisoara hospital in a coma.

—•—

The Securitate then moved against Balaton and Lajos Vargas, another close friend of Tokes's, arranging for their workplaces to transfer them to Galati, a town in the eastern part of Romania. A Securitate agent paid a visit to both to ensure the banishment would be enforced. Each was given only a day to pack and forbidden to return for several weeks.

The campaign against the congregation was starting to take its toll. Tokes wrote a desperate appeal to Ceausescu to publicize the persecution.

> I, the undersigned Laszlo Tokes, appeal to you with regard to my situation and that of the Hungarian Reformed Church of Timisoara. In collaboration with local city officials, Bishop Laszlo Papp of Oradea is seriously violating not only our church statutes, which have been ratified by the state, but also the laws of the state itself. He is conducting a veritable campaign of harassment against the leadership and members of our congregation in Timisoara. At the same time, Hungarian Reformed believers are being subjected to harassment and threats.
>
> For several months now, the Securitate and local officials have gone about creating an atmosphere of uncertainty and provoking outrage not only among church members, but among respectable citizens as well. The persecution of church members has gravely affected the lives of their family members, especially the elderly and the ill among them.
>
> I respectfully invoke our country's laws, the principles of human rights and of freedom of conscience and religion guaranteed under our constitution. I request that you initiate an investigation into and put an end to these unlawful acts against the Timisoara Reformed Church and thereby guarantee our right to a dignified and peaceful existence.
>
> Rev. Laszlo Tokes, October 15, 1989

—•—

One quiet November evening, Tokes and his wife were entertaining some friends, a married couple who had somehow slipped through the net of surveillance surrounding the church building. It was a rare opportunity to talk to someone. Tokes and his family were living under virtual house arrest now. All eight windows of their apartment were boarded up. They felt trapped inside, cut off even from the outside light. It was like living underground.

The visit was a welcome relief, helping them escape, if just for the evening, the prison that had been erected around them. Around

7:30, their conversation was interrupted by a muffled thud at the door, then what sounded like a supersonic boom.

The door flew off its hinges and came smashing in. Tokes's wife, Edith, let out a scream as four hulking forms wearing stockings over their heads rushed in with knives. Mate watched in horror as one of the masked intruders came at his father. Tokes picked up a chair to protect himself, but the attacker lunged at him and slashed him across the forehead. Edith instinctively grabbed their three-year-old and ran to the window to call for help.

Though the church premises were under twenty-four-hour surveillance no help appeared. The two friends battled back with whatever they could find, turning over tables, throwing bottles, vases, lamps. They somehow managed to fight them off. After a brief skirmish, the intruders were gone.

Tokes put his hand to his forehead. It came back a deep scarlet. He winced as Edith pressed a rag to his brow, wiping the wound clean. It stung. Fortunately the cut wasn't too deep. Tokes embraced his pregnant wife. She was still trembling from the terrifying murder attempt. The intruders were obviously surprised to find they weren't alone. His visitors seemed to have thrown off what appeared to be a carefully planned attack. Tokes thanked God for their presence. The next time, would he be so lucky?

After the attack, Tokes and his wife sent Mate to live with Edith's parents in Dej. The situation was becoming too dangerous, and they didn't want to subject him to the risks they were now facing.

The couple braced themselves for the next scheme the authorities would devise. It came in the form of a summons from the Securitate. The agents thrust a familiar-looking paper in Tokes's face. The pastor recognized it. It was a letter he had mailed to an international Christian organization thanking the group for supporting him.

"You see," one of the officers shouted. "This is proof you're spying against Romania and receiving payment for it."

The agents then produced several photographs taken of Tokes's relatives, apparently snapped when they were detained at the Timisoara train station and barred from visiting him. The pictures showed them with food they were bringing for three-year-old Mate, including hard-to-find oranges and bananas.

"And take a close look at these. Where is your family finding oranges and bananas? You know very well you can't get them in Romanian shops. What more evidence do we need that your family is dealing on the black market?

"You know you can be imprisoned on these charges," they threatened. "You can get fifteen years for being a foreign agent paid by the West. Dealing on the black market can get you another seven to eight years. On the other hand, we don't have to bring these charges against you. They can be disposed of quite easily. All you have to do is stop creating a scandal for the Romanian authorities. If you'll just comply with the transfer order, we can promise you won't have any more trouble with the authorities."

Again, Tokes refused to give in. No one had the authority to remove him except for his congregation. And they wanted him to stay.

The next move against Tokes came from the civil court in Timisoara. After proceedings brought by Bishop Papp and the Ministry of Cults, Tokes was ordered to leave his parish apartment. Papp argued that since Tokes refused to comply with his transfer order, the eviction was entirely justified. "It is clear to any person of good faith that Laszlo Tokes broke the oath he took on his ordination," Papp wrote later. "Laszlo Tokes is a victim of his own actions, inspired and encouraged by hostile, anti-Romanian circles abroad, especially Hungary, and under no circumstances can one say that he was sanctioned for his religious activity."

The court sided with Papp, ruling that since Tokes was no longer the legal pastor of the Timisoara congregation, he no longer had the right to live in the parsonage. Tokes appealed the decision. On December 7, the court quashed his appeal. The hearing took just five minutes. The eviction was set for December 15.

The Sunday before the deadline, Tokes stepped behind the pulpit. The sanctuary was packed, with people spilling over from the pews into the aisles. But there was no uncomfortable rustling. They sat, hypnotically hushed, hanging on to their pastor's words. "On Friday, they are coming to take me away," he announced in a quiet but deliberate voice. "I have no intention of leaving. They are evicting me illegally. I invite anyone who wants to see this revolting action, to see how a pastor can be removed from his own home, to come and watch. Come and be my witnesses."

10

East Germany

The Iron Curtain was starting to fall, quite literally. In May of 1989, the Hungarian government began cutting down a 150-mile stretch of the rusty barbed wire fence along the Austrian border. As word spread that the physical barrier was coming down, East Germans began flooding into Hungary on tourist visas. But their real destination was Austria, and hundreds began slipping through the now tattered curtain.

Then, in September, Hungary agreed to let East Germans cross legally, and Austria dropped its normal visa requirements. A steady stream of Trabants, laden like packhorses with luggage, TV sets, even mattresses, sputtered toward Hungary and its wide open border. The gleaming, neon life East Germans had seen on West German television beckoned; the material goods and the freedom to travel where they pleased, were within reach. They could now virtually waltz right up to the border in broad daylight and promenade right past smiling Hungarian border guards into Austria.

Brigitta Treetz watched the images of the mass emigration shown on West German TV with mixed emotions. Now everyone who wanted to leave for the West could do so unhindered. In a journal she was keeping, she wrote: "Is this the beginning of the end for this country? We hope that it is, and yet we fear it."

Leipzig, East Germany
June 1989

It was the beginning of summer, a perfect night for a cookout. Brigitta was celebrating Johannesfest, the German summer solstice festival, with her *Hauskreis*, her church small group, at the cottage of a couple who belonged to the group. The savory smell of plump bratwursts sizzling on the grill wafted through the pleasant garden where they had gathered. Their conversation and laughter drifted off into the cool night air like the smoke wisping from the grill.

There was so much to catch up on. Everyone seemed to be talking at once. It was times like these, people like these, that made living in East Germany bearable and gave Brigitta hope that things could change. These were thinking people, concerned people, people committed to working for change within the country. Meeting together with them gave her a sense that together they could actually make a difference.

Brigitta, like most of the others in the group, lived in one of the city suburb's typical Socialist-style high-rises, a building virtually indistinguishable from the others clustered haphazardly around it in the concrete complex, a maze of uniformity. But she took care to make the interior of her apartment rise above the dull mediocrity of the surroundings. It was important to her to create an open comfortable space, both in her life and in her home. The apartment reflected her own carefully cultivated style; it was modest, but attractive, with sleek, modern furniture and Scandinavian-style bookshelves neatly packed with the latest literary fare.

Brigitta worked at a music publishing house and drove a Trabant, the toy-like auto made in the surrounding region of Saxony that sputtered all over East Germany; that is, when they weren't broken down, littering the side of the road, which was more often the case. The motorcycle-sized engine, with its horsepower just above that of a lawn tractor, coughed up clouds of smelly exhaust, earning the nickname "little stinker." The plastic bodied cars were also dubbed "suitcases," because of their miniature size, and they were the butt of all kinds of jokes. Brigitta was always eager to tell the latest one. Her favorites: How do you double the value of a Trabant? Answer: Fill it up. And: How many people does it take to build a Trabant? Two, one to fold and one to paste. She would tell the jokes with relish, punctuating the punchline with a hearty, carefree laugh. Somehow, they seemed to summarize all the absurd aspects of life in East Germany. Perhaps the biggest joke of all, though, was that she had to spend ten years on a waiting list just to be able to buy the wretched little car, and it took her nearly that long to scrape together the money.

Brigitta was single. She regarded the church small group as her extended family. The group of about twenty-five people reflected the mixture of professional and working class people from the suburb of Grunau where they all lived. They were professionals and blue-collar workers, shop assistants and students from the university, even a couple of non-Christians interested in examining this faith for themselves. Every month they studied the Bible and struggled together over how to apply the Christian faith to life in East Germany.

There was the time Brigitta came to the group in a muddle over the "System of Solidarity" instituted by the government. Like everyone in the government trade union, a percentage of her salary was taken out to fund certain state-supported causes. She didn't want any part of her paycheck going to a cause she knew nothing about, especially one selected by the government. She found out from the group discussion that instead of having her paycheck automatically deducted, she could choose to give the same amount to the charity of her choice. Now her money was going to a hospital for mentally disabled children, and she felt that she was being a better steward of her resources.

Brigitta thought about how close the group had become. During the past few years, they had done so much together. The deteriorating situation in their country had forced them to pull together. That closeness had given them the courage and strength they needed for resisting the system.

During Brigitta's exhausting, drawn out battle with kidney disease four years before, the members of the group had been a constant source of strength for her. They stood by her throughout the painful years of kidney dialysis and through the first trauma of her kidney transplant: the anxieties beforehand, not knowing whether the operation would be successful; the anxieties afterward, wondering whether her body would reject the new kidney. They were by her bedside, encouraging and praying with her during the seemingly never-ending period of recuperation, when she wondered whether she would regain the strength to resume a normal life. They helped yank her out of her feelings of doubt and self-pity, and prodded her into searching for the will to recover. When she was weak, they were strong.

Brigitta felt especially close to Uwe and Ulrike Jaeger, a married couple in the group she had come to consider two of her closest friends. All evening, though, she sensed something might be bothering them. In the midst of the uproar and the children banging in and out of the house, they stood off by themselves.

Toward the end of the evening, after all the children were put to bed, Brigitta and the others sprawled on the lawn, content in each other's company. When the conversation died down, Uwe cleared his throat and looked at his wife. She nodded at him, and as if on cue, he announced to the group, "Ulrike and I have something we would like to bring to your attention."

Brigitta noticed they both looked very uncomfortable. "Bring to our attention?" she thought. She wasn't prepared for what they said next.

"We have to leave East Germany," they announced.

Brigitta felt like she had been punched in the stomach.

"What?" she stammered in disbelief.

"We've applied for exit visas to emigrate to the West."

The whole group seemed flabbergasted. At first, there was silence. Then a barrage of questions.

"Why? You have a nice apartment. You have great jobs."

Uwe worked in an environmental institute, Ulrike was a geologist at an academic institute.

"I want to do something for peace and the environment, and I can't do it here in the GDR," Uwe said.

"But with your job, you're one of the few people who can make a difference and help clean up this filthy air we have to breathe,"

Brigitta said, countering. "And what about all your talk about working together for change? Were those just empty words?"

"I do want to make a difference," Uwe said, getting defensive. "I'm just worn out trying to do it here. We've lost hope. We feel like we can't breathe here anymore. Nothing's ever going to change."

The group pleaded for them to reconsider, throwing out argument after argument: "But we're seeing some changes starting to happen now. *Perestroika* may be slow in coming here, but it's taking root in the minds of the people. Look at our group."

"We're just tired of always running and never getting anywhere," Ulrike said. "And the children. We have to think of them. What's here for them?"

"But you can't leave now," Brigitta said, almost pleading. "We need you."

The group's appeals weren't being heard. Brigitta realized Uwe and Ulrike had made up their minds. Nothing any one of them could say would talk them out of it. She was hurt and bitter that they had not let anyone know they were contemplating leaving; they had not even bothered to ask for prayer and advice while they decided what to do. No! They just dropped their decision on them out of nowhere and retreated. End of discussion.

"But we need you until we go," Ulrike said with a slight smile of superiority.

Brigitta's response was curt. "But we need you to stay."

Although she planned to stay the night with the others at the summer home, Brigitta drove back home to Leipzig with Father Bernhard Venske, a Dominican monk in the house circle. Neither one of them could say anything. She was so sad and so angry she felt as if she had the flu. Everyone was leaving.

Several weeks later, the house circle met at Uwe and Ulrike's. There was only one subject of discussion: their departure. The group took it almost as a personal betrayal. Their discussion degenerated into an angry quarrel, with bitter accusations tossed back and forth. "One day you'll leave, too," Uwe and Ulrike said with a hint of condescension. "But it may be too late then. For those who still want to remain, nothing more can be done. Don't you see that it's too late to change anything here? Everyone who is capable and confident in their abilities is leaving now for the West."

Brigitta left in tears. She was angered most by the way they justified their departure. "Certainly parting is part of life," she thought. "But in this way? Why must they, because of this step that has clearly brought them pain, hurt us in such a conscious and calculated way. Don't we mean enough to them to deserve a bit of honesty? Why aren't they capable of simply saying: 'We are leaving, because we and our children will be able to live better in the West, and we'll miss you'? Was that so difficult?"

LEIPZIG, EAST GERMANY
September 1989

The peace prayer service at the Nikolai Church had almost turned into an emigrés convention. It was overrun with *ausreisen*, East Germans who had applied for exit visas to leave the country but had their applications refused. Because the church was the only place to speak openly and freely, more and more people were drifting in to voice their complaints, until the number of those who simply wanted out overwhelmed those who wanted to stay and work for change.

The hordes of *ausreisen* taking over the services put Pastor Führer in an awkward position. As the sign posted outside said, the church was open to all. He couldn't very well say, "Welcome, come in, but please leave your ideas and desires at the door."

On the one hand, Pastor Führer felt he had to take up the concerns of the *ausreisen* because of the discrimination being mounted against them. The Protestant church in East Germany traced its theological heritage to Dietrich Bonhoeffer, with his emphasis on the church's need to be there "for others"—the weak, the friendless, the persecuted. This new breed of activists, the *ausreisen*, were fast becoming the class of the oppressed. The moment they announced their decision to leave East Germany, they were often harassed, stripped of jobs, persecuted. They came to the church seeking legal help and financial aid. The church had always championed the right to travel and emigrate as basic human rights, and planned to continue to speak out for that right.

But on the other hand, Pastor Führer in no way wanted to encourage the massive wave of emigration. The official position of the Protestant church in East Germany positioned it as the "church within socialism." As Pastor Führer liked to explain, this position didn't mean the church was *for* socialism, or *against* socialism, but rather *in* socialism. The church had opted to work within the system, and had a duty to discourage those who simply wanted to give up and leave it.

At first, the *ausreisen* numbered only fifty or so. Now they crowded in by the hundreds. The issue of whether to stay or whether to go sparked heated discussions in private groups during the services, some of them dragging on for hours.

At the beginning of one service, Pastor Führer rose to address the controversy. "I have to point out that this is a peace prayer. All of us are gathered here to do something for peace, to create a more open, democratic society. If you're not interested in that, then perhaps you're in the wrong place. The church is open for everyone, but not for everything. As our synod has proclaimed, 'The feeling that nothing will ever change here is a fundamentally un-Christian thought.' Being a Christian means staying and bearing witness. We want to transform this land so there will no longer be any reason to leave."

When he finished his appeal, the church was like a morgue. One thousand silent, blank faces stared back at him. The *ausreisen* did not want to hear this message. They didn't even want to discuss the idea. They wanted out, and that was it.

In fact, soon afterwards, on September 11, after the regular peace prayer service, hundreds of *ausreisen* filed out of the church, shouting with one loud voice: "We want out! We want out!"

The protest was well-timed. Leipzig was swarming with Western media covering the city's annual international trade fair. Their presence guaranteed a modicum of protection and media coverage at the same time. It still didn't stop the police standing by outside the church from moving in and hauling off the demonstrators. In the melee, young Stasi provocateurs began ripping the hand-painted posters out of the protesters' hands and trampling them. More than seventy people were detained and ordered to pay fines of up to five thousand marks, roughly $2,500, or about five times the average monthly salary.

As Brigitta watched the demonstration that evening on West

German television, she trembled at the terrible pictures. "This is how they deal with the freedoms of those whose thinking is different than their own," she thought. She quickly ran over to a friend's apartment to discuss it with her. She couldn't stand being alone with those pictures in her head.

LEIPZIG, EAST GERMANY
September 18, 1989

Father Bernhard Venske looked a little like Martin Luther as he hurried across Leipzig's Karl Marx Platz, Bible tucked under one arm, the white cassock and long black cape of his Dominican order fluttering behind him. He felt a little like the Reformer, too, though he wondered whether Luther felt such fear on his way to nail the 95 Theses to the door of the Wittenberg Castle Church, not so far away from Leipzig.

The thirty-year-old monk was on his way to give the sermon for that Monday's peace prayer service at the Nikolai church. He was intrigued when Brigitta told him about the weekly meeting where different groups met to pray and voice their opinions on everything from the environment to the arms race. His parish, St. Martin's, and Brigitta's church, St. Paul's Evangelical, stood side by side, their steeples rising like twin lighthouses in the city's working class district of Grunau. The two congregations often met and ministered together. They even shared the same promotional flier. Catholics could find information on the ministry and time of services at St. Martin's on one side of the brochure. Protestants could find out all about St. Paul's on the other side.

Perspiration started to bead up on Father Bernhard's doughy, round face. He usually didn't wear his monk's habit. He donned it today as a sort of invocation for protection. Surely the Stasi wouldn't bother a meek-looking monk who looked like he belonged to another century.

The very thought of the secret police made him shudder, like feeling someone's clammy hands on the back of his neck. He was seventeen when he first came into contact with the Stasi. His outgoing personality had attracted the attention of the local unit in his hometown, a border city with no man's land for a back yard.

The Stasi was always on the lookout for bright young people with good connections, people who were tuned in to everyone and everything around them. And the secret police were particularly interested in getting information on any plans for making a break across the border into West Germany. Young Bernhard, with his many friends, would know this kind of thing; so he was summoned for a four-hour "chat."

"Bernhard, we understand your brother was in jail," the Stasi officer told him in a falsely gentle voice.

Bernhard glanced around nervously. His older brother was a political prisoner who had only been out of jail for a short time.

The interrogating officer took note of Bernhard's fear and anxiety at the mention of his brother's name. The officer prided himself on the way he handled his subjects, mentally probing them like a welder examining a piece of metal, until he found the weak spot, the flaw that made them malleable in his hands. He had obviously hit on that spot in Bernhard.

"I understand he wants to rehabilitate himself," the officer continued, "to go to the university to study. We've been keeping an eye on him. It would be a shame if he slipped up again, wouldn't it?"

The insinuation was clear.

"All we want you to do is keep your eyes and ears open for us. Let us know if you notice anything unusual with your friends, if you spot any suspicious strangers in town. We can have these friendly conversations from time to time, and you can tell us what you've seen and heard, the latest gossip, that sort of thing."

The officer produced a pen and sheaf of paper. Bernhard seemed to see the faces of his family staring back at him from the blank white sheets of paper placed in front of him. His mother's visage was streaked with tears. She had nearly suffered a nervous collapse when his brother was imprisoned. It would be too much for her to live through that again.

Bernhard took the papers. He was forced to write out the contract himself. When he handed it to the Stasi officer, he felt dirty, stained with the ink of the agreement he signed promising to inform for them. He wanted to run out of the room and wash his hands. He waited to hear from them, to be brought in for another "friendly" conversation. But they were silent.

Father Bernhard always wondered over the years when that piece of paper would be retrieved from the file drawer, when the Stasi would collect on this Faustian contract. Now, as he walked toward the peace prayer service, he felt like he was re-experiencing a bad dream, a recurring nightmare. Just ahead of him, in the cobblestone plaza outside the church, a cordon of police officers stood guard. Construction work on the twelfth-century church's decaying facade had reduced access to the church to only one narrow entrance, making the security police's job that much easier. The only way into the church was through the cordon and past the officers' attentive gaze. This was the same group of police who had violently broken up the *ausreisen* demonstration and hauled off several young protesters the week before. Father Bernhard felt as if he were walking right past the jaws of the dragon as he entered the church.

The cool stillness of the air inside washed over him like a refreshing wave. He took a seat in the chancel and looked out into the nave. The sanctuary was nearly filled.

A young woman, a mother of four, started off the prayer service with a song. As her clear voice sang out the lyrics full of peace, hope, and love, a strange feeling descended on the young Dominican, an awareness of a battle raging all around him and within him, an almost visible clash of forces without and within. The embodiment of his anxiety and terror surrounded him outside. Yet inside, he was pervaded with a curious peace.

His attention focused again on the terror outside when Pastor Christian Führer rose to address the congregation, wearing nothing but black. He pointed to his clothing: "Today you see me dressed in black. This is because of last Monday. What happened then made up the minds of those who want to leave the country and those who are still trying to decide whether to go. And for those who have consciously decided to stay here, it's getting more and more difficult not to be filled with either resignation or aggression. Because of those police actions, slow changes through peaceful means are becoming ever more improbable.

"However, we have to differentiate among the officials. I ask you especially to try to understand the riot police on the first row. These are young enlisted men, who can't choose their own deployment.

This could also hold true for some of the other security officers. And for us as Christians, even those who use force against us are human beings, because God created everyone in his own image, and that applies without exception to all human beings."

He paused, then began reading a list of names, twelve protesters still in detention.

"Today, we are including them in our thoughts and prayers," he continued.

"Our church remains a house of hope in the middle of this city. Help each other, so that the hope will also pour out into the plaza in front of the church."

When he finished speaking, Pastor Führer turned the program over to Father Bernhard. The young monk took his text from the book of Joshua, the story of the fall of Jericho. After reading the passage, he looked out into the thousands of faces waiting on his words and asked: "All right then, so let's all grab trumpets and blast down the walls? I'm afraid seeing the story this way would be naive and stupid, and we would be waiting for the results for ever.

"Not every wall is a product of evil. The walls we see here, the walls of the Nikolai Church, offer protection. They're good walls. But on the other hand, there are walls we've built around us that are unbearable."

Father Bernhard then turned the direction of his sermon into a public confession he had been wanting to make for a long time.

"I have to face the walls I've built within myself, and this creates fear, because it can lead to finding out things about myself I'd rather ignore or have no idea how to handle. We all have this kind of fear, everyone here today, and I'm no exception. It's the fear of the unpredictable, of what we're coming up against in these walls, whether they're walls of men or walls of stone.

"This fear is simply either ignorance or arrogance. To run away from it, as I've done for a long time, until today, is cowardice. Dear sisters and brothers! I have a confession to make. I stayed away from these peace prayers out of cowardice and fear. That is the guilt I bear.

"But there is a way out of this. We can see it in the story of Jericho: The first way is through prayer. Okay, I can hear you now; here he comes with the pious stuff. But bear with me. The message of the Holy Scriptures, the testimony of thousands of believers, meeting together with genuine Christians, all these things allow me to communicate with God. And from talking with God, I can realize that he loves me the way I am. That's the only way I can expose myself to this fearful situation, to learn something about myself, for example, from the walls which are taking shape outside, the police cordons and so on. For a Christian, this should be easy. But it isn't. This kind of self-examination is constantly being undermined, sometimes even by the church itself. But not until I'm ready to accept the walls erected within myself can I overcome the walls outside myself. Not until then will I be able to find the right note for my trumpet, and discover it's not the same note blown by everybody else. Only then will the walls come tumbling down. Now, the walls remain. But they can be overcome. It's up to us to bring them crashing down. Amen."

When Father Bernhard sat down, he realized his own walls of fear and cowardice were crumbling. He had faced his fear; he had called it by name. And in the naming of it, he found new strength and courage.

When the prayer service ended, as Father Bernhard was walking out of the church, a friend pointed up to the window of an apartment across the narrow alley. Just behind the window's reflection, they could make out a TV camera taping away as the crowd emerged from the church. The two looked up at it and, feeling a boldness they had never felt before, began to wave.

Then Father Bernhard strode straight toward the wall of policemen stretched in front of him, well aware that Stasi eyes were riveted on him. When he reached the human barrier, the policemen made a break, parting before him like the Red Sea. Father Bernhard hoped the Stasi were getting a good video of this: a wall of heavy security, armed with shields, clubs and menacing-looking dogs, opening up for a meek-looking monk with a billowing black cape, armed with nothing but a Bible.

Leipzig, East Germany
Late September 1989

When Brigitta emerged from the peace prayer meeting the next week, the narrow area outside the Nikolai church was filled with young people who were not able to get inside for the service. The entire crowd began to move toward Karl Marx Platz, the town center. Police and reserve units stood close by, on alert, holding their dogs at bay. The scene was bedlam. Traffic was snarled. Horns honked. There were screams and whistles. Brigitta thought she heard the Internationale, the revolutionary Socialist anthem. She heard people humming the melody at least, though no one seemed to know the words.

A friend of Brigitta's, a young woman named Gisela, began passing out handbills that proclaimed: "We don't want any violence." Brigitta incredulously watched her handing them to police officers and obvious Stasi agents, marveling at her courage. When a group of policemen detained Gisela and began taking down her name and address, they were immediately beset by a crowd of people like a flock of pigeons drawn to a pile of bread crumbs. "Leave her alone!" they shouted. "What are you doing to this woman? She's done nothing to you!"

Again, Brigitta gawked in disbelief. It was amazing to see how the crowd watched out for their own. But she wondered just how effective their protection would be in the face of the superior police force.

The group of about eight thousand reached Karl Marx Platz, and the crowd began shouting, "We want out! We want out!"

Brigitta and her friends stood on the edge of the demonstration. Against the forceful chant, they took up a competing call: "We're staying here!" It was a new signal to the authorities. "We're staying here!" Meaning, we're making a commitment to this country and we're not backing down. The new affirmation was picked up by more and more people, until it drowned out the chants of those wanting out and became the new rallying cry for the burgeoning demonstrations.

The next evening, an article on the demonstration appeared in the Leipzig newspaper:

> On Monday evening, in Leipzig's center, an illegal riotous assembly gathered without permit and disturbed the public peace and for a time interfered with traffic. Due to the level-headed and guarded behavior of the security forces, this

new riotous assembly with clear antisocial tendencies remained in check.

With that, Brigitta realized, the persecution had begun.

Part 3

Lanterns and Trumpets

11

Poland

Solidarity was formally outlawed on October 8, 1982. After spending a year in internment, Mazowiecki was released along with most of the other political detainees on December 23, in time to share the next Christmas wafer with his family. The state of martial law was formally lifted one week later, on December 31, but the government's war against Solidarity continued for the next six years.

Many Solidarity activists were driven into hiding, where they continued their active opposition to the regime through an underground network of samizdat *and illegal lectures in the Flying University. The Catholic church offered its tacit support for the opposition with financial, legal, and medical assistance. Some priests even harbored activists hiding from the authorities. While the opposition welcomed the church's support, there was growing dissatisfaction with the church hierarchy's moderate stance toward the Jaruzelski regime. After the brutal murder of the popular pre-Solidarity priest, Jerzy Popieluszko, by the secret police in 1984, the divide between the church and the authorities widened, while the rift between the church and opposition began to diminish. Another wave of strikes in May 1988 bridged the gap even further.*

NOWA HUTA, POLAND
May 1988

Halina Bortnowska waited until the shift change at the Nowa Huta steel works outside of Krakow to try to sneak inside the factory gates. The huge foundry, Poland's largest industrial works, was crippled by a wildcat strike, and she wanted to find out the situation firsthand. Bortnowska, a Catholic intellectual who had helped establish the Solidarity trade union at the steelworks, still maintained contact with the steelworkers, even though Solidarity had been banned.

About seventeen thousand workers began occupying the steelworks in a new wave of strikes again spurred by hikes in food prices of up to 200 percent. A group of workers at the Lenin shipyard in Gdansk also went on strike. The original strike at Nowa Huta had not been started by Solidarity, now operating underground, and Bortnowska feared that the strike might be a ploy by government collaborators to lure Solidarity supporters out of the woodwork. Her job was to discover just what kind of support the strike enjoyed, and what kind of assistance any legitimate strikers might need.

Nowa Huta was built as a model Socialist steeltown, and in a model Socialist steeltown, there would be no church. Nevertheless, out of that supposed sea of atheism rose a structure in the shape of a large ark, the local Catholic church. It was built by the workers themselves after a twenty-year struggle mounted by the pope-to-be himself, Karol Wojtyla, when he was Archbishop of Krakow.

When the mass of workers who decided to stay out of the strike began clocking in, Bortnowska nonchalantly joined their ranks, stealthily melding into the mass. This was illegal. She, a notorious Solidarity activist, was entering the strike-bound factory without permission. She fell in step with the shift change, acting as if she knew what she was doing, careful not to attract undue attention as she marched past the security unit stationed around the factory grounds. The ruse worked.

Once inside, she immediately searched out the strike leaders and discovered that their demands were strictly economic. They wanted higher wages to offset skyrocketing food prices. They didn't even want to talk about Solidarity. When she started to draw the distinctive red and white Solidarity logo on a strike poster, one leader snapped at her, "Put that away! It's different now. Everything's changed. We can't even think about the legalization of Solidarity. It's too soon for that."

But before she left, the strikers put in a request. "Send us the Warsaw lawyers," they pleaded, meaning Mazowiecki and the other advisors who had helped negotiate the Gdansk accords eight years earlier.

After slipping out of the foundry grounds unnoticed, Bortnowska headed to Warsaw to Mazowiecki's apartment to fulfill their petition.

"The strikers are asking for help," she told him after describing the scene at the steelworks. "Management has declared the strike illegal, and is refusing to talk to them. I'm afraid if negotiations aren't started soon, there's a real danger the strike will be aborted."

"We need to establish two mediation teams, one to go to Gdansk, and one to Nowa Huta," he counseled. "You should be a part of the Nowa Huta team, to go back in legally, as an official mediator."

"But will they give me permission to enter?" she asked.

"I'll discuss it with the other KIK members. We can work with the bishops to secure legal permission."

The Warsaw KIK chapter was in constant contact with the Catholic episcopate. The bishops acted in this case as go-betweens to secure permission from two moderate party bosses, Deputy Secretary Stanislaw Ciosek and Politburo member Jozef Czyrek, to send a team of negotiators to each strike-bound enterprise. The Communist authorities hesitated at first to allow Bortnowska back into the Nowa Huta shipyard, but finally relented.

For her part, Bortnowska was glad to leave the job of dealing with Ciosek and Czyrek to the bishops, and a masterful job they did, she thought. She could not conceive of having good relations with the two officials, or "Rosencrantz and Guildenstern," as she called them.

GDANSK, POLAND
May 4, 1988

Mazowiecki arrived at the Lenin shipyard bearing something of an imprimatur. His partner on the mediation team, Wielowieyski, had a special dispensation from the bishops' conference to try to mediate a solution to the stand-off. Bortnowska headed back to her old stomping grounds at the Nowa Huta steelworks, accompanied by

Andrzej Stelmachowski, now president of KIK, and Janusz Olszowski, another Catholic intellectual.

The scene at the shipyard took Mazowiecki back eight years earlier. Hundreds of tough-looking workers, their faces darkened with coarse whiskers and grime, straddled the iron gates singing lustily and chanting Solidarity slogans. The signs of their loyalty were pinned to their grease-stained overalls: the distinctive red-lettered Solidarity logo, under an icon of the Black Madonna.

Just across a divide from them stood row after row of gray-uniformed riot police. "Smurfs," the workers called them, after the cartoon characters popular in Poland. These were a new breed of strikers, a youthful bunch. Many of them weren't even working at the shipyard when Solidarity was legalized. But unlike their fellow workers at Nowa Huta, the spirit of Solidarity still inspired their actions. One of their key demands was for an end to the ban on the independent trade union. Their new battle cry: "No freedom without Solidarity."

As he walked into the shipyard, his head swimming with memories, Mazowiecki told reporters, "Our job is to work up a solution and to push it forward. [Society] must evolve toward more pluralism." He desperately wanted to help revive Solidarity. That's where his heart was.

Walesa was already entrenched in the shipyard, schooling the new generation of strikers. Mazowiecki joined him in the shipyard's unappetizing cafeteria next to the main gate, which served as the strike headquarters.

Wielowieyski and he were welcomed by the strike leaders, who thanked them for the support of the bishops.

Walesa corrected them. "The bishops aren't supporting the strikers," he said sternly, like a teacher scolding a pupil who had gotten out of line. "They're just offering their assistance in trying to find a solution to end the strike."

Nowa Huta, Poland
May 5

It was after 10:00 P.M. Bortnowska had just gotten off the phone with the director of the Nowa Huta steelworks. She had high hopes for some kind of breakthrough. The plant's management had finally agreed to meet with the three mediators and members of the strike committee. The meeting was set for the next morning.

It had been an exhausting day. She spent hours listening to the strikers' stories and demands, and hours more discussing those demands with the director—what kind of pay raise was realistic, what wasn't. She was surprised at how much the atmosphere had changed in just two days. Before, the legalization of Solidarity wasn't even an issue. Now that's all the strikers wanted to talk about. She began to feel that the strike was viable. The workers were together again, under the banner of Solidarity, and it wasn't over yet. Victory could still be theirs, but the only proof of its reality would be the relegalization of Solidarity. Now none of the workers wanted to accept a resolution without Solidarity.

After midnight, the mediation team left the shipyard to go back to the neighboring parish where they were staying. Bortnowska fell asleep with high hopes for some kind of breakthrough.

At 2:00 A.M., hours after getting the guarantee that negotiations would begin, the sleeping strikers were jolted awake by the sound of percussion grenades. ZOMO squads were storming the shipyard. The heavily armed units rushed in, firing tear gas, and in a flash of terror, began flailing at the fleeing strikers with night sticks. Dozens were dragged off and put under arrest, including Father Tadeusz Zaleski, a pro-Solidarity priest who had been giving the strikers spiritual support. The vicious raid was over quickly. The ZOMOs left the grounds littered with bloodied strikers, dazed and writhing in pain.

In one corner of the yard, Father Zaleski's vestments lay ripped and scattered across the floor. Just in front of the altar where he had celebrated mass for the strikers, a crucifix dangled, freshly pierced with bullets.

Cardinal Franciszek Macharski of Krakow, an instrumental figure in initiating the church mediation plan, got a first-hand account of the violence from Father Zaleski. The police dumped the priest off at the cardinal's office immediately after the predawn raid.

The next Sunday the cardinal preached a forceful sermon at a Krakow church deploring the action. Ironically, that Sunday was the feast of the patron saint of Poland, St. Stanislaw, who was killed by the Polish king for his outspoken criticism of the ruler's behavior.

"I assure you of my determination to wipe away the recent tears," the cardinal told the congregation. "I am making the following demands: that those who have been arrested and detained be released and all those who participated in the social unrest be guaranteed freedom. This is essential for public order, so that on the strength of our deepest convictions we can start the great task of rebuilding our country."

GDANSK, POLAND
May 5, 1988

Mazowiecki was indignant when he heard about the raid on Nowa Huta. The sketchy details he knew he had gleaned from scratchy reports over Radio Free Europe. Just two hours earlier, he had been given assurances from members of the Central Committee that force would not be used to end the strikes. Here he thought things were heading in the right direction again, toward more openness, toward pluralism, perhaps toward the re-establishment of Solidarity as a legal entity. The crackdown seemed to crush those ideas.

What was baffling was that the mediators in Nowa Huta had been given assurances that dialogue would begin. Either the mediators had been betrayed, or it was a sign that the hardliners in the Politburo were gaining the upper hand against the more liberal members who had authorized the mediation effort.

Tension gripped the shipyard. The strikers had been holed up inside for four days, cut off from their families. The riot police blockading the shipyard had it bottled up so tightly that even food and supplies couldn't get through. The relatives usually clustered outside the main gate had been cleared, leaving a stark Golgotha of three steel crosses jutting out of the open plain, a memorial to the 1970 massacre erected soon after the 1980 strikes, one of the concessions won in the Gdansk Accords.

At three in the morning, ZOMOs stationed around the yard began taunting the strikers, rhythmically beating their plastic shields like war drums as they marched toward the gate followed by a line of trucks. When the strikers jumped up from their beds to check out the disturbance, the phalanx retreated into the uncertain darkness.

Inside the yard, underneath the table where he slept, Mazowiecki wondered whether the authorities would use force here as well. The Gdansk shipyard was an almost sacrosanct place, the cradle of Solidarity. Violently ending the strike in Gdansk would be a much more forceful statement than crushing the one at Nowa Huta. But it happened there, he thought. That meant it could happen here.

GDANSK, POLAND
May 10, 1988

The strikers processed out of the Lenin Shipyard with heads held high, but feeling defeated. Some of them were weeping. Others were stoically silent. The strike was over, nine days after it started, abandoned without getting any concessions on the legalization of Solidarity from the government.

The decision to call off the strike came after hours of talks pushed forward by Mazowiecki's mediating team between management and members of the strike committee. At first, management refused even to negotiate, arguing that the strike was illegal. Mazowiecki's partner on the mediation team, Wielowieyski, left three days into the strike, convinced that the authorities weren't serious about negotiating.

Mazowiecki had finally been able to convince the shipyard management to sit down with the strike leaders, only to watch the talks break down when management refused to consider the legalization of Solidarity. The government offered instead a nominal pay raise and a vague promise not to take any disciplinary action against the strikers, a compromise offer soundly rejected by the workers.

After the talks had broken down, the authorities put an even tighter stranglehold on the shipyard, raising the specter that the strike in Gdansk would meet the same violent fate that befell the one in Nowa Huta. Walesa then delivered an emotional plea to the workers, urging them to abandon the strike, calling it a "truce, not a defeat."

Before leaving the shipyard, the workers issued a statement: "We are not giving up the fight for Solidarity. We remain faithful to the slogan of our strike: No freedom without Solidarity."

At the head of the grim-faced procession of about five hundred workers was Mazowiecki, holding high a rough-hewn wooden cross.

He was flanked by Walesa and some of the strike leaders carrying large pictures of the pope and the Black Madonna. The weary-looking band walked on to St. Brygida's church while squads of riot police glared at them in silence. Scattered shouts of "There's no freedom without Solidarity" sprang from the small crowd that gathered to watch the solemn parade. None of the workers joined in.

When they reached the church, KOR activist Adam Michnik, met them at the door, embraced Walesa and handed him a bouquet of white flowers. Inside, Father Henryk Jankowski, Walesa's priest and spiritual advisor to Solidarity, tried to bolster the workers' spirits in his sermon: "Please be proud of your fight, and don't stop fighting for the rights of Polish workers."

Walesa may have declared a truce, but to Mazowiecki, these events certainly felt like defeat.

August 1988 - April 1989

After the strikes ended unsuccessfully in May, it was only a matter of time before Polish workers staged another labor revolt. Poland's slipshod economy was wearing thinner and thinner. Waiting lines grew longer and longer, and the zloty, *Poland's currency, was buying less and less. The difference between the zloty's official exchange rate and the black market rate for the dollar widened exponentially. Often, the only placed stocked with needed goods was the local dollar shop, a store that accepted only hard currency—either there or the black market, where the* zloty *was also worthless. In effect, the dollar had reduced the* zloty *into little more than Monopoly money. On top of it all, Poland was still saddled with a whopping foreign debt of nearly 40 billion dollars.*

The Polish government had its hands tied. Part of the problem plaguing the economy was a system of government price subsidies that kept the cost of goods at an artificially low level. But every time the government tried to raise prices and bring them to a more realistic reflection of the true cost of production, the workers vetoed their actions with protests and walkouts. Again and again, in 1956, 1970, 1976, and 1980, the government was forced to back down on the measures needed to keep the economy from sliding into catastrophe. And the Communist regime lacked the support of the Polish populace to institute the kind of reform needed to stop the steep descent.

It was becoming evident to General Jaruzelski that he had no chance to reform the economy without popular support. At a meeting of the Polish Central Committee in June, he had mentioned the rather enigmatic idea of a dialogue with all segments of Polish society to discuss how to pull Poland out of its economic slide. But this proposed summit remained an enigmatic notion.

It came as no surprise when the latest shock on the seismological scale of labor unrest in Poland came in August, a month replete with anniversaries in a country where anniversaries are a vital link to the all-important past. It was in August that the Warsaw Uprising, the ill-fated revolt against Nazi occupation, began. August saw the first strikes start up at the Lenin Shipyard in 1980. And August was the month Solidarity was founded. The new series of strikes started when coal miners in southern Poland walked off the job demanding higher pay and the legalization of Solidarity. The labor unrest soon spread to a dozen other mines.

Some of the Catholic intelligentsia in the Warsaw chapter of KIK saw in this latest wave of strikes an opportunity to again play the part of mediator. Perhaps this latest eruption could help shake the government into reaching some kind of accord with the opposition once and for all.

WARSAW
August 1988

The Polish government had been making overtures for contact with the Solidarity opposition and saw the members of KIK as a possible bridge to renewing dialogue. One of the deputy secretaries of the Communist party, Jozef Czyrek, had proposed setting up a discussion with KIK members on the country's political problems. In a first for the Catholic group, KIK had invited the Party *apparatchik*, Czyrek, to a discussion that ended up stretching into five hours. Nothing came of it, though.

The chairman of the KIK Warsaw chapter, Andrzej Stelmachowski, thought now would be an opportune time to make use of the contact with Czyrek. He called him and reached his secretary. The boss wasn't in, he was told. When he made a second phone call, he was told the same thing. Maybe Czyrek doesn't want to talk to us, he thought. The KIK group got together again to decide how to proceed. The members decided to give it one last try. Stelmachowski called a third time, and got the same curt response from the secretary. He decided to give up. It was obvious the government wasn't interested in talking.

To his surprise, several hours later, Czyrek called him back.

"What do you want, Professor?" he asked.

"You know, a while back, Jaruzelski mentioned this idea of a round table discussion with the opposition," Stelmachowski said. "Don't you think it's time to get something going?"

"What do you have in mind?" Czyrek asked warily.

"The group at KIK has come up with a proposal for opening talks."

"If you have such a proposal, why don't you bring it to me?"

Saturday evening, Stelmachowski showed up at the home of the Communist official clutching an outline of the plan.

"You must start with some spectacular step," Stelmachowski suggested. "We propose a meeting between Walesa and someone from the government. That would be a sign to the entire society that you're being realistic about your desire to talk to the opposition. Otherwise, the people will be suspicious, and there won't be any possibility of normalizing the situation. The talks would be broad-based, covering political and economic themes, including the relegalization of Solidarity."

Czyrek was taken aback. The government had branded Walesa a fomenter of revolution, and Solidarity a gang of terrorists. "You know the government's view of Walesa. It's asking a lot. I'll have to get the approval of General Jaruzelski himself for this."

At midnight the next night, Stelmachowski got a call from Czyrek.

"I finally succeeded in getting the okay from Jaruzelski,"he said. "But now it's too late. The Gdansk shipyard just went out on strike, and Walesa's joined them. It's impossible for the government to talk to Walesa while he's leading an illegal strike."

Over the next few days, the situation changed from hour to hour. One minute the talks were on. The next minute they were off. In the meantime, the church episcopate had been informed of Stelmachowski's talks with Czyrek and began exerting pressure of its own. Channels between the church and government leaders had remained open over the last several years. The church took advantage of these channels to persuade the Party hierarchy to pursue the proposal.

Stelmachowski had almost given up hope for any chance of success when he was again contacted by Czyrek.

"Jaruzelski has decided we need to renew our talks," the Communist official told him. "We're ready to go along with your proposal. But you have to understand that talking with Walesa is a great concession on our part. Before we sit down with him, we need to get a written declaration of his intention to stop the strikes."

Stelmachowski promised to do what he could, and headed to Gdansk. When he got there, he went to St. Brygida's church, where Mazowiecki and Michnik were waiting. They had turned the parish assembly hall into a temporary strike headquarters.

Mazowiecki accompanied Stelmachowski to the shipyard. When they got there, it was surrounded by police. As Mazowiecki sauntered toward one of the main gates with Stelmachowski, he was collared by one of the policemen standing guard.

"Where do you think you're going?"

"I'm accompanying my friend here, Professor Stelmachowski, to convey a message from the government to the strikers."

They surveyed Mazowiecki's lanky form. "We've been instructed to let *him* in," they said, pointing to Stelmachowski. "No one else."

Mazowiecki was shoved aside, while Stelmachowski was allowed entry.

Stelmachowski found the strike committee conferring with Walesa in a wood-paneled room above the cafeteria.

"The government is offering the possibility of round-table talks if you end the strike," he told them. "It's up to you to decide whether to take them up on it. I can't give you any guarantee these talks will end in success. But you see the wave of strikes isn't nearly as strong as in 1980. If they end as they did in May, with nothing, it could be far worse."

The strike team realized Stelmachowski was right. The strikes were slowly dwindling. Out of the twelve mines that walked out at the height of the unrest, only about five were still out.

"Will we be guaranteed the legalization of Solidarity?" one of the strike leaders asked.

Stelmachowski's reply was circumspect. "The government has agreed to discuss it. The only guarantee they're giving is to talk, nothing more."

After a heated debate of several hours, Walesa retired with Stelmachowski and a group of twelve strike leaders outside, out of sight, where no one could eavesdrop.

"In our proposal, we have to insist on the relegalization of Solidarity as a point that must be discussed," Walesa emphasized. "Otherwise, the talks are doomed to failure. The church must also be involved," he insisted. "The government mistrusts us; we mistrust the government. Only the church has the trust of both sides. The church ought to be a part of the talks as an observer."

The two points were inscribed into a proposal to give to the government, and a letter drafted to Cardinal Glemp asking for the church's involvement in guaranteeing the talks.

Stelmachowski emerged from the shipyard six hours after he arrived, and headed back to Warsaw with the secret proposal spelling out Solidarity's position. It was now up to the government to decide whether to accept it.

Warsaw
August 31, 1988

One week later, Walesa met with representatives of the Polish government for the first time since Solidarity was outlawed. Before traveling to Warsaw for the meeting, he issued a call urging all strikers to return to work, a call the young Turks in the Gdansk shipyard accepted only reluctantly. They wanted a guarantee of Solidarity's restoration before calling off their strike.

The scene in Warsaw where the meeting took place marked a dramatic turnaround: Walesa, a man regarded by the government as the non-leader of a non-union, entering a government house to talk to two party leaders, Gen. Czeslaw Kiszczak, the Interior Minister, and Politburo member Stanislaw Ciosek. During the two-hour talks, both sides agreed to get together again for round table talks that would include the possibility of restoring Solidarity's legal status.

The meeting took place eight years to the day after Solidarity was signed into existence in the Gdansk shipyard, underlining the importance of Polish anniversaries.

WARSAW
September 1988

Father Bronislaw Dembowski, the priest who presided over the hunger strike at St. Martin's Church back in 1977, was summoned to see Cardinal Glemp. In the sumptuous surroundings of the primate's residence, the archbishop got right to the point of why he had called for the priest.

"These upcoming round table talks are of vital importance to our country," the cardinal told him. "I would like you to attend them as one of the church representatives."

"My archbishop already mentioned the possibility to me," the priest replied.

"Good, then you aren't surprised."

"No, and I would be glad to serve as a representative of the church."

The cardinal then relayed the church's position on the talks. Dembowski would not be an actual participant in the discussions. Even though both sides had invited the church's participation in discussing the different reforms laid on the round table, the church did not want to get involved in the nuts and bolts of a political agreement. Instead, Father Dembowski would serve as an impartial observer. Dembowski knew why the church's presence was important. It would be a sign to the Polish people that the talks would not be the dirty work of politicians with dirty hands.

As the priest turned to go, Cardinal Glemp called after him. "Wait. You didn't ask me for any instructions."

Father Dembowski looked sheepishly at his superior. "Oh, I'm sorry. It slipped my mind."

"I have only one piece of advice," the cardinal said, pausing for effect. "Do your best to make sure that the first meeting won't be the last."

Father Dembowski realized the weight of those words.

Considering the gulf between the two sides, carrying out the cardinal's command would be anything but easy.

MAGDALINKA, POLAND
September 16, 1988

The first official session between the government and Solidarity representatives got underway at an Interior Ministry facility in Magdalinka, a village just south of Warsaw. It was full of cantankerous debate. Mazowiecki joined Walesa and other Solidarity figures to meet with General Kiszczak and his delegation of Communist party leaders and representatives from the Communist-led union, OPZZ. Watching the so-called "Magdalinka Group" were Father Dembowski and another priest, Alojzy Orszulik.

The talks were convened to discuss the issues that would be dealt with at the round table. But they quickly bogged down over the usual sticking point, the relegalization of Solidarity.

"It's impossible to have two trade unions in the same factory," Romuald Sosnowski objected. He was one of the government representatives for the official trade union.

"What's the problem with having a second trade union in the same factory as the official trade union?" the Solidarity side demanded. "The two can exist side by side."

Sosnowski wouldn't budge. "I have no problem with your being an independent trade union, as long as you stay out of factories where the OPZZ already exists."

The debate dragged on past the appointed time for supper. Up to now, Father Dembowski and Father Orszulik had kept quiet. But Father Orszulik's stomach had been rumbling for the past twenty minutes. And the kitchen had been serving up some delectable meals. The general was feeding them well.

"Excuse me," he interrupted, raising his hand. "It's twenty minutes past supper time. We need to have some consideration for the cook, who has already prepared supper. I think a short break would be very much in order."

The innocent suggestion turned out to be a turning point in the negotiations. During supper, Walesa, Mazowiecki, and Kiszczak excused themselves to discuss the deadlock between just the three of them. They returned to the table with a short communique, a somewhat skimpy statement that avoided the issue of relegalizing Solidarity altogether. It simply stated that "the positions of the sides were brought closer" and that both sides agreed to begin the round-table talks in the near future. The statement with its lack of concrete proposals, was disappointing to many Poles. But to Father Dembowski, they were welcome words. He had been faithful to the cardinal's instructions. The first meeting would not be the last.

WARSAW
February 6, 1989

After months of haggling, the round table talks finally commenced with a bizarre tableaux—General Kiszczak, the short, weaselly-looking Minister of Internal Affairs, shaking hands with Mazowiecki and other former inmates of his internment camps as they filed into the Palace of the Council of Ministers for the first session. The fifty-seven delegates took their places around a vast doughnut-shaped table with a centerpiece of red and white flowers, former prisoners facing their former jailers. The specially constructed table was nine meters in diameter because, according to a joke making the rounds, the world record for spitting was seven and a half meters.

Father Dembowski assumed his place at the table as an observer. "A knight of the round table," he liked to call himself. On his right sat General Kiszczak, head of the government delegation, on his left, Walesa. The arrangement struck him as fitting—the church representative smack in between the epitome of Poland's political right and left.

The talks kicked off with speeches by Kiszczak and Walesa, followed by short addresses delivered by three representatives from both sides.

Kiszczak was the first to speak. "We have come here guided by a sense of responsibility for the future of our homeland. We have come here convinced that our country faces a great historic opportunity. We are all responsible for Poland's future, and this is the essential message of today's meeting."

He went on to enumerate the conditions for reaching some sort of national agreement. First, he said, socialism would have to remain the country's system of government, although he was careful to point out it should be socialism with a human face. Second, the renewal would be the responsibility of both sides. Third, change was necessary. Everyone recognized that. But the change had to come gradually. Finally, he said, no one should overlook the achievements of forty years of Communist rule.

Walesa's speech certainly didn't overlook the nation's Communist legacy. In fact, he minced no words in blaming the Communists for Poland's dire situation. "We know it, the country is ruined," he said. "And it wasn't some elves who ruined it, but a system of exercising authority that detaches citizens from their rights and wastes the fruits of their labor."

If the Communists were upset with Walesa's forthrightness, the speech by opposition representative Jerzy Turowicz, editor of the Catholic daily *Tygodnik Powszechny (Universal Weekly)*, was the crowning blow. He stood up and accused the authorities of reneging on their promises to society so often that they had lost the confidence of the Polish people. "The first task must be to restore the confidence between the authorities and society, a confidence that is lacking now," he said. "If restoring society's confidence in the authorities is to succeed, it's not enough merely to introduce formal changes in the legal structures of the state. It's also necessary to make profound changes in the practice of government, in its means of exercising power."

He continued his assault on party politics, calling for an end to the Party's leading role and for the abolition of the *nomenklatura* system.

"In the forty-year-long history of the People's Republic, we have a period euphemistically called the 'time of errors and distortions,' which in fact was a period of brutal violation of fundamental human rights, even more a period of violence and crime which victimized tens of thousands of innocent people, allegedly in the name of the law. We have now started talking about this, but that is not enough for creating an atmosphere conducive to reaching a national agreement. We must clearly expose the relation between this lawlessness and the Stalinist political system and its heritage, and expose the whole truth about this period of 'errors and distortions.' "

The speech deeply distressed Politburo member Stanislaw Ciosek. To challenge the sacred institutions of the *nomenklatura* and the Party's leading role was blasphemous.

"It's all over," he wailed to Father Orszulik during the coffee break that followed. "After this speech by Turowicz, the Party will call off the talks. It will be impossible for them to continue, after this diatribe."

Father Orszulik tried to reassure him. "I'm sure it's not that bad," he said. But Ciosek became more and more agitated. He was sure all his efforts at helping bridge the two sides were now washed away.

Ciosek went over to a small table where Mazowiecki was conferring with Kiszczak. Mazowiecki noticed Ciosek's agitation and tried to settle him down. Just then, a party functionary came over to Ciosek and said, "General Jaruzelski wants you to call him immediately."

Ciosek's face flashed crimson. He blustered off to the telephone. Right after he took off, Mazowiecki turned to Kiszczak and, in a quiet, unwavering voice, said: "General, you need to go and calm Ciosek."

The general blinked. "Yes, of course," he stammered, not used to taking orders, and rushed off in the direction of Ciosek.

Moments later, the two party leaders returned. Ciosek was considerably calmed down. Jaruzelski had been spared the disastrous assessment. The talks would go on.

WARSAW
February 11, 1989

The talks convened around the actual round table only during the first and last sessions of the negotiations. In between, the delegates broke up into smaller working groups to discuss the fine points of a national agreement, such as the economy, political reform, and the media and censorship.

Mazowiecki served as the opposition chair for the working group on union pluralism, a committee saddled with the tricky task of coming up with an agreement on the relegalization of Solidarity. The topic was a well-worn road for Mazowiecki. The same old obstacles that hindered his negotiations with the government during the strikes of 1980 and 1988 cropped up again. The official trade union representatives continued to insist that Solidarity and the official trade union could not exist side by side in the same factory. They also demanded that the relegalization of Solidarity proceed gradually, factory by factory.

Mazowiecki stuck by Solidarity's insistence on an immediate nationwide bill legalizing the independent union.

"The road to this meeting has been difficult and long," Mazowiecki declared to the committee. "For us, the main issue is the introduction of union pluralism, the relegalization of Solidarity." That was the bottom line, a *sine qua non* he refused to concede over the next two months of tedious negotiations.

WARSAW
April 5, 1989

At the end of the round table talks, both sides came away with what they were looking for. In a historic accord the government finally promised to relegalize Solidarity. In exchange, Solidarity promised to participate in upcoming parliamentary elections, a prospect the Solidarity side did not particularly relish. The elections would be the first free and open elections in Poland since the Communists consolidated their power after World War II. But the outcome would still be rigged. The Communist party and its puppets would be assured of 65 percent of the seats in the lower house. A newly created Senate made up of one hundred members would be freely voted on without any restrictions, and have veto power over the lower house.

Solidarity was hesitant to agree to elections that would give the Communists a certain degree of legitimacy. The opposition was also wary of getting saddled with Poland's problems and sharing the blame for Poland's devastating economic situation in a system still fettered by the bureaucratic chains of the *nomenklatura* and Communist control of industry. And the upcoming election was coming up so fast that Solidarity would barely have enough time to crank up a campaign that could compete with the Party's well-oiled political machine. There was the horrifying possibility that Solidarity would lose.

Nevertheless, Solidarity walked away from the round table with the prospect of emerging from an underground existence into a coalition government in the short space of three months. Walesa concluded the talks by pronouncing the round table accord the "beginning of the road to democracy and a free Poland."

WARSAW
April 17, 1989

Mazowiecki stood at the top of the courthouse steps, grinning broadly and raising a bouquet of red tulips over his head. He had just submitted the court application for the restoration of Solidarity's legal status agreed on in the round table talks.

"For me, today means the restoration of justice," he said in a jubilant voice to the smattering of supporters and reporters gathered there. "I was here in 1980 when the union was first legalized. Let's hope I won't have to come here a third time."

12

Hungary

The political opposition in Hungary was not nearly so well-defined as that in Poland. The tolerant atmosphere under the Hungarian Communist party succeeded in lulling the populace into political apathy.

Nevertheless, an opposition movement did begin to emerge. Pastor Gabor Ivanyi's involvement in the fledgling movement started in 1976, when he was asked by a circle of literature students at Budapest University to discuss the Bible with them. The students were for the most part atheists whose privileged position at the university generally meant their parents were prominent members of the Communist party. But like many Hungarian young people, they were questioning the Marxist values they were indoctrinated in. When they invited Ivanyi to discuss the Bible as a cultural piece of literature, he was all too happy to accept. Through this group, he got to know philosopher and dissident Janos Kis, one of the leaders of the emerging opposition. By the end of the 1970s, the group began organizing unofficial lectures much like Poland's Flying University. Up to three hundred people attended the seminars organized in private homes.

Kis lectured on Sovietology. Ivanyi's topic was "Why the Hungarian Free Churches Are Not Free." Despite constant surveillance, house searches, and interrogations, the group coalesced into a loose political movement called the Network of Free Initiatives.

Church involvement in the opposition was rare. Aside from a few dissenters such as Father Gyorgy Bulanyi, a Catholic priest who publicly denounced mandatory military service, most church leaders were either coopted by the Communist government or wary of the worldly business of politics.

Ivanyi was criticized within his own church. He defended his involvement by arguing the gospel compelled him to work for the well-being of the city where he lived, and that meant speaking out against the persecution he perceived around him. Besides his regular outreach at the Kispest church, he often preached among the gypsies, where he observed first-hand their horrendous social situation. He tried to explain to his colleagues that he was not interested so much in political ideas as in concrete cases of oppression. Despite his arguments, Ivanyi found himself a lone voice crying in the wilderness.

By the late 1980s, the voice of the opposition began growing louder. In May 1988, the mounting demands for change and Hungary's growing economic crisis caught up with the aging Communist party leader, Janos Kadar. He was ousted and replaced with reform-minded leaders. When Kadar stepped down, he was remembered not so much as a man whose hands set in motion Hungary's liberal economic and political policies, but as a man whose hands were stained with the blood of Imre Nagy.

During the 1956 uprising, Nagy vaulted to the position of premier and assumed the post of First Secretary of the Communist party. Nagy's push for a pluralistic democracy, mixed economy, and neutrality from Moscow brought Soviet tanks into Hungary to crush his far-reaching reforms. During the bloody fighting that followed, Kadar was secretly spirited to the Soviet Union, where he proclaimed a government loyal to Moscow and called on the Red Army to crush the rebellion. While Nagy was being arrested by Soviet security forces, tried in a kangaroo court and hanged, Kadar was riding to power atop the invading Soviet tanks.

The leadership that succeeded Kadar in 1988 needed to distance themselves from his treacherous legacy if they were to gain any amount of popular support. So in January 1989, the Communist party declared the 1956 revolution a justified popular uprising, not the counter-revolution steadfastly proclaimed by the Party line. Then in June, Hungary's Communist leadership sanctioned a funeral they hoped would bury the past once and for all.

BUDAPEST, HUNGARY
June 16, 1989

For Gabor Ivanyi, it was the day the whole country cried. The maverick Methodist pastor had been invited to participate in the funeral of a man who had been dead thirty-one years. Imre Nagy, the former Hungarian prime minister who was hanged and tossed into an unmarked grave in an obscure corner of a city cemetery, was finally getting a proper burial.

The political opposition helped organize the ceremony under the auspices of the Committee for Historical Justice. Ivanyi was one of eight religious leaders chosen to officiate at the solemn ceremony, all of whom had either been imprisoned or persecuted because of their criticism of church corruption. When a group of official church leaders known for their cooperation with the government asked to participate, the Committee for Historical Justice turned them down.

Ironically, Nagy's funeral was not only a political resurrection for the disgraced leader, it also served as the rebirth of the opposition, a sign of its newfound power. Not only had the opposition successfully pressured the government into allowing the reburial, it also convinced the Party to initiate a review of his case. Just a year earlier, a demonstration held to commemorate Nagy's execution was forcefully broken up by police.

As many as 200,000 people gathered for the solemn ceremony in Budapest's Heroes Square. Banners of black and white, the traditional colors for mourning, draped the classical columns of the art museum at the head of the huge square. Arranged on a modernistic wooden and metal structure were coffins bearing the names of Nagy and the four other officials sentenced to death as traitors and counter-revolutionaries after the 1956 uprising. A sixth stood as a reminder of the nearly three hundred victims of the purge that followed. Ceremonial torches burned between each one. In another bit of grim irony, the stark set was designed by architect Laszlo Rajk, son of the former Interior and Foreign Minister who had been executed in 1949 after one of the most infamous Stalinist show trials.

Four top party officials, including Prime Minister Miklos Nemeth and Minister of State Imre Pozsgay, showed up to pay their respects, even acting as honorary pallbearers. They skulked off before the speeches started—speeches that shocked Gabor Ivanyi with their forthright denunciation of the Communist party.

The pastor noticed how people began to fidget nervously when Viktor Orban, the young spokesman for the opposition group called the Federation of Young Democrats, called for an end to Communist dictatorship and for the withdrawal of Soviet troops, the very demands that had brought the Soviet tanks in three decades earlier.

"We do not understand that the very same party and government leaders who told us to learn from books falsifying the history of the revolution now vie with each other to touch these coffins as if they were lucky charms," he said. "We do not think there is any reason for us to be grateful for being allowed to bury our martyred dead. We do not owe thanks to anyone for the fact that our political organizations can work today. . . . If we can trust our souls and strength, we can put an end to the Communist dictatorship; if we are determined enough we can force the Party to submit itself to free elections; and if we do not lose sight of the ideals of 1956, then we will be able to elect a government that will start immediate negotiations for the swift withdrawal of Russian troops."

After the ceremony in Heroes Square, Ivanyi joined the funeral procession that plodded toward the huge cemetery where Nagy and his revolutionary compatriots of 1956 were first buried in the unmarked graves of Plot 301. The plot had been freshly cleared of a tangle of weeds and garbage. Six gaping holes lay open for the reburial. As two actors intoned the names of the dead in alphabetical order, a torchbearer stepped forward, lifting high the flame, and said: "He lives in us; he has not gone." Then any relative who had requested a religious ceremony stood silently as Ivanyi or one of the other religious representatives stepped forward for a quiet prayer. After all

250 names had been read, the religious leaders marched toward the tomb reserved for the coffin of the unknown martyrs and said a prayer together.

As Ivanyi surveyed the columns of grave posts carved into traditional Hungarian symbols, he realized this was the first chance for most of the victims' relatives to mourn in public. Before now, they didn't even know where their family members were buried. He knew he was experiencing a historic moment. Forty-year-old wounds were being healed. The whole nation was grieving for its past.

But much more than that, it was a human moment, a day of personal grief. Ivanyi was deeply moved by the pain and sorrow of the family members he prayed with that day. In that way, it was really no different than any other funeral.

BUDAPEST, HUNGARY
July 6, 1989

On the day the Hungarian Supreme Court announced the full legal rehabilitation of Imre Nagy, a note was passed through the chambers where the action was being discussed. Janos Kadar was dead. History had come full circle. While Imre Nagy was being resurrected as a hero, the man ultimately responsible for his death had passed away into ignominy, together with his legacy of Communist party rule.

13

East Germany

The winds of Gorbachev's glasnost *blowing across Poland and Hungary died out when they reached the borders of East Germany. The political atmosphere remained stagnant and motionless, with not even the hint of a breeze of political change. Disenchanted East Germans continued to leave the country in droves. Border guards once under orders from Honecker himself to shoot escapees stood by as citizens clogged the available escape routes leading West. Not only did they flood Hungary's open border, they also began stampeding into the West German embassies in Prague, Warsaw, and East Berlin seeking political asylum.*

After more than five thousand people crammed into the embassy grounds in Prague, the East German and Czechoslovakian governments finally relented and allowed them to leave for the West. When the momentous decision was announced, one harried West German diplomat at the Prague embassy exclaimed, "The Berlin Wall is history, and they don't realize it yet in Bonn."

Those leaving Prague were routed in sealed trains through their homeland, a route the East German government insisted on so the refugees could be properly marked with stamps expelling them as "anti-social elements." Honecker's ploy blew up in his face. When the trains pulled into Dresden, a riot broke out as thousands of East Germans trying to get on board were beaten back by police. News of the riot only served to convince his subjects of how desperate their situation was becoming.

With more and more people leaving, the peace prayer service in Leipzig began to take on a more political character. The would-be emigrés were shoved into the background, while those wanting change were taking their place at the forefront. The Nikolai church was fast becoming the focus for political reform.

As the dissident basis groups meeting behind the church's protective walls began to emerge, they took refuge under an umbrella group called Neues Forum *(New Forum), a citizen's initiative formed to act on behalf of the united opposition. New Forum immediately issued a statement calling for democratic dialogue with the government about the need for reform, an end to censorship, and the immediate release of all demonstrators still in detention. The group's application to field candidates for the upcoming election in May was summarily rejected by the Interior Ministry. The government accused the group of having a "subversive platform" and ordered its members to cease all activities immediately. Buoyed by the growing demonstrations and swelling exodus, though, the group vowed to defy the ban and continue its campaign for reform.*

One West German official keeping an eye on the developments in Leipzig told the Washington Post*: "There is obviously a growing number of people who are willing to expose themselves to risk to try to change things. This drama of the exodus has stimulated concern, stimulated the feeling that the time is ripe for change."*

LEIPZIG
September 27, 1989

"You're a naive and starry-eyed counter-revolutionary!"

The words came flying at Brigitta from Bettina, a young co-worker at the music publishing house. Brigitta had been handing out a petition supporting New Forum's call for democratic change when the two got into a heated political discussion. Everyone else in the room remained silent and stayed out of it.

When Bettina stamped out of the room, the other co-workers began expressing their sympathy with the demonstrations. What cowards! Brigitta thought. They had to wait for Bettina to leave before they dared to speak up. Bettina had let it slip one day that her husband was an unofficial member of the Stasi. The blunder had obviously been brought to everyone's attention.

Brigitta really didn't care whether she told her husband about her involvement in New Forum. She wasn't afraid of Bettina! What could she do to her? Get her fired? She was already in hot water at work. Her boss had actually told her, "If you stand on the streets during the demonstrations, you'll stand on the streets without a job."

She could do without the job, she thought. There were better ones out there. Bettina was just trying to make life difficult for her, probably because she felt so insecure herself. For some reason, Brigitta had this uncontrollable urge to tell her all about the peace prayers at church. She chuckled to herself. Then Bettina would at least have something important to talk about at home. Who knows? Maybe even she would wake up.

It bothered Brigitta that everyone always talked about the fact that someone needed to do something to bring about change. But whenever she asked, "Who is this someone?" they would just shrug their shoulders.

"Gorbachev should finally do something," one colleague volunteered. Once again, she thought, they were delegating the problem to someone else. For years, any suggestions coming out of the Soviet Union were considered patronizing. Now, all of a sudden, a Russian was supposed to help.

Brigitta continued handing out the New Forum petitions for her co-workers to read. She saw anxiety in the eyes of everyone she approached. They seemed afraid she would ask them to sign it.

"What's the use?" they all said after reading it. "You know we can't change anything."

Brigitta wanted to respond, "That's right. *You* can't do anything." But she held her tongue.

LEIPZIG, EAST GERMANY
October 2, 1989

Father Bernhard dredged two large fistfuls of mustard seeds out of the deep pockets of his white cassock and spread them on a table set up in the Reformed Church's entrance. The Monday peace prayer service at the Nikolai church was getting so crowded that he had been asked to lead a second prayer service there. The tiny seeds were for the sermon he had prepared. Everyone filing into the church was asked to take one.

The young priest had been expecting maybe a handful of people to show up. But by the time the service started, the table was swept clean of the minuscule mustard seeds. There must have been two thousand people in the church, spilling over from the cramped pews into the aisles. And to Father Bernhard's surprise, many of them were elderly, not the usual young crowd who came on Monday afternoons. As he looked into some of the wrinkled faces from the front of the church, he was so moved he had to turn around to hold back the tears that were welling up inside him and threatening to spill over. He cleared his throat, rescuing his voice from the emotion that had choked it of sound, and turned back around to start the prayer service.

The church was hushed. "Sisters and brothers," Father Bernhard began, "we must do this prayer service together. To the members of the Stasi here I want to say: here in this place you are our sisters and brothers. What you do outside the church is your problem. But here you are our sisters and brothers.

"Yesterday we celebrated our Harvest Festival. As we think about this celebration, we realize we are harvesting much more than we have sown. Much of what was planted before our time is now blooming, from both good seed and bad. Jesus said, 'You shall know them by their fruits.' We now have before us the fruit of our deeds. Isn't it time to ask ourselves whether some of the things we don't like about our situation came from our *own* bad seed. Isn't it time to ask ourselves whether some of the fruit we are harvesting now has been sown by us Christians and the church as well?

"We're always complaining about the economic situation. But how often have we declared in the church that our everyday work should be done out of service and love for each other, and that is our mandate from God. We complain about the lack of open criticism. But has the church always been ready to handle and to accept criticism? How has the church dealt with those who have different opinions? We deplore aggression. Yet hasn't the church been quick to label its enemies? We smiled secretly at the mass exodus of people escaping our society. But didn't that smile freeze on our faces when some of our own people left? Don't be mistaken. I love the church. Otherwise I wouldn't stay with her in service to the Lord and to mankind. But it's precisely that love that makes me ask these questions.

"The seed has come up and borne its fruit. Let us follow the gospel and sort out the good seed. And even if it's as tiny as the mustard seed you hold in your hand, it can still bear new fruit, good fruit. We have hope, like this grain of a mustard seed. But we must give it away. We must take it into the world and plant it in good soil. Then we will bear good fruit, even if it takes generations to come. . . . Amen."

Father Bernhard gazed out into the congregation and opened his hands in a gesture of release. "Now I ask you to give your neighbor this grain of hope."

He watched with satisfaction as a chain reaction erupted in the pews, with one person turning to the next and placing in his outstretched hand a splinter-sized seed. The church broke out into a peaceful sort of pandemonium. Amid the din, a young man squeezed out of his pew and headed toward the open microphone. Father Bernhard blanched. He had been warned there might be some kind of disturbance, some kind of provocation. He wasn't prepared to handle such a situation. Should he head him off before he reached the microphone?

The young man came straight for him and stretched out his open hand. In his palm lay the barely visible speck of a mustard seed. "I didn't want you to go without," he said.

LEIPZIG
October 2, 1989

When Brigitta's mother arrived in Leipzig from their hometown in the Thuringia district about forty miles away, they both knew why she was there. Her mother didn't say it on the phone when she announced she was dropping in to go shopping. And Brigitta tiptoed around the topic, too, while on their shopping tour through downtown Leipzig. But Brigitta knew it, and her mother knew it. Frau Treetz had come to keep her daughter from participating in the demonstration that day. She knew or sensed somehow that Brigitta was taking part in them.

The subject didn't come up until they neared the vicinity of the Nikolai church. Brigitta had arranged things so they would wind up in the center of the city around 5:00 P.M. She saw the anxious look in her mother's eyes. When they approached the church, there was already a crowd standing outside. There was no room for anyone else inside.

Frau Treetz watched the line of security forces stretched out around the church with wariness.

"Brigitta, I don't like the idea of your getting involved in these demonstrations," she blurted out.

Brigitta almost laughed. It was finally out in the open. "But mother, something is finally starting to happen. People are finally beginning to wake up out of their apathy. I have to be a part of it. Do you think we all ought to remain silent?"

"It's not that, dear," she said. "You know I don't disapprove of your political involvement. God knows, this country needs to change. I'm just worried about you, about your safety. These demonstrations could be so dangerous. And after your kidney transplant, how can you even think about endangering your health again?"

"But I'm perfectly all right now, mother," Brigitta said, trying to reassure her. "Yes, I lost my health at one time. But it's been given back to me."

"And do you want to lose it again?" her mother retorted. "If the demonstrations get violent, who's to say you won't lose that expensive kidney? After all you've been through! Have you forgotten all those years of dialysis, those painful trips every three months to East Berlin? It would be agony to have to go through that again."

Her mother looked around at the crowds and police force. "I don't like the looks of this. Let's go, Brigitta," she said, her face almost ashen.

She tried to pull her away, but Brigitta resisted.

"We really can't go now, Mother." Brigitta protested. "Don't you see? If there are lots of people, the police can do nothing. It's in our numbers that we provide protection for each other."

Brigitta realized she was trying to convince herself with her arguments as much as her mother.

In the end, her mother prevailed, and Brigitta promised to take her home. Back at Brigitta's apartment, they spent the entire evening talking about courage, fear, and hope. Brigitta had never felt so close to her mother. Frau Treetz began to understand why Brigitta felt compelled to take part in the demonstrations. Yet when she left town the next morning, she feared for her daughter's safety more than ever.

EAST BERLIN
October 5, 1989

For eighteen-year-old Ilonka Schmidt, her poem was an act of protest. It summed up all the feelings of disillusionment with the government she had grown up with, the only government she had ever known. She was born after the Wall went up and raised in the isolation of its shadow. The poem was entitled "Forty Years," and it was a personal look at the forty years of history she so desperately wanted to help change.

Ilonka was reluctant to let anyone read the poem. She had shown it to some of the leaders at the Gethsemane church earlier, hesitantly handing it over like a shy teenager proffering flowers on a first date. But they dissuaded her from reading it aloud at one of the church's daily services. It was too direct, too open. Yet what good was a protest that remained forever silent? What good was her dissent if it was stuffed away out of sight in her scrapbook?

She was attending the 8:00 P.M. service at the red-brick church later that evening when she first heard about the hunger strike. The sanctuary of the Gethsemane church was bathed in a warm, orange glow, bright with the almost surreal light of hundreds of candles. Just a few steps away from the low, wooden altar, a wall was covered with newspaper clippings on East Germany from various West European newspapers. Hanging on another wall was a large New

Forum poster with red and blue letters, surrounded by notices giving the names and addresses of opposition members. On the left side of the nave, just across from the pew she had sidled into, she noticed ten people sitting cross-legged on sleeping bags spread out on the floor like a squatter's camp. The candles scattered around them seemed to cast a protective wall of light around them. They were singing along with the rest of the congregation.

Ilonka wondered who those people were, and why they were camping out in the church. Her curiosity was satisfied when the pastor leading the service that night announced the church was harboring hunger strikers who were now in the fourth day of their fast. They were demanding the release of pro-democracy protesters arrested at earlier demonstrations.

For Ilonka, the announcement brought her an epiphany, the words trumpeted straight from heaven. This was it—the form of protest she had been searching for! She had been wanting to do something more than just take to the streets, although she knew that was important, of course. She wanted to demonstrate more openly, somehow, the hunger for justice she had tried to express in her poem. Fasting was the perfect act of protest, a visible incarnation of that hunger. She would make her body her poem, the act of fasting a work of physical poetry. She decided to start that very night.

Immediately after the service, Ilonka headed home to get a sleeping bag. She took the terminally slow elevator up to the twelfth floor apartment where she lived with her parents. On the way up, she thought about how she would tell her parents she had decided to join the hunger strike.

Ilonka's faith hadn't won her any points with her family. She had been going to church on her own since she was twelve, much to her mother's consternation. Her grandmother was a member of the Party, and she had inculcated Ilonka's mother with an aversion to Christianity. Though Ilonka's father was raised a Christian, he was not a churchgoer. When Ilonka felt compelled by her faith to drop out of the Free German Youth, the German Communist youth organization, she did it despite her parents' disapproval. She was throwing away her future, they argued, and almost certainly giving up any chance to go on to the university.

Her mother eyed Ilonka suspiciously as she pulled down her

sleeping bag from the jumble of things in her closet.

"What are you going to do with that sleeping bag?" she asked curiously.

"There's a hunger strike going on at the Gethsemane Church," Ilonka said, brushing her stringy blond hair out of her eyes. She was working up the courage to announce her decision.

"So?" Her mother's hard-edged voice demanded more.

"So, I've decided to join it."

"When did you decide to do that?" her mother asked.

"Tonight. I just found out about it at the church service."

"You mean you're going to deliberately starve yourself? Just how long do you plan to go without eating?"

"I'm not sure yet. I guess until the government releases the demonstrators who've been arrested. That's what we're fasting for." Ilonka realized she hadn't really given the question much thought.

"You know going without food isn't good for you. Your body needs daily nutrients. You'll ruin your health." Her mother was a doctor.

"It's something I feel I have to do."

"Well, I know I can't stop you. You're eighteen. You can do what you want. I just get so worried with the situation the way it is now. These are dangerous times."

"I'll be inside the church," Ilonka said, reassuring her. "That's the safest place to be. It's the only place where there aren't any police."

"You know what I mean. The demonstrations—people are getting arrested."

"I promise I'll be careful." With that, Ilonka was out the door.

As she walked through the cramped corridor to the elevator, she glanced around to see if anyone was watching her. She knew she looked suspicious walking out of her apartment carrying a sleeping bag late at night. Of the twelve families on her floor, six were suspected of having connections with the Stasi.

LEIPZIG
October 7, 1989

Gabriele Schmidt headed straight for the farmer's market with a few friends from the factory where she worked. She bought some cut flowers, did a little window shopping, wandering through the alley-like streets of the old city, and then dropped by the Nikolai church to lay the flowers at a shrine-like display set up to show support for the political detainees. It was around 1:00 in the afternoon. There were a number of people standing outside the church, engrossed in intense conversation.

She spotted a couple of friends, and walked over to exchange pleasantries. There were a few policemen patrolling the area, but she didn't think that was unusual, until the police started to line up around the square.

Then, without warning, one of them shouted "Action!" and riot police were everywhere, their night sticks flying, beating anyone in sight. Troop transport trucks started rolling in. They pounced on one forty-year-old man, clubbing his face. Some of his teeth were knocked out, so that all you could see was a black hole in the middle of his blood-encrusted face. He was dragged to a truck and tossed in like a dead animal. One of the riot police grabbed Gabriele's hair and began dragging her across the square to one of the waiting trucks.

A woman dressed in civilian clothes was standing in the gaping entrance at the truck's transom. She reached down and clutched Gabriele by her clothes to haul her onto the truck. Others were tossed in. The matron grabbed at them to herd them onto the hard benches set up at the back of the truck. Gabriele could hear shouts of "swine" and "sow" as people were pushed into the truck.

They lurched off with eight detainees and three guards aboard. The truck drove into a courtyard completely enclosed by tall buildings and jolted to a stop. Where were they? A guard grasped her by the clothes and pulled her off the truck. She felt the sharp pain of the night stick once more against her upper left arm.

"Male or female?" a guard barked out, and the detainees were lined up accordingly and marched up some steps into a building.

Orders were flung at them from all sides.

"Hands at your sides!" "Stand up straight!" "No leaning against the wall or you'll be punished!"

They were taken one at a time into a dimly lit hallway where they had to show their identification papers. Then they were marched off to a small room at the end of the hall. Everywhere Gabriele looked, there were guards.

After waiting there for hours, she heard her name called. She followed an official dressed in civilian clothes upstairs. He pulled out a key and unlocked one of the rooms. They made her sign a confession. Then it was downstairs to a dank cellar lined with bars. Several male detainees were already waiting there. The guards forced her to empty her purse, then opened the door and threw her inside like an animal in a slaughterhouse.

It seemed only seconds later that the cell door creaked open and she was dragged out again. She followed a uniformed woman down a dingy corridor. *Where are they taking me now?* Gabriele wondered. Her thoughts were a muddle of anxiety and uncertainty. They emerged into the courtyard, then into another building, up some more stairs. She didn't even know what floor she was on anymore. She was led into another room where a few more detainees were being watched by three guards. Hours went by.

One of the detainees dared to ask whether they would get anything to eat or drink. As punishment, he was forced to stand leaning against the wall, feet spread apart.

Gabriele worked up the courage to make a request. "I'm supposed to attend an engagement party for someone in my family," she told one of the guards. "I'm sure they are worried about me. Could someone contact them and let them know where I am?"

"It's being taken care of," came the gruff reply.

Somehow, she found that hard to believe.

Another roll call—9:30 P.M. They were marched downstairs and into the open courtyard again where the transport trucks were waiting like cattle cars. Riot police swarmed around them. They seemed inhuman, almost otherworldly, with their visor-covered faces, night sticks, and plastic shields. A few carried machine guns. The detainees were packed shoulder to shoulder, like sides of beef. The guards kicked the last few prisoners on board so they could close the truck's gate. Images of the Gestapo flashed into Gabriele's mind. They had taught her about the Nazis in grammar school. Now they were showing her.

As the second journey began, so did the rain. She felt the heavy drops. The heavens are weeping with us in compassion, she thought.

The truck pulled into the grounds of the city's agricultural exposition. The gate was removed, and they started to climb out. Gabriele saw that more police were there waiting for them, glowering like bulls getting ready to stampede. They yanked the men out of the truck and snatched away their jackets.

"Hands against the wall!" they growled.

When the men complied, they kicked their feet out from under them, sending them sprawling onto the ground.

"You swine!" the police howled. "Keep your lousy hands against the wall!"

The men were frisked and rounded up into cold, smelly horse stalls.

Then it was the women's turn. Gabriele had to hand over her jacket and stand against the wall, arms and legs spread apart. A policewoman began body searches.

"I'm having my period," Gabriele told her when she approached.

"What of it, you sow?" a policeman standing nearby shouted.

Another policeman corralled her into a horse stall filled with other women. His eyes had the malicious look of a rabid dog. He seemed to take perverse pleasure in packing as many people as he could into the stalls.

A very elderly woman incarcerated there was sobbing and trembling uncontrollably with a look of terror on her face like a cornered mouse. They called to one of the guards to at least take pity on the elderly and free her. He snickered and moved on, as if he didn't hear them. He could have been her son, Gabriele thought.

At 1:00 A.M. they were finally given something to eat: a hot dog, stale dinner roll, and swallow of lukewarm tea. Gabriele's body was numb with exhaustion. She felt like her legs would buckle any moment from the long hours of standing motionless. It was impossible to sleep.

At 6:30 in the morning, another transport truck drove up and its cargo of older men unloaded. As they filed by, Gabriele saw some of them had blood streaming down their faces. The police must have been promised a bonus for each battered head, she thought. At noon, a final roll call. Gabriele was given back the belongings that they'd confiscated and bundled off yet again in one of the trucks parked in the courtyard. It stopped periodically and let the detainees out three at a time. They were each released after being fined one hundred dollars and presented with a bill of thirty-seven cents for the hot dog and dinner roll.

An account of the demonstration appeared in the *Leipziger Volkszeitung*:

> Throughout Saturday, October 7, the normal life of the city and inner city traffic were temporarily disrupted by groups of primarily adolescent rowdies. The groups appeared organized and influenced by the Western mass media. The German people's police force prevented further disruptions through level-headed actions and allowed the day to pass in an orderly fashion. It was noticed that most of the troublemakers who had to be berated by the police were not from Leipzig or the Leipzig region. Several of the troublemakers and leaders of the pack were taken in for questioning. From phone calls to city officials and the editors of the *Leipziger Volkszeitung*, it is obvious that the citizens were disturbed by the rowdiness and disruption of their lives and demanded that the instigators be apprehended.

Berlin

October 8, 1989

The first day of the fast had been the hardest. Thoughts of food gnawed at Ilonka. She tried not to think about it. But the more she tried to suppress the thoughts, the more she was plagued by mouthwatering visions that set off the rumblings of her stomach. She depended on the company and camaraderie of her fellow hunger strikers for strength. Most of them were women in their thirties. Ilonka stood out somewhat because of her youth. Her rail-like figure and the traces of acne still lingering on her boyish-looking face made her look even younger than her eighteen years. But she felt a real kinship, a real solidarity with them, despite the age difference. She knew she couldn't have sustained her fast without their support. Singing and praying with them gave her a renewed feeling of spiritual power and strength, even though physically she felt very weak.

Each day, people from the neighborhood would drop by with

candles, coffee, and juice. Their visits helped nourish her. They were always so friendly. It was important for her to see their hunger strike was being supported by the people around them. That was one of the paradoxical purposes of their protest, she realized, for the people to draw power from her powerlessness, strength from her weakness.

On the third day of her fast, the hunger pangs began to disappear. Ilonka felt a clearness of mind she had never experienced before. She fed on the knowledge that her action was a visible sign of nonviolence to the people of East Germany, who were following the hunger strike through West German TV. And she felt the satisfaction of living out her commitment to change. As the fast went on, more and more people joined them, basking in the warmth of the candles and each other's company by day, joining the growing demonstrations by night.

The wave of demonstrations in East Berlin started as monthly protests called to denounce the country's May 7 local elections. The people were furious about the obvious falsification of the results by the Communist party. The returns failed to register the many blank ballots cast in an organized abstention campaign to lodge a protest against the Party. The church council of the Lutheran church wrote a letter to Prime Minister Willi Stoph to denounce the election fraud.

Every seventh day of the month, young Berliners converged on Alexanderplatz, the city's main square, to protest in ever more creative ways. There was a different theme each month. On June 7, they stood around the landmark television tower that rises out of the concrete plain and did nothing but laugh, holding their bellies in one long hoot of derision. On the seventh of July, everyone was urged to bring a whistle to Alexanderplatz. When the date arrived, there were so many protesters you couldn't find a whistle left on the store shelves. Altogether, they blasted their whistles as a symbolic representation of a German expression, "*Ich pfeiffe auf Dich*," literally, "I'm whistling at you," but figuratively meaning, "Get lost!"

The visit of Soviet leader Mikhail Gorbachev to East Berlin on October 7 to mark the fortieth anniversary of East Germany's Communist government emboldened the demonstrators even more.

"First, I should tell our Western partners that matters relating to the German Democratic Republic are decided not in Moscow, but in

Berlin," Gorbachev told an elite group gathered at the Palace of the Republic. "The GDR of course has its problems, demanding solutions. They arise from the internal demands of a society moving toward new horizons and the gradual process of modernization and renewal in which the Socialist world now finds itself."

These words were taken almost as an endorsement of the *perestroika* the East Germans were seeking in their own country. As Gorbachev stood side by side with Honecker, smiling and waving to a torchlight procession celebrating the anniversary, he was hailed with shouts of "Gorby, Gorby!"

Those officially organized celebrations soon turned into spontaneous demonstrations for democratic reform. Spurred on by Gorbachev's visit, demonstrators in East Berlin followed Leipzig's lead and took to the streets with chants of "Gorby, Gorby!" and "No violence." They, too, were met with riot police swinging truncheons and blasting them with water cannons.

For Ilonka, it was particularly dangerous to join the Berlin demonstrations. She knew that the Stasi could identify all of the hunger strikers by face. Their pictures were broadcast on the West German evening news. And there were always cameras snapping away inside the Gethsemane church. It was impossible to distinguish which ones belonged to the press and which ones to the Stasi. One of her fellow hunger strikers was arrested when she made a brief trip to fetch something from home. She arrived to find her apartment ransacked, and the Stasi waiting there for her. She had apparently been targeted because of her role in the hunger strike.

On the night of October 8, Ilonka ventured onto the street after the evening service. She went out arm in arm with her fellow protesters, linking up in a human chain to stand firm against the security forces. There were probably ten thousand people demonstrating that night.

Ilonka held tightly to the friends linked up next to her in the crush of people. It was important to keep tabs on them, so if they were arrested, someone could inform their families. People were pressing from behind, but there was nowhere to go. A massive line of security police in front of the demonstrators had blocked off the streets around the church and was pushing the crowd back. It was like being caught in a massive vice.

When the riot police ordered the demonstrators to leave a street just outside the church, they answered with cries of "We're staying here!" and "No violence!"

Suddenly, security police rushed the demonstrators, swinging their clubs and beating them back with their shields. The human chain broke apart. The demonstrators scattered. People were running wildly. Ilonka tried to stay with her friends, but they got separated in the melee. She was so preoccupied in trying to find them that she didn't notice the security officer behind her. He tried to grab her. But she shook off his grasp and slipped away, getting swallowed up by the chaotic crowd.

When word reached Ilonka's family that dozens of people had been arrested outside the Gethsemane church, her father made a frantic trip to the church to determine whether Ilonka was among them. He wanted to tell her how worried they were about her, and perhaps talk her into giving up her fast and coming home with him.

When he arrived at the church, he could hardly move for the people that had been herded inside, seeking shelter from the riot police. He tried searching for his daughter, but it was impossible in the mass of people. He spotted several of her friends and made his way to them through the press of people. But they didn't have any answers. They had lost track of Ilonka in the melee. He finally gave up the search and left, disappointed and anxious.

When he walked in the door of their apartment, the phone rang. It was Ilonka. She was calling to let them know she was safe and no, they couldn't talk her out of abandoning the hunger strike.

West Berlin
October 8, 1989

Checkpoint Charlie was blocked off on the East Berlin side by heavy concrete and metal barriers erected by the East German border guards overnight.

"What do you mean, you won't let us through the border?" Brigitta asked one of the border guards standing in front of the barrier. She was in West Berlin to see Barbara and George McDonald, some American friends she met during a recent visit to Seattle. Because of her kidney problems, she was on a select list permitted to travel freely outside the country. The East German government afforded the special status to the ill and the elderly; the country could afford to lose them if they decided to defect.

Brigitta was trying to take the McDonalds from West to East Berlin for the Gorbachev visit when they were stopped at the checkpoint. The border had been closed all day, and the guards were turning away visitors who were usually let through on one-day tourist visas.

"We can allow you through as a citizen of the GDR," the border guard told Brigitta in a bureaucratic tone. He was dripping with sweat. "But your friends are undesirables. We can't allow them into the country."

"Undesirables?" Brigitta was outraged. How could they get away with this spiteful treatment? What were they so afraid of? She argued, but it was no use. They tried three other crossing points, but got the same story.

So her American friends and she stood at the Brandenburg Gate and gazed into the eastern sector of the city. Next to the gate stood the familiar sign, "You are leaving the American sector."

East Germany
October 9, 1989

The rumbling of tanks through Tiananmen Square still echoed through the streets of Leipzig. The image of the bloody crackdown was still fresh. The massacre had occurred just five months before. And it was common knowledge that Egon Krenz, then Politburo member in charge of internal security, had issued a telegram commending China's Communist regime for the brutal repression of the unrest. Rumors were running rampant that the Communist Party Central Committee had come up with a ten-point program at a recent party meeting aimed at crushing the so-called "counter-revolution," and that D-day for the blitzkrieg would be October 9. The question on everyone's mind in Leipzig now: Was the government considering a "Chinese solution" to stop the growing demonstrations? Had Honecker given the order to shoot?

Tension permeated the city like a thick fog. Leipzig was now surrounded by army troops. In addition, several thousand riot police stood on alert in the inner city. The *Kampfgruppen*, East Germany's equivalent to the national guard, had been called out. Water cannons lay in wait behind the Stasi headquarters. Some of the security forces had been issued weapons and live ammunition. And in a chilling article in the local newspaper, the *Leipziger Volkszeitung*, one of the national guard commanders warned they were prepared to defend socialism "if need be, with weapons in hand."

The city's hospital was put on alert: rooms had been cleared, extra staff called in, and additional blood supplies trucked in. Pastor Christian Führer received threatening phone calls throughout the day warning him to call off that afternoon's peace prayer. The anonymous voices on the other end of the line threatened that the forces would open fire if the demonstrations were allowed to continue.

But the church refused to back down. In fact, four additional churches would be opened up for peace prayers to get out the message of nonviolence to as many people as possible, and to provide a place for protesters to flee if things got bloody.

Helga Wagner, a lecturer at the Karl Marx University and Communist party member, got a call very early that morning informing her that the Party was mobilizing its forces against the counterrevolutionaries, and she should get in touch with her party leadership. She drove to the university at 9:00 A.M. for her faculty party meeting, where the order was issued: five comrades were needed to go to the Nikolai church. She immediately volunteered, more out of curiosity about the growing demonstrations than a sense of duty to the Party. Her first set of instructions came from the local party secretary. She was to keep a low profile in the church and quickly separate herself from the demonstration after the prayer service. The second set of instructions came at a meeting of other party members convened at city hall at 1:00 P.M. They were to go to the Nikolai church in small groups. Anyone wearing the Party symbol should remove it so as not to be conspicuous.

One student piped up that he thought the whole thing was a trick. He was immediately silenced.

A shout came from someone near the door: "How long are we going to sit around and talk? The church is already filling up!"

By the time Helga reached the church at 2:00 P.M., it was already standing room only. The sanctuary's two thousand available spaces were all occupied, most of them by party functionaries. When Pastor Führer saw the situation, he opened up the seldom used church balcony, allowing another thousand people in. By 3:30, the doors of the church were shut. There was no more room available.

Helga sat reading the thicket of announcements handed out while waiting for the service to begin. She was surprised to see a report from one of her former students denouncing the recent arrests, asking why the demonstrators were being met with so much hate and antagonism. That's odd, Helga thought. Those were her feelings exactly, even though she was on the other side.

LEIPZIG, EAST GERMANY
October 9

Dr. Peter Zimmermann, a theology professor at the Karl Marx University, had been on edge all day. He had been under pressure ever since sending back the special medal he had won in conjunction with the country's fortieth anniversary. After reading the threat by the *Kampfgruppen* commander in the newspaper, he decided he couldn't keep the award in good faith, and shipped it back along with a letter of explanation to Party leader Erich Honecker. In the United States, it would be akin to sending back the Congressional Medal of Honor out of disagreement with the President's policies. The controversial action hit the newspapers and thrust him onto the city's center stage.

Zimmermann's hopes for a renovation of East Germany's Socialist system were eroding. He reflected on the demonstration a month before, when a small group of students at the edge of the crowd shouting "We want out," countered with their own slogan, "We're staying here." It was a signal. A group of people was finally urging everyone to stay in the country to work for change, so there would no longer be a need to flee. But to see those shouting that slogan beaten and jailed was a terrifying revelation. It meant the authorities could get along far better with those who simply wanted to give up and get out than with those who wanted to work for change.

His thoughts were interrupted by the jangling of the telephone. It was Dr. Roland Wötzel, the regional party secretary in charge of academics.

"Dr. Zimmermann, could you meet me in the city today?" he asked with a sense of urgency.

"What for?" Zimmermann asked suspiciously.

"I've been very distressed at the events in the city over the last several days. As you know, the situation is explosive. Something's got to be done to avert a bloodbath. I read with interest the item in the newspaper about your bold action. And of course, I remembered our discussions in the past. I'm trying to get together a group to take some kind of action, and I immediately thought of you."

Zimmermann was a member of the Christian Peace Conference, one of the country's Communist-sanctioned "official" peace groups. He was also a regular at the peace prayers at the Nikolai church, and served as something of a go-between for the church peace groups and Communist party functionaries. Wötzel and his fellow party members had insisted that getting rid of the peace prayers would cause the opposition to lose interest. Zimmermann had argued that the movement around Nikolai church was only the symptom of a greater disease, and cutting out the peace prayers wouldn't bring about a cure. They didn't seem to listen then. Perhaps his words were starting to sink in now.

"What do you plan to do?" Zimmermann asked.

"I'm not sure. I just know that someone has to take the first steps to keep violence from breaking out. I'll call you back to let you know the time and place."

After they hung up, Wötzel dashed out of his office to meet with Bernd-Lutz Lange, a prominent political satirist. He was trying to solicit his support as well for some kind of initiative. On the way out of his office at the regional party headquarters, Wötzel saw two other party secretaries, Kurt Meyer and Jochen Pommert, in the hallway.

Meyer flagged him down. Wötzel could see whatever he wanted couldn't wait.

"I got a call from Kurt Masur today," Meyer told him, referring to the world-renowned conductor of the city's Gewandhaus orchestra. "He wants to get a group of people together who are willing to try to come up with a non-violent solution to this current madness.

He wants to get together this afternoon to talk about what kind of action we can take."

Wötzel couldn't believe the coincidence. "I've been in touch with Dr. Zimmermann from the university and Bernd-Lutz Lange for the very same reason," Wötzel said.

"Wonderful! That's just what we need, a group of well-respected, high-profile people," Meyer said. "I'll call Masur back and recommend we all get together to talk."

Pommert, the other Party official, was a little wary about the plan. "You know what this means for the three of us," he cautioned. "It means expulsion from the Party. The Party leadership views the masses on the streets as counter-revolutionaries. We could be seen as traitors going to the other side."

"There's no time to worry about that," Wötzel said. "We've got to act now, without delay, or people could soon be dying in the streets."

The group of six assembled at the house of the conductor, Kurt Masur, at 3:00 that afternoon. Wötzel and Lange arrived together. They were so overwhelmed by the tension of the moment they barely noticed the elegant furnishings of the famed conductor's home. Zimmermann and Pommert were already there.

"Welcome, gentlemen," Masur graciously ushered them in. "I think we all agree that if we don't come up with some kind of way to prevent violence today, we will be looking at civil war."

"I myself witnessed the brutal action of the police last Saturday," he went on. "We are reaching the boiling point. This morning, I was practicing with the orchestra for this evening's performance. We were playing a piece by Strauss, a rather whimsical composition. And it hit me that while we're performing it this evening, this comical piece could very well be the background score for the first shots that are fired, for the killing of our people."

"But what can we possibly do this afternoon to avoid violence?" Zimmermann asked.

"We need to come up with some kind of personal appeal, an appeal from all of us that reaches out to both sides, the demonstrators as well as the security forces," Masur answered. "We all have some degree of influence."

"We also need to guarantee we're doing everything in our power to create an open dialogue between the activists and the authorities. And not just here on a regional level, but with the national party leadership too," Zimmermann said with emphasis.

"I've already jotted down some ideas," Masur said. He pulled out some scribbled notes he had made and the group began to assemble a draft of an appeal, point by point, while Lange wrote it down.

When they were satisfied with a final draft, they started for the concert hall, the Gewandhaus, to issue the appeal. Time was growing short. It was already nearly 4:30, and the peace prayers started at 5:00. Wötzel would arrange for the appeal to be read over the city loudspeakers. Zimmermann would distribute them to the churches.

They drove into town in three cars: Pommert and Meyer in one, Wötzel and Lange in another, and Zimmermann in Masur's car. Traffic was terrible. It was rush hour, and the number of security forces and demonstrators already massed in the city made for even more gridlock than usual. Zimmermann was already starting to sweat. They got stuck behind a student driver. Masur blasted his horn and tried to zip around him, but there was too much traffic headed straight for them in the passing lane. He had to grit his teeth and poke along behind. To make matters worse, an old Skoda stalled in front of Wötzel's car. It didn't look like they could possibly make it in time.

When they finally reached the Gewandhaus, Lange started banging out the appeal on a typewriter.

"You only have to type it once," Zimmermann said, pacing nervously. "They have copy machines here."

"Oh, come on," Lange retorted. "This is the GDR. You know nothing ever works here. I'll use carbon paper."

When he had finished typing out the appeal, they read it over once more together. Satisfied, Zimmermann grabbed the copies and bolted out the door.

In the meantime, someone with the Leipzig radio station arrived. Masur read the appeal on tape to be broadcast later over the radio and the city's loudspeakers.

Wötzel then got on the phone with his boss, Helmut Hackenberg, who had given the go-ahead for the meeting with

Masur. "Comrade Hackenberg," he said, "Dr. Peter Zimmermann is on his way to the churches with an appeal we drafted. Make sure the security forces let him through the barriers to deliver it."

They all agreed to meet back at the Gewandhaus at around 7:30. As Wötzel and Pommel were leaving, they promised the security forces would be restrained. But they all knew there were really no guarantees.

Issuing the appeal was comparable to a group along the lines of theologian Martin Marty, conductor George Solti, and cartoonist Gary Trudeau getting together with three local politicians to put out a statement on behalf of the White House. The group was well-known and well-respected. But they were taking a bold step, issuing a local appeal that had implications for the entire country without consulting the national leadership.

—•—

It was nearly five o'clock. Zimmermann felt the time slipping away. Masses of people spilled over into the streets of the inner city, making it impossible to drive to the churches. He would have to make his rounds on foot. He headed off, looking almost comical as he dodged through the pockets of people waiting for the demonstration to begin. He sprinted furiously, his long graying hair streaming behind him, his ample beard ruffled by the wind, until he reached the Nikolai church, where hordes were already assembled outside.

He pushed his way through to the front, past the police barricade, and went in.

He nearly had to hurdle over the people sitting in the aisles to get to Pastor Führer at the front. Looking completely unnerved, he thrust the appeal at Pastor Führer and two other pastors sitting next to him. They began to read it over.

"It's a political appeal," Zimmermann told them. "Its terms will be completely upheld by the riot police, at least as far as we can rely on the promises of the three party secretaries." His voice was vehement now. "You've got to read it aloud at the end of the prayers with as much emphasis as possible," he implored.

The three gawked at him in disbelief, but then nodded in agreement. A member of the New Forum sitting with them volunteered to take a copy to Saint Michael's Church. Then Zimmermann was down the aisle, out the door, and on to the three other churches.

—•—

Johannes Richter, rector of the St. Thomas Church, had a strange feeling, a feeling of fear tinged with excitement, like waiting for war. That morning, he had met with the dean of the Roman Catholic church to discuss how to respond to the volatile times. As the two walked along after their meeting, Richter looked into the eyes of the people they passed and saw faces full of fear. One woman who noticed their clerical collars stopped them on the street. "You are leaders of the church. Please do anything to stop the demonstrations," she begged. "I know there are orders to shoot. Please keep all the children off the street."

Richter looked at her. There was no trace of the usual gap-toothed grin on his corpulent face. "I'm sorry," he said grimly. "We cannot do anything."

Her appeal weighed on him as he sat waiting for the prayer service to begin. He surveyed the congregation, overflowing with more than two thousand people, and realized what a great responsibility he had in preaching the sermon that evening. He would be preaching to mostly unbelievers. This would be a new experience.

He felt buoyed by the tradition of belief that had gone on before him. This Gothic church on the edge of the medieval Market Square had stood for 750 years, a mighty fortress in the vicissitudes of German history. Napoleon turned it into a military storehouse. Martin Luther claimed it for the Reformation. And Johann Sebastian Bach filled it with the magnificence of his music as the church's choir director for nearly twenty-five years. A statue of the famed composer stood outside, and his visage also gazed down at the church from a stained-glass window along with other such luminaries as Kaiser Wilhelm I, Luther, and Elector Frederick the Wise. Perhaps history will be decided here again, Richter thought.

The prayer service started with an address by Johannes Hempel, the bishop of Saxony, the jurisdiction that included Leipzig. He had been dispatched to the city to issue a special appeal to all the churches.

"Dear brothers and sisters," Hempel addressed the congregation. "Quite frankly, I would like to be at all four churches, and that isn't easy to do in only forty-five minutes. So I'll keep my comments brief. God is keenly aware of what's going on in the GDR. He is adding his powerful word to the events as they are unfolding before us. For the sake of these convictions, based on my faith, whether or not you share them with me, I am asking you to keep a cool head, to be prudent, and to observe unconditional nonviolence. Violence destroys everything that is dear to us, and the highest value above all is life. I ask you to observe non-violence so that no blood is shed."

While Dr. Hempel was speaking, the church sexton tiptoed up to Pastor Richter and tapped him on the shoulder. "There's a Dr. Zimmermann at the door. He wants to see you right away," he whispered. "He says it's urgent."

Richter walked over to a side door where Zimmermann was waiting. He was panting, drenched with sweat and exhaustion. His usually neat beard was scraggly, the face behind it blanched and contorted, wrung with tension. Richter had never seen such a fearful look. His hands were trembling as he handed Richter the appeal.

"Pastor Richter, please take this paper and read it to the people," he said. "It's very important."

Richter skimmed the appeal. "If you hadn't brought this in person, and if Wötzel's name weren't on it, then I would think this was a very sick prank."

He took the appeal and walked back to his seat at the front of the church. When Hempel finished speaking, he stood up and read it.

"The following is an appeal to all the citizens of Leipzig from conductor Kurt Masur, theologian Peter Zimmermann, Cabaret player Bernd-Lutz Lange, and SED secretaries Kurt Mayer, Jochen Pommert, and Dr. Roland Wötzel:

" 'Today our common concern and responsibility has drawn us together. We are alarmed about the developments in our city and we are searching for a resolution. All of us need a free exchange of ideas about the future direction which socialism must take in our land. Therefore we six persons vow to all citizens that we shall assert our fullest strength and authority that this dialogue will occur not only in the district of Leipzig, but also at the level of our national government. We urgently implore you to exercise utmost prudence and restraint in order to enable peaceful dialogue.' "

You could almost hear a collective sigh of relief in the congregation. The cloud of tension hanging in the air seemed to dissipate.

Then Richter stood up to give his sermon.

"In my search for a word which could be meaningful to us today, I found in the 25th chapter of Proverbs the following passages:

Through patience a ruler can be persuaded,
and a gentle tongue can break a bone (v. 15).
Like a city whose walls are broken down
is a man who lacks self-control (v. 28).

"During many conversations I've had in recent days, I have reached the following conclusion: There is a great restlessness among us. People are tired of having someone else do the thinking for them. They are tired of having others making decisions on their behalf. They are tired of having others determine if they may or may not travel to another country. . . .

"Restlessness is growing out of our lack of patience. And on top of our feelings of restlessness is a mounting anger. . . . How much longer do they expect us to tolerate the tension between reality and the partial truth portrayed in the news media? And so they are understandable, this restlessness and anger. . . .

"Let's not misunderstand each other. Patience is altogether different from cowardice. And a gentle tongue is not referring to the meaningless prattle of charlatans. The truth always has two sides: comfortable and uncomfortable.

"For us, there is no alternative to dialogue. For us, there's nothing else but . . . fearlessness in truth. These verses from Proverbs contain their own irrefutable logic:

Like a city whose walls are broken down
is a man who lacks self-control.

"The message is clear: in antiquity, in the middle ages, the walls surrounding a city were the guarantee of security. A city without walls was defenseless, vulnerable, and could be attacked, harmed, and damaged. The same applies to human beings who think in anger, who act in anger. For us, as well as for our society, everything depends on whether we give in to our own restlessness and anger, or

U.S. Secretary of State ***James Baker*** recognizes ***Laszlo Tokes*** during meeting in Bucharest two months after the fall of dictator ***Nicolae Ceausescu.*** *AP/Wide World Photos*

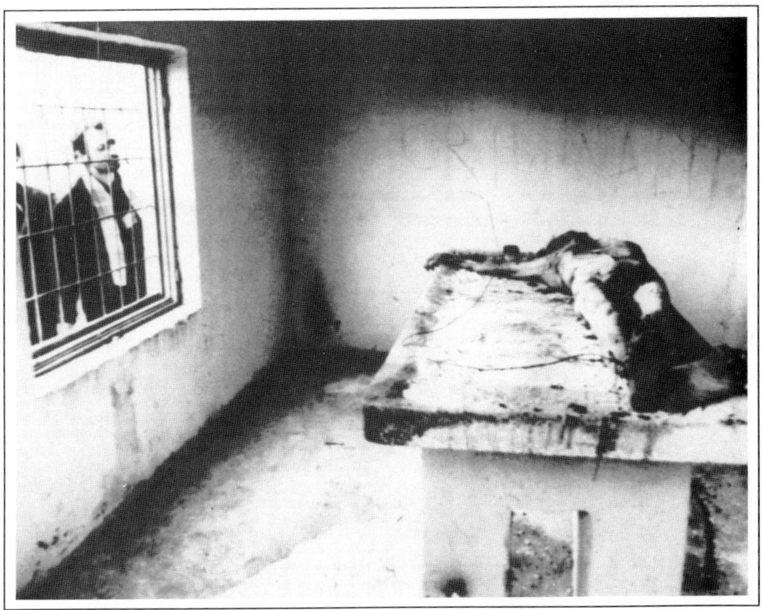

People look through a window at the body of an elderly man lying in a small morgue in Timisoara. Hundreds of people were killed. *Reuters/Bettmann*

Top: A demonstration in Timisoara against government economic policies and soaring prices. The banner reads, "*What is left of the revolution*," a reference to Timisoara uprising which led to the collapse of Romanian communism. *Reuters/Bettmann*

Left: Young Romanians celebrate in the streets of Bucharest, carrying a portrait of Ceausescu behind bars.
AP/Wide World Photos

Top: **Tadeusz Mazowiecki** gives victory sign as he leaves Parliament in Warsaw as the Eastern bloc's first non-Communist prime minister. *AP/Wide World Photos*

Bottom: **Tadeusz Mazowiecki** (speaking) with *Solidarity* leader **Lech Walesa** addresses crowd of 10,000 Solidarity supporters. *AP/Wide World Photos*

Hundreds of workers rally at Lenin Shipyard in Gdansk. *AP/Wide World Photos*

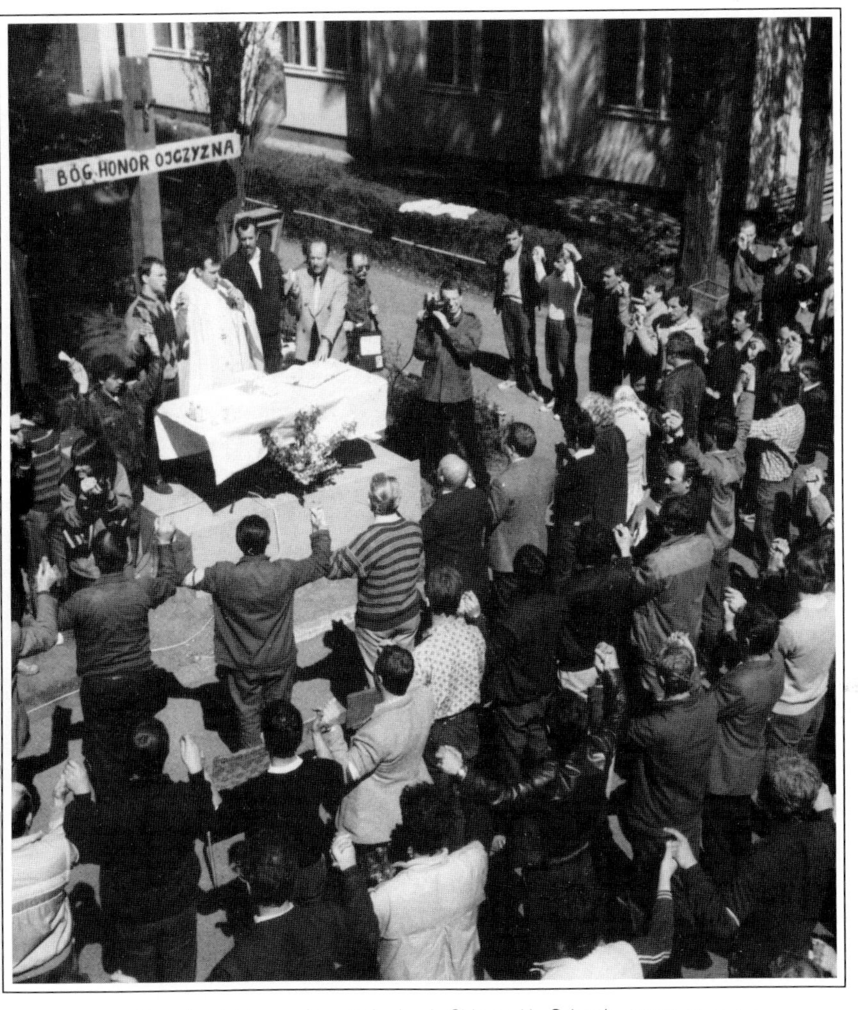

Mass for striking workers at the Lenin Shipyard in Gdansk. *AP/Wide World Photos*

Crowd stands outside the gates of the Lenin Shipyard in Gdansk.
AP/Wide World Photos

Top: Prayer service for imprisoned pro-democracy protesters at Gethsemane Church in East Berlin. *AP/Wide World Photos*

Below: Protest march in Leipzig following prayer service. *Harald Kirschner*

Top: Candles are lit outside church in Leipzig. *Harald Kirschner*

Left: **Brigitta Treetz** and **Bernhard Venzke**. *Harald Kirschner*

Below: East German citizens shake hands with West German citizens through a line of East German police. *Reuters/Bettmann*

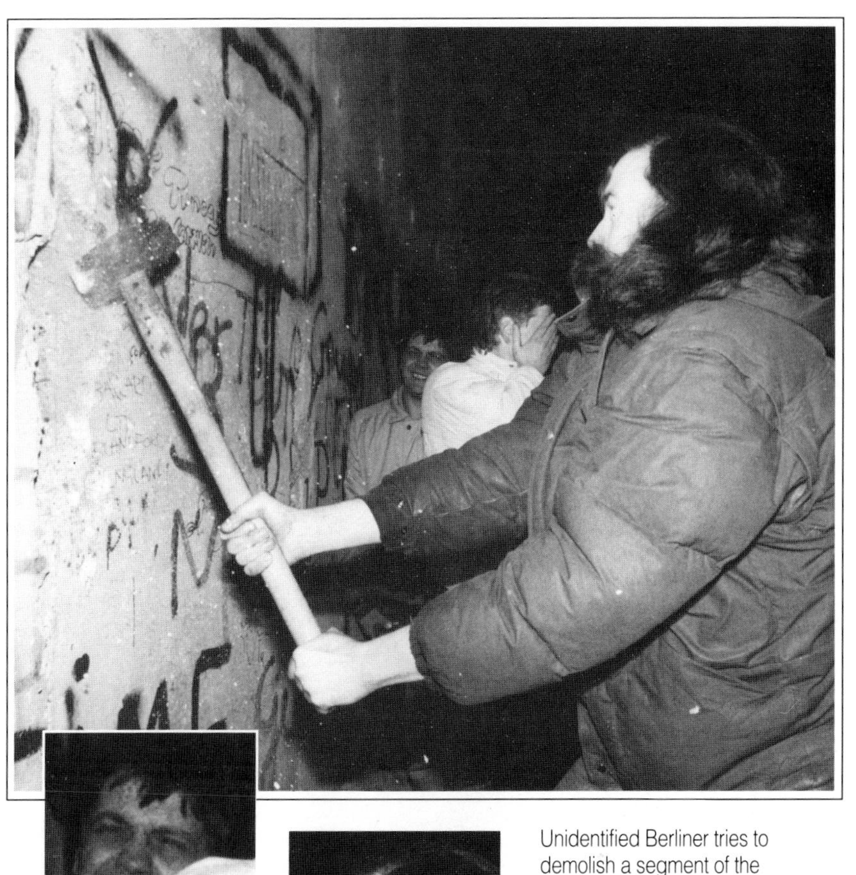

Unidentified Berliner tries to demolish a segment of the Berlin Wall. *AP/Wide World Photos*

East German couple exchanges a kiss in front of the Brandenburg gate as crowd burns sparkling candles after East Germany opened new border crossings.
Reuters/Bettmann

Tens of thousands crowd around the Wenceslas monument during mass demonstration demanding free elections. *AP/Wide World Photos*

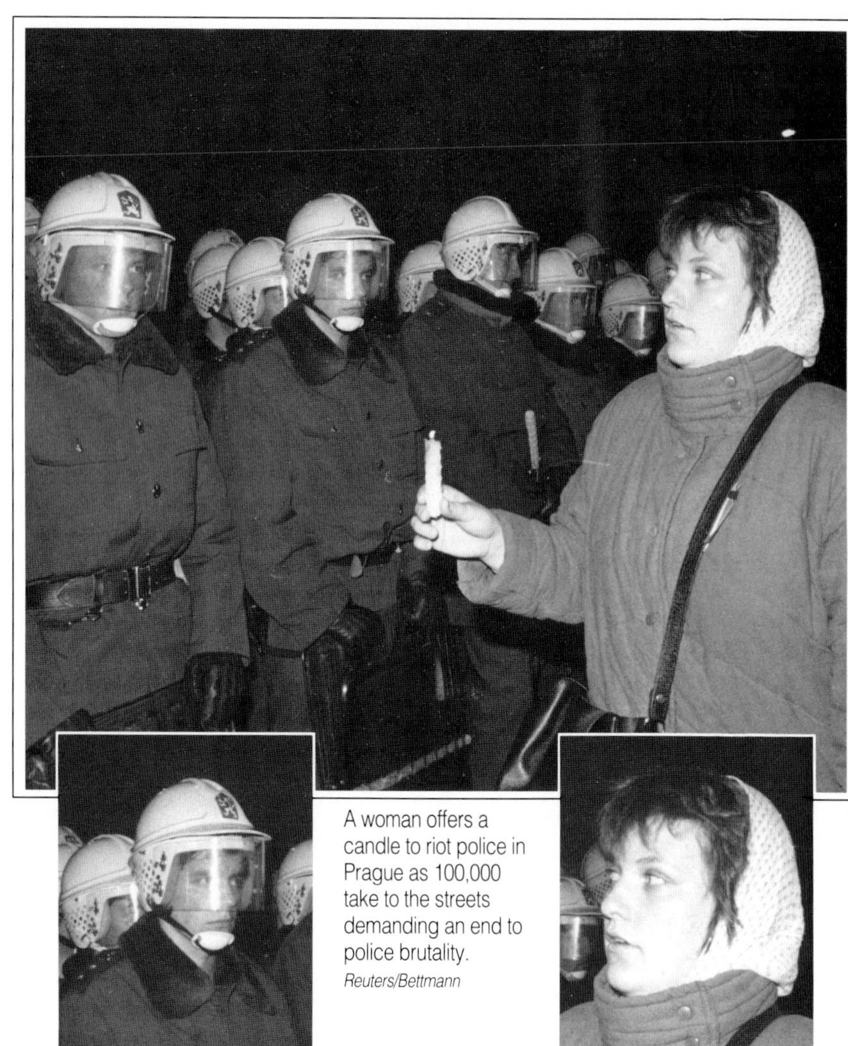

A woman offers a candle to riot police in Prague as 100,000 take to the streets demanding an end to police brutality.
Reuters/Bettmann

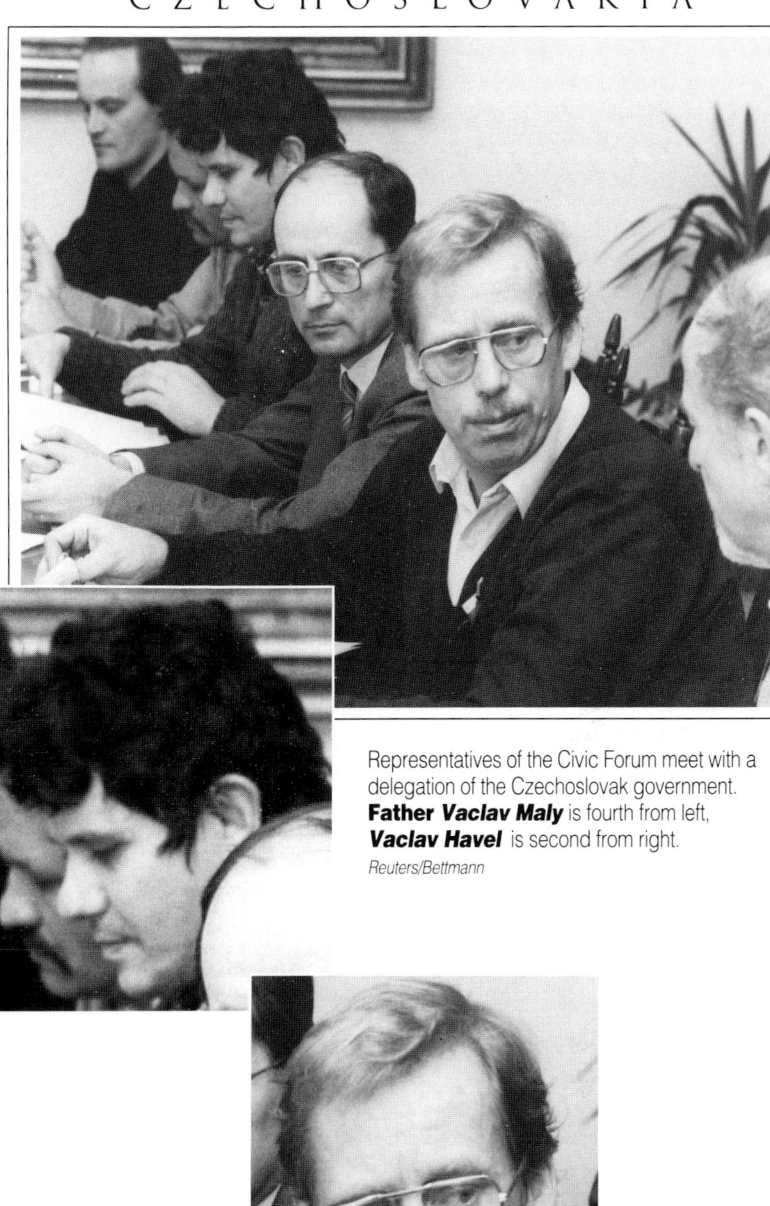

Representatives of the Civic Forum meet with a delegation of the Czechoslovak government. **Father *Vaclav Maly*** is fourth from left, ***Vaclav Havel*** is second from right.
Reuters/Bettmann

Vaclav Havel reads out the names of Czechoslovakia's first non-Communist government since 1948 as thousands celebrate the success of their peaceful revolution.
Reuters/Bettmann

Above: Members of the diplomatic corps and representatives of churches stand at attention during the funeral ceremony for Imre Nagy at Budapest Heroes Square. *AP/Wide World Photos*

Left: ***Gabor Ivanyi*** (second from right) leads worship service in front of his church in the Kispest district of Budapest. *Keston Research*

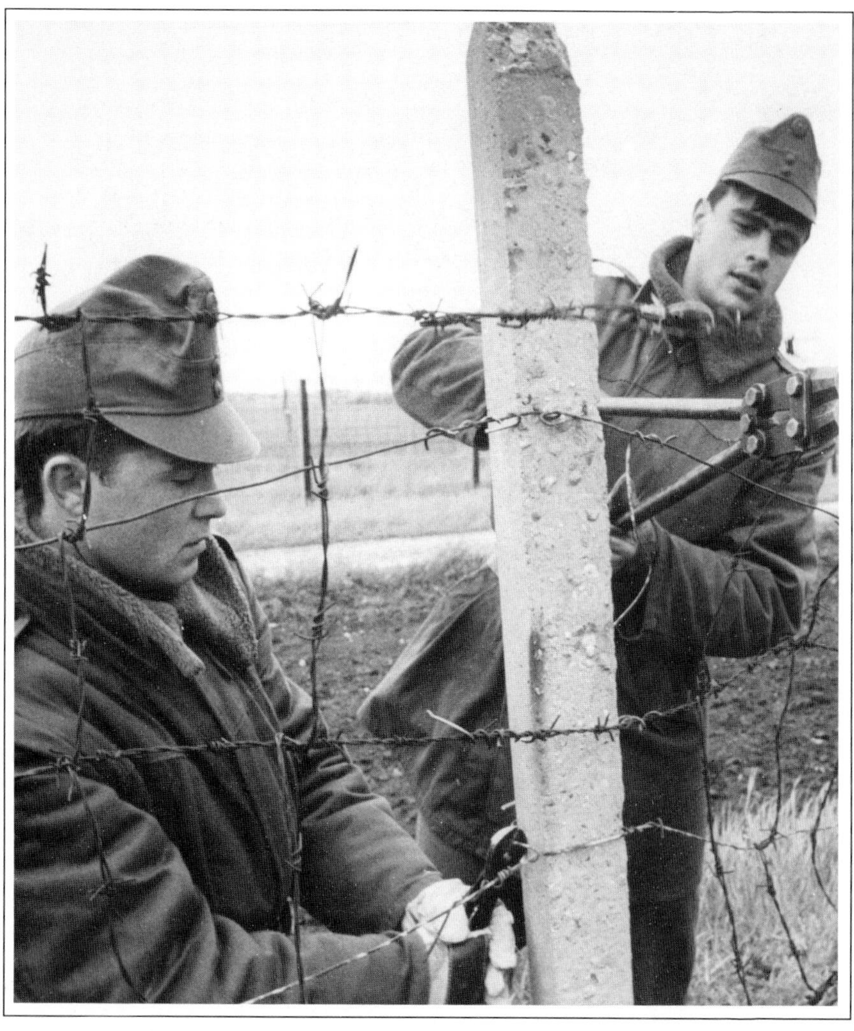

Top: Hungarian border guards cut the barbed wire fence as Hungary starts dismantling 354 km of the Iron Curtain toward Austria and the West.

AP/Wide World Photos

whether we develop in ourselves the freedom which our Jewish predecessors had.

"I ask you for your own sake and for mine to have the courage to be patient. I ask you for your own sake and for mine to exercise the power of wise words. I ask you for your own sake and for mine to have the courage to resist anger. Amen."

—•—

The prayer service at the Nikolai church was surprisingly calm, even though the tension seemed to build minute by minute, heightened by the chants, whistling, and applause that occasionally filtered in from the crowd outside—shouts of "Gorby, Gorby!" "We're staying here!" and loudest of all, "No violence!"

Pastor Führer started off the service by addressing all the Party people who had been ordered to fill the church. "You know the sign outside the church says, 'Open for all.' And that includes members of the Party. We stand by that. All are welcome. But please allow us to conduct our service in an orderly and peaceful manner."

He then read out the appeal hand-delivered by Zimmermann. The words prompted the same collective feeling of relief they elicited at the St. Thomas Church. Bishop Hempel issued his same plea for restraint as he made the rounds to all the churches.

When the service ended, Pastor Führer feared the people exiting the church would have no room to move because of the thousands of demonstrators packed so tightly around the church. But as they filed out, the people pressed against the church parted to make room. The people coming out of the church were singing "Dona Nobis Pacem" [Give Us Your Peace]. The lilting melody began to spread through the crowd outside, blowing through the courtyard like a gentle breeze.

The streets of Leipzig were now congested with the traffic of some seventy thousand people. The city's inner ring was a mass of human gridlock. Lining the ring truck after truck of riot police sat, watched, and waited. In front of the line of trucks, some officers stood talking into walkie-talkies, their chests emblazoned with decorations. The protesters passed column after column of white shields. And everywhere dogs were barking, straining at their leashes held by the security forces.

As one woman passed the line of troops, she shouted: "I know my son is somewhere among you. Dear son, if you can hear me, don't shoot!"

The demonstrators began to process around the city. Amid the shouts of "We're staying here," and "Democracy now," a new chant broke out from the crowd. "We are the people." The chant sounded over and over again, louder and louder, as if the protesters were fully convincing themselves of the power of those words. It was a declaration of their unity, and at the same time an invitation to the troops: "We are the people," meant "We're no different from you. We're on the same side. Come join us."

—•—

When Brigitta left Berlin for home, she had such a good feeling. All of her test results were encouraging. The doctor had pointed a chubby index finger at her and said with a good-natured chuckle: "I hope you're not going to the demonstrations in Leipzig, are you?"

And Brigitta laughed back and said, "Well, why not?"

Now, as she approached her hometown on the train, that feeling was rapidly fading. There was talk on the train that the city was surrounded by security forces, and the plan was to shoot down the demonstrators.

The train pulled into Leipzig's main station, but it was cordoned off. The station was shut down. She looked out the window and saw police scattered everywhere in the darkness, and convoy after convoy of canvas-colored trucks full of soldiers. The sight filled her with terror. *What is happening?* she wondered. Had the troops violently crushed the demonstration?

She got off the train and had to wander through strange, darkened passageways to get outside. As she plodded toward the downtown area, struggling with her luggage, she could hear the demonstration in the distance. Faint chants of "We're staying here!" and "We are the people!" became more distinct as she neared the city center. The chants gave her hope.

She continued following the sound, carried along by the crowd from the train station. She desperately wanted to locate her friends, to seek comfort in their familiarity, but she knew that would be impossible. It seemed like it took her forever to make it to the city center. When she reached the pedestrian bridge next to the town's main department store, it was crowded with people.

Just ahead of her, she saw the mass of people coursing through the city center, cascading around the inner ring like a mighty river, and the overwhelming number of security forces containing them. She felt an overpowering chill, both of fear and joy. Fear that just one stone could be enough to provoke a violent police attack. Joy that there were so many people of all ages and backgrounds.

Shouts of "We are the people!" sounded over and over, magnified a hundred thousand times. The cry was so simple, yet so ingenious, Brigitta thought, because it's the people's army and the people's police standing face to face with the people themselves. Perhaps the security forces would realize they, too, were the people. In the jumble of her feelings of fear and joy, Brigitta could barely muster a shout.

By the time she reached the inner ring, she was worn out from carrying her heavy baggage. She felt the fearful trembling. But she had come too far to stop now, so she stepped into the flow, luggage and all. Now there was no turning back.

—•—

Pommert and Meyer went to the regional party headquarters after they left the Gewandhaus. There they found their boss, Helmut Hackenberg, on the phone with a military commander.

"Withdraw your forces!" he was yelling into the phone. "Withdraw them even further. Do whatever you can to make peace!"

When he hung up, he began chastising his two comrades. "I didn't know you were going to issue this appeal. I don't think it was such a good idea acting so independently. Either the entire Secretariat should have approved it, or no one.

Meyer was unshaken. "But the Secretariat can endorse it early tomorrow," he suggested. "We can print it in the Leipzig newspaper with the signatures of the entire secretariat."

"It's already done now," Hackenberg groused.

The phone rang. It was Egon Krenz from Berlin, inquiring about the situation in Leipzig.

"Everything's proceeding without any violence," Hackenberg told him.

Krenz and the rest of the Politburo were obviously in the dark about the appeal. They decided to keep it that way for the time being and headed back to the Gewandhaus.

—•—

Peter Zimmermann was heading back to St. Michael's church when the appeal was read out over the town's loudspeakers. The chants died down as Masur's authoritative voice boomed out over the city like a message from on high. The masses were silent for a moment, then erupted in thunderous applause.

Zimmermann felt tremendously relieved that their appeal was so well received. But his fears still nagged at him. He knew the three party leaders weren't important enough to know what orders were coming down from Berlin, from Honecker, and from Krenz. And he also knew a bloodbath was just a hair trigger away. One provocative act, one overzealous security officer, and a conflagration of violence could be ignited. His mind flashed back to just two days before, when he witnessed a security officer holding back a ferocious-looking dog. Someone in the crowd asked the officer when he planned to remove the dog's muzzle. "When things get feisty," was the ominous reply.

Back in the city center, he saw the demonstration march begin. As he surveyed the sea of people walled in by the security forces, he realized the volatility of the situation, and just how much pressure the security police must be feeling. Panic gripped him when the demonstrators halted in front of the Stasi headquarters, the very symbol of all they were protesting against. "*Ohrenburg*," it was derisively dubbed, meaning "Fortress of Ears," for its Orwellian intrusion into their lives.

Zimmermann was on the front row of the demonstrators. He could almost smell the danger. The crowd was whistling and jeering, tossing taunts and epithets at those inside. "Stasi to the sloth farm!" "Stasi, get out!" "Get a real job!" Just twenty feet away, a row of riot police looked on.

Zimmermann watched in amazement as the security forces began to back off and slowly withdraw. A few even removed their helmets, and laid their shields and nightsticks aside. The demonstrators were encouraged by the sight. They saw the security forces were not looking for confrontation.

A few people in the crowd later began placing candles on the steps of the Stasi building. More and more candles were added, until the steps blazed with the brightness of hundreds of candles, forming a symbolic barrier of peaceful protection. The flickering flames cast an eerie shadow against the backdrop of the oppressive looking building, the light dancing with the darkness.

Zimmermann went back to the Gewandhaus around 7:45, where the other five drafters of the appeal were already there waiting for him. They watched together from the concert hall as the first wave of demonstrators rounded the city's inner ring and marched past the Gewandhaus. The demonstration had passed without incident.

Masur turned to his colleagues and smiled.

"Excuse me, gentlemen," he said matter-of-factly. "I have a concert to conduct."

On his way back to Masur's home to pick up his car, Zimmermann passed through the inner city. People were heading home. Trucks from the security forces still lined the streets, as if they were standing at attention. But the riot police were no longer poised for action. They were milling around in the streets, uniformed but unarmed. Zimmermann looked more closely to convince himself of what he was seeing. Some of the riot police were actually chatting casually with groups of demonstrators, as if they were mingling at a cocktail party. Then he saw one of the demonstrators offer a security officer a cigarette. Zimmermann knew they had won the night.

East Berlin
October 10, 1989

Ilonka ended her fast and returned home after going without food for five days. She left the Gethsemane church feeling a little light-headed, a little wobbly-kneed, emerging from the church's dusky darkness and blinking into the bright day. She was stepping out into the realization that the words of her poem were made flesh in her fasting, that forty years would soon be over.

Leipzig
October 15, 1989

Several days before Uwe and Ulrike left for West Germany, Brigitta helped them pack up their belongings. It was official now.

Their emigration visas had come through. They were going to live outside of Hanover.

It was a difficult afternoon for Brigitta. The Jaegers were her friends. She still wanted to help them, but she didn't want to help them leave.

The apartment where they stayed up so many nights engrossed in never-ending debate, where they laughed and drank and commiserated together, was now nearly barren. They said little while boxing up books that once sparked spirited conversations. The silence between them was painful. Uwe tried to joke around, but nobody laughed.

When they finished packing up, Brigitta kissed the children goodbye. As she was walking out the door, the couple reminded her of the farewell party they were throwing at their apartment the next night. The small group was invited.

But neither she nor Father Bernhard could force themselves to go. They didn't feel like celebrating.

LEIPZIG
October 16, 1989

Brigitta and Father Bernhard emerged from the Reformed church together illumined by the light of thousands of candles. The awesome sight of the warm candlelight and the haunting sound of many voices singing "Dona Nobis Pacem" filled Brigitta with peace. She thought about how candles were the perfect symbol for their nonviolent demonstrations. Using one hand to hold the candle, and the other to protect the fragile flame left the demonstrators no hands free for violence.

The anxiety that had marked the previous weeks' demonstrations had almost subsided. The police so prevalent beforehand were almost nowhere to be seen. The rally that night had taken on a relaxed, almost jovial atmosphere. They sang songs from Taize, the ecumenical community in France. In the midst of the mass of people, Brigitta felt herself incredibly strong. So much was finally beginning to change.

As Brigitta passed a young reservist standing by, observing the demonstrations, she heard a passer-by ask him: "How can you stay here? Do we look like enemies of the state that you have to stand watch and oppose us? We are the people. Come join us."

He replied in a quiet voice: "I only have six more weeks in the reserves. After that I will gladly join you."

After the demonstration that evening, Brigitta and Bernhard drove with friends in several Trabants back to his apartment to watch the incredible images of the demonstration on TV. They couldn't believe how many demonstrators there were. Aerial shots showed the city's entire inner ring filled with protesters. The media estimated the crowd at 150,000. They were filled with such a sense of joy and euphoria they couldn't sleep, staying up until 1:30 in the morning talking.

In her journal entry for that evening, Brigitta jotted down some thoughts on a quote from Galileo that seemed to sum up the past week:

> Finally things are on the move
> And we are on the move with it.
> Or is it the other way around?
> It's all the same! And it moves indeed.

Over the next few weeks, the huge rallies proceeded peacefully, growing exponentially. Slogans and posters began to take on an almost humorous bent as the demonstrators became bolder and bolder. A sign that appeared at one rally: "That was the shirt, now we want the trousers!" At another demonstration, the crowd gathered in front of the main train station and pointed up at the surveillance camera mounted there, chanting: "We see you! We see you!"

But it was the overwhelming shout of "We are the people!" that finally convinced the government of the people's power. The people spoke; the government listened. On October 18, Honecker resigned. Egon Krenz replaced him and began calling for dialogue. On November 7, the entire East German cabinet resigned, followed by the Politburo the next day. The East German government, with one of the most powerful and extensive security forces in the world, had been toppled by a bloodless revolution, a revolution not of weapons and violence, but of candlelight and peace. And the demonstrators liked to point out that the revolution occurred in typical German fashion, after working hours. The East Germans didn't even call it a revolution. They called it *die Wende*, the turning point. And it was a true turning point in history. The Eastern bloc, indeed the world, would never be the same.

At the height of the demonstrations, the city's populace stretched a huge banner across one of Leipzig's streets. It read in big, bold letters: "*Wir danken Dir, Kirche!*" (We thank you, church!)

14

Czechoslovakia

The Czechoslovakian government was keeping a nervous eye on the events unfolding next door in East Germany. The hard-line government had been cozying up to East Berlin as the two like-minded regimes banded together against the encroaching reforms of Poland and Hungary. Now, with the changes convulsing East Germany, Czechoslovakia found itself even more isolated in the Eastern bloc.

The government also feared the repercussions of letting thousands of East Germans gain free passage to the West from Czechoslovakia, while its own citizens were still trapped within their country's borders. The Czechoslovakian regime couldn't hide the East German crisis from its people. Evidence of it filled downtown Prague: hundreds of abandoned Trabants littered the downtown streets. The area around the West German embassy had been cordoned off.

After the decision to allow the East Germans free passage was finally announced, the massive exodus got underway in a strangely dignified fashion. The rowdy throngs of East Germans pressed into the embassy grounds suddenly became orderly, waiting patiently in line to board the buses that would take them to the train station and on to freedom. Prague's inner city was crowded with shoppers when the buses pulled out onto the narrow street outside the West German embassy.

As the buses rolled up the hill to a square at the end of the street, the two hundred or so Czechs going about their everyday business stopped what they were doing. Then, as they watched the busloads of East Germans pass by, in a true gesture of empathy, the people of Prague broke into spontaneous applause.

PRAGUE
November 1989

The legend had been passed down in Czechoslovakia from generation to generation: "When Blessed Agnes is canonized, great things will happen in the land."

Agnes was born a princess in thirteenth-century Bohemia, the daughter of King Premysl Otakar I and the sister of King Wenceslas, the good king of the Christmas carol who later became Czechoslovakia's patron saint. When Agnes was growing up, all of Europe was in the throes of a severe economic crisis. Protected behind the royal palace's walls of lavish comfort, she felt far removed from the growing poverty of her people. She was so moved by their misery she renounced her royal heritage to follow in the footsteps of the woman history knows as St. Clare of Assisi. The two contemporaries were good friends. They corresponded regularly about how Christian charity could help the continent's growing urban poor. Clare once called Agnes "half of my soul."

Agnes was besieged by European monarchs asking for her hand in marriage. Her kindness and intellect were well-known across Europe. Emperor Frederic II and King Henry III of England were among the rulers who tried to convince her to become their bride. Her family pleaded for her to marry. A royal wedding would mean a powerful diplomatic liaison. But she resisted the advances of her suitors and her family's pressure and left the castle for the convent. She founded the First Order of the Poor Clares in Prague, where she served as mother superior. The order started a hospital and established housing to take in the city's poverty stricken residents.

While Agnes was serving the sick and the poor, she was also serving her country. Her brother would often turn to her skills in languages and diplomacy for help in solving some vexing problem of state.

Because of her devotion to the sick and the poor, Agnes was beatified in 1874. But because she was the daughter of a small nation, her canonization was not a priority for the church hierarchy. The Catholic church in Czechoslovakia had been actively lobbying for her sainthood since 1947, but she was continually passed over.

On November 12, 1989, fifteen thousand Czechs and Slovaks from all over the world converged on Rome to celebrate what the Czechoslovak people had been awaiting for nearly eight centuries. Agnes was finally being canonized. Despite the obstacles thrown in their way by the Czechoslovak government, ten thousand people from inside the country made the trip. It took months to get a visa, and many who applied were denied. Those who did get permission to go to Rome had to pay the state travel agency, Cedok, seven thousand crowns to make the trip, more than twice the average monthly salary. Trains and buses headed to Rome were slowed, and many pilgrims traveling to the ceremony were stopped at the Czechoslovak border and subjected to humiliating strip searches.

But they had no doubts the trip was worth it. The ceremony itself was resplendent. John Paul II sung the praises of Agnes in both Czech and Slovak, as Prague's renowned choir of St. Jakub added its own paean of praise. Czechoslovak TV gave in to the demands of the people to broadcast the ceremony. At the solemn moment of consecration, however, the Mass was abruptly cut off.

At the end of the service, the Pope prayed, "Holy Agnes, protect us on our way," an invocation the worshipers took to heart as they left the cathedral and the jubilant week of festivities in Rome to head back to Czechoslovakia.

As one of the buses neared the border, the passengers inside were grumbling about having to return to the stringent controls of their homeland. It was hot and stuffy inside the bus. They had already been on the road for hours. The time in Rome was already starting to pass away like a pleasant dream.

"Have you ever experienced such a feeling of freedom?" one

passenger reflected. "It's too bad we have to go back home."

"I hate having to go back," another said. "Things are so hard at home."

The bus soon filled with a chorus of complaints, with passenger after passenger adding to the mournful litany.

"It's such a terrible place to live," someone else groused. "And things will never change."

"Now, wait a minute," an old nun dressed in street clothes piped up from somewhere in the back of the bus. "Agnes was not only a saint. She was also from a diplomatic family. She can arrange it for us."

The bus got quiet for a moment, then erupted in raucous guffaws.

PRAGUE
November 17, 1989

The demonstration started as a commemoration for a student killed during an uprising against Nazi occupation fifty years before. It was organized by a Communist-sanctioned group, the Charles University Union of Student Youth, and even approved by the Communist authorities. About seven thousand students gathered at the cemetery where the student martyr, Jan Opletal, was buried for what started out as an innocent memorial service. They laid flowers at his grave and lit candles. They sang the national anthem. There were speeches, poems, and tributes. But there was an undercurrent of dissatisfaction from some of the student activists who had helped organize the rally. Some of them had been involved in "unofficial" discussion groups or had contacts with Charter 77. Others were part of the growing number of disillusioned young intellectuals turning to the church for answers.

When one of the leaders of the Communist-sanctioned group gave an innocuous speech about the need for constructive cooperation in the country, he was roundly booed, and someone unfurled a banner saying "We Want Freedom for Christmas." The rally had been hijacked by the circle of student activists. One of them, Martin Klima, addressed the group: "Oppression is worse than death!" he declared. "We should not only remember the past with piety, we must care for the present and even more for the future! We must fight for freedom because we cannot live without it."

His words fired up the rally. The group had grown to about fifteen thousand. They decided to march on to Wenceslas Square, the half-mile long pedestrian plaza in the heart of Prague. As they moved en masse, their numbers made them bolder. Some of them shouted defiant slogans. The number of demonstrators seemed to multiply minute by minute as they shouted for others to join them. When they reached the square, they came up against a roadblock of riot police. The protesters tried to talk to them, offering them flowers, and placing lighted candles at their feet. But the police stood firm and ordered them to leave.

The protesters moved up Narodni Street. There they were met by another line of riot police. Now they were surrounded, hemmed in on every side. The students on the front row facing the heavily armed units stretched out their hands, palms upward, in a gesture of nonviolence, pleading with the police, "We don't want violence. See our bare hands."

The response was vicious. The police charged. The only route of escape was a narrow arcade lined with riot squads. The protesters were trapped. Police began clubbing them like seal pups, until blood streamed down many of their faces. Heavy batons and boots came crashing down on those who fell. Others were chased into buildings, dragged out, and beaten mercilessly.

Watching the horrifying display of violence from the windows above were actors from the National Theater. Some of the students had run into the theater for shelter. Seeing their battered bodies and bleeding faces galvanized the actors into action.

The theater shut down at intermission and went on strike, opening its stage for an improvisational dialogue, providing an open mike for free speech. Anyone who wanted could grab the microphone and engage in free discussion. The curtain went up on the real-life drama unfolding around them.

PRAGUE
November 19, 1989

The basement of another theater, the Magic Lantern, located just off Wenceslas Square, was clouded with the stale smoke of cigarettes, the "perfume" of the opposition, as one dissident writer called it. It was late in the evening.

News of the brutality against the student protest had spread. The students had sprung into action to publicize the violence, distributing leaflets and grisly pictures of bloodied protesters to offices, to factories, to people on the street. They were calling it a massacre. No one was killed—one student was rumored to have been beaten to death—but hundreds were injured. As a sign of their outrage, the students started a sit-down strike in the university and called for a two-hour general strike a week later.

Father Vaclav Maly sat at a table surrounded by members of VONS and Charter 77 and other dissident groups. Havel had hurried back from his country cottage in northeast Bohemia when he heard about the protest and hastily assembled the group. He even turned down the government's offer of a passport to travel to Sweden to accept a humanitarian award because of the growing tension at home. There was a feeling that this could be the moment of change they were looking for, that the authorities had sounded their own death-knell.

One unexpected face among the dissidents seated in the theater's basement was that of Jan Skoda, the leader of the Socialist party. Up to now, members of his party had been known more or less as the lackeys of the Communists. In a surprising move, the Socialists and another satellite, the People's Party, were breaking ranks. This gave the opposition an even broader base of support.

Maly was asked to be the group's spokesman. His charisma, commitment to human rights, and especially his credibility among young people, Havel had argued, made him a perfect candidate for the position. Maly hesitated for a moment. He wasn't a professional politician. He didn't want to make politics. But then he thought: here's a chance to work for a better political atmosphere, to make sure that ethics will be the basis of any political change; here's a chance to put on the pressure to destroy once and for all the barrier between the powerful and the powerless. He had no choice but to accept.

Maly faced the members of the press who were quickly summoned to the meeting and announced that those assembled there had decided to establish an umbrella group for the opposition. He then read from a declaration the group had hastily written.

"This forum will act as a spokesman on behalf of that part of the Czechoslovak public which is increasingly critical of the existing Czechoslovak leadership and which in recent days has been profoundly shaken by the brutal massacre of peacefully demonstrating students. . . .

"We demand the immediate resignation of the Communist leaders responsible for preparing the Warsaw Pact intervention in 1968 and the subsequent devastation of the country's life, starting with the president, Gustav Husak, and the Party leader, Milos Jakes, the immediate resignation of the federal interior minister, Frantisek Kincl, and the Prague first secretary, Miroslav Stepan, held responsible for violent repression of peaceful demonstrations; the establishment of a special commission to investigate these police actions; and the immediate release of all prisoners of conscience."

"We also announce our support for a two-hour general strike on Monday, November 27, from noon to 2:00 P.M.

The group known as Civic Forum was born.

PRAGUE
November 20, 1989

Cardinal Tomasek was returning from a conference in Rome with Father Halik when he first heard about the growing demonstrations in Prague. The two eagerly snatched up the newspapers in the Rome airport to get the latest news of the growing unrest before boarding the Czechoslovak airliner that would take them back home. On the plane, they were limited to reading the accounts in the Communist party daily, *Rude Pravo*, describing the student protests as a provocation and violation of public order.

When they arrived back in Prague, the Cardinal summoned Father Zverina and another banned priest, Father Otto Madr, to discuss how to respond to the demonstrations. The two priests, along with Father Halik, comprised an inner circle of unofficial advisers to the Cardinal.

"I must do something to show my support of the people," the Cardinal told the group.

"But what opportunities would we have to publicize the church's support?" Father Halik asked. "The official media would never publish a statement from you. There's Radio Free Europe or Voice of America."

Father Zverina had been in touch with the leaders of Civic Forum over the past several days. "The Socialist party newspaper has offered its balcony to Civic Forum to address the demonstrations in Wenceslas Square," he said. "Father Maly is serving as moderator."

The Cardinal knew Maly well. Maly's arguments had largely convinced him that human rights and religious rights were inseparable.

Zverina continued. "We could put together a letter declaring your support and give it to Father Maly to issue at Wenceslas Square."

The rest of the day was a swirl of activity. The three priests spent their time shuttling back and forth between the archbishop and the inner sanctum of the Magic Lantern, the dressing rooms in the theater's bowels where Havel, Maly, and other key Civic Forum leaders were perpetually huddled together, banging out communiques and working out strategies.

By the end of the evening, they had drafted a letter of support. Back at the Archbishop's Palace, the cardinal was handed the typewritten pages. The ninety-year-old archbishop put on his reading glasses and began perusing the statement. He nodded his approval, took out his pen, and placed the nation's Roman Catholic church squarely behind Civic Forum with his signature.

By four o'clock the next afternoon, Wenceslas Square was overrun with demonstrators. The number of people teeming in the square had grown every day since the suppression of the student protest. At the far end of the square, where the plaza sloped down from the National Museum, the colossal statue of King Wenceslas on horseback was covered with candles. The square was awash with some 200,000 people.

The masses were still incensed over the brutality that took place in the same spot five days before. An occasional cry went up from the demonstrators: "Punish, punish, punish!"

The square burst into applause when Vaclav Maly appeared at the balcony of the Socialist Party newspaper overlooking the square and repeated the demands of Civic Forum. This publishing house of the Socialist party, which had formerly echoed the Communist party line, was now echoing calls for democratic reform through a public address system Civic Forum had set up on its balcony, conveniently located halfway down the square.

Maly then took out the statement from Cardinal Tomasek. "I have a letter here from one of the great symbols of our movement, Cardinal Frantisek Tomasek," he announced.

"Dear friends," he read aloud. "I express my support for all those calling for justice. It is only right that those guilty of brutality against the student demonstrators should be brought to justice, but I plead with you not to resort to violence yourselves. We will fight for good only using good methods.

"It is impossible for me to remain silent when my people have joined the mass protest against four decades of unjust rule in Czechoslovakia. It is impossible to have faith in the leadership of a state that refuses to tell the people the truth and give them the rights and freedoms that are common even in third-world countries. We can wait no longer. I urge all Roman Catholics not to stand apart in this decisive hour in our history. Instead, I ask you to raise your voices again, this time in union with non-Catholics, Czechs and Slovaks, and people of other nations, believers and nonbelievers. For the right to faith cannot be separated from other democratic rights. Freedom is indivisible."

When Maly finished reading, the square resounded with chants of "Long live Tomasek!"

There were cheers when Havel appeared at the balcony, and more cheers when he announced the Czechoslovakian prime minister, Ladislav Adamec, had promised the government would not impose martial law and there would be no more beating of protesters.

When the rally continued, the vast audience of 200,000 all took out their key chains and began jangling them, until the square reverberated with the taunting tintinnabulation, chanting at those in power, "The bell tolls for you."

PRAGUE
November 23, 1989

Two nights after Maly read Tomasek's rousing letter of support, a prominent figure from Czechoslovakia's Protestant church appeared at the same balcony to address the crowd. Josef Hromadka was the leader of the Evangelical Church of Czech Brethren, the country's second largest Protestant church, and chairman of the Czechoslovak Ecumenical Council of Churches.

The Protestant church in Czechoslovakia was small compared to the country's Roman Catholic church, numbering about 1.5 million out of a population of 15 million. Most of the nation's Protestants were concentrated in the Czech republic; the republic of Slovakia was more like Poland, traditionally Roman Catholic. Czech Protestants proudly traced their roots back to Jan Hus, the fifteenth century religious reformer burned at the stake by the Catholic church. Conflicts between the two republics and the two traditions could be dated back to the same period, and on through the Reformation and Counter-Reformation. The Catholic church was closely aligned with the Hapsburgs of the ruling Austro-Hungarian empire and viewed with suspicion by the Protestant Czechs. When the independent state of Czechoslovakia was founded after World War I, Tomas Masaryk, the president of the new republic, tended to see the Catholic church as a force used to oppress the Czech national character and tried to reduce its influence.

The Communist party took full advantage of the division between Czechs and Slovaks in seizing power after World War II, and exploited the tension between Protestants and Catholics as well. Because of the strength and numbers of the Catholic church, it received the brunt of the regime's campaign of religious repression. As long as the Protestant churches walked the tightrope of compromise, they were allowed a limited amount of freedom in church life and protected, for the most part, from systematic repression.

The leadership of the Czech Brethren had always been careful not to be openly critical of the government. For his part, Hromadka had always tried to maintain good relations with the state. He had occasionally expressed criticism of the government, but was always careful to do it privately, without calling attention to it in the press. Now he stood in the public eye, under the scrutiny of television cameras and 300,000 people.

"We live in a society that's sick and needs a remedy," he told the crowd. "By speaking truthfully and critically we hope we can overcome many things . . . but words and judgments are not enough; this time, this gathering in itself is a judgment on all that is bad and has to be overcome. . . . We must all have the courage for a new lifestyle, perhaps with less material wealth but with more of the values that have been missing from people's lives. . . .

"Remember the figure of Jesus Christ. Our long history is full of Christianity. Let's look at this history, and take note of its value. Don't lose sight of Christian values—love, truth, compassion, fidelity and sacrifice—in your search for meaningful lives."

Earlier, Prague's Comenius Protestant seminary students had issued a statement saying "Black Friday," as they called the bloody crackdown, compelled them to speak out against government injustice. Their statement posed a provocative question: "Would this have happened if it had not been for the bloodshed? Our situation has fundamentally changed. We are happy and behaving like people again. We are no longer afraid. But we are guilty of remaining silent. We have sinned enough, let us sin no more."

PRAGUE
November 24, 1989

The news spread through the crowd assembled for the eighth straight day in Wenceslas Square: Dubcek was coming!

Alexander Dubcek. The very symbol of change, of the high aspirations of 1968, that time of hopes raised, then dashed.

There was an electric excitement in the square. Nearly a third of the city's population had turned out. It was no longer a mass of mostly young people. Now there were people of all ages and backgrounds, mothers with children wrapped up against the cold in tow, factory workers still wearing the sweat and dirt of the day's labor, and silver-haired men and women, their faces lined with the hardship of the past twenty years.

When Dubcek walked out onto the balcony, it was like a ghost had appeared from somewhere in the distant past, a past that had dissipated into an ethereal mist, exorcised in a government campaign of official "forgetting," as Czechoslovak writer Milan Kundera characterized it. But here he was, in the flesh, looking much the same as he did in his last public appearance in Prague, more than twenty years before. After the Soviet-led invasion that cast a permanent chill on the reforms of his "Prague spring," the former Communist party chief had been working in an obscure post in the forestry administration in Bratislava, almost in internal exile. His once dark hair was white now, his face lined with age. But there was no mistaking the thin six-foot four-inch figure and the stiff way he carried himself.

At the first sight of him, the crowd below let out a shout that shook the city. "Long live Dubcek!" they cried. They stomped and clapped and wiped away the tears, applauding for a full minute.

Then he spoke. "I am standing before a people who have again raised their heads," he said. "The ideal of socialism with a human face is living in the conditions of a new generation. We must unify to raise our country to a higher level, a free Czechoslovakia.

"An old wise man said, 'If there once was light, why should there by darkness again?' Let us act in such a way to bring the light back again."

After the rally, the Civic Forum leaders convened on the stage of the Magic Lantern theater for their daily evening news conference. A newly built set for the play *Minotaur* provided an ironic backdrop to the press conference: an eerie-looking maze guarded by the mythical monster with a light glowing just at the end of the tunnel.

Havel and Dubcek were responding to a question about socialism.

"I believe in the reformability of socialism," Dubcek said. "We must look truth in the eyes and depart from everything that is wrong."

Havel disagreed. "For me, socialism is a word that has lost its meaning in our country. It has been only a sham word the bureaucrats used to justify their existence. I identify socialism with men like Communist party chief Jakes. I believe in social justice, and I think the only thing that can guarantee social justice is a free economy, to reintroduce the market mechanism."

The news conference was interrupted when Havel's brother, Ivan, walked on stage and whispered in Havel's ear. Havel then leaned over to Dubcek and whispered to him. Dubcek gasped in surprise, then broke into a broad grin.

Havel announced the news. Communist party chief Milos Jakes and the entire Politburo had resigned.

Applause broke out. The Civic Forum members jumped to

their feet and began hugging one another. Someone popped open a bottle of champagne, and Havel gave the toast: "Long live a free Czechoslovakia."

Prague
November 25, 1989

Clouds of sweet smoky incense drifted up to the vaulted ceiling of St. Vitus Cathedral, traversed by beams of brilliant purples and reds breaking through the rose window high at the back of the church. At the front of the church, past the massive marble columns of the magnificent cathedral, a simple portrait of St. Agnes hung suspended over the altar.

Ten thousand people were gathered inside for the first solemn liturgy in Czechoslovakia to commemorate the canonization of St. Agnes. Hundreds of thousands of others overflowed outside on the grounds of Hradcany Castle next door, despite the brittle bite of the cold morning air. This time, the entire ceremony was being broadcast on national TV.

The crowds outside chanted the name of Cardinal Tomasek, using the familiar form of his name in the Czech language as if he were an old friend. Inside, the cardinal delivered a sermon aimed at emboldening their calls for political change.

"We cannot trust these people," he said, his voice still strong and resonant, like an old church bell. "I must not be silent when you have united for a mighty protest against the injustice committed against us for four decades. . . .

"All of us, wherever we are, let us fulfill Christ's call: 'You will be my witnesses.' In this grave hour of struggle for truth and justice in our country, the Catholic church and I are on the side of the nation. We remember Christ's words: 'Blessed are those who hunger and thirst for justice, for they shall have their fill.' None of us can remain uninvolved when the future of our nation is at stake. I beg you in these days: unite courage to wisdom and refuse violence."

The injunction rang in the crowd's ears, like the cathedral bells tolling in the background, as they left the solemn liturgy and moved as one down the winding streets of Prague's castle district to join the daily protest organized by Civic Forum.

PRAGUE
November 26, 1989

The day's demonstration, the tenth in ten days, had to be moved to the Letna parade ground just across from the city's soccer stadium because the number of protesters had outgrown Wenceslas Square. Even so, the broad esplanade, an area about the size of three football fields, was covered with more than half a million people. Rising behind the crowd in the distant haze were the twin spires of St. Vitus Cathedral, ascending out of the sea of faces like the mast on a great ship.

It was so cold on the snow-swept field that journalists had a hard time taking notes; the ink in their ballpoint pens kept freezing. The demonstrators massed together, bundled up in scarves and ski caps. Clumps of people jumped up and down together to ward off the bitter cold. Yet the mood of the people was warm, joyous, even euphoric. It was more like a political pep rally than a demonstration. Banners and the familiar red, blue and white Czechoslovakian flag dotted the crowd, waving in the wind. Someone had decorated the spot where the cold bronze figure of Stalin once glared across the field with a poster of the Soviet dictator and an accompanying caption: "Was he really the last?"

Standing on a huge soundstage facing the crowd, flanked by a battery of speakers, media equipment and TV soundtrucks, was Vaclav Maly, wearing a blue parka. His broad, cherubic face beamed from behind the bank of microphones. A huge banner emblazoned with "Civic Forum" hung below the podium and its bank of microphones.

Maly was once again the moderator for the rally, leading the crowd like a cheerleader at a football game. He laughed, he cajoled, he joked, keeping the crowd's spirits high. The huge audience answered him with good-natured chants. Someone would start a chant, others would pick it up, until it spread like a wave through the entire throng.

Maly glanced at his watch and looked over at Vaclav Havel waiting in the wings. It was time to start the procession of speakers lined up for the day. He turned the microphone over to Havel. The crowd greeted him with a thunderous roar.

"Long live Havel! Long live Havel!"

"One week ago, a people's movement began in Prague," Havel told the cheering crowd. "For seven days, Prague and the entire republic have been living through great dreams. After forty years of totalitarian rule that manipulated them, citizens have started to think and act freely.

"On behalf of the Civic Forum, I can announce that what we have been calling for has happened: dialogue has begun between the power and the people. This morning, Prime Minister Adamec has met with the Civic Forum. On Tuesday, we will meet again. I thank the Prime Minister for his good will."

He paused as chants of "Adamec! Adamec!" fluttered through the crowd. The prime minister's meetings with the Civic Forum leaders were the first talks of any substance to take place between the Communist regime and the opposition.

"Tomorrow we will show our determination to achieve democracy, freedom, and peace by a symbolic general strike," Havel said. "We ask you to make sure that this strike will not threaten any vital functions of the industry, the health of the people, and lives. We do not want to disrupt our economy. We want it to function better.

"Civic Forum is ready to create a bridge for a peaceful path from totalitarianism to civil freedom, which will later be guaranteed by free elections. The Civic Forum is prepared to negotiate all stages of the peaceful journey across this bridge. . . .

"We know what we want—truth, humanity and freedom. From now on, we are all participating in the management of this country and we are responsible for its fate."

While Havel was speaking, Adamec was waiting in the wings. He was the first Communist party official to put in an appearance at the pro-democracy demonstrations. Maly introduced him after Havel finished his speech, and the crowd took up chanting his name once again.

The prime minister warily approached the microphone, looking very regimented in his hat, coat, and tie next to Havel's casual, Saturday-afternoon-at-the-professor's house, attire. Adamec wasn't used to addressing such a spontaneous demonstration. Any public appearances by the country's Communist leadership were usually before crowds carefully choreographed to show their support.

"I would like to thank the organizers of this rally for inviting me," he began. "I will gladly explain my ideas, and I will listen to the demands of any representatives of the public who are interested in finding joint solutions of the problems that exist. That is why I came here to join you."

The crowd roared its approval: "Thank you! Thank you!"

"In only a few hours, the general strike will begin," he went on. "There is some concern about what will happen and what the strike will bring. That is why I proposed to look for an approach that will keep to a minimum the damage it brings to the national economy. I am glad that all participants in the negotiations agree that it should have a symbolic character. To state your views, it is not necessary to strike for two hours. Two minutes will do."

At the suggestion to shorten the general strike, the crowd suddenly turned on him, pelting him with boos, catcalls, and derisive whistling. The prime minister seemed taken aback by the rude outburst, but continued making his point.

"We must look for unity, without suspicion. We must try to understand each other. That is why the government is prepared to negotiate with everybody caring for the good of our country. Throughout the country, there is agreement in principle on the need to speed up the reforms. Therefore it is necessary to limit the social tension as soon as possible, to end strikes and demonstrations.

"The enforcement of political demands must be in full agreement with the efforts to improve the economic situation. This is what I regard under the present conditions as the principal question."

Adamec ended with a promise to give the Central Committee a list of demands for democratic change presented to him by the Civic Forum leaders at their meeting earlier in the day. The demands included an end to one-party rule and an end to censorship. With that pledge, the crowd once again broke into cheers. When the prime minister left the microphone, it was evident to those on stage and those in the crowd that the Party was in full retreat.

Alexander Dubcek was next in the parade of speakers. He spoke with a thick Slovak accent peppered with Communist jargon, making it difficult for most of those in the audience to understand him. They interrupted him with jubilant applause just the same, and gave him a thundering ovation when he finished.

Maly appeared back on stage.

"I was ordained a priest," he said. "But because I signed Charter 77, I had to clean toilets: that's why I'm asking you now for one minute of silence for all the oppressed."

A hush suddenly fell on the boisterous crowd. There was a long silence, and the cold air was so still that those who shut their eyes could hardly believe they were standing in a field filled with half a million people.

After the moment of silence, Vaclav Benda, the political activist imprisoned with Havel, took the stage to read out a list of names of political prisoners just released on orders of the new government. Among the names on the list, Jan Carnogursky, a leading Slovak Catholic and human rights activist, and Father Stefan Javorsky, a sixty-four-year-old Slovak priest. The crowd let out a cheer for every name Benda read. After the last name on the list, they took out their keys and shook them in that CHINK CHINK CHINK CHINK peal that had come to symbolize their clamor for freedom.

The parade of speakers continued, and the protesters responded with the same enthusiasm. As folk singer Jaroslaw Chudka performed, they sang along lustily, swaying, their hands held high in the victory sign. He had just returned to his homeland from a twenty year exile. The crowd knew every word of his songs, despite the regime's ban on his music. The authorities' attempt to enforce "forgetting" had obviously failed.

The crowd was exuberant. They laughed, then cried, for joy. But then a serious note.

Havel led two people forward and Maly introduced them as high-ranking members of the security police responsible for the brutality against the student demonstration the week before. The crowd started jeering.

"They have come to apologize," Maly shouted over the loudspeaker. The crowd fell silent. He could almost sense their desire for revenge.

A tall, good-looking man wearing a fatigue-colored parka stepped forward and looked at the stony faces.

"My name is Ludwig Pinc," he told the crowd. "I'm a lieutenant in the Prague police department. We see that it's a tragedy that we were enlisted to stop the democratic changes now taking place. Most of us joined the public security with the understanding that we would use our power to fight against the criminal element, not to oppress regular working citizens."

The statement elicited cheers from the crowd.

"We share some of the blame for what happened during the last days," he said. "After the unpleasant events on November 17, there's a growing animosity of citizens toward the police. We want to tell you that none of our members had the legal right to use force to suppress the people. But this order didn't come from the police. This was a decision made by the higher-ups in the government."

He was interrupted by jeers. "What lies!" the crowd shouted together.

Maly put up his hands to hush the crowd. The young officer continued facing them, standing stiff and formal. He raised his voice to be heard over the angry chants. "We want to give you our support for the new democratic changes in our country. I want to express our profound apology that our leaders set us against the people of our own country. Last week, the striking students offered their hands to us in friendship. We want to reach out and accept their outstretched hands now."

It was an emotional moment. A few in the audience wiped away tears with their sleeves. One of the other junior officers standing to the side joined his colleague at the podium. He was wearing the red-banded green cap of the security police.

"I just want to add that I hope I never see the day when the people of this country stand against one another," he said.

When the two finished speaking, Maly took the microphone. His face was solemn. The crowd was still.

"We have to be proud of these members of the security police who came forward to apologize," he said. "They could be risking jail for their actions, and we have to protect them. Thank you for your understanding. Whenever there's political change, there's always the danger of the powerless seeking retribution against the powerful. Now, I'm not asking you to forget what those in power have done.

But I am asking you to show forgiveness. Forgiveness is more than a word. There's power in forgiveness. There's hope in forgiveness. Now, will you accept their apology?"

There was an ominous silence. Then, a chant commenced, faint at first, but growing louder and louder, until the voice of half a million became one voice.

"We forgive you! We forgive you!"

Maly stood there, tears in his eyes. When the chanting subsided, he said, "I would like to end this special moment with a prayer. Those of you who know the words, I invite you to say them aloud with me. Those of you who don't know the words, pray with me in your hearts."

He began reciting the Lord's Prayer. Some in the audience prayed along, others fumbled for the words, until Letna field rang with the sound of a prayer that no one had dared to utter in public in more than forty years.

PRAGUE
November 27, 1989

The lecture hall was filled with university students listening in rapt attention as Maly instructed them in the fine points of publicizing their cause, points he had learned from years of working with Charter 77 and VONS. The students trusted him. He had developed a certain rapport with many of them as he had come to know them over the past few years during the unofficial lectures and masses held in various apartments.

"Now the tables are turned," he exhorted the students from a podium in front of the classroom. "Instead of being educated, it's up to you to educate the people. You have the power of the truth on your side."

After the pep talk, off they went. The students had set up working battalions in their classrooms, gymnasiums, and lecture halls to rally support for the general strike. Volunteers in the bustling basement of the Magic Lantern churned out posters proclaiming slogans remarkably reminiscent of the Communist Manifesto like, "Workers, join us for freedom!" Others grabbed the signs and plastered them in the city's subways, shop windows, and on street corners.

Students ventured out two by two to factories and enterprises, armed with pictures and videotapes documenting the violence used against them in Wenceslas Square. They stood in factory yards in the cold morning air, puffing out their strike appeals as workers filed by to start the day. Some were kicked out. Others were given the chance to come back and make their case after work.

It was crucial to get the backing of the workers. Intellectuals had always been the vanguard of the opposition. The country's working class had been bought off by the state, their mouths filled with food and beer, both cheap and plentiful, to keep them shut. In return for higher salaries and a better standard of living than most Eastern bloc countries, the workers tacitly agreed not to speak out. Without the support of the country's factories and farms, the crescendo of voices calling for change would drop off into a faint, isolated voice. For the Civic Forum leaders, the general strike was high noon.

When twelve o'clock finally arrived, it was as if the entire country had walked off the job and into the streets. Shops were darkened, factories shut down, mass transit ground to a halt, and the city of Prague was filled with the sound of church bells clanging out their protest.

At a brewery in the working class district of Branik, a worker in grimy overalls named Zdenek Janicek climbed onto a platform and addressed his fellow strikers,

"We hold these truths to be self-evident," he said, "that all men are created equal, that they are endowed by their creator with certain inalienable rights, that among these are life, liberty and the pursuit of happiness. Americans understood these rights more than two hundred years ago. We are only now learning to believe that we are entitled to the same rights."[1]

Prague
December 4, 1989

Maly appeared at the speaker's balcony overlooking Wenceslas Square after dropping out of sight for several days. The crowd below was restless and angry. The sense of victory and euphoria that marked the demonstrations the week before had vanished. In its place was shock, disappointment, and defiance.

A new cabinet had just been announced. Instead of the broad-based coalition Adamec had promised in negotiations, only five of the twenty-one positions had gone to non-Communists, and only one of the new ministers was even remotely close to Civic Forum. The people's spirits were deflated. Civic Forum had to do something to revive their flagging hopes.

Maly had spent the week holed up with other Civic Forum leaders behind the door in the Magic Lantern theater marked "Smoking Room" in crudely painted letters. In the room's cloudy confines, he had been pushing to keep up the pressure on the government. While others were hailing the prime minister's pledge to put together a new government based on a broad coalition, Maly told the group, "It's premature to celebrate. We still have a difficult stage of negotiations ahead of us." When the National Assembly voted to abolish the leading role of the Communist party, Maly still wasn't satisfied. "The changes are merely cosmetic," he stated flatly. "They don't go far enough." And while some Civic Forum members were talking of a willingness to compromise with the more moderate Communists, Maly held his ground. "For me, there are no reformists in the Communist party," he argued. "There are only those who try to accommodate to save themselves."

A moratorium on public protests had been declared during the past week to give Adamec time to form a new government. But when the new positions were announced, Civic Forum called for renewed mass protests and threatened another general strike if a new government wasn't formed within a week. Now was the true test of the opposition's strength and will. As the light of the cold, gray day began to fade and darkness settled over Wenceslas Square, it was up to Maly to resurrect the people's hopes for real change and get the opposition moving again.

"We will not sit idly by as the neo-Stalinists continue to hold onto power," Maly said, his voice reverberating over the crowd. His youthful face seemed somehow older, suddenly aged with a new seriousness and intensity. The crowd erupted to life, clapping, chanting, cheering, as he launched into a rousing speech outlining a new list of demands from Civic Forum and its counterpart opposition group in Slovakia, Public Against Violence.

"The basic objective of Civic Forum and Public Against

Violence is to form a situation for free elections, which must be held by July 1990 at the latest," he shouted over the agitated crowd. "Civic Forum and Public Against Violence can ensure the holding of free elections if they become an organization and consistent coalition of all the political forces in our society. We therefore recommend that Civic Forum and Public Against Violence enter into these elections with a common list of candidates."

It was the first time Civic Forum had announced its intention to become a political party in direct competition with the Communists.

"After the elections, individual political parties can spin off Civic Forum and Public Against Violence," Maly continued. "We also assure that we will at the same time serve as a guarantee of the whole process of development toward a democratic state."

The crowd was with him now. The momentum was rolling again.

"We need your support now more than ever!" he shouted.

"You have it," the crowd cried, and then began chanting, "Long live Maly! Long live Maly!"

The Czechoslovak government met Civic Forum's deadline to the day. Adamec resigned as prime minister. He was replaced by another Communist, but for the first time since the Communists took power, they were reduced to the minority in the cabinet. Of the twenty-one other ministerial posts, only ten went to party members, and two of those were closely aligned with Civic Forum. Civic Forum and Public Against Violence filled seven of the positions, while the Socialist and People's parties received two seats each.

The new government was sworn in on Sunday, December 10, by hardliner Gustav Husak, who then promptly resigned as president. It was an appropriate day for the changing of the guard—UN Human Rights Day.

Note

1. Esther B. Fein, "Unshackled Czech Workers Declare Their Independence," *New York Times*, 28 November 1989, 1.

15

Romania

Romanian president Nicolae Ceausescu was making it clear that his country would have nothing to do with the trends toward democracy sweeping the Eastern bloc. The point was driven home at a major Communist party congress. "Some Socialist countries have adopted measures with a view to increasing the wealth of some people and increasing the number of the poor," he said. "This focus is not Socialist, and we cannot admit it in any way."

But in Timisoara, a town where nothing ever seemed to change, except for the worst, where the drudgery of waiting in line and putting up with the scarcity of essential items had worn the people down into a surly subservience, the people were waiting, hoping for a change. They were tired of the corruption, tired of only being able to buy things on the black market. The official economy had virtually collapsed, while the country's second economy, the black market, was thriving. That could be seen in front of the Continental Hotel, where small groups of black marketeers carried out their transactions surreptitiously, always on the lookout, like crows picking at a carcass on a busy highway. The lei, *Romania's currency, was worthless here. Swiftly changing hands instead were dollars and Kent cigarettes. (For some unknown reason, Kents had been elevated to a symbol of status in this topsy-turvy economy, and Kent Golds were like gold itself.)*

With its ethnic mixture of Hungarians, Germans, Serbs and Romanians, the city of Timisoara was a volcano bubbling with discontent. The people knew it was ready to explode anytime, but the repressive measures employed by Ceausescu kept everything bottled up, everyone fearful of taking any action. Nevertheless, there was a saying being repeated from mouth to mouth in Timisoara: "Christmas will come soon, and with it will come our salvation." Perhaps they sensed the demonstration around Tokes's church was the advent of their long-awaited deliverance.

TIMISOARA, ROMANIA
December 15, 1989

It was an unusually warm day for December, beautiful, clear, spring-like. Word had spread through the city, the way word spreads in a country starved for information: today was the day Tokes would be evicted. The news was also being broadcast by the Hungarian media. The members of Tokes's congregation knew the power of publicity. It was their only weapon against the powerful regime. They had contacted friends in Hungary to ask them to publicize the impending eviction. One of Zoltan Balaton's contacts, a journalist, called him at three in the morning each day when there was less chance of security listening in for an update on the situation.

The first to arrive outside the church Friday morning was a handful of old ladies from the congregation, looking anything but revolutionary in the traditional garb of Hungarian widows, tightly wrapped babushkas, plain black dresses, and black shawls.Other parishioners started to join them. The group soon swelled to about forty or fifty people, filling the narrow side street beside the church entrance.

People waiting at the tramline across the street noticed the crowd starting to build beside the church. In Romania, where the only organized demonstrations are those officially sanctioned by the Communist party, a gathering of any size is an unusual occurrence.

The number of people jammed together, elbow to elbow, in the alley-like street looked like a huge demonstration.

There was no sign of any uniformed police yet. But a few plain-clothes members of the Securitate could be spotted in front of the church entrance, moving their heads from side to side in a tell-tale motion that looked like a nervous tick, keeping an obvious eye on developments.

Tokes was also watching the crowd congregate from the window of the church office where he was waiting. It was a complete surprise to him. So many people! He really had not expected such an outpouring of support. A feeling of joy and satisfaction flooded over him. At the same time, he was filled with terror. He knew the power of the Romanian authorities and just how ruthlessly they could wield it.

He opened the window, poked out his head and greeted his new-found group of supporters. "I'm not sure what's going to happen," he shouted over the hum of the crowd. "No one's showed up yet, and I don't know when they're coming for me. But as far as I know, I'm still being evicted."

A voice rang out from the back of the crowd. "We won't leave you, Pastor. We're standing with you, Pastor." There was a sense that as long as the people stayed there, perhaps the authorities would reconsider the eviction. As a sign of their support, the crowd began passing food to the isolated apartment through the windows, loaves of bread, followed by milk, eggs, even meat. Tokes was humbled by the generous gesture. He knew what a sacrifice it was in the face of such severe shortages. He thanked them for their support and with-drew back inside.

The crowd continued to multiply hour by hour. At first, there were just members of Tokes's parish. Then they were joined by members of the Baptist church down the street, and later by believers from other denominations. Then townspeople getting off work stepped down from the trams clanging to a stop across the street and joined the throng. By the time darkness fell, a human chain stretched around the church, members of the Reformed congregation joining hands with Baptists, Baptists linking arms with Orthodox, Orthodox with Catholics, believers with unbelievers. Most miraculously of all, for perhaps the first time in their history, ethnic Romanians stood side by side with ethnic Hungarians, joining hands in a common cause.

Word of what was going on had also reached the town's Communist party headquarters. The nervous party officials inside were trying to decide what to do. The images of Leipzig, Berlin and Prague haunted them. The Romanian regime had stood fast, vowing to protect the Socialist gains under Ceausescu from capitalist encroachment. They could not let things get out of hand like their Communist counterparts had over the past two months. The town's mayor, Petru Mots, was dispatched to get the situation under control.

Mots arrived with a delegation to the unsettling sight of hundreds of his townspeople surrounding the church of this "renegade" pastor. He elbowed his way through the mass of people until he stood on the sidewalk, just under the window where Tokes was taking refuge.

The mayor had to yell over the din of the crowd. "Pastor Tokes, I want to talk to you." Tokes agreed to meet him at the gate of the courtyard.

"I have an offer for you," the mayor told him. "If you'll just speak to the crowd and tell them to go home, we'll work it out so you can stay on at the church. The eviction will be called off."

Tokes debated what to do. He feared a violent confrontation would erupt if he remained holed up inside. He didn't want to be a revolutionary. He just wanted the right to minister freely.

He deliberated, then returned to his apartment, threw open the window and addressed the people massed outside. "It looks like we've got what we came here for," he shouted. "The authorities promise I can stay. The problem's solved. I'm not out for any political gains. I'm asking you to trust God, be peaceful, and leave."

The appeal met with a wave of grumbling from the crowd. A voice rose up somewhere in the midst of it: "We don't trust them. We don't trust them."

More shouts erupted: "Don't leave, Pastor. We love you. We'll protect you."

The mayor then turned to face the vocal mass. When he tried to appeal to them, he was shouted down, his words drowned out by their angry chant: "You leave! We'll stay!"

They were glaring at him, anger in their eyes, rage in their voices. Boos and catcalls followed him as he pushed his way back through the crowd and departed, their derision echoing in his ears.

After the mayor departed, a twenty-four-year-old railway engineer from the Baptist church named Daniel Gavra took out a bundle of candles hidden under his coat and passed them out. He lit the first one and watched the warm glow spread as the flame flowed from candle to candle. In the pale candlelight, the crowd began to sing hymns and pray.

The vigil continued throughout the night, several hundred people strong. The morning light found demonstrators sprawled all around the church, still singing, praying and refusing to move.

By Saturday afternoon, the crowd surged to several thousand as more and more townspeople joined the demonstration. The narrow street beside the church was jammed with people.

From inside, Tokes heard the strains of a familiar song. He listened more closely to place the melody. He couldn't believe his ears. The crowd was singing a Romanian national hymn called, "Romanians Awake!" It was a popular song dating back to the revolution of 1848. The sound overwhelmed him, his eyes brimmed with tears. Here they were, ethnic Romanians, singing their own patriotic hymn for a Hungarian pastor who had been pilloried as a chauvinistic anti-Romanian enemy of the state. The words once repugnant to him took on new meaning. He heard them with new ears, their power nearly wounding him as they cut away at the very heart of his prejudices. Romanians and Hungarians had always been at odds, their age-old hatred fostered by the regime. This hymn once divided them, Tokes thought. Now it was uniting them.

As it grew dark, a lone voice from somewhere in the middle of the crowd, the voice of a young factory worker, finally expressed what the people so desperately wanted to shout: "Down with Ceausescu!"

The three simple words struck the crowd like an electric jolt, galvanizing opposition against the hated regime. Years of dissatisfaction and discontent came spewing out in a cacophonous chorus. "Down with the dictatorship!" "Ceausescu, come and get us!" "We want bread!" "We want liberty!"

The people were sensing their power now, and the vulnerability of the Party that had been in power for more than forty years.

Suddenly someone began to shout "On to the Party headquarters!" and everyone took up the cry and started marching toward the center of town. Inside his apartment, as the sound of the crowd's chanting became fainter and fainter, Tokes prepared himself for a violent fate. "It's our destiny," he thought. "I can do nothing at all to control this crowd, to control their feelings. The streets are now full, and that means the hour of our death."

The volatile crowd converged in front of the Communist party headquarters, a steely gray building on the Boulevard of August 23, just down from the Continental Hotel. Thousands of people were moving through the city, as legions of workers and students streamed into the city center from the campuses of Timisoara University and the city's Polytechnic Institute and outlying factories.

The group outside the Party headquarters continued shouting their defiant slogans and demanded a meeting with the authorities sequestered away behind the granite facade. The Prime Minister, Constantin Dascalescu, appeared on the balcony with the local party leader. Dascalescu was there on the orders of Bucharest to restore order. When they told the crowd to go home, they were met with a round of boos and jeering and more chants of "Down with Ceausescu!"

The two retreated back inside, and the crowd, more of a mob now, surged toward the entrance to the Party headquarters and pushed their way inside. They rushed through the corridors lined with pictures of Ceausescu, ripped portraits off the wall and threw them out the windows. Another group broke into a storeroom, where they discovered cases of hard-to-get goods like coffee and salami. This enraged them even more.

Thousands tore through the city, ripping down the ubiquitous red banners and posters inscribed with party slogans and setting them on fire. They tore down the Romanian national flag and ripped out the Communist emblem at the center to create the donut-hole flag that would become the symbol of the uprising. Bonfires dotted the streets where people broke into bookstores, grabbed Communist party literature and books of speeches by Ceausescu, piled them up outside, then torched them.

A group of teenagers armed with sticks broke off from the demonstrators and went on a rampage through the downtown area, breaking all the shop windows. The teenagers were apparently provocateurs, young toughs hired by the Securitate to stir up violence and give the local militia an excuse to break up the protests.

Several fire trucks pulled up, their sirens screaming. Water hoses were turned on the demonstrators. But the mob began to fight back, seizing one fire truck and setting it on fire. They attacked another truck parked on a bridge, turning it over into the river below.

Militia squads, along with Securitate and army troops, moved in with truncheons, bayonets, and tear gas. They fired blank shots to disperse the crowds. As the panicked protesters began running, police armed with sticks, shields, and helmets chased them, flailing their billy clubs and forcing bloodied protesters onto buses under arrest.

Many of the protesters were brutally beaten. Others were tortured later. But the crackdown failed to stop the protest. A large contingent of demonstrators who fled the assault made their way back to the church to continue the vigil there. There, as the chill of the night began to set in, they circled the church and waited once more for the security forces to arrive.

Timisoara, Romania
December 17, 1989

It was four in the morning. Tokes and his wife had fallen into bed exhausted. Six friends who slipped into their apartment during the confusion of the day's events were keeping vigil with them.

Tokes woke with a start, "Laszlo, wake up!" One of his friends was shaking him. "The militia's here. They're breaking down the doors."

It sounded like a battering ram was pounding on the gate to their courtyard. Laszlo quickly roused Edith and the two of them scrambled into the pitch-black basement and took the secret way into the church, climbing the 30-foot ladder in the darkness, followed by two of their friends.

What seemed like a battalion of soldiers, police and Securitate had surrounded the church and were hauling off demonstrators, beating those who tried to resist.

Inside, the security officers seemed to be coming from every direction, pouring into the courtyard like storm troopers. Using the butts of their rifles, they smashed in the doors protecting Tokes one by one, ripping through them like cardboard.

The invading Securitate officers tackled the four friends who had stayed behind to create a diversion. When they struggled to get up, the militia men slammed them back against the cold, hard concrete, and began kicking and beating them. The four groaned in pain as they were led away to a van waiting to take them to Securitate headquarters downtown where more brutal beatings awaited them.

Laszlo and Edith Tokes barricaded themselves inside the sanctuary with the two others, Edith's brother-in-law and a student. They waited, panting for breath, listening for footsteps, hearing the heavy thud of the militia bounding up the stairs. Their eyes were fixed on the heavy wooden double doors, the last barrier between them and their would-be captors.

The officers were just outside, battering the door. The rhythmic pounding shook the whole sanctuary, the sound vibrating throughout the cavernous space. The group trapped inside watched as the doors began to buckle, inch by inch, gradually giving way under the force of the methodical hammering. Suddenly, in a blur of motion, the doors flew open and the police were upon them.

Tokes was ready, dressed in his clerical robe, Bible in hand. The police grabbed him, ripping his robe, and began savagely beating him. They carted him downstairs, bloodied and bruised, and then began dragging Edith after him, heedlessly disregarding that she was three months pregnant. The two were trundled to Tokes's office, where they were met by two officials from the Office of Religious Affairs and forced to sign an eviction notice.

They were then pushed outside to a waiting convoy of five automobiles. Tokes was shoved into one, his wife into another. The friends arrested with them had disappeared in the darkness, surrounded by a host of militia men.

Tokes looked out the window as the convoy made its way through Timisoara. He had no idea where they were taking him, but he feared the worst. He surveyed the streets of the city, shocked by the signs of the clash between the demonstrators and police, the shattered shop windows, the smoldering wreckage of a fire truck, the mutilated pictures of Ceausescu littering the streets. And everywhere, soldiers. The city had been turned into a battlefield. The revolution had begun.

BUCHAREST
December 17, 1989

Nicolae and Elena Ceausescu were enraged that troops held back their fire and failed to use live ammunition to crush the demonstrations in Timisoara. On Sunday, the ruling couple convened an emergency meeting of the Romanian Communist party's Political Executive Committee. With the use of a closed circuit television hookup from the room where they were meeting in Bucharest, they got in touch with the remote sites where some of Ceausescu's generals and top men were monitoring events. Emil Bobu, the Party's ideology chief, and Ioan Coman, the secretary of the Communist Party Central Committee, had joined Prime Minister Dascalescu in Timisoara.

"Why didn't they shoot?" President Ceausescu demanded of his defense minister, Vasile Milea. "They should have shot to put them on the ground, to warn them, shot them in the legs."

He was livid, threatening to fire him, along with the Internal Affairs Minister, Lt. Gen. Iulian Vlad. He decided to give them another chance only after several members of the executive committee argued that they should not make any personnel changes until after the protests were quashed.

"Starting today, all units of the Interior Ministry, the militia, security troops, and border guards will have fighting weapons in them, including bullets," Ceausescu ordered. "Anyone who tries to enter a state institution or party headquarters, or who breaks a shop window must be immediately shot. Everybody who doesn't submit to the soldiers, I've given the order to shoot. They'll get a warning, and if they don't submit they'll have to be shot. It was a mistake to turn the other cheek.

"Relay my order to all officers," Ceausescu barked at Gen. Coman. "I want calm restored in Timisoara in one hour. Call everybody. Give orders and execute them. Understood?"

"Yes, Comrade Secretary General," Coman said. "I can inform you that right now three columns of soldiers are entering Timisoara. I report to you that I have ordered them to shoot."

TIMISOARA, ROMANIA

All was still quiet when Cornel Marincu passed by Tokes's church Friday on his way to work. There were only about fifty people assembled there. He knew a little of what was going on. He had heard about the vigil from a member of Tokes's congregation who worked with him at the Polytechnic Institute. He himself was a member of the Pentecostal Church. In fact, he was one of the leaders in the church, although you would not know it by the looks of him. Everything about him was understated. You almost had to lean forward to catch what he was saying. His voice barely seemed to rise above a whisper; the earnest expression in his quiet eyes never seemed to change. Hardly the boisterous, charismatic figure you might expect to find in the forefront of a church noted for its lively, emotional services. Yet his soft-spoken seriousness commanded respect, his straight-forward manner earned him the trust of his fellow church members.

Marincu cast a sympathetic glance at the budding protest as he hurried to the Polytechnic. Theirs was a bold action. He knew all too well the problems of putting up with government restrictions on religion. He himself had gotten into a bit of trouble at work. His job involved instructing ten to fifteen students in using a lathe machine. He worked closely with them, standing behind them and guiding them while they worked on the lathe to hone large chunks of wood. As he got to know them, he began telling them about his faith. Word reached his superiors that Marincu was proselytizing. He was summoned for a talk with his supervisor and warned that speaking so freely could cost him his job.

As Marincu performed at his lathe, he hardly gave the vigil a second thought. Not until Saturday night, when he was returning from visiting some friends in town to his simple home on the outskirts of Timisoara and heard people shouting slogans against the government, did he realize the small demonstration had ignited a fuse that threatened to blow the city apart.

He drove back into town Sunday morning. He had to see what would happen. As he approached the center of town, he felt like he was entering a city he'd never seen before, a completely different one from the place where he lived and worked and raised his children. It was a city under siege. The Securitate and army units had received substantial reinforcements during the early morning hours. Columns of tanks were rolling into the city from their secluded bases around the country. Some armored columns had already taken position throughout the city, their long-barreled guns glinting in the sunlight. Riot police with shields and young soldiers with mounted bayonets stood guard on every street corner.

The authorities moved quickly to ban all tourist travel into Romania and sealed off the country's borders with Bulgaria, Yugoslavia, and Hungary. The official news agency, Agerpress, offered a rather implausible explanation for the action. "Romania cannot receive any foreign tourists, as there are no free places in Romanian hotels," the news agency said. "All are occupied."

It seemed the entire city had taken to the streets. Tens of thousands were crammed in the city center, shouting their defiant slogans. Students and workers had rallied their colleagues to the cause. They were spurred on by the rumors running rampant, rumors that Tokes had been molested, that his pregnant wife, Edith, had been beaten. The couple's whereabouts was still unknown.

Marincu navigated his Soviet-made Skoda through jammed streets, backtracking, detouring around road blocks. He headed toward the sound reverberating throughout the city, the sound of chants echoing and ricocheting off the high-rise apartment buildings lining the streets, until he joined the mass of protesting people. He noticed the number of young people, even children, in the crowd, hundreds of teenagers standing on the front-lines, shouting fearlessly. "We want bread!" "We want heat!" The stone-faced soldiers opposite them, just a couple of years older really, watched, ready for confrontation, rifles in hand. Marincu thought to himself, "Surely the soldiers won't shoot."

—•—

Later that afternoon, a crowd of people gathered in front of the

Party headquarters. The mass pulsated with fervor like a huge heart, drawing courage from the rhythmic beat of their chanting, hurling their defiant demands at the phalanx of security forces facing them. "Come with us!" they yelled. The forces responded with a volley of machine gun fired into the air as warning shots. When the protesters stood their ground and refused to disperse, the guns were turned on them. The troops opened fire, mowing down a line of children standing in front of the crowd. They fired again, and another three rows fell to the ground, dead or wounded.

But people were still standing, still shouting. "What are you doing?" they screamed in disbelief at the approaching soldiers. "We are the people, without guns." And then, staring straight into the face of death, the chants continued: "Down with Ceausescu! Down with communism!"

Zoltan Balaton was in the Continental Hotel where his wife worked as a waitress when he heard the first shots. He ran over to a window and saw thousands of panicked people running helter-skelter toward the hotel from the direction of the Party headquarters. A line of tanks rumbled after them, herding them like cattle past the sundial-like clock next to the Continental into the tree-lined park behind the hotel. People were screaming, nearly trampling one another to get out of the tanks' path. The armored column continued its deadly pursuit, corralling about fifteen thousand people inside the park. When there was no room left for the people to run, the tanks kept coming, one crushing a forty-year-old woman under its tread.

The war was on. Soldiers from both the army and the Securitate shot at the crowd of demonstrators on the ground, from tanks and from moving cars. Helicopters swooped in and joined the attack. Snipers appeared on the roofs of buildings and fired on protesters below. It was the same bloody story throughout the city.

A group of twenty-five uniformed Securitate soldiers confronted a crowd of mostly teenagers shouting slogans in front of the Chemistry High School.

Their cries of "Freedom!" were answered with a long burst of machine gun fire. The protesters standing at the front of the crowd crumpled to the ground in a bloody heap.

After several minutes, the voices, though fainter, started up again: "Freedom!"

Another savage round of gunfire.

A feeble chant rose up again, only a few voices now: "Freedom!"

After a third blast of machine-gun fire, the voices fell silent.

In the city's Liberty Square near the army garrison's headquarters, a young mother got caught up in a stampede of protesters fleeing the approaching tanks. She was cradling her baby in her arms, and dragging another child by the hand, desperately trying to get to safety. She felt the child slip out of her grasp and jump from the sidewalk onto the street. When she rushed over to retrieve the child, she looked up to see the tank's caterpillar track heading right for them. All three were killed instantly.

In the downtown area, security forces chased escaping protesters into the eight-story apartment buildings along the streets, shooting into windows and dragging them out of the staircases where they were hiding. A soldier spied two children from the fourth-floor balcony of one of the buildings shouting anti-Ceausescu slogans and tossing rocks onto the forces below. He ran into the building, bounded up the stairs, broke into the apartment and shot all eight people inside.[1]

Another group escaping the melee in Opera Square rushed toward the Orthodox Cathedral for refuge. They thought it would be safe. As they stumbled up the steps into the church's columned portico, the troops fired on them, directly into the cathedral. A barrage of bullets riddled the mosaic tiles decorating the cathedral's entrance. About twenty-five people fell dead, their blood trickling down the cathedral steps.

—•—

Cornel Marincu's wife, Mary, was attending evening services at the First Baptist Church when she heard the news of the shootings. At the end of the service, the pastor of the church, Peter Dugulescu, approached the pulpit visibly shaken.

"I've just received a message that the police are shooting people in the city, and that many people have been killed tonight," he announced. "We need to pray that God will show his mercy on Timisoara and Romania."

While Mary's face flushed with anxiety at the news, she was

relieved that Cornel had decided to return home from the city just before she left for church. At least he was home safe. He had told her about the volatile scene he witnessed that morning in the city and warned her to be careful.

On her way home from church, Mary heard the distant crackle of gunfire. She picked up her pace on the way to the car. She discovered later that two young girls who left the service that evening were gunned down by marauding Securitate. She rushed home to find Cornel there waiting for her. She nearly jumped into his arms, as if they'd been apart for years, sobbing softly, her tears dampening her husband's shirt as he pressed her against his chest. They were tears of joy and relief, that her husband was home safe, mingled with tears of grief over the deaths in the city.

Cornel took her face in his hands and stroked her moist cheeks, using his thumb to wipe away the splotches of tears.

"Did you hear?" she asked, looking up into his gentle eyes. "They're shooting people in the city."

"I heard," he answered softly. "I was afraid it would come to this."

"Thank God we're safe at home," she said.

He pulled her against his tall, wiry frame, trying to reassure her of his presence. Then he looked down into her face, his eyes dark with determination.

"Mary, I've been praying about this, and I think I need to go back on the streets."

"What?" She recoiled from his embrace. "Tonight?"

He nodded in resolute silence.

"You can't be serious! You'll be killed! People are still dying on the streets."

"I know," he said. "But I don't think it's right for us to stay inside while others die for us. It's not right to receive a blessing bought with the price of other people's blood."

"But what about the children? We have to think of them, too."

They had six children. The oldest, Andrea, was only eleven. The youngest was still in diapers.

"You can stay at home to be with the children," he answered slowly, still thinking through the decision. "That way, you'll be here to provide for them if," he hesitated a moment, his voice trailing off, "anything happens to me."

"But why do you need to put yourself in danger?" she protested. "We can stay here together and pray for the situation. We're always talking in church about the power of prayer. Staying here and praying is just as important as going out on the street."

"There's a time to pray and a time to be involved," he answered. "This is a time to be involved."

A little later, the phone rang. It was a friend from church who worked at the phone company, calling to warn them to stay at home. Someone at work had overheard Ceausescu give the order to destroy Timisoara.

The words of the warning hung there, then came thundering down on Mary. "You see how dangerous it is. You can't go back out there," she pleaded. She wanted to throw her arms around him and hold him there.

"I can't stay at home," he said quietly. Mary knew that voice—a gentle, confident voice that seemed to be able to quiet any storm. "I have to be on the streets. God is with us. We have to trust Him. He can give us the strength to stand against the government."

"I know you have to go," she said with resignation.

The two embraced, lingering in each other's arms, aware that this could be their last moment together. They bowed their heads and prayed together. Then Cornel sneaked into the living room to get a glimpse of the children, pulled away and headed out the door, back to the center of the city.

—•—

Back in the fray, Cornel Marincu wanted to rip out his eyes. They burned with the painful reminder of the tanks and troops coming at them, tossing tear gas, firing shots.

People were running everywhere, running to escape, running to tend to the bodies of their friends, children, wives, and husbands lying on the pavement—people who just minutes before were full of life and passion and glory. He could barely see, his eyes blinded by the sting of the tear gas. He tried to run for protection from the marauding troops, dodging other protesters running for safety.

Ambulances were screaming back and forth from the hospital,

picking up the dead and wounded strewn across the city. Scattered crowds of demonstrators still clinging to their ideals continued sporadic protests throughout the city, some even shouting, "We do not care if we die!" Marincu was amazed at their courage.

A car whizzed by, and in the blur Marincu could just make out some men in civilian clothes pointing snub-nosed barrels out of the window, taking pot shots at the clumps of people. Marincu froze and dropped to the ground. He saw two people hit by the gunfire, knocked over backwards by its force, before the car sped out of sight.

Another car screeched to a halt just in front of him, and two people in plainclothes got out. Marincu started to dash away, then realized they were stopping to load a wounded companion into the car. It was hard to know whom to trust. He had to be on the lookout for plainclothes Securitate officers as well as uniformed troops.

He picked himself up and took off again, trying to reach the relative safety of the nearby apartment buildings. All around him, troops were rounding up demonstrators, beating them and stabbing them with bayonets before forcing them onto trucks for unknown destinations. Out of the corner of his eye he saw several uniforms running toward him, pointing their rifles in his direction. Marincu took off sprinting. He heard a quick POP, POP, POP. They were shooting at him. He spotted a side street ahead and quickly darted into it, listening for the clatter of footsteps in pursuit. There were none. They must have found another quarry.

Marincu edged his way along the high-rise buildings, staying in the shadows and off the street. Just ahead, he spied another uniformed army patrol. He quickly ducked out of sight, but he could hear the soldiers' conversation in the distance. It sounded like they were arguing. One of them—the commander, he presumed—was yelling at another soldier.

"When I issue an order, I expect it to be obeyed! Our orders are to fire on the anti-Communist hooligans. Understood?"

"But they're our own people," the soldier protested.

"So you're refusing to obey a direct order?" The voice was full of rage.

"I refuse to shoot my own people."

Marincu flinched at the next sound he heard, the sound of a weapon being fired at close range.

Mineu, Romania
December 19, 1989

Tokes was being interrogated for the third time that day. He and his wife never knew when they were going to come for them and cart them to the militia headquarters in the nearby town of Zalau for more questioning. The sessions seemed never-ending, one after another, often in the middle of the night. His eyes told the story of the relentless psychological pressure they were exerting on him. They were laced with spidery lines of red and ringed with black, not by beatings, but by lack of sleep.

Edith was not exempt from the interrogations either, even though she was pregnant. She was taken to a separate room where they used all kinds of psychological tricks to coerce her into testifying against her husband. Laszlo feared she was on the verge of a nervous breakdown.

The couple had been transported to Mineu, the remote village where they were to be exiled originally, and placed under house arrest. They were taken to the primitive wooden cabin that once served as the village's Reformed parsonage. It hadn't been used for years. There was little heat, no running water. The rundown cottage became their prison. Barbed wire was erected all around the house. It was patrolled night and day by Securitate agents with vicious dogs. Blinding floodlights illumined the house by night. After they arrived, a few of their belongings were unceremoniously dumped on the bare, wooden floorboards, all jumbled together.

Special Securitate interrogators were brought in from Bucharest to conduct the interrogations. They seemed to be preparing Tokes for some kind of show trial. The Securitate wanted him to go on radio and TV to confess to his "crimes" against the Romanian state, to admit responsibility for the revolt in Timisoara.

"Admit that you're an agent of Hungary and Western capitalism," they said. "We know you were paid in dollars to organize an uprising against the Socialist Republic of Romania."

They thrust a declaration into his face to sign. When he refused, the line of questioning started all over again.

That evening, after the grueling round of interrogations, Laszlo and Edith shivered together in their cold cabin prison around a short-wave radio they had found among the disorderly pile of their possessions. They had quickly hidden it away before their captors discovered they had forgotten to remove it. Of course, Laszlo realized, perhaps this was another psychological trick. Maybe his interrogators wanted him to hear about the bloody suppression of the uprising in his hometown, hoping the news would pressure him into signing their prepared confession. If so, the ploy was working. The news he heard was chilling. There were reports of thousands being massacred in Timisoara. He wondered about the members of his congregation, his friends and supporters. How many of them were still alive?

BUCHAREST
December 20, 1989

Ceausescu returned to Bucharest from a state visit to Iran hoping to have a written confession from Tokes in hand. He apparently planned to read it at a massive rally the next day as proof the uprising in Timisoara was the work of Western agents. Tokes disappointed him.

Word was already spreading throughout the country of the massacre in Timisoara. People listening to the BBC and Radio Free Europe were shocked to hear about their people's blood being spilled by their own government. Some residents of Timisoara were also doing their best to publicize events there, sneaking past roadblocks to visit other towns, using veiled language on the telephone to communicate to their friends in other cities what was happening.

The aging leader went on state-run TV that night to denounce the demonstrations. Standing at his side, at rigid attention, were his wife Elena and other top-ranking government officials.

"These demonstrators in Timisoara are nothing but a few groups of hooligan elements," Ceausescu raged. "On the basis of data available so far, one can say with full conviction that these actions of a terrorist nature were organized and unleashed in close connection with reactionary, imperialist, irredentist, chauvinist circles, and foreign espionage services in various foreign countries."

He was using code words familiar to Romanians throughout the country. "Irredentist, chauvinist circles" meant the country's Hungarian minority.

"The purpose of these provocative anti-national actions was to provoke disorder, to destabilize the political and economic situation, to create conditions for Romania's dismemberment, and to destroy the independence and sovereignty of our Socialist homeland," he said. "It was no coincidence that during these anti-national and terrorist actions, the radio stations in Budapest and other countries had already launched a shameful campaign of slander and lies against our country."

Tokes heard the speech on the radio from his isolated captivity, and knew it was directed at him.

The next day at noon, thousands of people assembled in Bucharest's Palace Square, duly rounded up for the contrived propaganda rally orchestrated by Ceausescu, carrying the usual laudatory placards handed out by their factory Party leaders.

Ceausescu strode to the second-floor balcony of the Central Committee headquarters adjoining the square, looking comical in his oversized black fur hat. His wife Elena stood beside him, as always.

The obligatory cheers of adulation rose to greet him as he walked forward to the microphone for the televised speech. "To begin with, I would like to extend to you warm revolutionary greetings."

The ritual cheers of "Ceausescu," "Romania," and "Communism" mingled with the echoes of his raspy voice still resounding through the square.

The president launched into an attack on what he called Hungarian "revanchists" intent on taking back Transylvania, vowing: "We will do all we can to defend the sovereignty of Romania, and the freedom and life of our people, and the well-being of the whole nation."

As he pounded the podium, his voice rising to a shout, from somewhere in the back of the crowd came the chant, "Timisoara, Timisoara!"

Then he was drowned out by a chorus of angry boos and shouts of "Down with Ceausescu!" and "Free elections."

A startled look appeared on Ceausescu's face. "What? No . . . No . . . hello, hello?" he stammered, suddenly looking very old and very vulnerable.

At that moment, Romanian TV quickly voiced over the booing with a soundtrack of canned applause, then cut into the broadcast and began playing patriotic music to cover up the jeering crowds.

After three minutes, the cameras came back to Ceausescu. He tried to resume the speech, but he was badly shaken. After bringing the rally to an abrupt end, the dictator darted back into the palace, and protests sprang up throughout the city. The revolution had come to Bucharest.

Cornel Marincu was watching the address at a neighbor's house. When he saw Ceausescu falter and the broadcast cut off, he rushed outside and, practically dancing along the dust-swept cobblestone street, began yelling: "The government has fallen!"

Neighbors leaned out of their windows, enjoying the spectacle of the one-man parade. "You're crazy," one of them hooted.

But if he was crazy, then so was all of Timisoara. It was the moment they had been hoping and praying for. They knew if the fire of the revolution they had ignited spread to Bucharest, they would be saved. They saw their own victory written all over Ceausescu's astonished face.

Bucharest
Thursday, December 21, 1989

Since Romania had been sealed off, no Western reporters were allowed in to Bucharest to cover the violence sweeping the capital. Ironically, the most accurate source of information were reports filed by East European press agencies such as Yugoslavia's *Tanjug* and the Soviet news agency, *TASS*.

One such report in *Tass* read:

> Truckloads of troops and fire engines are massing in the center of the Romanian capital.
>
> Approaches to Republic Square have been closed by Romanian Army units. The police made an attempt to disperse demonstrators and to prevent new people from joining them, but failed. The initial crowd of several hundred protesters has swelled to several thousand.
>
> The demonstrators are chanting: "Freedom!" and "Down

with dictatorship!" They are stopping buses and other passing vehicles.

Sympathizers are cheering and applauding the main group of demonstrators.

Tanks are following soldiers toting submachine-guns who are pushing the demonstrators along Bucharest's main thoroughfare. Automatic fire can be heard. Panic-stricken people seek shelter inside building entrances and yards.

At least two people were crushed to death by an armored vehicle, according to a number of demonstrators leaving the University Square.

When a group of onlookers rushed to take the victims from under the wheels of the vehicle, submachine guns were fired. The people scattered. Several people were hit and fell next to those crushed by the vehicle.

By 6:30 P.M. Moscow time, demonstrators gathered in Mageru Street, Bucharest's central thoroughfare, adjoining Republic Square. They are sealed off by Romanian troops, special militia units with clubs and plastic shields and security forces. Helicopters are patrolling over the city.

Protesters continue to shout anti-government slogans. Anti-government leaflets are plastered on houses. City streets are thronged with people. Romanian radio is broadcasting patriotic songs and reports about the country's economic achievements. Romanian television is off the air.

A submachine-gun burst has just ripped through the city's center. The reason for the shots and details of the incident are not yet known.[2]

—•—

TIMISOARA

The day before Bucharest erupted in violence, a huge protest had been called in Timisoara to storm the Party headquarters. The demonstrators were demanding the bodies of those killed during the massacre two days earlier to give them a proper burial. The brutal crackdown had successfully crushed any massive demonstrations until now. Troops dissected the city, cutting off the university, the Polytechnic, and the outlying factories to isolate the students and workers from each other. But the military buildup could not stop what was going on inside the factories and schools. Committees were forming, strikes were being called. There were rumors that workers had taken over some factories and threatened to blow them up if their demands were not met. Among the demands: that the country's leadership resign and that the army units massed in the city withdraw.

When Cornel Marincu heard about the planned protest, he went racing through his office building at the Polytechnic Institute, pounding on doors, poking his head into classrooms, corralling colleagues in the corridor, until he had rounded up a group willing to stand up to the regime's massive military force once again.

Marincu looked like some kind of Romanian Pied Piper, marching out of the building. A rag-tag line of fellow teachers and students followed him out and converged with the thousands of people filing past the Institute toward the center of the city.

Commotion ruled the streets as the procession inched through the city. The crowd waved up at office buildings and apartments, beckoning with sweeping strokes of their arms, calling out to anyone passing by: "Come join us!"

Just ahead of them was Opera Square, an expansive, manicured area at the center of the city about the size of two football fields. It looked more like an armored camp now. Troops and tanks sat in front of the city's Opera House with its alabaster balcony overlooking the square. The security forces lined the marigold-colored shops that enclosed the square, and extended clear to the other end, where the diamond-patterned cupolas of the Orthodox Cathedral, crowned with gold crosses, spired in juxtaposition to the turrets of the tanks.

The crowd continued until it could go no further, stopped by the wall of troops ringing the square. They stood face to face, deadlocked, the emotional faces of the people confronting the emotionless expressions of the soldiers clutching their automatic rifles. Yet the eyes staring back at the protesters were the eyes of the Romanian army, the country's sons, brothers, and husbands, not the blank, vacant eyes of the brainwashed Securitate units. Seemingly unaware of the consequences, the crowd shouted appeals at the troops. "The army is with us." "We are the people." "Come join us."

For fifteen minutes the stand-off lasted. Frenzied demonstrators facing stoic-looking soldiers. In the midst of the crowd, Marincu felt the tension build with the crescendo of the crowd's chanting. Just two days before, he saw his people gunned down by these soldiers. The danger was palpable. He prayed for God's protection.

Then, as if on cue, the tanks turned and began to withdraw. One by one they rolled out of the square.

The crowd stared in disbelief. Their chants fell silent as they watched the troops depart. They didn't know why, whether the withdrawal was ordered by the local army commanders or whether the Communist party leaders overseeing the operation in Timisoara gave the order. All they knew was that, miraculously, unbelievably, the army was now on the side of the people.

The scene turned delirious. Throughout the city, people ventured back onto the streets, whooping and dancing, embracing the departing soldiers, climbing onto tanks and waving the Romanian tricolor with its ragged hole in the middle. Soldiers began fraternizing with the people they had been ordered to shoot.

At least 150,000 people, nearly one-third of the city's population, swarmed into the square. It got so crowded that some teen-age boys looking for more room shinnied up the trees and lampposts edging the square and were hung onto them like banners.

It was the turning point in Timisoara. The authorities had effectively lost control of the city. The demonstrators were in charge now. They set up a committee made up of protest leaders, took over the Opera House, and turned its balcony into a platform for their demands. The spontaneously formed group called itself the Action Committee of the Romanian Democratic Front. Among its demands: the resignation of Romania's leadership, an investigation into the violent crackdown in the city, freedom of speech and the press, and free national elections.

Prime Minister Dascalescu and the other Communist officials in Timisoara were forced to enter negotiations with the newly formed leadership. On Friday, December 22, the Democratic Front formally took over power in Timisoara and declared the city free from Communist rule.

A string of speakers appeared on the balcony of the Opera House to address the huge crowds that massed in the square for pro-democracy rallies. Pastor Dugulescu was one of those invited to speak on Friday. His voice boomed from behind a microphone set up on the balcony and drifted through the square.

"Let me introduce myself," he told the massive audience. "I am Peter Dugulescu from the First Baptist Church of Timisoara. I want you to know that I myself was harassed by the Securitate. They even tried to kill me. In 1985, they staged a car accident. I survived, but as you can see, it left me with a deformed arm." One of his arms was slightly crooked, and hung limp at his side. "I've been through a lot of difficulties and problems. But I want you to know that God has been with me through them all. He has protected me. I'm alive through his grace.

"The Communists tried to take God out of our minds, out of our souls, out of history, but I tell you, God exists! God exists!"

The crowd hung on his words, and in a burst of spontaneous enthusiasm, began shouting along with him. "God exists!" "There is a God!" "God is with us!" The chants filled the square and rose heavenward, 150,000 voices rejecting the Communist creed of atheism that had been forced upon them and publicly affirming the belief that had so long been suppressed.

Dugulescu gazed from the balcony toward the Orthodox Cathedral towering behind the mass of people. Ceausescu had once threatened to turn the magnificent Byzantine church into an apartment building, because he couldn't bear the sight of it whenever he addressed the people of Timisoara from that very spot.

"Please, my friends," Dugulescu continued. "In this great, historic, and critical moment, we need to turn our face back to God, kneel down, and pray."

Without any prompting, the crowd turned and faced the cathedral, dropped to their knees, and began repeating the words of the Lord's Prayer after the Baptist pastor.

Cornel Marincu, kneeling among the crowd, was overwhelmed

with joy to hear his people praying. He now knew, deeply and fully, that God would give them victory.

Mineu, Romania
December 22, 1989

Tokes braced himself for yet another interrogation. His guards were due in half an hour to take him and Edith to the militia headquarters in Zalau. The worst part was the waiting, not knowing what to expect, what new psychological tricks they would spring on him like a sadistic jack-in-the-box, catching him off guard. Or maybe they would beat him this time. They hadn't tortured him yet. But there was always that possibility. They seemed to be holding the threat of physical abuse over him, making him squirm, toying with him like a puppet, pulling on the strings of his anxiety and fear.

Trying to get his mind off what awaited him, he switched on the concealed radio. Edith and he had tuned into Ceausescu's speech earlier and heard what sounded like boos and derisive comments in the background. That gave them a glimmer of hope, enough to hang on and endure another grueling round of interrogation. They were keeping abreast of the swirl of events in Bucharest, listening to the news of the demonstrations and fighting that had gripped the capital over the last several days.

"Edith, come listen to this," he beckoned his wife.

They strained to hear the announcer's voice through the crackling static. He was saying something about Ceausescu. Tokes turned it up. The Romanian dictator had fled the palace in a helicopter after the army switched over to the side of the demonstrators. The country was now in the hands of a provisional government calling itself the National Salvation Front.

Laszlo and Edith looked at each other in disbelief. Could this be true? He picked her up and nearly smothered her with a wild embrace. The news was more than enough to bolster him for the next interrogation.

A half hour came and went without the dreaded knock at the door summoning them to the Securitate headquarters. An hour passed. Still no one showed up. Was this another psychological game? Tokes wondered. Making him wait? Getting his hopes up, only to dash them later?

They began to sense something different about their captivity. It was so quiet outside. They listened for the sound of the guards surrounding their secluded cabin, the occasional bark of the dogs patrolling the area outside. Nothing. Just the snowy hush of the wind sifting through the drifts blanketing their mountainous hideaway.

Tokes padded over to a steamed up window and wiped it with the ball of his hand to peer outside. He blinked through the blinding whiteness until his eyes adjusted to the light and swept the snowy terrain. The guards had disappeared. They had apparently heard the news about Ceausescu and fled.

"Edith, we're free!" he exclaimed. "We've escaped death!"

It was the happiest moment of his life. He felt as if he could reach out and grab a handful of God's mercy, it was so tangible, so real to him at that moment.

TIMISOARA, ROMANIA
December 22, 1989

"Where are you going? What are you going to do?" the neighbor called out after Marincu as he hurried to his car.

"I have to go to the city. I have to find out what happened," Marincu answered back.

"But you'll be killed. You heard the news."

Marincu did not have time to argue. He hopped into his car and sped toward the city center.

He had been listening to the news at his neighbor's house. The announcer on the Bucharest television station, which was now in the hands of the new provisional government, said there was another massacre in Opera Square. According to the TV report, the Securitate forces had fired on a huge crowd of demonstrators.

Marincu was in the square earlier that day. There must have been 200,000 people there at the time celebrating the fall of Ceausescu. If Securitate forces had fired on the massive rally, it would have been a slaughter. He prayed it was not true. He had to see for himself, see what he could do to help.

He really thought they had finally won. Ceausescu was out. The army was on their side. He should have known the ruthless Securitate would not give up so easily. Now the secret police were apparently back to continue their reign of terror.

He drove up to his office at the Polytechnic Institute and jumped out of the car. As he neared his office building, shots rang out. A limb came crashing at his feet where the barrage of bullets struck the tree he was standing under. The gunfire came from his right. Someone was shooting from the student dormitory across the street from his office. He kept running toward his building, hunching over like a fullback plowing through the defensive line. The sniper opened fire again. Marincu hit the ground. He heard the shattering of glass as the bullets ricocheted into one of the windows of his office building. He got up and made a run for it into the building.

Once he was safe inside, Marincu walked through the halls, searching for anyone who could tell him what happened. His hollow footsteps sounded like those of an army as they echoed through the empty corridor. No signs of anyone there.

Marincu dashed out of the building's back entrance, listening for sniper fire. He ran across the street to the hospital. "What happened in the square?" he asked a nurse hustling past him in the entryway.

"The secret police . . . they're back . . . they're roving in packs through the city shooting people. We're treating lots of wounded here."

"In the square? Did they shoot into the square? Was there another massacre?"

"I don't know."

Marincu ran outside and cornered a man coming toward him from the direction of the square.

"Were you in the square?" Marincu asked feverishly.

"I just came from there."

"How many people were there when the shooting started?"

"Just a few. We were warned the Securitate was going to stage a comeback. Most of the crowd left before the shooting started."

Marincu felt a burden lift from him, like waking up from one of these dreams where he was running and running from some unknown pursuer, but never able to get anywhere.

"It's dangerous to go there now," the man called after him as he continued heading toward the center of town.

But Marincu was still determined to complete his self-appointed mission, to see the situation in the square for himself and offer his services to the wounded.

He continued cautiously, choosing each step carefully. Just ahead in the darkness, he saw the Bega Canal that sliced through the city. He had to cross the bridge over it to reach Opera Square. When he reached the foot of the bridge, he heard an explosion of shots from across the canal. He dropped to the ground, feeling the pain as his knees hit the hard pavement. He crawled back across. He lifted his head and squinted through the darkness, trying to determine where the shots were coming from. Nothing moved in the shadows across the bridge.

He continued crouching there, shrouded in the shadow of the bridge, hoping to outwait the sniper. Behind him, two figures suddenly appeared out of the darkness like apparitions. He jumped when he saw them. They were unarmed.

"Get down," he hissed through his teeth. "There's a sniper across the bridge."

They dropped prostrate beside him. They wanted to get to the square themselves, they told him in a hoarse whisper. The three of them waited another fifteen minutes. Then Marincu started out across the bridge again. He had just made it to the middle when CRACK . . . another shot was fired from across the canal. The sound sent him diving back to the spot where his two companions were waiting.

Another fifteen minutes passed. They glimpsed a light flickering behind them. Headlights were heading their way! The three quickly rolled down the embankment of the canal, just before the beam of light exposed their position. They lay there prone, out of sight, as the vehicle approached the bridge. It was a jeep with the special markings of the Securitate. Had it spotted them? It continued rolling across the bridge, until it disappeared out of sight.

The three waited another hour before attempting to cross the bridge again. They ventured several feet, then stopped. No sniper fire. Another few tentative steps. Still no shots. They continued the trek, almost scraping their bodies across the pavement a few feet at a time. Finally, they were across.

From there, they made their way to the back of the Orthodox

Cathedral at one end of the square. There was still a knot of people milling about the square. One of the leaders of the army was speaking from the balcony, appealing for everyone to leave so his troops could fight the Securitate without endangering civilians.

Marincu was relieved to hear the army had returned to the city to repel the attacks of the Securitate. There was nothing left for him to do there. He left the square obediently and walked back to the hospital, to do what he could to help. He had survived sniper fire. Others were not so fortunate. Ambulances were pulling in and out of the hospital, unloading blood-soaked stretchers bearing the victims of the latest wave of Securitate terror and roaring off for more. Marincu was there all night, watching the grisly procession of casualties pass by.

No one really knew how many had died when the bloodletting finally stopped and the Securitate terrorists finally admitted defeat and turned themselves in. At first it was reported that thousands had been killed in Timisoara during the two weeks of fighting. The new government later revised that estimate down to 689. It was hard to tell. Securitate agents were seen picking up dead bodies from the street and loading them on trucks to be burned. They also confiscated lists of victims from the city's hospital to keep the extent of the massacre from ever being known.

But they were not able to bury their dark deeds entirely. Their atrocities soon became apparent, dug up with the corpses discovered in mass graves, bound together with barbed wire, some with no fingernails and no hair; laid bare with the bodies found at the morgue, lying lifeless and exposed on the cold concrete slabs, still bearing the bruises of brutal beatings; uncovered in the gruesome torture chambers found in the deep recesses of some cemetery vaults.

The hospital was overflowing with hundreds of injured and wounded. Ironically, some Securitate terrorists lay side by side with their victims in the same ward, bound to their beds with rope to restrain them. Many of them showed no sign of remorse. One of the terrorists told a television interviewer: "I haven't killed enough."

Mineu, Romania
December 23, 1989

The Securitate guards who had so suddenly disappeared were soon replaced by an army unit loyal to the new provisional government sent to protect Tokes. The National Salvation Front, the leaders who stepped in to fill the vacuum left by Ceausescu, urged Tokes and his wife to remain in Mineu under armed protection because of concerns that roaming pockets of Securitate resistance might still be out to kill them.

Tokes also received an unexpected invitation from the National Salvation Front to become a member of the new government's ruling council. As soon as it was safe for him to travel, he made the trip to Bucharest to accept the offer, although he was a little suspicious of some of the former Communists who made up the ruling council. When he arrived, he was hailed as a hero by Romanian television.

"I feel a little uneasy being with the greatest people of the country," he told Romanian television upon his arrival. "When I came today to Bucharest, I did not trust the representatives of the army. I feel a little embarrassed. I have come to trust no one."

He also felt a little overwhelmed at his sudden elevation from serving under house arrest to serving on Romania's governing body. Looking back over the events of the past two weeks, he had only one explanation. "For me," he told the Romanian TV interviewer, "it is a miracle."

Notes

1. An eyewitness account of Rev. Peter Duguleseu, Pastor of Timisoara's First Baptist Church, "Timisoara, the Martyr City," (The Romanian Missionary Society).

2. "The Romanian Turmoil through Soviet Eyes: Chance and Sudden Violence," *The New York Times*, 22 December 1989, A14.

Part 4

Lighting the World

16

Poland

The Polish Communist party leaders were devastated by the election results. In the first round, the Solidarity-backed candidates won ninety-two out of the one hundred uncontested seats in the Senate, the upper house of Parliament, and all but one of the 161 seats they were allowed to run for in the lower house known as the Sejm. *Not only that. In a humiliating rejection of the Party, voters barred virtually all of the regime's thirty-five unopposed candidates, including General Kiszczak, from taking office by simply striking their names off the ballots.*

"This is not just a lost election, gentlemen," Jerzy Urban, the government spokesman, told his Communist compatriots. "It's the end of an era."

Warsaw
June 8, 1989

When the final disastrous election returns were in, the government's inner circle met with Solidarity leaders back in Magdalinka to try to work out a power-sharing formula in a tension-filled meeting.

The Communists were irate. General Kiszczak opened the meeting by lashing out at the opposition.

"These elections were patently unfair," he said. "Solidarity violated the spirit of the round table by conducting a confrontational campaign."

"Listen, general," Walesa shot back. "It's not our fault the national list lost. You lost the election by yourself. You had forty years to campaign for this election. And the people said no. You lost because, for the first time, the people could choose without manipulation. When I had the chance, I marked out your name, not once, but so many times I wore holes in the paper."

Walesa's caustic comment drew laughs from the Solidarity side of the table. The Party leaders were not amused.

The meeting dragged on for ten hours, until Solidarity agreed to add thirty-three new candidates to the Communist ballot in a run-off election. But the compromise in no way ended the Party's political problems. The Communists saw their power disappearing over night.

Two months later, Jaruzelski barely squeaked into the presidency with a parliamentary majority of just one vote. Then General Kiszczak, picked by Jaruzelski to be prime minister, admitted he was hard-pressed to form a government. Walesa was convinced the time was ripe for Solidarity to take the helm.

In a flurry of masterful backroom wrangling, Walesa managed to persuade the delegates of the Democratic and United Peasant parties, long-time Communist bedfellows, to Solidarity's side. With the two puppet parties in their pocket, Solidarity deputies forced a vote in the Parliament calling for the formation of a new government under Walesa's leadership.

Now Solidarity had to come up with a choice for prime minister. Walesa didn't want the job, opting to continue coaching from the sidelines. Instead, in his own increasingly autocratic style, he ramrodded through his own candidate, Mazowiecki. The suggestion encountered resistance from Solidarity's Parliamentary Club. Mazowiecki was seen as too indecisive, not vibrant enough. They favored Geremek for the post. But Walesa had made up his mind. Mazowiecki had the all-important backing of the church and would be much more palatable to the Communists than either Geremek or the other candidate whose name popped up, KOR activist Jacek Kuron, an archenemy of the government. Michnik once joked that when the Communists wanted to scare children, all they had to do was mention Kuron's name.

Walesa visited Mazowiecki's apartment late at night with the unexpected proposal. Since the legalization of Solidarity, Mazowiecki had gone back to editing the newly resurrected Solidarity weekly after turning down pleas to run in the elections. He had decided to sit them out because he was uncomfortable with the undemocratic way Solidarity candidates had been selected to run.

"Tadeusz, I want you to be prime minister," Walesa told his close adviser.

Mazowiecki was taken aback by the suggestion. When the idea of a Solidarity-led government was first floated in an editorial by Adam Michnik in the new opposition paper *Gazeta Wyborcza* entitled, "Your President, Our Prime Minister," Mazowiecki helped talk Walesa out of it. Solidarity wasn't ready to run the new government, he counseled him. Did Solidarity want to assume the blame for the country's economic problems? Not to mention the fact that the trauma would be too great for the Party, and there could be a backlash from the Party hardliners. Now here was Walesa asking him to throw away his reservations and head up the government himself.

"You have a night to think about it," Walesa said before he left.

Mazowiecki felt like a huge burden had been placed on his shoulders. Did he really have a choice?

The next day, Walesa placed a slip of paper on Jaruzelski's desk with three names on it: Mazowiecki, Geremek, and Kuron.

"This is my choice," Walesa said, pointing to Mazowiecki's name. "But you can also say you considered the other two."

Polish Press Agency Report
August 18, 1989

> As a result of talks and consultations held with parliamentary and non-parliamentary representatives of socio-political groupings, President Wojciech Jaruzelski presented a proposal to Tadeusz Mazowiecki to take up the post of chairman of the Council of Ministers of the Polish People's Republic.

> Tadeusz Mazowiecki is a long-time Catholic activist. He was a Sejm deputy between 1961 and 1972. Later on he started activities in Solidarity. He is one of the leading activists of this organization. At present, he is editor-in-chief of the Solidarity weekly.
>
> In the nearest future, the president will table a motion to the Sejm speaker on the appointment of Tadeusz Mazowiecki to the post of premier and entrusting him with the mission of forming a government.
>
> In the present situation, the president sees a need to create a government enjoying the necessary support of parliamentary floor groups and to build it on foundations of broad agreement between Poland's political and social forces.
>
> The president thinks that the formation of such a government will be conducive to expeditiously overcome economic difficulties, continue reforms stemming from the philosophy and essence of the round table, and satisfy the needs and aspirations of Polish society.[1]

Warsaw
August 18, 1989

After accepting Jaruzelski's offer to become prime minister, Mazowiecki was rushing from meetings with Jaruzelski and Cardinal Glemp to report back to his Solidarity colleagues in his new chauffeur-driven government car when the car coughed to a halt. It was out of gas. What an ignominious thing to happen to a prime minister! he thought, appreciating the irony as he got out and began pushing the automobile to the nearest gas station.

At the station he received a first-hand reminder of the economic problems now resting on his shoulders. The line of cars waiting to fill up stretched interminably. He decided to abandon the car and call one of his three sons to drive him to the meeting, where he arrived twenty minutes late to a barrage of reporters inundating him with questions. When asked about the difficulties he would face as prime minister, he cracked a smile and answered, "My biggest problem is that I ran out of gas."

The first day after his nomination, Mazowiecki took refuge at Laski, the home for blind children run by the Franciscan sisters of St. Martin's Church. It was the place he always returned to when he needed time to reflect or go for a much-needed walk in the woods. His wife was buried there. As he sauntered through the forest, the leaves crackling under his feet, he stared into the face of the problems before him. They were huge, seemingly insurmountable. But he told himself they could be overcome. If he didn't believe that, he never would have taken on the job. After all, he was a believer, and he believed that providence would take care of them. After the past ten years, how could he doubt that God always wills for people to live in freedom and justice—despite the often contrary will of man.

He gave his first television interview since his nomination from a peaceful glade on the grounds. He seemed relaxed. His collar was open, his coat slung casually over his shoulder, a breeze ruffling his graying hair. "I find my inspiration here, where there is so much suffering and yet these young children maintain their optimism," he told the interviewer. "A man can gather strength here, and that's what I needed."

WARSAW
August 24, 1989

One week later, Mazowiecki entered the Sejm chamber for his inauguration. His mind went back to the unsuccessful strike in 1988. He had no inkling then that leaving that shipyard, disappointed and dejected, would lead to entering this hall. Now he was about to walk into history. He took his place at a bench at the front of the hall, looking more like a condemned man about to receive his sentence than someone about to be confirmed as prime minister. The vote was taken. 378 votes for, 4 against, 41 abstentions. When the results were announced, he stood and took a deep bow as the legislators rose to their feet in a rousing ovation. Then he strode to the podium, stepping forward to become Poland's first non-Communist prime minister since 1947.

"I want to create a government capable of acting for the good of society, the nation, and state," he told the hushed Parliament. "It will be a government of a coalition in favor of profound reform of the state. Today, such a task can be undertaken only by a government open to the cooperation of all the forces represented in Parliament, formed according to new political rules.

"The mechanisms of normal political life must be restored in Poland. The transition is difficult, but it doesn't have to cause a shock. On the contrary, it will be the road to normality. The principle of struggle which sooner or later ends up eliminating the opponent must be replaced with the principle of partnership. Otherwise, we will never abandon the totalitarian system to democracy.

"I want to be the premier of all Poles, regardless of their views and belief. . . . I will take pains to make the rules of government clear to everyone. What will help will be an understanding on the part of the church, which has always stood up for human rights and felt the worries of the nation as its own. The church was and continues to be a stabilizing power in Poland.

"The future government must tell society the truth. It must also . . . listen to the voice of public opinion."

Fully aware that eyes in Moscow were focused on his address, he went on to stress the importance of maintaining friendly relations with the Soviet Union, and his government's intentions of remaining in the Warsaw Pact.

"I count on this moment becoming significant in the consciousness of my compatriots," he said concluding, "so that we can revive Poland by common effort, not because of my person, but because of the needs of Poland and the historic moment."

One of Mazowiecki's first acts as prime minister was to place two phone calls, the first to his old friend Pope John Paul II, the second to Walesa.

He then decided to get acquainted with his new office in the Council of Ministers building, a mammoth stone structure just down from the Lazienki park filled every summer Saturday with the sounds of an open-air Chopin concert. He found the government building a little overwhelming. It was dark, the windows were small, and the enormity of the space imposing. As he surveyed the labyrinthine halls, Mazowiecki promised himself he would do all he could to make the space warm and human.

He then returned to his old familiar office at *Wiez* to fetch just the thing for his new office. He entered the modest quarters, just off the offices used by the Warsaw Chapter of KIK. The space held so many memories, held the breath, the spirit, of the past in anticipation, now, of an expansive future. This was the scene of his many hard-fought battles with government censors. The place where the Appeal of the 64 was first conceived and formulated, the site of a make-shift strike headquarters during the labor unrest of 1980 and 1988. With a look of satisfaction, Mazowiecki walked over to the wall and took down the picture of the idealistic crusader, Don Quixote, tilting at his windmills. He would take this with him into that once-impossible tomorrow.

WARSAW
September 12, 1989

It had been almost three weeks since Mazowiecki's nomination, and he had been working feverishly eighteen to twenty hours a day, trying to put together a new government. During that time, Parliament and the Polish people were growing increasingly impatient with his painstaking efforts at selecting a cabinet, a process no one expected to take more than a few days.

The job ahead of him was a daunting one. It would not be easy heading an uneasy coalition of old foes working together with him to resurrect Poland's moribund economy. Finally, after three weeks of political bickering and infighting, he was ready to announce his government. He had decided to name eleven Solidarity members to the cabinet and appoint an independent as foreign minister. Four posts would go to the Communists, including the key positions of the Defense and Interior Ministries to head off any Soviet concerns. The Communists had demanded more positions, but Mazowiecki refused. The remaining seven spots went to the Peasant and Democratic parties.

The strain of the past several weeks showed on Mazowiecki's gaunt face as he strode to the podium of the Polish Parliament to outline his policy and finally present his cabinet. Forty minutes into his policy speech, he began to falter. The packed parliament started to fidget. Mazowiecki turned pale and clutched the lectern, gasping for breath. "I don't feel too well," he muttered under his breath, then turned to the assembly speaker to request a short recess.

A nervous buzz broke out as he moved haltingly toward the wooden double-doors behind the podium. Doctors scurried in and out of the back room. Nurses suddenly appeared with an electrocardiogram machine. Frantic conversations started to break out among the delegates, their eyes fixed on the closed doors for any clue to the fate of their new prime minister. He had a history of heart and lung problems. The chamber hissed with sibilant whispers. Maybe he was having a heart attack.

After an anxious hour that seemed more like several, Mazowiecki emerged from the double-doors at last and took his place at the podium to a resounding ovation. He waited for the applause to die down. "Excuse me," he said wryly, "I have reached the same state as the Polish economy. But I have recovered, and I hope the economy will recover, too."

The relieved Parliament exploded in laughter, and Mazowiecki resumed his speech. After publicly presenting his Cabinet, Mazowiecki concluded, "We do not promise it will be easy for everyone. But we do not stand as a nation in a losing position, if we display effort, patience and the will to persevere. Let us have confidence in the spiritual and material strength of the nation. But I believe that God will help us to make a giant step forward in the road that opens before us."

This simple invocation of divine guidance seemed to echo through the chamber's marble halls where even the mention of God's name was once anathema—a sign of the changes to come.

The parliament voted unanimously to confirm his cabinet, and Mazowiecki stood at the Prime Minister's bench, raising his arms in the two-fingered salute, the symbol of both Solidarity and of victory.

Note

1. *Daily News*, No. 160, 19 August 1989, (Polish Press Agency), 11-12.

17

Hungary

The Hungarian Communist party was no more. In October, the Party took the unprecedented action of basically voting itself out of existence by changing its name to the Hungarian Socialist Party. The Party's new incarnation promised to transform itself from a Soviet-style Marxist body to a party based on the ideals of European democratic socialism, including more democratic methods of choosing its leadership. As Gabor Ivanyi saw it, the fleas were jumping off the drowning dog.

Ivanyi had helped pave the road for this dramatic conversion of reformed Communists into transformed Socialists through his involvement with the Alliance of Free Democrats, one of the political groups that had recently spun off the network of opposition activists. The Alliance was one of eight opposition groups at Hungary's own version of Poland's Round Table. Only the Hungarian version was dubbed the "triangular table," because of the three sides represented in the meetings: the government, the opposition, and a collection of other organizations loosely connected with the former Communist party.

In September, after three months of meetings, the "Triangular Table" agreed to hold parliamentary elections that would be completely free and open. Unlike Poland, the ruling Socialists would have no reserved seats. The country's president, however, would be chosen before those elections, while the Socialists still controlled the Parliament. Ivanyi's Alliance of Free Democrats objected to the plan as patently unfair, and refused to sign off on the agreement. They argued the early presidential elections would give the Socialists an unfair advantage, with the press, state-run TV, and all important government offices still within their grasp. In league with another opposition group, the Free Democrats pushed through a referendum on the question and won, despite the government's call for a boycott of the vote.

The parliamentary elections were set for March 25. When the campaign got underway, Ivanyi faced a dilemma. The Free Democrats were urging him to run for a seat, while his church was pressuring him to drop out of the Party. His church members didn't think it was appropriate for a pastor to be a member of any political party. Ivanyi compromised and left the Party, but ran as an independent with the Free Democrats' backing.

When the final results of the election were in, a rival opposition group, the Democratic Forum, won 60 percent of the vote and 165 seats. The Alliance came in second with nearly 24 percent of the vote, taking 92 seats. The Socialists trailed at fourth with 8.5 percent of the vote, garnering only 33 seats in the Parliament it once dominated.

Ivanyi emerged from his race a winner. The pastor whom the Hungarian government locked out of his own church had won the right to enter the exclusive halls of Parliament as a member of the government.

—•—

The thirty-foot-high red star atop the Hungarian parliamentary office building along the rolling Danube River was now removed. The building's front entrance opened into a huge hall draped all around with beige curtains. Hidden behind those curtains, veiled from sight, bronze plaques proclaimed the sayings of Marx, Engels, and Lenin. The Marxist slogans were now silenced; the building that for more than forty years served as the domain of the Communist party was now stripped of any allusions to the country's Communist legacy.

On the third floor, off a seemingly endless corridor, was the office of Gabor Ivanyi. He held in his hands files he had just acquired from the State Office of Church Affairs. Things had come full circle. Before he was at the government agency's complete mercy. Now the entire agency was abolished, and as a member of the Parliamentary Committee on Human Rights, Religion and Charities, it was part of his responsibility to oversee church-state relations.

The files he had in his possession would finally reveal the truth of the relationship between Hungary's church leadership and the government. During the stormy years of meeting outside his locked church, during the long campaign of harassment against him, his family and his church colleagues, Ivanyi was sometimes nagged with doubt about the rightness of their cause. They were accused of being inflexible, narrow-minded and naive about the issues involving church leadership. At times, he wondered whether he and his defiant church were too uncompromising, too harsh in their condemnation of the church hierarchy. Living in the shadow of communism's big lie often obscured the light he knew to be the truth.

As he perused the files, what he found was shocking. The documents more than vindicated his church's accusations of corruption at the highest echelons of church leadership. It seemed everyone was dirty. One well-known church leader had turned over to the State Office of Church Affairs tapes of secretly recorded conversations between two other pastors. In another document, a pastor wrote about a colleague's problems with his wife. That statement was underlined and marked with an exclamation point, indicating the information would be put to use.

The file was full of reports dutifully filled out by church leaders after returning from trips abroad for Christian conferences. Every question was answered in detail: Who was there? What foreigners were there? What Hungarians were there? What did the Hungarians say? Scribbled on one such report was the suggestion that the pastor be called in to provide another, more thorough, account. The record of his compliance with the request was there, attached to the first report. There were reams of reports made by church leaders from virtually every denomination, as well as transcripts of exchanges between the Office of Church Affairs and the state security. The more he read, the more he became convinced the agency was obviously intent on destroying the church.

Ivanyi felt a certain amount of disgust as he waded through the files, but also a strange satisfaction about his own unwavering stand. He shook his head in disbelief. It seemed almost everyone in the church had been tempted by the ripe government promises of small advantages in exchange for a little cooperation. Now he realized why the church in Hungary had been exempt from the outright oppression of the other Soviet bloc countries. Their semblance of religious liberty had been bought with a price, the cost of collaboration. The politics of small steps as practiced in Hungary had led right into the deceitfully spun web of the Communist government. Now, as a member of parliament, it was his responsibility to start removing the church from its moral entanglements.

18

East Germany

The announcement came almost as an aside during a news conference given by East German Politburo member Günter Schabowski. East Germany was immediately lifting restrictions on travel and emigration to the West. "We know this need of citizens to travel or leave the country," Schabowski said. "Today the decision was taken that makes it possible for all citizens to leave the country through East German crossing points."

Just two hours after his announcement, an East Berlin couple tentatively approached the Berlin Wall border crossing at Bornholmerstrasse. With just a flash of their identity cards, they were through. After a brief exchange with West Berliners on the other side, they returned home. They were just trying out the new regulation. But as word spread, the tentative steps taken by other East Germans through the newly open border turned into a stampede. Soon tens of thousands of East Berliners were streaming back and forth unhindered, and one of the world's biggest block parties got underway. The wall that had gone up on August 13, 1961, to staunch the hemorrhage of East Germans to the West was coming down for the same reason—to keep people from leaving by other routes. No man's land was now everyman's land. The wall had fallen.

Leipzig
November 9, 1989

Brigitta was driving to a restaurant for a get together with friends from the publishing house when she heard the report on the radio. She turned it up. It was Schabowski's announcement on the new travel regulations. She couldn't believe what she was hearing. She must be dreaming.

Brigitta was astonished. Or there was some mistake. He couldn't possibly mean what he was saying. When she reached the restaurant, her astonished co-workers had heard the same announcement. They couldn't believe it either. If this were true, it meant the end of a barrier so taken for granted they couldn't imagine a world without it. Finally, their curiosity got the best of them. They had to know if this were real. The gathering broke up almost as soon as it started, and Brigitta rushed home to see what West German TV was reporting.

There she saw the pictures that thrilled the world. Young people standing on top of the wall, dancing and drinking champagne, West Berliners lining up at checkpoints to greet dazed East Berliners with cheers and hugs, revelers chiseling away at the graffiti-covered wall while East German border guards who would have shot them the day before now looked on. It was true. The wall was history. Brigitta stayed up all night glued to the TV, hypnotically switching from channel to channel, trying to convince herself the incredible images before her eyes were real.

The next day dawned cold and clear. Brigitta had the day off, so she rushed to the train station to try to get to Berlin to witness the scene first-hand. But there were no trains available. They were all overbooked. It seemed as if the whole city had converged on the station to test the new waters of freedom, turning Leipzig into a ghost town over the weekend. Brigitta returned home and turned on the television once again, reveling in the sweep of events over the last three months.

Back in September, she thought, sitting in the sanctuary of the Nikolai church, it all seemed so unthinkable, so utopian. Their voices then seemed so faint, so insignificant.

Now the political machine was forced to bow to the pressure from the streets. In school and at the university, they all had to read Marx. This much they understood from him: when an idea takes hold of the masses, it becomes a material force.

Over the next few weeks, the changes were happening so quickly, Brigitta could hardly keep up with them: a parliament with open discussions broadcast over TV; constitutional change—the leading role of the Communist party abolished; the prosecution of ministers and high government officials for misuse of their political office. The end was still not in sight. She thought at first that many people would be content with the opening of the border and the freedom to travel. The first weekend the wall opened up, more than half a million people crossed into West Berlin. However, on the following Monday, 250,000 people took to the streets of Leipzig again, demonstrating for free elections and more democratic reform.

In the meantime, the media was changing so radically that Brigitta spent several hours a day reading the newspaper and watching the news on all channels. Hardly anyone was listening to West German television anymore; incredibly enough, reliable information was now coming from the East German media. Journalists who were finally able to investigate and report unhindered were uncovering things about the government that no one had ever suspected. Not a day went by that Brigitta wasn't deeply shaken by the extent of the state's deceptions.

Wandlitz, the compound of twenty-three homes that was once off-limits to all but the hard-line government's upper crust had been opened up. TV camera crews allowed into the opulent homes and vast hunting grounds showed East Germans just how privileged life was at the top. With its swimming pool, movie theater showing Western movies banned in East Germany, and private store stuffed with consumer goods unavailable to the general public, Wandlitz stripped the East German regime of the modest mantle of moderation in which it had so carefully cloaked itself. The revelation outraged the people of East Germany.

Brigitta wondered how they would be able to put faith in a government again. In light of all that was happening, she could hardly sleep. She was so worked up, and caught up in the prospect of creating something new and honest.

The fact that Uwe, Ulrike, and the children had left still caused her a good deal of anguish. The more people who left now, the more doubtful the outcome of upcoming elections. They would miss them at the ballot box and in the restructuring of the country.

It was exciting to be in Leipzig, even though things were becoming more difficult. The economic collapse hadn't bottomed out yet. But the West Germans were descending on their East German cousins like shoppers in a bargain basement, snapping up goods as quickly as possible. They could obtain East German marks dirt cheap. On the black market, one West German mark could buy ten East German marks, making everything in East Germany incredibly inexpensive. The equivalent of one dollar could buy a full-course dinner at the finest restaurants. For one pfennig, a little over a penny, West Germans could buy two rolls that would cost them the equivalent of fifty cents at home. As a result, many subsidized goods, like food and children's clothing, were rarely available anymore. "If this doesn't stop," Brigitta thought, "they'll have to close down the 'GDR-store.' If the West delays much longer with their promised aid for the reconstruction of our economy, they will be able to buy us out, and the longer they wait, the cheaper our price."

She hoped they had gone through the past few weeks out of moral concerns and not just for material improvement. The idea of reunification with West Germany was being bandied about as a quick fix for the country's economic problems. Voices at the demonstrations calling for reunification were starting to swell, the chant of "We are the people," gradually overwhelmed by the slogan, "We are *one* people."

The development distressed Brigitta. Like most people at the forefront of the demonstrations, she felt reunification might just turn East Germany into an impoverished vassal state of the German Federal Republic.

LEIPZIG, EAST GERMANY
December 3, 1989

On the first Sunday in Advent, Brigitta left her apartment to join hands with all of East Germany. She jumped into her Trabant and puttered off to pick up Father Bernhard and a few other friends, then headed out to the *autobahn.* When they reached the highway, a line of people was already gathering all along the road. Brigitta looked for a sparse spot in the crowd and pulled over. Her party pried themselves out of the car and scoured the roadside for a place to stand. It was a bitterly cold morning, well below freezing, but they hardly felt it. They were flushed with the excitement of what they were about to do, something they really didn't believe was possible. Cars zipping by on the *autobahn* honked their horns in support, as more and more people joined the throng along the road.

It was almost noon. Brigitta looked all around her. There were thousands of people standing along the *autobahn* on both sides of her, stretching as far as she could see. The human chain actually extended from the south through Leipzig and East Berlin all the way to the country's northern border. Another line of people standing side by side reached from east to west across the country, converging in the middle of East Berlin. At exactly 12:00, the millions of people standing all across East Germany joined hands. For a quarter of an hour, they stood in silence, as a human cross took shape across the face of the entire land.

19

Romania

"Good news this Christmas day. The Antichrist is dead."

With those words, Christmas came to Romania. They were uttered by a TV newscaster announcing the execution of Ceausescu and his wife.

The two were tried by a military tribunal and sentenced to death for "genocide" and "crimes against the people." Romanian TV broadcast a videotape of the hated couple awaiting execution, the president looking defiant while getting his blood pressure taken, his frightened wife beside him—both very tired and very old. They had been held for three days in an armored car driven around an army post near the town where they were captured. Before the execution, Elena Ceausescu turned to her captors with a bewildered look and asked, "Why? Why? I raised you like a mother." It wasn't until late the next day that Romanian television showed the graphic pictures of the Ceausescus lying dead in a pool of blood, an image splashed around the world. There were so many volunteers for the firing squad that soldiers had to draw lots to win a spot.

In Timisoara, on Christmas Day, the people were still burying their dead. Thousands of candles burned in front of the Orthodox Cathedral, the flames serving as reminders of those who died in the uprising. Tanks stood in front of the Opera House, protecting the people now instead of threatening them. The churches were still closed; the shops boarded up. Sporadic street battles between the army and Securitate holdouts continued breaking out.

But for the first time in more than forty years, it really was Christmas in Romania. Out of the pain and travail of labor came the nativity of new hope. The Front was promising democracy, religious freedom, free elections in April, and an end to the village destruction campaign. Christmas carols played on Romanian radio for the first time almost anyone could remember. And on the balcony of Bucharest's Central Committee Headquarters, in the very spot that Ceausescu made the speech that preceded his downfall, a Christmas tree glittered.

Laszlo Tokes celebrated the holiday a free man. He led Christmas services at the Hungarian Reformed Church in Mineu, still under the protection of the Romanian army. Afterward, he accompanied a delegation from the church in a visit to the local Orthodox church to show their solidarity with the nation's ethnic Romanians. For Tokes, the message of Christmas was a message of reconciliation, a message he was able to deliver to the entire country on Romanian TV. It was an appearance in stark contrast to the televised confession Ceausescu tried to orchestrate. Tokes used the Christmas address to impress upon the people the need for unity between ethnic Hungarians and Romanians. That, he told the nation, would be the only way for democracy and freedom to survive.

TIMISOARA, ROMANIA
December 1989

Daniel Gavra could still feel his left leg, even though it was not there. It had been amputated just below the knee. But sometimes he swore he could feel it tingle, like it had gone to sleep. He had to look at the sheet covering his body and see it flattened against the bed, a starched empty plane, to convince himself it really was missing.

Rev. Peter Dugulescu was making the rounds in the hospital when he spotted Daniel across the crowded ward. The young engineer was a member of his congregation. He remembered running into him the night of the vigil around Tokes's church. Daniel had told him then he was on his way to defend Tokes, and showed him the candles he planned to distribute among the demonstrators when it got dark.

Dugulescu walked over to the bed where Daniel was lying and greeted him.

"Daniel, it's good to see you. How are you feeling?"

Daniel's youthful face brightened a bit when he saw his pastor.

"Pastor Dugulescu, it's nice of you to stop by. I'm doing much better now, thank you."

The pastor looked down at the bed, then tried to shield the shock of what he saw. But Daniel saw it in his eyes.

"As you can see, one of my legs had to be amputated. But I'm lucky to be alive."

"What happened?" Dugulescu asked.

"It was the first Sunday of the demonstrations," the twenty-four-year-old replied. "I was leading a group of students back to the university campus that afternoon. We were going to try to get some more of our friends to join the demonstration. We were marching and shouting and waving a Romanian flag, one that we'd ripped the Communist emblem out of.

"We had just gotten to the Michelangelo Bridge when we saw a detachment from the Securitate waiting there for us. They pointed their rifles at us and, before we could even start to run, they started shooting. I was on the front row, holding the flag. I felt bullets tear into my leg. I tried to get away, but I couldn't even walk. Blood was pouring from my leg. I fell down. There were people falling all around me. Altogether, I think about two hundred people were shot in that spot.

"Things began to get a little blurry then. But I remember a private car pulling up, and somebody loading me in it to take me to the hospital. I'm fortunate I wasn't picked up by an ambulance."

"Why is that?" Dugulescu asked.

"I found out later that everyone there who was picked up by an ambulance was killed right afterward. They must have been taken straight to the Securitate."

Dugulescu stood silently, letting the sobering story sink in. As he turned to leave, Daniel called after him. "Pastor Dugulescu, you remember how I showed you the candles that I brought to the vigil?"

Dugulescu nodded his head.

"I lost a leg, but I lit the first candle."

ORADEA, ROMANIA
May 8, 1990

The graffiti scrawled on the side of the Hungarian Reformed church in Oradea told the story of the dramatic changes sweeping the church. Someone had spray-painted an invective aimed at Tokes's persecutor, Laszlo Papp, the English equivalent of which would be something like, "Bishop Papp, go home."

So, the handwriting was on the wall, quite literally. In the aftermath of the revolution, Papp fled the country for France. When an angry crowd broke into his house during the uprising, they discovered he had already left. They found instead his old mother-in-law, crying forlornly in a corner, deserted. She died of a heart attack soon after.

Outside the grafitti-marred church, a crowd started to gather. It was a sun-drenched day, a perfect day for a church celebration. A smattering of applause broke out at the sight of the solemn-looking line of pastors clad in black cassocks processing into the church. In the middle was Laszlo Tokes, carrying a single red rose. He smiled beatifically, resplendent in his church regalia. He was about to be inaugurated as the Reformed church's bishop of Oradea to replace Papp.

Since emerging from hiding in Mineu, he had remained on the run; remnants from the Securitate were apparently still trying to track him down. After his first visit to Bucharest, the unidentified assailants opened fire on the train carrying him out of the city. Bullets struck his compartment, but Tokes escaped unharmed.

Since the revolution, everything had changed, but nothing had changed. The Communist bureaucracy entrenched under Ceausescu was still in power, just under a different name. The oranges, red meat, and other scarce items that suddenly appeared on the shelves after Ceausescu's vast storehouses were broken open had long since disappeared. There were still shortages of heat, electricity, and food.

The government of Ion Iliescu, Romania's new head of state, abolished the old Department of Cults, but replaced it with a new ministry level department called the Ministry for Religious Affairs.

Now as Tokes took the pulpit, his booming bass voice announced the Reformed church would no longer be subservient to the government. "The year 1990 will mean the beginning of a new chapter in the life of the Reformed church. The new leading body of our church is assuming its job under the condition of the revolutionary transformation of society. We're leaving behind perhaps the darkest period of our history, and facing new conditions that offer the unique possibility of rebirth, conditions that compel us to action.

"God has used our church to liberate our country, sending the Timisoara congregation against the dictatorship like David against Goliath in days of old.

"As Jerusalem was under siege in biblical times, so was our church under attack from a dictatorship trying to deprive us of our last refuge, our faith, to drive us out of our strong fortresses, to break up our communities. Although we didn't give up the fight, and the best of our pastors struggled desperately against the powerful authorities, the endless siege took its toll. There were traitors and weaklings. Many of them gave up or ran away, others died in the fighting.

"Our church deteriorated, in its structure, in its faith, and in its moral point of view. A significant portion of its people became alienated. The youth slipped out of its hands. The remains of the flock were divided by anxiety and fear, given over to despair.

" 'There's a time to break down, and a time to build up,' says the preacher. The duty now before us, with God's help, is to 'build up again the ruins,' to resettle the church as the people of Israel did, returning from captivity, to make it once again a powerful fortress against the enemy.

"We must bring to an end the one-sided state of dependence which damaged the church in its most important interests and in freedom. The church's autonomy must be reestablished, to realize the ideal of a free church in a free state. That is the only way to assure real freedom of religion."

WASHINGTON, DC
March 15, 1990

Several months before his inauguration as bishop, Tokes found himself once again in front of the camera of Western TV journalists. This time, instead of a clandestine interview conducted in the risky setting of his church balcony, the interview was out in the open, in the studios of the "MacNeil-Lehrer NewsHour." Tokes was in Washington to meet President Bush.

During the interview, MacNeil-Lehrer's Judy Woodruff asked Tokes about the suffering he had endured: "You were held in custody, you were threatened, you were beaten, you were stabbed at one point. What was it like going through those experiences? How frightening?"

"For Christians, suffering is natural," Tokes responded. This matter-of-fact reply prompted a look of astonishment from Woodruff. Tokes continued, "The sacrifice of Christ embodies our suffering, the sufferings of humankind. So for me, it was natural, in this sense of the word. But every time these sufferings were near, there was the hope that they will end as the sufferings of Christ ended—in Easter."

20

Czechoslovakia

After the new Czechoslovakian government was formed, the issue remained of filling the post of president. Civic Forum proposed Vaclav Havel for the position. After some backroom bargaining with the Communists, the idea was approved. But Havel was reluctant to accept the post. He was a playwright, not a professional politician. He agreed on one condition: that free elections would be held for parliament during the next year, with a new president elected to a regular five-year term.

The drama being played out on the Czechoslovakian political stage was far more ironic than anything Havel, a master of irony, could ever have dreamt up. Six months before, he was in prison. Now he was poised to become president.

PRAGUE
December 29, 1989

Vaclav Havel fidgeted with his tie. He looked ill at ease in his somber blue suit. He was more at home in jeans and a sweater. As the country's new president, he was going to have to get used to it.

He was waiting outside the medieval Hradcany castle to be inaugurated as Czechoslovakia's first non-Communist president in more than forty years. Inside, in the crowded Parliament chamber, Marian Calfa, the country's new Communist prime minister, was singing his praises.

"He has won the respect of all," Calfa told the Parliament. "He never accepted the suggestions of friends or foes that he go into exile, and bore the humiliation of a man oppressed and relegated by those in power to the margins of society. Your vote for Vaclav Havel will be a vote for insuring the human rights of every citizen of our country."

The vote was taken, and all 323 deputies in the Communist-dominated parliament raised their hands in support of Havel as president.

After the vote, the doors to the sixteenth-century coronation hall flung open, and as a band struck up Czechoslovakia's version of "Hail to the Chief," Havel strode down the aisle shoulder to shoulder with Alexander Dubcek, the new chairman of the Parliament. The powerless were taking power. The dissident playwright had indeed risen from prisoner to president in just half a year. And the reform-minded Communist chased out of power by Soviet tanks in 1968 had emerged from disgrace and exile to give the Czechoslovak government a human face once again.

The oath of office used to swear Havel in had to be hastily rewritten to delete a clause pledging allegiance to the cause of socialism. After the inauguration, he ventured out onto the castle balcony and looked down onto the inner courtyard overflowing with people shouting their adulation. Banners bearing Civic Forum's logo waved alongside Czechoslovak flags. All over Prague, it looked like a giant New Year's Eve party, with revelers popping open champagne bottles and dancing in the dazzling light of hundreds of sparklers to usher in a new era.

"Thank you all for your support," he shouted into the microphone, like a host trying to get his guest's attention at a raucous party. "I promise you I will not betray your confidence. I will lead this country to free elections. This must be done in an honest and calm way, so that the clean face of our revolution is not soiled. That is the task for all of us."

The noise from the crowd swelled into a rushing river of sound as Havel made his way through the courtyard to St. Vitus Cathedral for an inaugural Mass. Just weeks before, another jubilant crowd had come to the same cathedral to celebrate the canonization of a saint; now they were lauding a leader. Both events told miraculous tales about the power of the powerless.

The new president followed behind Cardinal Tomasek in a procession of robed priests and mitred bishops down the wide aisle past the ornate tomb of his namesake, King Wenceslas (Vaclav being a derivative of Wenceslas). This would be the first time since World War II that the inauguration of the country's president was being blessed by the Catholic church. But then, it had been a year of firsts. When Havel reached the front of the church, he bowed in reverence before the Host placed in a glittering monstrance upon the altar.

"We have come today to the cathedral to thank God for the great hope that has opened up for us in the last few days," Cardinal Tomasek said at the start of the ceremony.

Then the sonorous strains of the *Te Deum* by Czech composer Antonin Dvorak filled the Gothic cathedral. As the music enveloped the great space with its glorious words of praise, one of Havel's aides was heard to remark, "St. Agnes had her hand under our gentle revolution."

PRAGUE
January 1990

After any revolution, the first evidence of change can be seen on the street signs of the capital. Streets and districts bearing names associated with those formerly in power are stripped of their old identity, and plastered over with appellations more in keeping with the country's current political reality. Prague quickly changed in just this way: Gottwald Street, named after the Communist leader who took power as president after the coup of 1948, was out. Masaryk Street, so named for the founder of the first Czechoslovak republic, was in. And the subway stop once called "Moskevska," after the Soviet capital, was now called "Andel," the Czech word for "angel." At the top of the steep escalator leading out of the metro station, a terra cotta statue of an angel stood watch with wings spread in vigilance.

The Red Army had obviously been replaced as the country's Keeper.

Not far from the station, overlooking the racket of pounding jackhammers and construction crews perpetually polishing up the tarnished-looking working class district, stood a church also bearing the name of an angel: St. Gabriel's. From outside, it was a cold-looking building of dark brick and a design so heavy it looked like it would drop right through to the center of the earth. Inside the rundown sanctuary, where the paint was peeling and the roof was leaking, Vaclav Maly was getting ready to celebrate Mass in his own parish for the first time in more than a decade.

It was still a strange feeling to say Mass in public, he thought to himself while vesting in the small sacristy. He wondered whether he had made the right decision. Here he was, in an obscure run-down parish, while his friends were occupying powerful positions in the government. Havel was now president, Benda was head of the Christian Democratic party. Maly had been offered his pick of political positions. What about an ambassadorship, possibly to the Vatican?

Maly smoothed out his alb and slipped the chasuble on over his head. It had been so tempting to take a plum position in the new government. He could still hear the accolades shouted from the mass of people in Wenceslas Square—"Long live Maly!" "Long live Maly!"—the chants feeding his personal ambitions. God's grace had stopped him, though. He really believed that. He had seen firsthand how dangerous political power can be, so easily misused to manipulate others and take away their freedom. He was not a professional politician, he told himself. He was just an imperfect servant of God. That is where his real power lay, in being a servant. When he took his vows of celibacy, he was taking a vow of serving others, of giving joy to others. His success would come only from living in the truth; his happiness only from leading others into the truth. For eleven years, all he had wanted to do was serve as a parish priest. Now he finally had the opportunity. He was fulfilling the true mission of his life.

That mission is not an easy one, he thought as he placed the stole around his neck. The country needs a change of heart. Life had been so gray under communism. It would take years to wipe out the acquiescence ingrained in his fellow citizens, especially in the young people who had never known any other way of life. It was his responsibility to help instill in them the trust, hope, mutual help, forgiveness, sacrifice and other virtues essential for political life. People were angry with the Communists. He understood that anger. He had felt it himself. To forgive, to remain peaceful, was the great task ahead. Politics would still play a part in his personal ministry. After all, he thought, the gospel isn't only for the heart; it also speaks to public activities. But the church had to play a moral role, not a political one, to serve society, not be the master of it.

The breathy notes of the small pipe organ at the back of the church sounded, signaling the service was beginning. Maly kissed the fraying ends of his stole and took his place in the procession, filing through the Byzantine interior of the church past the sweeping arches up to the four gold columns surrounding the altar. The entire sanctuary was a portrait straight out of the Book of Revelation. Though the picture was marred, water-stained, cracked and smudged with the smoke of ages of incense, it was a striking likeness nonetheless, like an old masterpiece in need of touching up. The walls were covered with primitively painted icons of patriarchs, prophets, and apostles. Ascending the sepia-toned arches in front of the altar were the seven stars and seven candlesticks, reaching up to where the Lamb of God was seated triumphant on his throne.

Maly had been saying Mass in secret for nearly fifteen years. Now he could finally celebrate it openly, with no fear of recrimination. When he picked up the gleaming chalice to celebrate mass in the midst of this run-down sanctuary where the roof leaked, the angels and archangels and all the company of heaven looked on and celebrated along with him.

PRAGUE
April 21, 1990

Pope John Paul II stepped off the plane that brought him from Rome and kissed the soil of Czechoslovakia. He was on his first visit to an East European country outside his native Poland. Five years before, he had been refused permission by the government to preside over a religious service there. Now he was making this hastily arranged trip at the invitation of President Havel.

After Havel's government took power, *Pacem in Terris* was abolished, all ten empty bishop seats filled, restrictions on seminary enrollment lifted, and the right to religious education in the church restored. Just two days before the pope's arrival, the government had renewed diplomatic relations with the Vatican.

The president embraced the pope in the cold wind and greeted him with words that spoke for all the nation. "I do not know whether I know what a miracle is. Nevertheless, I dare say that I am at this very moment a participant in a miracle: a person who was arrested as an enemy of the State is welcoming today, as the president of the state, the first pope in the history of the Catholic church to stand on the soil where this state lies.

"I do not know whether I know what a miracle is. Nevertheless, I dare say that this afternoon I shall be a participant in a miracle: on the same spot where five months ago—the day we celebrated the canonization of St. Agnes—the future of our country was being decided, the head of the Catholic church will today celebrate Mass, and most probably thank our saint for her intercession with the One who has in His hands the mysterious course of all things.

"I do not know whether I know what a miracle is. Nevertheless, I dare say that I am at this moment a participant in a miracle: into a country devastated by ideologies of hatred comes the herald of love; into a country devastated by the rule of uneducated people comes the living symbol of culture; into a country until recently destroyed by the idea of confrontation and division of the world comes the herald of peace, dialogue, reciprocal tolerance, respect, and loving understanding—the messenger of brotherly reconciliation of all our differences.

"For long decades the Spirit was being chased out of our country. I have the honor to witness the moment when her soil is being kissed by the apostle of spirituality."

21

The Enduring Light

Nineteen eighty-nine was a year that shook the world, a year the world witnessed the collapse of communism. We in the media watched in astonishment as the walls of totalitarianism came crashing down. But in the rush to cover the cataclysmic events, the story behind the story was overlooked. We trained our cameras on hundreds of thousands of people praying for freedom, votive candles in hand, and yet we missed the transcendent dimension, the explicitly spiritual and religious character, of the story. We looked right at it and could not see it. Too often we in the media preferred to discuss the story, to use George W. S. Trow's phrase about television, "in the context of no context."

The religious and philosophical backdrop was crucial to those who stood at the forefront of the revolution. When dissident playwright Vaclav Havel addressed the United States Congress as the new president of Czechoslovakia in February 1990, he provided us with that context.

Havel noted that while the legacy of Communist totalitarianism included "countless dead, an infinite spectrum of human suffering, profound economic decline, and above all enormous human humiliation," it also brought with it a specific knowledge, an experience he could pass on to the West as an in-kind payment for the West's defense of European freedoms.

> The specific experience I'm talking about has given me one great certainty: Consciousness precedes Being, and not the other way around, as the Marxists claim.
>
> For this reason, the salvation of this human world lies nowhere else than in the human heart, in the human power to reflect, in human weakness and in human responsibility. . . .
>
> We still don't know how to put morality ahead of politics, science, and economics. We are still incapable of understanding that the only genuine backbone of all our actions—if they are to be moral—is responsibility. Responsibility to something higher than my family, my country, my company, my success. Responsibility to the order of Being, where all our actions are indelibly recorded and where, and only where, they will be properly judged.[1]

Havel summarizes the experience of Communist totalitarianism as a massive social experiment, which left no measure untried to verify its premises. This social experiment pitted the Marxist view of human nature against the West's traditional, Judeo-Christian view. The Marxists believe that humankind can be freed by virtue of a new order of liberating social arrangements. The Judeo-Christian conception of human nature has always taught that humankind's freedom consists in obedience to that higher authority of which Havel speaks, the judge of our actions, as interpreted by the still, small voice of conscience. Once again, and with what a measure of suffering, we have been taught that the first truth is the truth of the human heart; that men and women must first be reconciled to their God before they can find the means of reconciliation among themselves to bring about just and peaceful societies.

Havel's words were widely applauded, but little understood, much like the events of 1989. Havel's rise to power is a case in point. His ascent from prison to the presidency was for the most part told as a Cinderella story, an "accident in history" to use the words of one newspaper account. But Havel's presidency was no accident, if the backdrop of his leadership of the Charter 77 movement and his political philosophy are taken into account. The coverage by the mainstream media was devoid of this crucial context, stripped of the philosophical notions of the "power of the powerless" and "living in the truth" that helped answer the "why's" of Czechoslovakia's Velvet Revolution. The media's preoccupation with power and tangible events doesn't mesh with concepts like "powerlessness" and "Being." Havel's philosophy doesn't translate into good pictures; his ideas just don't make for good soundbites.

Instead, the media tended to focus on Eastern Europe's sudden plunge into the free market, and the coming dawn of capitalism as savior. Little attention was given to the peace prayer services in Leipzig and the moral movement for change. Instead, the predominant picture on TV screens after the fall of the Wall showed the East Germans' fascination with the capitalist lifestyle of their West German cousins, portraying them as little more than kids in a candy store. Economics and the politics of capitalism were the prevailing themes of media coverage.

Certainly, these were real issues, but not the primary ones for those at the forefront of the revolution. Pastor Tokes told *USA Today's B*arbara Reynolds that "stories about God's intervention in the transformation of the Eastern Bloc often are edited out by the media."[2]

Throughout his writings, Havel has stressed the importance of "living in the truth" as the antidote to the environment of lies created by totalitarianism. The truth has a force of its own little understood in the West. During the height of the campaign against Charter 77, Havel told *The Register*, a British journal, "Many people who live in the open societies of the West don't understand how important the role of the truth is in totalitarian conditions. It really doesn't matter so much whether Charter 77, for example, has a thousand or a million signatories. What's more important is whether or not it has the truth on its side. And the truth exercises an indirect and invisible influence which represents a special kind of power. This is not something which can be easily understood by people from Western countries, where power simply depends on votes and on the perspective strengths of different parties and politicians."[3] For those who made the revolutions of 1989 in Eastern Europe, truth reigned as the primary issue.

"What is truth?" Pilate's question occurs almost immediately to those of us in the cynical West. We understand civil liberties and the existence of free markets because these are practical benefits. But we, ourselves, have forgotten the philosophic basis—the view of human nature—which nurtured them. As Tom Wolfe told the American Society of Newspaper Editors, "We have in the West a sense of immunity brought on by prosperity."

As the prospect of reunification loomed before them, the same concern kept cropping up among East German church leaders, the fear of exchanging the dialectical materialism of Marx for its mirror image, practical materialism. The West's forgetfulness of its own philosophic underpinnings suggests that we have acquired the habit of seeing only what is reflected in this mirror image. We have turned away from the church in our public square. Like the Romanians in Timisoara's Opera Square, we need to turn around and face what the church teaches once again. Only a view of human nature that sees men and women as sovereign creatures whose first loyalty belongs to God leaves enough room in social obligations for true human freedom. Adam Michnik, a self-described "pagan," sums it up eloquently. He writes, "The Church is the most important institution in Poland because it teaches all of us that we may bow only before God."

Many hazards and difficulties still confront Eastern Europe in the years ahead. After the euphoria of the revolutions, Eastern Europeans have settled into the hard and sacrificial business of rebuilding their nations. All the bills of past abuses have come due. The usual rancorous debate of the democratic process, where competing interests exaggerate their opponents' failings while minimizing their own, quickly replaced the unanimous voice of opposition against a common totalitarian enemy. Walesa and Mazowiecki ran against each other for Poland's presidency in a particularly nasty campaign that split the Solidarity camp.

In some cases, those who stood on the front lines of the revolution have felt betrayed by what the revolution wrought. The word heard later on the streets of Timisoara again and again: "We shed our blood for nothing." Romania's National Salvation front (NSF) turned out to be little more than the same party *apparatchiks* in power, only the names had been changed (to protect the guilty, in this case).

Ethnic tensions long suppressed by totalitarianism have begun to bubble to the surface again. Vaclav Havel was jostled in the streets by angry Slovaks seeking an independent republic. Laszlo Tokes's dream of reconciliation between ethnic Hungarians and Romanians is far from reality. In March of 1990, a celebration of a Hungarian national holiday in the Transylvanian town of Tirgu Mures turned into a deadly clash between mobs of Hungarians and Romanians.

The Eastern Europeans are also quickly discovering that democracy and a free market system are no sure cure for the problems of their societies. On the contrary, the transformation has often been a bitter pill to swallow. The West has not rushed in with massive recapitalization efforts. Many workers have lost their jobs, and inefficient factories continue to close. After reunification, the unemployment rate in Leipzig soared, and the same demonstrators clamoring for freedom were back on the streets clamoring for jobs.

All of the emerging democracies are saddled with the problems of rising unemployment, soaring inflation, and a deteriorating environment. Yet, as documentary filmmaker Piotr Bikont pointed out to Lawrence Weschler of the *New Yorker*, the problems are the "real, normal problems of real, normal countries. You have no idea how long we've been yearning for real, normal problems instead of all the surreal, abnormal problems we've had to cope with in this crazy country for so many years."[4]

Now (with the partial exception of Romania) the pervasiveness of the totalitarian lie, the former climate of untruth, has been replaced with the opportunity of living in the truth. The populations have escaped the moral jail of totalitarianism. They are free. And the difference between freedom and enslavement, even if that difference has not translated immediately into much improved economic conditions, is still immense. Michnik is a man who knows the difference.

> If we look into the mirror or into the depths of our hearts, we must realize how much totalitarian communism has depraved us. We lack democratic culture and institutions.

> We lack the democratic tradition of coexistence according to democratic rules. . . .
>
> In the face of the many ethical traps of contemporary politics, we stand helpless. It is then that we reach for the truth of our own roots, to the ethic of the power of the powerless, to the morals of the Ten Commandments. The rest is a lie and has the bitter taste of deceit.[5]

Now that the church is no longer the church of the opposition, it faces the temptation of identifying itself with those in power, with one or another political party, and entering politics as an equal player. Pastor Christian Führer of the Nikolai church cautions against yielding to the temptation: "The church must be independent, strictly separate from the state. If the church receives a privileged status, it loses its power and the gospel is neutralized. And if it loses its power, what good is it?"

In Poland especially, a country where more than 90 percent of the population is Catholic, there is the danger of the Catholic majority imposing its will on the rest of the country. In September 1990, the Polish government hastily introduced voluntary religious instruction in public schools, stirring fears of Catholic indoctrination among non-Catholics and growing concerns that Poland was exchanging the "red" dictatorship of communism for the "black" dictatorship of the clergy.

Again and again, church leaders of various traditions from various countries voiced the same opinion: though the church is no longer the church of the opposition, it must continue speaking out for the poor, the oppressed, and the lowly. In the words of East German theologian Walther Bindemann: "We now have to raise the question of what will happen with Bonhoeffer's heritage. We have said the church in the GDR should be a church without privilege. Now we're a church living in privilege. Bonhoeffer taught us to be a *kirche für andere*, a church for others. Now there's the danger that the church will narrow its concentration away from outward service. Bonhoeffer helped us understand that we must bring together religious and social activity. Now there's the danger of becoming exclusively religious by excluding others. We have to ask, 'What will happen to this heritage?' "

Perhaps the best counsel for the Eastern European church in finding its role in the post-revolution comes from one standing outside the church looking in—again, Adam Michnik:

> We need . . . a church that will teach us moral values, defend national and human dignity, provide an asylum for trampled hopes. But we do not expect the Church to become the nation's political representative, to formulate political programs and to sign political pacts. Whoever wants such a Church, whoever expects these things from Catholic priests, is—whether he likes it or not—asking for the political reduction of the Christian religion. For we do not need a Church that is locked up, that is hidden behind the walls of a particular political ideology. We need an open Church, a Church that "takes the whole world onto the arms of the Cross." It is such a Church, I think, that all Poles need today: those who believe in the "madness of the Cross," those who are blindly searching for the meaning of Christian transcendence, those who define the meaning of their lives in the categories of lay humanism.[6]

In fulfilling its role, the church and its members will find themselves doing what to the world may seem foolish. But only this kind of foolishness can help heal these cultures so damaged by forty years of totalitarianism, the kind of "madness of the cross" so evident in the story of an East German pastor named Uwe Holmer.

Pastor Holmer was not sure how to respond when he was approached by leaders from his church district asking him to take in Erich Honecker, the hated former leader of East Germany. The seventy-seven-year-old had just been whisked from a state-run hospital, where he was recuperating from cancer surgery, to Rummelsburg prison to stand trial on treason charges. But he had hardly been there twenty-four hours when a court ruled he was too sick to stay in prison. After his release, the state refused to provide him with a place to stay. Honecker and his wife, Margot, had nowhere else to go. They were banished from their villa just fifteen kilometers away in Wandlitz, playground of East Germany's Communist elite.

Pastor Holmer was the director of a church-run convalescent center in the secluded village of Lobetal. He knew it would be the ideal setting for the Honeckers, a neutral, out-of-the-way spot where they could easily be protected. But to grant Honecker asylum! He had bitter memories of Honecker and his regime. Honecker had personally presided over the building of the wall, a wall that divided Holmer's family when it was erected, and prevented him from attending his own father's funeral. When Holmer's father died, he wasn't even allowed out to attend the funeral. He had even more reason to resent Honecker's wife, who ran the Ministry of Education as a ruthless, doctrinaire Marxist. Holmer's ten children had been denied admission to any university because of their refusal to join the Communist Youth League and go through the *Jugendweihe*, a secular ceremony for fourteen-year-olds. It was offensive to most Christians because of the oath of loyalty to the Communist party the teenagers had to swear.

But Pastor Holmer tried to put himself in Honecker's shoes. What would it be like to live at the very pinnacle of society and suddenly plunge to the position of being the lowest of the low? And how would he feel to have to accept the charity of the church he once suppressed, in the shadow of the place he once lived in privilege? Then there was Holmer's own responsibility as a Christian. He reminded himself that it was the church's mission, in fact, the very purpose of the ministry at Lobetal, to take in the poor, the sick, and the homeless. Honecker was now the poor, the sick, and the homeless.

But Pastor Holmer decided it would not be fair to put Honecker up in the church's retirement home. There was a long waiting list, and those on it would be justifiably angry if Honecker were given preferential treatment. The only alternative would be to take him into his own home as his private guest. He decided he had no choice but to shelter Honecker under his own roof.

When Honecker arrived at the Holmer's rambling two-story home, he looked dazed and confused, like a lost little boy. Holmer and his wife ushered the couple into a comfortable drawing room. "Welcome to my home," Holmer said in a quiet, soothing voice. "I know you have come here to convalesce and to rest, and I hope you will find the quiet and peace you need here."

The Honeckers lived upstairs. Their modest living conditions were quite a contrast to the luxurious trappings of Wandlitz. They had their own tiny kitchen with a sink and toilet, a sparsely furnished living room and a small bedroom almost completely taken up by their bed. The stairwell leading up to their quarters was decorated with smiling portraits of the Holmer children, subtle reminders, perhaps, of the price the family paid for the regime's repressive policies.

After the Honeckers arrived, Pastor Holmer wrestled with his own feelings of bitterness toward his new guests. His personal faith compelled him to forgive them for all the disadvantages he and his family had suffered under the Communist system.

In the many talks they had, Pastor Holmer saw that to forgive is no easy task. The bitterness, the anger over the injustices of Honecker's regime, kept creeping back. In his own struggle to forgive, God's own forgiveness loomed even larger. He saw over and over again how much it cost God to forgive his own sins. In the knowledge of that forgiveness, he somehow found the strength to forgive even a man like Honecker.

His sentiment wasn't shared by the rest of the country, however. Hate mail began pouring in, much of it from Christians. Some of his own parishioners threatened to leave his congregation. Loyal supporters of the ministry at Lobetal gave notice they were considering cutting off their funds. The Holmer household began receiving bomb threats.

Holmer defended his actions in a letter that was published in the East German newspaper *Neue Zeitung*. In the letter he noted that his actions in no way interfered with any judicial proceeding. Honecker and his wife were simply two people in need of help.

"In Lobetal," he wrote, "there is a sculpture of Jesus inviting people to himself and crying out, 'Come unto me all ye that labor and are heavy laden, and I will give you rest.' We have been commanded by our Lord Jesus to follow him and to receive all those who are weary and heavy-laden, in spirit and in body, but especially the homeless. We also felt compelled to act as we did because of Jesus' example in visiting Zacchaeus, the tax collector, his commandment to love our enemies, and his instructions that we pray: 'Forgive us our trespasses as we forgive those who trespass against us.' We are convinced that what Jesus asked his disciples to do is equally binding on us."[7]

The church, when it acts in accord with the absolute demands of its Lord, provides a light that clarifies the relative merits of actions in the temporal world—in the world of politics, economics, and human rights. Unarguably, the fidelity of the church to its vision provided a touchstone for the revolutions that rose up in Eastern Europe in 1989. The church, so long condemned for its venal collaboration with temporal rulers in the course of Western civilization, became again in the twentieth century era of totalitarianism, the church of the catacombs—the church of the homeless, of the destitute, of the poor. Throughout Eastern Europe, the church served as the guardian of the truth and a shelter for those, believers and unbelievers alike, who dedicated themselves to the politics of truth. "And you shall know the truth," that church's founder said, "and the truth shall set you free."

Notes

1. *Congressional Quarterly*, 21 February 1990, H 394-395.

2. *National and International Religion Report*, 4, 26 March 1990, 6-7.

3. Jonathan Luxmoore, "Dialogue," *The Register*, n.d.

4. Lawrence Weschler, "A Reporter at Large," *The New Yorker*, 13 November 1989, 99.

5. From *Tygodnik Powszechny*, excerpted in *World Press Review*, August 1990, 29.

6. Adam Michnik, *Letters from Prison* (Berkeley, Calif.: University of California Press, 1985), 237.

7. Translation from "The Pastor and the Homeless Despot," *Christianity and Crisis*, 18 June 1990, 198.

Glossary

Adamec, Ladislav [Ah-DAHM'-ets, LAH'-dih-slaf]—Czechoslovakia's prime minister during the Velvet Revolution.

Alliance of Free Democrats—One of Hungary's democratic opposition parties.

Balaton, Zoltan [BAH'-lah-tahn, ZHOLE'-tahn]—Member of Tokes's congregation.

basis groups—Small discussion groups held in East German churches on issues such as peace, human rights, and the environment.

Benda, Vaclav [BEND'-ah, VAHT'-slaff]—Czechoslovakian Catholic active in Charter 77 and VONS.

Bortnowska, Halina [Bohrt-NOFF'-skah, Hah'LEE'-nah]—Solidarity activist involved in Nova Huta strikes.

Ceausescu, Nicolae [Chow-CHESS'-koo, NIK'-oh-lye]—Romanian Communist party leader who controlled the country along with his wife, Elena, a member of Romania's ruling Political Executive Committee.

Charter 77—Human rights document in Czechoslovakia; the name also applies to the opposition activists who signed the document.

Ciosek, Stanislaw [CHOH'-sek, STAN'-ih-swaf]—Polish Politburo member and Communist party deputy secretary.

Civic Forum—Czechoslovakia's umbrella opposition group.

Czyrek, Jozef [CHEER'-ek, YOE'-seff]—Polish Communist party deputy secretary.

Dubcek, Alexander [DOOB'-check]—Czechoslovakia's reform-minded leader who presided over country's Prague Spring; ousted when invasion by Warsaw Pact troops crushed his democratic reforms.

Dugulescu, Peter [Doo-goo-LESS'-koo]—Pastor of Timisoara's Baptist Church.

Federation of Young Democrats—Hungary's first independent alternative to Communist Youth League.

Free German Youth—East Germany's Communist Youth Organization.

friedensgebete—Weekly peace prayer services held in East German churches.

Führer, Christian [FYOOR'-uhr]—Pastor of Leipzig's Nikolai Church.

Geremek, Bronislaw [Geh-REHM'-ek, BROHN'-ih-swaf]—Polish professor of medieval history who, along with Mazowiecki, became one of Solidarity's advisers.

Gierek, Edward [GEER'-ek]—Succeeded Gomulka as Polish Communist party leader; ousted after 1980 strikes.

Glemp, Cardinal Jozef—Succeeded Cardinal Wyszynski as Polish primate.

Gomulka, Wladyslaw [Go-MOOL'-ka, VLAH'-dihs-waff]—Polish nationalist Communist who headed the Communist party, forced out after worker protests in 1970.

Halik, Tomas [HAH'-leek]—Banned Czechoslovakian priest who became unofficial advisor to Cardinal Tomasek.

Havel, Vaclav [HAH'-vehl, VAHT'-slaff]—Czechoslovakian playwright and Charter 77 activist.

Honecker, Erich [HAHN'-ah-kuhr]—East German Communist Party chief ousted as nation's leader in October 1989 after eighteen years as country's leader.

Iliescu, Ion [Ill-ee-ESS'-koo, Ee-YOHN']—Leader of Romania's

National Salvation Front.

Ivanyi, Gabor [Ee-VAHN'-yee, GAH'-bore]—Pastor of banned Hungarian Methodist congregation; later elected to Parliament.

Jaeger, Uwe and Ulrieke [YAY'-guhr, OO'-vay and Uhl-REE'-kah]—Members of Brigitta Treetz's church small group.

Jaruzelski, Wojciech [Yah-roo-ZEHL'-skee, VOY'-check]—Polish general who became Communist party leader in October 1981; two months later declared state of martial law.

Kadar, Janos [KAH'-dahr, YAH'-nosh]—Hungary's Communist party leader placed in power after the ill-fated 1956 revolution.

KIK—*Kluby Inteligencji Katolickiej*—Polish Clubs of the Catholic Intelligentsia.

Kiszczak, Czeslaw [KEES'-chak, CHESS'-waff]—Polish interior minister.

KOR—*Komitet Obrony Robotnikow*—Polish Workers' Defense Committee, set up by intellectuals to defend rights of striking workers.

Krenz, Egon [Krenz, AY'-gahn]—East German Politburo member who succeeded Erich Honecker as Communist party chief.

Maly, Vaclav [MAH'-lee, VAHT'-slav]—Banned priest in Czechoslovakia who emerged as Civic Forum spokesman.

Marincu, Cornel [Mah-RIN'-soo, Kore-NELL']—Participant in Timisoara demonstrations.

Masur, Kurt [Mah-ZOOR']—Conductor of Leipzig's famed Gewandhaus orchestra, signatory of Leipzig Appeal.

Mazowiecki, Tadeusz [Mah-zoe-vee-ET'-skee, Tah-DAY'-oosh]—Prominent Polish Catholic intellectual who served as key adviser to Solidarity.

Michnik, Adam [MEEK'-neek]—Polish dissident historian active in KOR and Solidarity movement.

MKS—*Miedzyzakladowa Komisja Robotnicza*—Inter-factory strike committee.

Molnar, Janos [MOLE'-nahr, YAH'-nosh]—One of Tokes's colleagues in the clergy who spoke out against Ceausescu's village demolition policy.

Nagy, Gyala—Bishop of Hungarian Reformed Church in Cluj, Romania.

Nagy, Imre [NAD'-jah, IM'-reh]—Hungary's reform-minded prime minister who was executed after 1956 revolution.

National Salvation Front—Romanian umbrella group that declared itself in power after Ceausescu was toppled.

Navratil, Augustin [NAH'-vrah-teel]—Czechoslovakian railway worker who circulated Petition for Religious Rights.

Nemeth, Geza—Hungarian Reformed pastor who headed up ministry to Romanian refugees in Budapest.

Nemeth, Miklos—Hungary's prime minister.

Network of Free Initiatives—Umbrella group for Hungarian opposition.

Neues Forum—New Forum, East Germany's umbrella opposition group.

Public Against Violence—Civic Forum's counterpart in Slovak republic of Czechoslovakia.

Richter, Johannes [RICK'-tur, Yoe-HAH'-niss]—Rector of Leipzig's St. Thomas Church.

Schmidt, Ilonka—One of hunger strikers at East Berlin's Gethsemane Church.

Securitate—Romania's dreaded network of secret police.

Staniszkis, Jadwiga [Stah-NEESH'-kees, Yahd-WEE'-gah]—Polish sociologist who joined Mazowiecki's Committee of Experts during 1980 strikes.

Stasi—East German Ministry of State Security, East Germany's feared network of secret police.

Stelmachowski, Andrzej [Stel-mah-KOFF'-skee, AHN'-zhay]—President of Warsaw Chapter of KIK during 1988 strikes.

Tokes, Laszlo [TER'-kesh, LAHS'-loe]—Pastor of Hungarian Reformed Church in Timisoara whose criticism of Ceausescu's treatment of fellow ethnic Hungarians helped spark the Romanian revolution.

Tomasek, Cardinal Frantisek [TOM'-ah-sek, FRAN'-tih-sek]—Czechoslovakia's primate.

Treetz, Brigitta [TRATES]—Participant in Leipzig's *friedensgebete* and demonstrations that followed.

Ujvarossy, Erno [Oo-vah-ROSS'-ee, UHR'-noe]—Member of Tokes's congregation found dead after being harassed by Securitate.

Venske, Bernhard [VEHN'-skee, BARE'-nahrd]—Dominican monk who participated in Leipzig's peace prayer services.

VONS—*Vybor Na Obranu Nespravedlive Stihanych*—Czechoslovakia's Committee for the Defense of the Unjustly Persecuted; offshoot of Charter 77.

Walesa, Lech [Vah-WEN'-sah, Leck]—Solidarity founder.

Wiez [Vee-ENZH']—Literally "link" or "bond." Catholic monthly periodical edited by Mazowiecki.

Wyszynski, Cardinal Stefan [vih-SHIN'-skee]—Poland's well-respected primate, died in May 1981.

Zimmermann, Peter—East German theologian who was one of the six signatories of the Liepzig Appeal.

ZNAK—Literally "sign." The political umbrella group for Poland's Catholic intellectuals; Mazowiecki served with a small group of ZNAK deputies in Parliament until he was dropped from the officially approved list of candidates for condemning police brutality against student demonstrations in May 1968.

ZOMO—Polish security police. Name is derived from the group's Polish initials: Zmotoryzowane Oddzialy Milicji Obywatelskiej (Motorized Units of Civil Militia).

Zverina, Josef [Svare-ZHEE'-nah]—Banned Czechoslovakian priest who was one of Cardinal Tomasek's unofficial advisors.

Chronology

1989: The Year That Changed the World

January 16—*Czechoslovakia*—Playwright Vaclav Havel arrested during human rights demonstration; Father Vaclav Maly in police detention to prevent him from participating in protests.

January 22—*Czechoslovakia*—Maly interrogated; refuses to give evidence against Havel and other Charter 77 activists under arrest.

January 23—*Czechoslovakia*—Cardinal Frantisek Tomasek sends letter to Communist government condemning use of violence and calling for dialogue with the opposition.

February 6—*Poland*—Round Table talks between Solidarity opposition and Communist government get underway.

February 21—*Czechoslovakia*—Havel sentenced to nine months in prison.

March 20—*Romania*—Laszlo Tokes gives surreptitious interview to Canadian film crew denouncing Romanian government's village demolition policy.

April 1—*Romania*— Tokes gets word of his suspension as pastor of Timisoara's Reformed Church.

April 5—*Poland*—Government agrees to relegalize Solidarity.

April 17—*Poland*—Solidarity's legal status officially restored.

May 2—*Hungary*—Government begins dismantling barbed wire fence along border with Austria.

June 4—*Poland*—Solidarity wins landslide vote in Poland's first open elections in more than forty years.

June 16—*Hungary*—Imre Nagy, leader of 1956 revolution, is reburied as a hero.

July 1—*Hungary*—State Office of Church Affairs abolished.

July 24—*Romania*—Hungarian TV broadcasts Tokes's March interview with Canadian journalists.

August 8—*East Germany*—Hundreds of East Germans seeking political asylum crowd into West German embassies in Prague, East Berlin, and Warsaw.

August 24—*Poland*—Tadeusz Mazowiecki inaugurated as Poland's first non-Communist prime minister since just after World War II.

Early September—*East Germany*—Thousands of East Germans flee through Hungary to go West.

September 18—*East Germany*—Demonstrations centered in peace prayer services break out around Leipzig's Nikolai Church.

October 3-4—*East Germany*—Nation observes fortieth anniversary amid growing protests; during a visit to East Berlin, Soviet leader Mikhail Gorbachev backs calls for reform.

October 7—*Hungary*—Communist party renounces Marxism, changes its name to Hungarian Socialist party, and embraces the principals of Western-style democratic socialism.

October 9—*East Germany—Die Wende* (the turning point)—Massive demonstration in Leipzig ends without violence, and government begins granting concessions to opposition.

October 18—*East Germany*—Honecker ousted; replaced by Politburo member Egon Krenz.

October 25—Gorbachev delivers speech in Helsinki renouncing Brezhnev doctrine.

November 2—*Romania*—Tokes attacked by armed assailants.

November 9—*East Germany*—Berlin Wall falls.

November 12—*Czechoslovakia*—Agnes of Bohemia named a saint; legend has it that miraculous things will happen in Czechoslovakia after her canonization.

November 17—*Czechoslovakia*—Police brutally crush student protest in Prague.

November 19—*Czechoslovakia*—Opposition group Civic Forum born.

November 21—*Czechoslovakia*—Cardinal Frantisek Tomasek expresses support for Civic Forum.

November 24—*Czechoslovakia*—Communist party leader Milos Jakes quits.

November 26—*Czechoslovakia*—Maly leads crowd in Lord's Prayer at massive rally on Letna Square.

November 27—*Czechoslovakia*—Two-hour general strike paralyzes the nation.

December 3—*East Germany*—Egon Krenz steps down as Communist party chairman; Politburo and Central Committee resign.

December 7—*East Germany*—Church leaders join opposition for first of series of talks paving the way for a new constitution and free elections.

December 10—*Czechoslovakia*—Communist president Gustav Husak steps down after swearing in new government; Communists reduced to minority for the first time since seizing power.

December 15—*Romania*—Deadline set for Tokes's eviction; vigil forms around Tokes's church apartment.

December 16-17—*Romania*—Massacre in Timisoara; hundreds killed.

December 17—*Romania*—Tokes and his wife forcibly evicted to Mineu; undergo interrogation.

December 21—*Romania*—Speech by Romanian leader Nicolae Ceausescu interrupted by jeers; protests break out in Bucharest; Ceausescus flee.

December 22—*Romania*—National Salvation Front declares itself in charge; Tokes named honorary member.

December 25—*Romania*—Ceausescus tried and executed.
December 29—*Czechoslovakia*—Vaclav Havel inaugurated as president, just six months after his release from prison.

Special Acknowledgments

The information in *Revolution by Candlelight* is based for the most part on extensive interviews conducted throughout Eastern Europe in the fall of 1990. The public speeches and sermons contained in the book are reproduced exactly from translations, though condensed in some cases. The dialogue is reconstructed, since people recalling events a year before rarely remember their exact words. However, every effort was made to render the dialogue as exactly as possible.

I am also indebted to the following sources for additional information:

Introduction

Trevor Beeson, *Discretion and Valour* (Philadelphia: Fortress Press, 1982).

Part 1

Czechoslovakia: Keston News Service; "Dialogue: Two Czech Dissidents on Party, State and Faith," interview with Jonathan Luxmoore, *The Register* interview with Vaclav Maly conducted by Olga Sommerova of Kratky Film Praha. Some background information is taken from William Echikson, "A Leader Aspires to Step Down; Vaclav Maly Helped to Launch a Revolution; Now He Intends to Become a Parish Priest Again," *Christian Science Monitor*, 4 January 1990, 14, and Peter Hebblethwaite, "Czech Priest's Work Has Political Dimension," *National Catholic Reporter*, 2 March 1990, 7.

Poland: *Gdansk, Sierpien '80: Rozmowy (Gdansk, August '80: Conversations)*, Andrzej Drzycimski and Tadeusz Skutnik, Oficyna Wydawnicza AIDA, Gdansk 1990.

Hungary: "Special Report on Hungarian Methodists," *Keston News Service*, 15 June 1978. The description of the Kispest church is based on my own personal observations in 1978.

East Germany: I am deeply grateful to Brigitta Treetz for making her journal available to me. It is a moving, eloquent account of her involvement in Leipzig's peace prayer movement and her reaction to the events of 1989. I relied on the journal for the scenes involving Brigitta throughout the book, drawing on her reflections to create an interior dialogue.

Romania: Translation of Tokes's interview to Canadian TV provided by the Hungarian Human Rights Foundation.

Part 2

Poland: The depiction of the negotiations inside the Gdansk shipyard is based on an account by sociologist Jadwiga Staniszkis, "The Evolution of Forms of Working-Class Protest in Poland: Sociological Reflections on the Gdansk-Szeczin Case, August 1980," *Soviet Studies*, Vol. 33, No. 2, April 1981, 204-231. I also gleaned information from Timothy Garton Ash's thorough account in *The Polish Revolution: Solidarity* (New York: Charles Scribner's Sons, 1984). Other helpful resources on the Solidarity period: Lawrence Weschler, *The Passion of Poland* (New York: Pantheon Books, 1984); and Neal Ascherson, *The Polish August: The Self-Limiting Revolution* (London: Allen Lane, 1981). The exchange between Cardinal Wyszynski and Gierek is based on an account in Bogdan Szajkowski, *Next to God: Poland* (New York: St. Martin's Press, 1983), 91-93. The account of Mazowiecki's internment is adapted from Tadeusz Mazowiecki, *Internowanie* (Biblioteka Wolnega Glosu Ursusa, 1989). Other resources on the martial law period include Jonathan Luxmoore, "The Polish Church under Martial Law," *Religion in Communist Lands*, Vol. 15, No. 2, Summer 1987, 124-166; and *A Prisoner of Martial Law*, Jan Mur, translated by Lillian Vallee, Harcourt Brace Jovanovich, 1984.

Czechoslovakia: The material on Vaclav Benda is taken from Vaclav Benda, "My Personal File," translation by Keston College, first published in *Svedectvi* (Paris) No. 58, July 1979, 273-276. Information on the trial of the VONS activists comes from H. Gordon Skillings, *Charter 77 and Human Rights in Czechoslovakia* (George & Unwin, 1981). The account of Havel and Benda's imprisonment comes from Vaclav Havel, *Letters to Olga: June 1979 - September 1982* (New York: Knopf, 1988). Maly's interrogation is a composite based on several accounts in Keston News Service. He was interrogated more than 250 times. Biographical information on Augustin

Navratil comes from "Czechoslovakia—One Year after the Petition for Religious Freedom," *Religion in Communist Lands*, Vol. 17, No. 2, Summer 1989, 148-150.

Hungary: Ivanyi's trip into Romania is actually drawn from several trips he told me about during an interview. The story of Lajos and Eva Oszvath's escape from Romania is based on an interview with the couple. Additional information on the plight of Romanian refugees in Romania comes from "Refugees from Romania in Hungary," *Religion in Communist Lands*, Vol. 16, No. 3, Autumn 1988, 254-256 and William Echikson, "Waves of Refugees Wash across Romanian Border," *Christian Science Monitor*, 13-19 June 1988, 2.

Romania: Pastor Tokes graciously consented to an interview from a hospital bed in Budapest, where he was recovering from an automobile accident. Most of his story is taken from his personal account. Other sources include Keston News Service, press releases from the Hungarian Human Rights Foundation, and Felix Corley and John Eibner, *In the Eye of the Romanian Storm: The Heroic Story of Pastor Laszlo Tokes* (Old Tappan, New Jersey: Fleming H. Revell Company, 1990).

East Germany: Sermons from the *friedensgebete* are translations from *Dona Nobis Pacem*, a compilation of the peace prayer services held during the fall of 1989 in Leipzig, edited by Günter Hanisch, Gottfried Hänisch, Friedrich Magirius, and Johannes Richter, Evangelische Verlagsanstalt Berlin, 1990.

Part 3

Poland: In addition to interviews with many of the principals involved in the strikes of 1988 and the subsequent Round Table Talks, including Halina Bortnowska, Rev. Bronislaw Dembowski, and Andrzej Stelmachowski, I drew from the following sources: John Tagliabue, "Young and Wary Strikers Take Solace from Walesa," *New York Times*, 7 May 1988, 1A; John Tagliabue, "Security Forces Crush a Walkout at Mill in Poland," *New York Times*, 6 May 1988, 1A; John Tagliabue, "Gdansk Workers End 9-Day Strike; Key Demand Unmet," *New York Times*, 11 May 1988, 1A; John Reed, "The Strikes Continue: Special Powers Legislation in Preparation," Radio Free Europe Research, Polish SR/8, 13 May 1988, 7-10; "At a Round Table, the Party Seals Its Fate," *Los Angeles Times*, 17 December 1989, Q4; Lawrence Weschler, "Reporter at Large: A Grand Experiment," *The New Yorker*, 13 November 1989, 59-104; Anna Swidlicka, "The Round-Table Talks Convene," RFE Research, Polish SR/4, 3 March 1989, 3-8; Louisa Vinton, "Initial Round-Table Talks Signal Conflicts to Come," RFE Research, Polish SR/4, 3 March 1989, 9-13; Louisa Vinton, "Round Table Talks End in Agreement," RFE Research, Polish SR/6, 7 April 1989, 7-12; Polish Press Agency Daily News accounts,

7, 10 and 17 February and 5 April 1989.

Hungary: "Hungarian Who Led '56 Revolt Is Buried as a Hero," Henry Kamm, *New York Times*, 16 June 1989, 1A.

East Germany: The account of Gabriele Schmidt's arrest and detention is taken from an interview in *Neues Forum Leipzig: Jetzt oder nie—Demokratie! (Yes or No—Democracy!)*, Forum Verlag Leipzig, Hermann Duncker, Leipzig, 1990, 66-69. Other interviews in the book also served as source material. The sermons are excerpted from *Dona Nobis Pacem.*

Czechoslovakia: I relied on raw footage of the Letna rally supplied by Kratky Film Praha to describe that event. Other sources include: Tyler Marshall, "Eloquence of Uncompromising Priest Raises Spirits of Czechoslovak Opposition," *Los Angeles Times*, 8 December 1989, A15; "Riot Police in Prague Beat Marchers and Arrest Dozens," *New York Times*, 18 November 1989, 7A; "Two Church Leaders Address the People (Czechoslovakia), Keston News Service No. 339, 30 November 1989, 11; a presentation by Jana Kiely, Director of Education at St. Paul's Catholic Church in Cambridge, Massachusetts, to a Harvard University Conference, "Revolution in Eastern Europe: the Role of the Church," 25 April 1990, and Esther B. Fein, "In Wenceslas Square, a Shout: Freedom!" *New York Times*, 23 November 1989, 1A.

Romania: In addition to interviews with eyewitnesses from Timisoara, I referred to the following for helpful background: Robert Cullen, "Report from Romania: Down with the Tyrant," *The New Yorker*, 2 April 1990, 94-112; Celestine Bohlen with Clyde Haberman, "How the Ceausescus Fell: Harnessing Popular Rage," *New York Times*, 7 January 1990, 1A; Vladimir Socor, "Pastor Tokes and the Outbreak of the Revolution in Timisoara," RFE Report on Eastern Europe, 2 February 1990, 19-25. Other eyewitness accounts of the Timisoara massacre come from "Timisoara: The Martyr City, a transcript of the events that took place in Timisoara before, during and after the mass demonstrations December 1989—as given by Rev. Peter Dugulescu, Pastor of the First Baptist Church, Timisoara," an interview conducted by Rev. Josif Ton of the Romanian Missionary Society. The account of Marincu's encounter with the Securitate is somewhat compressed in time—the actual Securitate reign of terror occurred over several days, instead of one.

Part 4

Poland: The account of Walesa's offering the prime minister position to Mazowiecki is found in "It's the End of an Age—and a New Start," *Los Angeles Times*, 17 December 1989, Q6. Mazowiecki's addresses are translated from excerpts in a collection published by the Polish Press

Agency, Profile Series 7-8/148-149, Warsaw, 1989. I also drew on a description of Mazowiecki's collapse from Joseph A. Reaves, "Solidarity Takes Power, Makes History," *Chicago Tribune*, 13 September 1989, 8.

East Germany: Brigitta's thoughts on the changes taking place around her come from a personal letter she sent to friends in the United States dated 3 December 1989.

Romania: Daniel Gavra's story is taken from "Timisoara: The Martyr City." Tokes's inauguration sermon is condensed from a translation by Keston College.

Czechoslovakia: Havel's speech at the Pope's arrival ceremony taken from "Pope, on Sweep Through Prague, Sees a United Europe," Clyde Haberman, *New York Times*, 22 April 1989, 10A.

I also need to thank a number of people and organizations for their help with the research for this book. The staff at Keston College gave me the run of their extensive files and documentation. Keston's former Hungarian researcher John Eibner was especially helpful in providing me with background information and resources on the situation in Hungary and Romanian. Rom and Nancy Maczka were invaluable in putting me in touch with just the right contacts in Leipzig, and providing me with translations of the journal and letters of Brigitta Treetz. CNN's video library made me an eyewitness to the major events sweeping Eastern Europe in 1989. Anita Deyneka and the staff of Slavic Gospel Association provided me with helpful background material. Jan van den Bosch of Evangelische Omroep and Peter van der Bijl of Stichting Antwoord in the Netherlands shared the wealth of their contacts and experiences in Eastern Europe. Vitezslav Bojanovsky and Olga Sommerova of the Czech film production company Kratky Film Praha graciously made their raw footage and interviews available to me.

The interviews conducted in Eastern Europe would not have been possible without the help of the following people: Petr Kubka in Czechoslovakia, Marek Wosko in Poland, Geza Nemeth in Hungary, Zoltan Balaton in Romania, and Pastor Klaus Fritzsche and his wife, Eva, in East Germany. They helped facilitate my research trip, provided me with new contacts, and showed me overwhelming hospitality.

Miriam Falco, Nora and Agnes Balint, Pavel Randl, and Monika Sullivan also deserve credit for putting in many painstaking hours of translating. Susie Gough Harrison struggled through the many revisions and permutations of the book to produce a flawless manuscript. And if not for the inspiration of Harold Fickett, who came up with the idea for the book, and the dedication of Rick Christian, who sold the idea, the book would never have been written.